Praise for Kurt R.A. Giambastiani and
Dreams of the Desert Wind

"The author of the Fallen Cloud saga has done his homework on the Middle East as well as he did on the Cheyenne, the saga's people, and has created a compact, lyrical fantasy. The characterization, lyrical prose, and pacing are nearly flawless, and readers close the book hoping that it is only the first in a new series."

> • Roland Green
> *Booklist*

"Giambastiani takes you to a Middle East beyond the headlines—a place of mystery and fantasy, where the ancient past collides with the 21st century to create a remarkable future. An amazing tale that blurs the lines between mystery, fantasy, and science fiction to create a work of remarkable imagination."

> • Robert A. Metzger
> author of *Cusp*

"*Dreams of the Desert Wind* is a mystery as dark and complex as the eastern land that inspired it. This intriguing tale richly details old and new Jerusalem, the Bedouins of history, and the politics of the future."

> • Louise Marley
> author of *The Child Goddess*

"*Dreams of the Desert Wind* gifts us with a modern Middle East that is gritty as a sand storm, real as tomorrow's news, and marvelous as a genie's vision. Detailed and surprisingly beautiful, Giambastiani paints a sympathetic portrait of what living in a war-torn and violent part of the globe might be like while telling a story of what it could be, if only the ancient magic could work."

> • James Van Pelt
> author of *Strangers and Beggars*

Praise for Kurt R.A. Giambastiani and the Fallen Cloud Saga

The Year the Cloud Fell

"An entertaining alternate historical tale....The story line is fast-paced and will gain author Kurt R.A. Giambastiani much praise. Fans of alternate history novels know they have a new hero.

- *Midwest Book Review*

The Spirit of Thunder

"[An] informed, reverent extrapolation on Cheyenne culture."
- *Booklist*

"The exquisite detail and respect shown in this portrayal of Cheyenne society are enormously compelling."
- *Locus*

Shadow of the Storm

"The third book in Giambastiani's series set in an alternate world where dinosaurs survive in historical North America to become the steeds of the Cheyenne is a solid piece of work."
- *Booklist*

From the Heart of the Storm

"Giambastiani's knowledge of the Plains Indians continues to carry the story more than any other aspect of the book....Kudos to this unlikely but undeniably successful alternate history."
- *Booklist*

Ploughman's Son

Also by Kurt R.A. Giambastiani

Dreams of the Desert Wind:
A Modern Fantasy of the Middle East

The Fallen Cloud Saga
The Year the Cloud Fell
The Spirit of Thunder
Shadow of the Storm
From the Heart of the Storm

Ploughman's Son

Kurt R.A. Giambastiani

Mouse Road Press
Seattle

Ploughman's Son
Book One of the Ploughman Chronicles

A Mouse Road Publication
October 2005
Copyright © 2005 by Kurt R.A. Giambastiani

MOUSE ROAD PRESS
16034 BURKE AVE N
SHORELINE, WA 98133
UNITED STATES OF AMERICA

Cover and book design © 2005 Mouse Road Press
Cover image based on a photo from *http://philip.greenspun.com*

ISBN 1-4116-3779-8

First Mouse Road Press Edition: October 2005
Printed in the USA

To Ilene
For patience above and beyond the call

one

Face down on the cold granite boulder, Alain sought the power of the ley line. He knew it ran through the mountain's core with a great surging pulse, but he could not sense it. His pale hair fell across chestnut-colored eyes as he pressed his cheek to the cold, rough stone. He stretched his arms and legs out to their full, slender length, and with his fingers, he held onto tiny crevices in the rock.

Above his head, the twisted arms of ancient oaks shook their leaves in the morning wind off the Bretagne coast. Wadded clouds capered across the springtime sky, chasing their shadows over the moorland and on up the mountainside. The dappled sunlight came and went, and Alain was alternately chilled and warmed by its inconstant attention.

He wanted to feel the ley line, wanted to taste the power it held. More than anything else, that was what he wanted; that, and what would come with it. His thoughts dipped down through the granite and he plumbed the mountain's depth for the line of magic.

The wooded mountainside permeated his mind. He smelled the iron-tinged granite where his breath made it moist, and he could smell the damp, virile musk of the forest's leaf-strewn floor just a few yards away. He heard the groans of the heavy branches as they protested the wind's attention, and the *flrr* as a pair of sparrows flew by.

He opened his mind and let these sensations flow into him. He let them merge with his spirit, and tried to join his consciousness with the cold mountain. His mind looked down, deep into the stone, searching, searching. He imagined the slow thrum of power and envisioned the line's shimmering glow with his inner eye. Would it be warm? Or as cold as the stone beneath him? He clenched shut his eyes in concentration, feeling for the ley line of Dead Ox Wood and the magic that always eluded him.

"Where are you?" Alain whispered to the line beneath the silent granite. "Where are you?"

A stone sailed in and bounced near his head. He opened his eyes and scrambled toward the trunk of a nearby tree. He was not fast enough. Another stone followed the first and caught him before he got off the granite shelf, striking him in the forehead. His hand went to the wound and touched hot blood.

"Away!" came his attacker's grackled shout. "Go away, ye evil thing."

A thin old woman stepped out from behind an oak tree. Her ash grey hair hung in matted hanks past her shoulders, and her ragged clothes were coated with weeks of dirt and grease. A string of curved boar's teeth and glass beads hung from her neck, clattering as she moved, making her seem more like a puppet on strings than a human being. In her hand she held a stick thicker than her bony forearm and just as long.

"Go away," she snarled, and threw the stick with more force and accuracy than her thin physique foretold.

Alain batted the stick away with his hand and sat back on his haunches, the fingertips of one hand still in contact with the inscrutable granite. The woman took a small step toward him, shooing him away with hissed words and waggling fingers. Alain hung his head and stared at the ground, waiting for his heart to stop pounding and his impatience to abate. The woman picked up some fallen leaves and tossed them at him, muttering under her breath, "Evil one, evil one."

"Mother," he said in a firm voice, and then "*Mother*," as she continued to toss twigs and leaves at him. The woman froze, hands extended in mid-air, and she seemed to see Alain for the first time.

"Ach," she said, straightening in her stance. "'Tis only you." She spoke to him in the Old Tongue, the language of her Cornish ancestors. Alain didn't think she knew how to speak Brezhoneg anymore. "Well, don't just sit there. Come and move the sacks inside, Bastard Boy."

He ground his teeth together as he stood, but did not move to do her bidding. Still mindful of the blood that made its trail down past brow and eye, he let it drip as a sign of his contempt.

"I'm not a boy, Mother."

The woman stopped and turned toward him. She walked back and grabbed him roughly by the sleeve. He did not move.

"Ha," she said as she looked him up and down. "Married, are ye?"

"You know I'm not. Who would have a man who brings a mother-in-law such as you? But I'm not a boy anymore. I haven't been for some time."

She tugged on his sleeve. "Perhaps not. But you're still a bastard. Will always be." She tugged harder, and he jerked his arm from her grasp. She looked up at his face, and Alain felt the thin line of blood course down his cheek. She stared at him a moment more before she turned away.

"Come, Bastard Boy of mine," she said as she walked back the way she had come. "Come. Move sacks."

Alain pressed his lips into a tight, exasperated line and felt an ache in the clenched muscles of his jaw. He wiped his sleeve across his brow, smearing the impotent gesture of his disdain, and winced at the sting of rough fabric against his wound. Then he let out a growling breath and followed the old woman back to her hut.

His mother's ancient hut was built on an even older foundation—stream-washed stones piled in a waist-high circle, ten paces across the inside. Stripling trunks were bent over the foundation to form a dome, and thatch was laid over the lattice. Alain's mother, the Delphine of Dead Ox Wood, walked up to the twig and bark door and pulled it open.

"Back there," she said, pointing deep within the darkness of the hut. "Put them back there." She produced a withered apple from the folds of her dress and sat down at the base of a nearby oak.

"As if I haven't been doing this for years on end," Alain muttered in a quiet voice. He glanced over at the Delphine. She had not heard him, and would not have heard had he spoken more loudly. She was rocking back and forth, gaze intent on the old apple in her hand as first she whispered secrets to it and then held it to her ear to hear its replies.

Resistance had always been a fruitless exercise, but he had never learned how to let it go. Her barbs always hit, and his skin never grew tough enough to thwart their sting.

His walking stick was a few yards away, stuck deep into the forest loam. Reynald, the draft horse he had led up the mountain, stood placidly nearby, the thin halter rope looped around the walking stick. Reynald's size and the sacks mounded on his back spoke of the animal's strength, yet still he allowed himself to be ruled by the tether's thin length. He cropped disinterestedly at the scrollwork of a lace-leafed fern that grew near the root of one of the great trees, and raised his massive head at Alain's approach.

"She's in a state, Reynald," Alain said in resignation. He began to untie the ropes that bound the sacks of grain and fruit his father had sent up for the Delphine. "She's worse in the springtime, I think."

He was tall, but the horse was taller still—Alain's head barely came up to Reynald's withers—and as he reached up to pull down the first sack, he felt the thin-fingered tug and stretch of the scars that laced his chest and arms. Behind him, his mother barked a laugh at some jest only she and the apple knew. A wild flash of anger shot through Alain, anger at the madwoman by the foot of the tree, the woman who had so mutilated his body.

Reynald gave a deep whicker and nosed the young man's shoulder. Alain smiled, and forced his anger to ebb away.

"You're right. No use quarreling with her when she's like this, is there? No use ever, really." He patted the horse's muzzle, and turned back to unloading. Settling a sack of grain on each shoulder, he walked to the hut.

Inside, a clay hearth sent an arm of sharp, tangy smoke up toward the hole in the center of the domed roof. A pile of bedding and rude table served as the only furnishings, but hanging from the rafters, sitting along the ledge of the stone foundation, and lined up against the walls was the collection with which the Delphine made her magic. It was an amazing clutter.

Dried herbs, fruits and tubers, leafy branches, glossy pelts, the severed feet and extricated organs of animals, all lay in bunched piles between pyramids of shiny stones sorted by size and ranks of beetles arranged by color. Bundles of feathers bound by leather strips, dried flowers tied together with woven plaits of grass, and sewn cloth packets of seeds all hung like clappers in the bell of the hut's roof. Alain could smell the braid of drying garlic that hung near the door and the scent of pitch balls his mother had gathered from the far side of the mountain. The odors brought memories, harsh memories of his years as a boy in the Dead Ox Wood with the mad Delphine for a mother.

Memories of home.

He put down the sacks of grain in a clear space near the split log she used as a table. On the log lay the Delphine's only two items of iron: a small flat-bottomed caldron and a knife worn thin by constant use and incessant honing.

Next to the knife lay a piece of river-worn granite, scorched by the tiny hyssop leaves the Delphine had burned on it. So charmed, the stone would bring potency back to a failing husband when placed beneath the sleeping covers. When Alain had arrived, he had seen her working on the charm, and so he had gone up to the outcrop to try once more to feel for the ley line. One did not disturb the Delphine when she was casting.

But ley lines meant nothing to the Delphine, for she did not draw her power from them. Her magic was the magic of the earth. Simple but strong. She conjured and brewed, making amulets and warders and charms for the villagers down in Belvanetes. She concocted potions of great efficacy, too, and many times, exhorted by a frantic mother, Alain had carried a sick child up the mountain to be healed by the woman that same mother would never have deigned to visit on her own. All his life, he had seen the Delphine work her magic, with greater or lesser success, but it was not her sort of magic that he dreamed of wielding.

Alain wanted the greater magic, the magic of the ley lines. His mother had taught him of the lines, spinning tales of their strength and their connection to the mystical Summerland where the mysterious Fair Folk lived. But he had never been able to sense the lines, had never found the talent to cast such magic. To his chagrin, he had not even inherited his mother's baser skills. He looked about the hut with its conglomeration of scavengings and cast-offs, and suddenly envied his mad mother her tremendous affinity with simpler, earth-bound magics.

"What were ye doing over at the rock?" the Delphine asked when he emerged from the hut. Alain walked back to Reynald's side and lifted a sack of winter wheat onto his shoulder. He pulled down a sack of apples and carried it under his arm.

"You were casting when I got here," he said. The sackcloth was rough against his neck. "I didn't want to disturb you."

"Hunh," the old woman said around her leathery apple. "Good thinking, that."

Alain went inside, dropped the sack of wheat and put down the apples on top. The light inside the hut dimmed as the Delphine came to the doorway. "But what were ye doing is what I asked."

Alain felt a flush of rise to his cheeks and he paused to let his embarrassment cool before turning. When he did she was still standing there, framed by the doorway, a black and grey shadow-hag with bits of leaves stuck in her wild hair.

"What were ye doing?" she sang in teasing tones. "Were ye playing with yerself, Boy?"

Jaw set, Alain walked up to the tiny woman. "You know what I was doing," he said as he elbowed past. He walked back to Reynald and took two brace of rabbit and string of quail from the horse's sidebags. He carried them over to the Delphine and held them out to her. She made no motion to take them.

"You were feeling for the line again, weren't ye, Boy?"

He nodded.

She stepped closer and grinned up at him. Alain could smell the foulness of her breath. "Did ye feel anything?" she asked. "Was it warm? Or was it cold?"

Alain shook his head slowly. He lifted the strings of game toward her. "I felt nothing," he said.

"Ach!" she said with a disparaging wave. "Go back t'Marrec, Boy." She turned her back on him and went inside the hut. She squatted before the hearth and fed a few sticks to the coals. "Go back down the mountain, Bastard Boy. Marrec's been calling for ye, and yer no good t'me here."

Alain felt his hands shake with sudden rage. He tossed the quail and rabbits to the dust of her threshold and stormed back to Reynald. Yanking his walking stick out of the ground, he started down the mountain slope. Reynald whinnied as the halter rope came taut, jerking him away from his idle munching, but Alain pulled the horse along.

"It's not my fault," he said under his breath as he stomped down the slope, winding in and out between the boles of oaks. "I can't help it if I can't feel the lines." His voice grew louder with each step he took away from the hut, away from his mother, and away from her insanity. "I'm not to blame. Not for that." A moment later and his voice was louder still. "Nor for the other thing." A half-dozen strides later, he stopped and turned upslope. The hut was all but lost in the darkness of Dead Ox Wood.

"*You're* the one who wouldn't marry," he yelled. Reynald shied and pawed the soft ground with a huge hoof. "Marrec offered. More than I'd have done!" His shout died in the air, answered only by a raven's throaty caw. He stared at the hut a bit longer, but there was no response, no acknowledgment of his outburst.

"Ach," he muttered and started off again. "So I'm no good to you, eh? Well, I don't need you, either. So Marrec's been calling me, eh? Good. At least I'm wanted down there."

His frown deepened as he walked, recalling his mother's words. Above him, the heavy limbs of the Dead Ox Wood began to thin as he and Reynald neared the forest edge.

What was it she had said?

The boughs parted as Alain led Reynald out of the wood and into the gorse-brush of the uplands. Below him lay the rolling hillsides of heather, the meadows of wild wheat and waist-high grasses that led down to his village. Belvanetes sat on the valley floor next to the lazy southward bend of the river. He smelled the powdery sweetness of the pink and white blooms around him, and the sharp bite of woodsmoke from the village.

"Calling me?" he asked out loud. "Marrec's been calling me?"

Out at the far reach of the vale, he saw the white walls of the old Roman villa owned by Jessup, the owner of the land Alain worked with his father. Outside its walls were the huts Alain and the other workers shared. Then he saw the flames eating away at the thatch of his home, and saw men and women running from house to house in the village. Looking seaward, he saw the dragon boat that sat in the sheltered lee of the river's bend.

"Epona's Fillies," he swore. "She knew all along. She knew and said nothing!" He pulled Reynald over to an old stump and leapt up onto the horse's broad back. "Head up, Reynald," he told the horse as he twined his fingers in the coarse black mane. "You're not fast, but you're faster than I am.

"Home!"

Reynald trotted down the hillside. Alain drove him on, urging him to speed. When they reached the valley floor where Reynald had room, the horse broke into a heavy gallop and pounded across the sedge toward the village.

"Move, Reynald," he said into the horse's ear as he hunched over the beast's arched neck. Reynald's breath came in harsh snorts as they went up the low rise into the tiny village. Alain saw a man lying in the dirt in front of the travelers' inn. Farther on, he saw Anton, the Christian cleric, standing in the roadway in front of his small church. He held to his chest two young girls, while their mother wailed over the fallen body of her husband.

The smell of smoke grew stronger. Ahead, Alain saw the flash of sunlight on sword and shield, and it filled him with both fear and a terrible anger. The Viking raiders were straggling back toward the river and their longboat, weighed down by sacks of stolen provisions and whatever precious items the villagers had possessed.

Alain wanted to fight them, wanted Reynald to trample them into the ground. He wanted to see their skulls crushed under the Reynald's huge hooves like summer melons, but his mother's words echoed through his brain.

"Marrec's been calling," Alain said to himself, and rode on toward his home.

Two of the raiders walked across the pasture in front of his burning home, smiling and laughing. One carried a straining burlap sack over his shoulder while the other struggled with an overfull barrow-cart.

Alain's anger boiled up in a wordless roar and the Norsemen looked up in surprise. The first man had enough time to drop his bundle before Reynald plowed into him and sent him flying like a wind-blown leaf.

Reynald was not slowed by the impact and Alain tugged on the halter to turn him around. He slapped the horse's hindquarter with his walking stick, urged him back into a run, and steered him toward the second raider.

The second Viking let go the barrow and stepped to a clear space to draw his sword. Alain took the thin end of his walking stick in hand and swung the heavy end in a circle over his head. They closed. The Viking stood, sword up. The blade flared with sunlight like an angry tongue of flame.

With a jerk to Reynald's halter, Alain veered the horse out of reach of the sword and swung his walking stick in a low, rising curve. He caught the raider under the chin with a blow that sent him tumbling backward. Alain pulled Reynald to a halt, leapt to the ground, and dashed across the distance to the burning hut.

Smoke from the damp, flaming thatch was thick and acrid. Alain stepped into the one-room cottage and blinked away stinging tears. The place was a tumble, chairs and tables upturned, crockery shards on the floor.

"Papa!" he called through the smoke. He took a few steps forward but the heat kept him at bay. The roofbeams flared in a fire-fall of burning rushes, and Alain was forced back. In the hot light he spied a hand and arm poking out from beneath an overturned bench. He pulled the heavy bench back and found a Viking, his pale hair matted with dark blood. The heat surged again and Alain backed out of the cottage.

The two Vikings he had rushed in the yard were well across the pasture. They supported one another as they limped off, their booty left behind in a cluttered pile. Reynald stood close by, nervously eyeing the flaming hut. Alain stared at the burning ruin of his home. There was no saving it or anything within.

He walked over to the edge of the turnip field. The spring plantings had been trampled by raiders' feet, the clean furrows of dark earth broken and the seedlings scattered. Alain looked at the two retreating raiders.

"I should have killed you," he shouted at them.

A muffled scream broke through from the stable. It was a woman's voice and it screamed again, clearly, a hot and angry "No!" that tore at the screamer's throat. Alain began to run.

Beneath the fury of the shouted word, he recognized the voice of the landlord's daughter. He ran into the stable and found Josselyn, bare legs flailing, one of her arms pinned to the straw by a heavy hand. With her free hand she pummeled the grunting, red-bearded man who was atop her. The Viking's pale and hairy rear was exposed, buttocks tensing as he tried to position himself.

The man's sword lay near his feet. Alain grabbed it. It was heavy, but it was not the first time he had held a sword. He could stab, but he might miss and hurt Josselyn, so he dragged the point across the rapist's bare behind, drawing a red line of blood.

The man's grunts turned into a roar. He leapt up, only to be tangled by his leggings bunched at mid-thigh. He fell backward and roared again as he landed on his wound. Alain dashed in and pulled Josselyn away from her attacker.

The Norseman lunged and Alain struck at him with the sword. The clumsy blow was easily turned by the bronze plates sewn onto the Viking's thick leather doublet, but he did not reach for Alain again.

Josselyn was safely out of the man's reach, and Alain stood firmly between them, protecting his longtime friend. He held the sword in both hands as Josselyn's father had shown him. There was a moment of quiet as the Norseman got to his feet. Alain regarded the face of his enemy. He saw clearly the steadiness of the marauder's eye, the scars on his forearms, and the heavy breath of grey in his hair. Alain grew afraid, wondering if he could fight the man off if he charged.

The Viking snarled, gesturing and shouting. Alain did not understand him. They faced each other, the man raging on in his language of strange vowels, and Alain standing quiet and firm with upraised sword. The man was not as tall as Alain but he was heavier across the shoulders. He pointed to the sword Alain held and put out his hand, demanding its return.

"What?" Alain said, and shook his head. Indignation made him brave, and to punctuate his point he slashed the sword across the space between them. He held the sword as he'd seen the Count's soldiers do in practice. He took a step toward the raider and slashed again. The Viking stood his ground, watching Alain intently, looking for the best opening. If the man rushed him, Alain would definitely fail. He had to turn the tide.

Calmly, and with as much menace as he could muster, Alain spoke to the man. "I know you don't understand me, but I'll tell you this. I nearly killed your two friends out there with a walking stick. Now I have your sword, and unless you run right at this moment, I shall show you what I can do with it." He motioned toward the stable door with the point of the sword.

The raider's blue-eyed gaze moved from Alain to the sword and to the smoky yard outside. The man's brow wrinkled and he took a wincing backward step. Then he nodded, hitched up his breeches, and ran out. Alain watched for a moment, knees shaking, as the Norseman ran unevenly across the field toward his boat.

"Alain."

Josselyn beckoned him from the back of the stable. She knelt down and Alain realized there was a man lying in the deep straw. It was Marrec.

"Papa." He dropped to his knees next to the old ploughman. His father's shirt was soaked with blood and a great deal more covered his face. "Does he live?"

"Yes, though maybe not for much longer. Give me the sword."

Alain hesitated. "What?"

Josselyn showed him an open hand and a fierce look, and he handed her the weapon. With it, she pierced the hem of her dress and tore off strips.

"We have to get him up to the house, and quickly. Can you carry him?"

Marrec was a large man, almost as tall as Alain himself and a good bit stouter. Alain considered the distance from the stable to Josselyn's homestead.

"No," he said, but remembered the raiders he'd knocked down in the yard. "I'll be right back," he said.

"Hurry," he heard her say as he ran from the stable.

Out in the yard, Alain saw the burning remnants of his home, the timbers of its windward wall stabbing the air with smoky fingers. He gave thanks to the White Goddess that the wind blew sparks out toward the fields and not toward the stable or Jessup's buildings.

Then he ran to the barrow-cart, righted it, and made haste back to the stable.

Alain and Josselyn struggled to get Marrec into the cart. The big man moaned once. Alain looked to Josselyn hopefully, but her terse expression gave him little hope. He wheeled the barrow-cart out with its unconscious burden, then headed down the path that led between the plowed fields.

The whitewashed walls of Josselyn's homestead—built by Gallic hands for Roman lords—gleamed as a shower of sunlight broke through the clouds. The front doors and the gates hung open, and Alain heard wailing as they approached.

"Where is everyone?" he asked. "Where is your father?"

"Father is dead," she said and Alain stumbled, nearly upsetting the barrow. He glanced sidelong at the young woman, startled by the news and by the calmness of her voice. Her home attacked, her body assaulted, and her father slain, why did she not weep? Alain wondered at her lack of emotion. He felt that he should say something, but couldn't imagine what words to use.

Marrec moaned again, and Alain put his mind back on the task of saving his father's life.

"And the others?" he asked as they reached the gate.

"I do not know," she said. "Father told me to run as they struck him down. He wanted no hostages this time. Not like...not like Mother." Her stoic façade cracked, and Alain heard the grief and anger that roiled within her.

He understood. It had been springtime then, too, three years ago, when Jessup's ransom returned his wife to her family.

"Let's get Marrec inside," he said as he wheeled the barrow-cart through the garden gate. "Calin! Get your old bones out here."

The kitchen door opened a crack and an old, grey head poked out of the narrow opening.

"Get out here, Calin," Alain said. "Marrec's been hurt." The old steward opened the door farther and Alain saw a gaggle of kitchenmaids behind him, eyes red from weeping, necks craning to see what was astir. Calin turned on them sharply.

"Don't be standing there like hens in the road. Clear some room, girls. And get water."

The two men pulled Marrec out of the cart and carried him up to the kitchen. Inside, long planks were set up on trestles. On them and elsewhere about the large kitchen Alain saw the remnants of the interrupted preparations for the evening meal: broken jugs, overturned bowls, and scattered, half-trimmed vegetables. Bread dough sat on window sills to rise in the springtime sun and pots simmered untended over dying coals. The smell of stewing beans and the spirit of yeast were thick in the air, mixed with the stench of fear and blood.

Two of the trestled tables had been cleared, and they brought Marrec over to one of them. On the other lay the body of Jessup, Josselyn's father. Cold and grey, he lay unnaturally still. His torso had been bound with linen, but from beneath the wrappings Alain could see the bloom of blood, chest to hip. Beside him on the table lay his sword, the one with which he had instructed Alain the previous summer. Alain had thought it a thing of beauty then, all silver in the bright sun. In its shiny length Alain had seen the breath of gods. Now it looked different, an angry, earthly tool covered with clotted blood. Alain's hand went to his belt to touch the hilt of the Viking's sword he still carried.

Marrec moaned, and Alain turned his attention back to the other table. Calin was examining the wounds.

"It's bad," the old steward said.

"Will he be all right?"

Calin wrung out a cotton cloth and placed it to the cut on Marrec's head. "Hold that," he told Alain, and then tore at Marrec's tunic. Calin hissed as he saw the wound the tunic had hidden. Alain could only stare at the blood and the deep dark gash that cut from his father's neck across his chest and into his left arm.

"Will he live?" he asked, fearful of what the answer might be, for looking at the long, dark laceration, he believed only one answer was possible.

Calin emptied a pitcher of water Marrec's chest and neck. Reddened water coursed across the rough wood and down to the floor. "I've seen worse, much worse, at Jengland-Breslé when your father and I went up against bald King Charles." He looked up at Alain. "It's bad. But don't give up on the old ploughman yet."

"I won't," he said, and *I can't*, he added to himself. "What can I do?"

"Just hold that cloth to his scalp, for now. The wounds are serious, and'll take some sewing. We may need help from the Delphine."

Marrec's groaned and his eyes fluttered open. "Boy," he said as he looked up and saw Alain's face. The voice was cracked and weak, but his laborer's hand reached up and grabbed Alain's shoulder with a slow, urgent strength. "Boy," Marrec said again. Alain smiled.

"Yes, Papa. I'm right here."

Marrec pulled Alain down close. "By Epona's filthy tail, Boy, what were you doing up in the wood so long? I needed you."

Alain's smile died. "I..." he began, but could speak no more, caught in the tumult of his own emotions. He looked at Calin, then back at his father. Marrec squinted up at him, and Alain could see the old man's jaw working beneath the thick, grey moustache.

"Why were you gone so long?" he asked. "To deliver a few sacks of grain?" His grip tightened. Alain felt as if his collarbone would pop. "You're a foolish bastard, Boy. While you were jawing with that witch, our house burned and I've been killed." He pushed Alain away then, and turned to Calin. "Worthless, that boy. Worthless."

"Hush, Ploughman," Calin said. "And be glad he's here. I've got to send him back up to the Wood."

"You might as well kill me now than wait for him to do a chore."

"Hush, Marrec." Calin gave Alain a weak smile. "He doesn't know what he's talking, Boy. It's the blow to his head."

"I know what I'm saying," Marrec mumbled as his eyes rolled white and closed. "That boy will be the death of me. Mark my words."

Alain took a step back from the table, heart pounding and gaze gone hard. He stared at the ploughman on the table.

"Boy," the steward said. "*Alain.*"

Alain looked up at Calin, silent behind his armor of hurt.

"I need a poultice. From the Delphine. To draw out the bad humours from this wound. It's too close to his heart. You must go up to the Wood."

Alain stood, caught between his love, his desire to help, and his pain-fed anger.

"Go," Calin said, tipping the balance. "Do not prove your father right."

Alain turned and left the kitchen, pushing the ancient door wide and walking out through the garden gate with long strides. He headed directly across the turnip field and was halfway to the stable by the time Josselyn caught up with him.

"Stop," she said as she ran up to him, breathless.

"What do you want," he said harshly. He turned to find her standing a few paces behind him, fists on her hips and a scowl in her eyes. The sharp scent of bruised turnip greens rose from the path he'd broken through the field. "Josée, I'm sorry," he said.

Josselyn walked up to him, the torn hem of her dress whispering through the calf-high greens. She said nothing, only reached out and touched his forearm with gentle fingertips. Bronze bracelets at her wrist caught the sun and winked.

"I just wanted," she began. "To thank you."

Alain saw in Josselyn the same proud features that had graced her mother's face. With intense eyes of iron-grey, a wide mouth now turned down in an angry frown, the strong sweep of her jaw, and a long, thick braid of sun-gold hair across her shoulder, she was the greatest thing of beauty he had ever seen. He did not know what to say to her now, however. After so many years of friendship, Alain found himself tongue-tied by concern and love.

Josselyn caught him looking at her. She made a small shake of her head. "Don't fret," she told him. "I will grieve. Later, when there is time."

"I should go," he said. "I know what herbs Calin needs. I've helped the Delphine prepare a hundred such poultices."

Josselyn looked up and pulled back a stray lock of hair that had fallen across her face. "Take one of the other horses," she told him. "Reynald is tired."

Alain shook his head. "The Wood is a strange place. Reynald knows it better." He hesitated before leaving her. "I am sorry," he said. "About your father, about our cottage. About...about everything."

"I know," she said. "Hurry back."

Alain turned and ran for the stable.

two

Alain rode the long trail up into Dead Ox Wood, slashing at branches with the Viking sword. Even high atop Reynald's back, there were not many in his way, but he struck at them all the same, taking out his frustration on the greenery. Reynald, unused to such violence, flinched with every flash of steel, and with every word Alain spat into the air.

"Bastard." A branch fell to the forest floor.

"Fool." A bough shivered.

"Boy."

"Worthless."

Finally, a cut branch fell on Reynald's nose. The horse snorted and shied. Alain prodded the horse's flank with his heel, but Reynald refused to continue. Frustration mounted in Alain like a tide, building in his breast until he could contain it no longer.

"Move your carcass!" he yelled and slapped Reynald's rear with the flat of the sword. The horse's eyes showed white and his legs shivered, but he did not move. Alain could only sit and fume.

Beyond the trees, the sun dipped low in the sky. The air had begun to chill. Night was coming, and the fog was on its way. In his haste, Alain had forgotten a lamp or torch. His father's words closed in upon him like a cold, cold quilt. He rubbed at his chest to dispel the sensation, and his fingers felt the welts of the scars on his chest. His hands went to the ties of his shirt and tore at the cloth. Fabric parted and Alain looked down at the angry lacework that curled across his flesh, raised, dark, and polished in the fading light.

The scars were the marks of a magical rite, impotent marks as it turned out, a cruel gift from his mother. Memories flooded his mind: darkness, the touch of rope, smoke that burned his eyes, the faint song of iron heated cherry-red, the smells of sweet thyme and sharp rosemary, the slow kiss of pain, and then more darkness. They were images of his youth, his years living with the Delphine. He began to claw at the shiny tapestry, scrabbling at the scars with nails still bloody from carrying his wounded father. He scratched until he tore, and his own blood mixed with Marrec's, and still the marks lay useless on his breast.

Alain leaned forward against Reynald's massive neck and began to weep. "I am nothing but the Bastard Boy of Dead Ox Wood," he whispered, and truly did not care whether he—or anyone else—lived or died. He glanced up through the branches. The first blood of sunset touched the bellies of the clouds, and he thought of his father, lying on the table in Josselyn's kitchen, ruddy water flowing from his wounds down to the floor. Time was precious, and he was wasting it. He touched Reynald's side with his toe.

"Come on, old friend. I've caused enough grief, already. I don't want to cause more."

Reynald began to trot upward along the path the two of them had traveled many times before.

The wood was quiet in the hour before twilight, the only sound the muffled crunch of mulch and twigs beneath Reynald's hooves. The barest breath of a breeze whispered in the high branches, unable to penetrate to the forest floor. All else was still.

Alain felt the brooding presence of the Dead Ox Wood. He let his mind expand to meet the presence, to invite the power of the forest and the mountain into his soul. As always, the magic kept its distance. Alain imagined it dancing around him, above him, kept at bay by his absent talent. He gave up and urged Reynald into a faster gait. The wind freshened as the dusk deepened. The fog was coming and the forest was lost in hues of blue-grey and deep-green.

When they arrived at the Delphine's hut, Alain reined Reynald to a halt and jumped to the ground. He looped Reynald's tether over a branch and patted the horse's cheek.

"Stay here," he bade the horse. Then, sword still in hand, he ran toward the dim orange glow that came from the hut.

"Mother," he called as he opened the thin door. "Marrec's been wounded and Calin needs a—"

The scream was barely human. The dark lump of clothes that huddled before the hearth leapt up. Alain saw white-rimmed eyes, snarling lips, firelight on a sharp-edged blade. He defended himself with his walking stick, but it was not the walking stick that he held. It was the sword, the prize of his bravery, taken up the mountainside to slash at tree limbs.

The blow landed before he knew it, the blade cutting through thin cords in the Delphine's neck. Blood showered them both and she fell back. The blade of her knife scraped against stone, bringing sparks, and her head hit against the hearth with a crack. Then all was silent.

Alain stared. He stared and could not breathe. His lips formed a word.

"Mother."

He knelt and reached for the wound. Blood still pumped and he pressed his hand against it to hold in the tide. He felt it spurt hot and thick through his fingers.

"No," he said. "Epona, *no*," as if words could do what his hands could not. Then the blood simply stopped flowing, and Alain saw the Delphine's tiny body shrink the slightest bit, as if the thin breath in her lungs had made up a portion of her size. He looked about the room.

On the hearth, the caldron bubbled with a thick, resinous potion, filling the air with a pungency that cut through even the heavy smell of the Delphine's blood. Nearby lay a small clay flask. He touched the Delphine's limp hand and crushed herbs fell from her fingers. He had interrupted a casting. In her half-mad trance, she had not recognized him. And in his preoccupied state, he had killed her.

He stood, horrified by his deed. "No," he said again, repeating the word over and over. His hand gripped the hilt of the sword and the word grew, multiplied, became a river of negation. He turned away from the body, then turned back.

Within his breast, hatred mingled with filial love, merged, convulsed. Fury built, fed by the scars of his past, scars created by his mother's cruel insanity. The sword came up, raised by the power of anger and rejection, and what he had first done in innocent defense now became an outpouring of his rage. Sound burst past his lips, and his vision burned. The sword, once raised, fell with inevitable force and feral vengeance. The scars across his chest stretched as he raised the blade to scrape the domed roof, each blow slashing through a memory, a vision, a wound. And the sword fell, and fell, and fell, and when it finally came to rest, Alain wept, anguished. The woody bones of the roof were chipped and cracked. The body at his feet had fared far worse.

He ran from his second deed as he had not run from the first. He ran out of the hut and into the clearing. Above him, the clouds glowed hot with the last of their sunset fire. A gathering of starlings coursed the evening sky. Swooping, they turned. They flocked in toward the Dead Ox Wood and the clearing around the hut of the dead Delphine, filling it with their high and piercing whistles.

He ran into the darkness of the trees, blindly, arms up to protect his face from lashing branches. In every shadow and every darkened corner of the wood he saw the phantom of the Delphine, hacked and mangled by his own fury. He stopped in his flight, collapsing against the intertwining roots of two immense oaks. He looked up into their branches and tears ran from his eyes.

"What am I?" he asked the twin trees.

A monster, came his own answer. Evil one.

What have ye done to me, Bastard Boy?

Alain leapt up in shock. The words were the Delphine's, as was the voice. But the sound echoed within his head and not in his ears.

Where have ye gone? I cannot see ye.

It was her voice, panicked and trembling. Alain spun around, sword out, expecting to see her appear from behind every tree.

"Where are you?" he cried.

In answer there came only a moan, a rising pitch of maddened pain that chilled Alain's skin and sent him running back to Reynald and home.

Reynald was nearly wild with terror when Alain reached the hut. The wailing had grown and it was clear that Reynald heard it too. Alain grabbed the horse's tether and started to untie it.

"Marrec," he said, remembering the reason he'd come. "Hold, Reynald. A moment longer." The horse calmed slightly at the sound of Alain's voice, but his great hooves remained restless, and his eyes rolled white with each peak in the spirit's wail.

Alain willed himself not to look at his mother's body as he ducked into the hut. He kept his tear-filled eyes raised. In the dim light from the hearth, he cut down what he needed from the myriad items hanging about the room. He took seeds of psyllum, dried iris bulbs, drapes of moss, a branch of agrimony, white clay from the seashore cliffs, and a packet of dried bogberries. As he turned to go, eyes and arms full with their respective burdens, the spirit voice ceased. He looked down before he could stop himself.

The Delphine lay where he had left her, twisted and broken in blood-soaked rags, but her face had changed. Her eyes were now open, and her lips were drawn back in a brown-toothed rictus.

Heart hammering and gaze fixed on the corpse that lay on the earthen floor, Alain edged around to the door. He backed out into the night air. The branches above were alive with wind and the whistling of starlings.

"I am sorry, Mother," he said, remorseful grief tightening his throat. "I truly am."

Ye've killed me! Ach, my Bastard Boy, ye've killed me!

The keening began anew.

Alain ran to Reynald. The horse needed no urging to flee the terrible place, and they plunged headlong down the mountainside.

The Delphine's ethereal wail had subsided with the setting sun, but when Alain rode into the village, people were still out of doors despite the darkness of night. They had gathered in knots along the old Roman roadway that passed through the heart of the hamlet, and near the Christian church, a large group crowded together around Brother Anton and Robert, who was the machtiern for Count Vanes and charged with keeping the peace in the local villages.

As Alain rode past, conversation stopped. People pointed at him, eyes wide with fear. He rode on, fearing what their actions foretold.

He stabled the shivering Reynald and ran to the homestead. Calin met him at the gate, blocking the entrance. He lifted his oil lamp and looked Alain up and down.

"You look like the spirit of death," the old man said, making one of the Christian warding signs with his hand.

Alain looked down at himself. He was a frightful sight, pale and covered with blood. He hadn't had time to think, did not yet know how to tell the tale of the Delphine's death.

"There was an accident," he said. "But I brought—"

"We heard the Delphine's keening across the valley, Boy." His words were harsh, bitten off. "You killed her." It was not an accusation.

"I...it was an accident." The words sounded pathetic to his own ears. "I brought what you need for the poultice."

"Keep it. I'll not take anything from such murderous hands."

"But Papa needs—"

"I'll nurse the ploughman through this without your help."

"Calin," came Josselyn's voice from beyond the wall. Let him through."

"No, Mistress," the steward said over his shoulder. "I'll not. He's accursed. First a bastard and now a matricide. He may have killed the Delphine, but he'll not kill the ploughman. He's a demon. Evil."

"Calin, please. It's Alain. Stand aside."

"No, mistress. I cannot."

"Josselyn," Alain called. "How is Marrec?"

Josselyn forced her way under the steward's arm. She gasped as she caught sight of Alain in the lamp's flickering light. Alain looked down at the ground, unwilling to meet the horror he saw in her eyes. "Your father still lives," she told him.

"No thanks to you, Boy," the steward said.

"That's enough," Josselyn said. "Go back to the house." The old man began to shake his head but Josselyn put a hand on his chest and pushed. "Go. Don't worry, old soldier. I will not let him in."

With a last withering look at Alain, Calin handed her the lamp and went back inside the gate. Alain was certain the old veteran had not gone far, and was probably waiting in the shadows to bar his entry, should Alain insist on seeing his father.

"I'm sorry," Josselyn said when they were alone.

"He has reason," Alain replied, and then in a quieter voice said, "Take these things." He held out the bundle of items from the Delphine's hut. "Don't let Marrec die because of me."

"But what can I do with these things? I cannot cast."

"Neither can I," he whispered. "Most of the Delphine's

healing magic was no magic at all." In a few moments' time, he gave her instructions on the grinding of the elements and the application of the poultice.

"But Calin may not allow it."

"Is Calin servant or master in this house?" Alain asked her bluntly. Josselyn's cheeks blanched at his words and Alain felt a blush of shame rise to his own. "Forgive me," he said. "I'm just worried about Marrec."

She looked away, trying to manage her own grief. Her eyes filled with unspilled grief.

"Ach, every thing I touch turns sour," he said, unable to control the thousand emotions he felt. He felt worry for Marrec, love for Josselyn, grief for Jessup, anger for his past, fear for his future, and all of them about the Delphine. He held out the bundle of ingredients. "Here, use the poultice if the wound turns sour. Tell Calin...tell him you learned it from your own mother. He'll not deny you that, if you press him on it."

She looked at him, grey eyes searching his face, and then looked down at the bundle of herbs. "I don't know," she said. "So much has happened. What if..."

Now, it was Alain's turn away. He looked up into the night sky and smelled the scent of the sea in the breeze from the south. He smelled also the ashy remnants of his home.

"Alain," said the woman behind him.

He frowned at the mention of his name and felt the dried blood on his face wrinkle and crack. Without looking back, he dropped the bundle to the ground and walked off toward the stable.

"Alain," she said again.

He continued walking, heading across the trampled turnip field. Behind him, he heard the gate close and latch. When he looked back, Josselyn was gone. So was the bundle.

At least I've had been able to do that much, he thought as he walked on.

It had been a long and draining day, and Alain wanted nothing more than a quiet place to curl up and give vent to the ocean of grief that filled him, but he could not. Before he allowed himself the luxury of sleep, there was one last task he had to complete.

three

This time he did not take Reynald. The horse had done enough for one day.

The night had been half spent when he set out, and by the time he arrived at the hut, dawn was breaking through the darkness of the east. A thick fog lingered in the trees of Dead Ox Wood, and the starlings clustered in the dripping trees and sang to the green-roofed canopy. The Delphine's spirit, if it was still there, was quiet.

At the door to the hut, Alain prepared himself for what needed to be done. The rickety door stood open, just as he'd left it in his rush to escape his crime, but his guilt stopped him before he could enter. He said a silent prayer to the gods of the forest, asking for forgiveness and for strength. Then he entered, knelt down, and picked up the Delphine's broken body.

"So light," he said as he cradled the corpse in his arms.

He walked slowly through the blanket of mist that clung to the forest like a shroud. The black-jacketed starlings kept pace, flitting from branch to branch and hopping along beside him on the ground. They followed him in numbers that filled the forest with life and sound. At the edge of the rill where his mother had drawn her daily water, he laid her body down.

He removed the string of teeth and beads from around her neck. The leather knot was tight, but came loose under Alain's patient fingers. He removed the boar's teeth and set them on the ground. Then he removed the six snakestones, beads of blue glass with white clay laid into spiral engravings. Of the six, he chose the best two and, standing at the mist-wrapped edge of the mountain pool, tossed them into the deepest spot.

Ripples radiated outward, marking the twin points of their passage. Alain watched the circles grow, meet, fade across the water's surface. According to the ancient rites, he spoke to the powers beyond the Veil.

"May the spirits of this wood and of the mountain waters be pleased by our offering," he said. There was no response, but he felt his own burden lighten.

Hoping the gods were propitiated, Alain set about his work. He scrubbed his mother's clothing and washed her body with free-running water. His gorge rebelled at the evidence of his savagery, so he plucked shoots of sour-grass and chewed them, their tartness helping to keep his nausea at bay.

Her clothes washed and wrung out, her body cleansed, her hair rinsed and tied back, Alain found in her features a strange, fey beauty. With her cloak he bound her torso and with a stretch of cloth retrieved from the hut, he wound a shroud.

At the nexus of an oak's buttressing roots, he scooped out a grave. Lightly, solemnly, he laid the Delphine in the shallow bed, curled up on her side as if in sleep. He placed the curved boar's teeth about her in a warding circle, planting each one point up in the rootlets that laced the soft forest earth. The boar's virility and strength would protect her in her journey beyond the Veil. He retrieved apples and grain from her hut, wrapped them in a piece of oiled leather, and laid it near her head. With her, too, he placed her knife and her caldron, her only two items of true permanence. Then he gathered clean stones from the creekbed and placed them atop her. Their rounded shapes stacked with ease, building up to form a cairn.

It was a peaceful place. The restful splash of water in the creekbed created a fundament of sound atop which danced the shimmering jubilance of the still-present starlings.

He walked to the pool and bathed in clear water so cold it made his head ache. With gritty earth, he scrubbed away the blood and sweat that caked his skin. On the shore, he rubbed himself with thyme and lavender before he donned his sun-dried clothing. Then he turned to look upon his work.

"It is a good barrow, if a small one," he decided with a nod. Then he took the lace of leather with its four remaining snakestones and tied it about his own neck. With starlings still swirling through the wood, and only a straw bed and an uncertain future awaiting him in the valley, he headed back down the mountainside.

The sun was high in a cloud-patched sky when Alain walked back into the village of Belvanetes. Fearing the stares and comments of his neighbors, he avoided the old Roman road that went through the heart of the village and kept to the river path. He ducked under boughs and hopped over exposed roots, walking beside the green waters. Fatigue pulled at his limbs and the day's growing warmth sapped his strength, but when he came around the last bend, his heart thudded to life.

Josselyn and the men and women of her household stood in a circle down in the low pasture. In the center of the circle was a grave, freshly-dug. Brother Anton stood beside it, intoning the ritual words for the dead. Josselyn was sobbing, held upright by servants on either side. She reached out for the open grave, all dignity thrown away in her open mourning, her supporters keeping her from diving in to join her father's corpse.

Alain stepped off the river path and walked toward the group, but Calin caught sight of him, and with a small gesture and a mouthed word, barred him from the ceremony. He stood there, the scent of clover sweet in his nose, the warmth of the sun on his back, and waited until the cleric completed his words and the members of the house turned and made their way back to the house. Cook saw him, and so did the housekeeper, Judica, but they said nothing and did not tell Josselyn of his presence. Calin stayed, as did Hincmar, the house's porter. They picked up spades and began to fill the grave.

"Go on," Calin said when Alain walked up to the grave. "You're not welcome here."

"Calin," Hincmar said with a disapproving tone. "The boy can do no harm to Jessup, now. You'll show proper respect, won't you, Alain?"

"I will," he said. "I promise." He came closer and with a look and an outstretched hand asked Hincmar if he could help fill the grave. Hincmar glanced at Calin and noted first the old soldier's disapproving scowl and then his shrug of resignation. Hincmar gave the spade to Alain, and Alain set to work.

Jessup's grave had been dug alongside his wife's. Marisca had been buried here in the low pasture, instead of in hallowed ground near her beloved church, because her death was unsavory in the church's eyes.

When she had been returned after two years imprisonment, there was little left of the woman the Vikings had abducted. She had been a devout follower of the growing faith of the Christ, but in the end, she had come back to her Briezh heritage. The dagger that had been denied her as a captive she took up freely upon her return. It allowed her a small portion of the dignity she deserved as Jessup's wife, and her suicide wiped clean the shame of her captivity and violation.

Jessup had paupered himself to raise her ransom, but he had never berated her for her suicide. That she had died free and in her own land was worth the financial ruination. In the years after her death, Jessup had remained a good master, and had treated Alain well. He had never discouraged Alain's friendship with Josselyn, and had taken time to show him how to use a sword when Alain's own father barely took the time to say good morning. Showing proper respect for his fallen master was an easy thing for Alain to do, and the three of them worked in silence, the two older men spelling each other, and Alain working steadily to fill the grave. As he shoveled the black, moist earth into the dark hole, Alain thought back on the man they were burying, and to what lay ahead for his own future.

For Alain, he saw no answers. Only questions.

four

A face hove out of the darkness. Beautiful. Black beard, black hair, black eyes smiling. The face glowed with hearthlight. Full lips parted, formed a word.

"Delphine."

The voice was soft, a caress. Love bloomed as hands reached out, became confusion as they grasped, throttled. Pain. The face twisted into a cruel cousin of its former self. Breath grew scant through a throat painfully constricted. The hands strangled. The mouth laughed, revealing white, even teeth.

"Delphine."

The face changed again, grew younger. Black hair captured light and became blond, the beard withdrew to reveal wide cliffs of cheek beneath deep eyes of heartwood brown. Alain's face.

Silver flashed through the firelight. The sword struck. Disbelief. Darkness.

Alain woke, eyes open, staring at the rafters, the vision still vivid in his mind. He shivered, but not simply from cold. The face—and the violence—froze him to his core. He rubbed his eyes and chafed his arms to dispel the chill.

Pre-dawn light peeked through gaps in the stable wall, and lark-song drifted in from the fields. One of the dogs beside him dream-yelped with twitching feet. Alain curled up on his side and burrowed back down amid the straw and sleeping dogs, seeking warmth and freedom from the continued nightmares.

The night following her burial, the Delphine's wail of death had returned, bringing him a series of nightly visions. In the fortnight since, Alain had slept little, disturbed each night by the sounds and images that rolled down from Dead Ox Wood. He had worked each day as best he could, tending to the fields while Marrec convalesced. But every night, his mother's spirit railed on, sending madness down from the mountain to torture his sleep. Each night, the visions grew stronger, filling his head with chaotic visions, shadows in the dark, terrifying and undecipherable. Tonight's dream had been the strongest of all, and its clarity set it apart from all the rest. He wondered how long they would continue.

He knew he would be unable to get any more sleep, so he rolled over onto his back again and stared at the roofbeams. The face of the man in the dream haunted him. It was a regal face, one that seemed almost familiar, but it was no face Alain had ever known.

"He called her 'Delphine,'" Alain muttered to himself.

For as long as he had been alive, Alain had only heard his mother referred to as *the* Delphine, as if there were no other. It had been spoken such as a title might be spoken, like "the Machtiern," "the Abbot," or "the Count." He had taken it as such, and also as something more palatable to the villagers' minds than "the Witch," though he had heard her called that, too. It had never occurred to him that "Delphine" might have been his mother's name.

He heard a gruff cough and heavy step outside. The stable door opened. Marrec entered and walked over to Reynald's stall. Calin had not allowed Marrec past the homestead walls during his recovery, and Alain had not been allowed within them, and so he had not seen his father since the Viking raid. He got up from his bed of straw and ran to greet his father. Marrec glanced at his son, but paid him no mind. He ignored Alain's presence and backed the big horse out into the main area of the stable, but Alain was unperturbed, any hurt from his father's coolness washed away by relief at seeing the old ploughman on his feet once more.

Brushing chaff from his clothes, Alain lifted Reynald's harness from its pins on the wall and carried it to his father.

"You'll be working today?" he asked Marrec.

Marrec stared at his son, working his jaw from side to side. The old man's eyes were red and bags lay heavy beneath them. Alain saw the still-pink scar that ran across his father's brow, jumped to his neck, and dove beneath his heavy tunic.

"Aye," Marrec said. He looked as if he had tasted something bitter. "I've been long enough abed."

Alain held out the harness. The ploughman made no move to take it. This time the insult stung, and Alain felt blood rise to his cheeks. Instead, he refused to react, and began to harness Reynald himself, instead.

"Leave it be," Marrec said.

"I don't mind, Papa."

The ploughman's heavy hand grabbed Alain by the collar and threw the young man to the ground. Marrec stood above him, feet apart, hands clenched at his sides. "Leave it be, I said. I want no help from your evil hands."

Alain released the strips of leather he still held. He got to his feet and moved to the door. "You don't know what happened."

Marrec grunted. He picked up the leather and began to harness the patient horse. "I know enough."

"You know what Calin told you."

"I know what I've *seen*." He looked over his shoulder at Alain and tapped a finger against his temple. "Here."

"What?"

"At night," he said.

"The sendings? You've seen them, too?"

Marrec paused. "We all have." His shoulders sagged at the admission. "For nearly a week, now. You've cursed us all."

A moment passed. Alain stood by the door, arms hugging his own slender frame for warmth. Marrec stood near Reynald's head, unmoving, his back to his son.

"I'm sorry," Alain said quietly. "It was an accident. She just...." He drew a deep breath and let it out slowly. "I had no reason to kill her."

Marrec turned. "No?" he said. "No reason?" In two great strides he was face to face with his son. The young man cringed at the expected blow, hands protecting his face. Marrec grabbed Alain's collar and tugged down. Alain felt his father's callused finger trace one of the lines the Delphine had carved on his chest. He looked at Marrec through tousled hair and splayed fingers, saw the fury on his father's face, the anger with which he viewed his son's mutilation.

"No reason? None? After what she did?" He released Alain's shirt and turned his back on the young man. "After what I allowed?"

Alain stared at his father's back. "I had reason to hate her," Alain said. "Certainly that. But to kill her? No."

"Then why did you?"

He shrugged and shrank back against the stable wall. "There is no *why*. She was casting. I interrupted her. She didn't know who I was. She came at me with her knife and I...." Alain looked up but Marrec still had his back turned. The pain of remembering, the horror of his actions choked his throat. Tears brimmed his eyes and fell to the straw at his feet. "I didn't mean to kill her," he whispered slowly. "I'm sorry."

Marrec turned halfway, his gaze still fixed on the ground. The ploughman's jaw was working again, unshaven chin moving side to side beneath the thick moustache. He looked at his son.

"I'm sorry," Alain said again, voice pleading. He stood before his father and the grief struck him afresh. He hid his face in his hands and turned away.

A boot scuffed the dirt. Alain felt a hand on his shoulder. Marrec turned his son around and pulled him into his arms. Alain melted against his father's solid frame. The ploughman stroked Alain's long hair.

"Hush, now," Marrec said, soft words fighting heavy emotions. He held him a moment longer, rocking gently. "It could be just as you say. We'll leave it there and speak no more on it." He stepped back and held out the halter. He inclined his head toward the waiting horse. "Harness the old boy up, then. I'll go ready the plow."

Alain met his father's gaze. In it he saw, though not understanding, at least forgiveness.

"Yes, Father," he said.

The sun hung above a the grey lid of clouds, burning through the overcast in a circle of heady light that spoke of summer warmth but delivered none.

Alain walked the river-front field, following his father who followed the plow that was pulled by Reynald. Spring clover, cropped close by grazing sheep, disappeared, curling up from the plow's angled blade. Black soil came up. Alain trimmed the lines as he went, busting clods and cleaning the upturned earth of stray stones. Worms wriggled in the weak sun and drying air before heading down again into the earth. Robins stood by, eager to plunder the field. The air was thick with the scent of soil and springtime.

A group of villagers approached along the river path. Alain saw them first.

"Papa," he said, pointing. Marrec lifted his attention briefly to the road.

"Hmph," he said, and returned to the steering of horse and plow.

Men and women walked along the river path, a score or more, all unspeaking, eyes furtive. They stopped as a group at the edge of the field.

Robert, the machtiern for Guihomarc, the Count Vannes, stood at the front of the crowd. Even if Alain hadn't known him, the bright embroidery on his dark overshirt and the sword that hung from his belt would have told him of the office Robert held. His coif of Frankish curls alone set him apart from the rest of the crowd, as did his demeanor. Liaison between yeoman and noble, he stood confidently at the edge of the field while nearly half the village stood silent on the path behind him, afraid even to step on the land tilled by the man who had once slept with the Delphine of Dead Ox Wood.

"You must go up," Robert demanded, but Marrec only clucked his tongue and squinted into the light as he turned his dray for another pass. "Haven't you felt her presence?" the machtiern went on, his Frankish accent clipping the edges of his words. "She has been sending three nights running; dreams, terrible dreams. Hoël's girl is fair ill with their evil, and last night...last night Faustin's Amelie lost her unborn babe."

Alain saw the nodding heads of the men and women behind Robert. He could see Faustin's lean face among them, pale and drawn. To disturb the villagers' sleep was one thing, but to cause the loss of a child; his mother's insanity was hurting more people than himself. It needed to stop.

Marrec pulled rein on his horse and brought a kerchief to wipe the sheen from his brow.

"Marrec," Robert said, adding a note of pleading to his voice. "You must go up."

Alain's father looked at the grey morning sky, at Alain, and then at the long, brooding line that was Dead Ox Wood.

"No," Marrec said at last, looking up into the sun. "I'll not go up." There was a murmur from the villagers.

"Then we'll go up and burn her out!" cried a voice. Alain did not have to look to know that it was Faustin who spoke so. Nor did it matter, he thought, judging by the number of voices raised to second Faustin's threat.

"I'll not go up!" Reynald shuddered at Marrec's shout, tack and harness jingling in the sudden silence that followed it. Alain felt shame burn his cheeks and looked down at the dirt, at the clean lines that were his father's trademark, furrows drawn straight and even, back and forth across the field. "Anyway," he heard his father say. "She would never listen to me."

"Marrec," Robert said, voice now placating and diplomatic. He smiled and indicated the people behind him. "These are honest people, innocently embroiled in the affairs of your family. If you refuse to assist these people, you leave them no choice but to—"

"*I* leave them no choice?" Marrec wheeled on the machtiern. "I? It was *your* ruling kept the Delphine alive in the first place."

"'Twas my lord Count's ruling, Ploughman, not mine."

"Ah," Marrec said, sarcasm twisting his mouth into a sneer. "'Twas, indeed. 'Twas the *count's* ruling kept her alive, then. And 'twas the *count's* ruling kept me feeding her instead of killing her for bewitching me. And 'twas the *count's* ruling kept me snared here in a town filled with hatred instead of free to find a new life. The *count's* words. Tell me, Machtiern, where's our noble count now that his people are beset by dragon-boat raiders from Carnac to the Vilaine? Where's he, now that the woman he had me keep alive is dead and her spirit haunting our valley?"

The machtiern stood a bit straighter and the smile on his lips grew strained. "The Count Vannes has many homes which he must visit from time to time. Just now Lord Guihomarc is in Cornwall, seeing to his holdings there."

"As he does every spring and summer."

"Travel is impossible in the winter. Storms—"

"He's run away! He's abandoned us, taken his men, and left us here alone with you and a few men that I could whip with a walking stick."

"Marrec!" Robert warned. "Remember to whom you speak."

Alain saw that the machtiern's hand now rested on the

pommel of his sword. All friendliness was gone from the official's expression.

"Will you go up?" the machtiern asked. "These sendings are beyond—"

"I know of the sendings she's been casting down from that place." Marrec took a step as he spoke, then another. "I've had the dreams as well! Evil things. Foul. I've not slept for days for fear of their coming." He stepped again and again, destroying the even lines as he closed on the machtiern. Alain feared that the machtiern would strike Marrec down but he dared not move. "If you go up there and burn out her hut, you'll do nothing! Nothing but keep her from finding her way."

Marrec and the machtiern were a hand's breadth apart. A trampled line of strewn earth made a path from the plow to the edge of the field. "You burn out that woman's home and you'll make her madness greater than ever it was in life. Go. Do that. And *then* let us see what manner of sendings come our way."

The machtiern's gaze was a smoldering fire and his lip twitched. His breath ran in and out of flaring nostrils. The two stood there, immobile but for their own breathing. When the machtiern spoke, it was so softly that Alain could barely catch the words.

"Erol's Helena is with child," he said, and watched as Marrec's fierceness cracked and began to tumble. "Will you have the loss of that babe on your head? As well as your other sins?" Marrec took a step backward. "I have spoken with the abbot," Robert went on. "He is of the opinion that the Delphine, this demon woman, this...witch, may have infected your soul as well." Marrec turned away and put his head in his hands and Alain saw his father's chest heave with a shuddered breath.

It was too much. Alain couldn't bear any more of it. The sendings, the threats, all because of him and his own stupid actions.

"I'll go up, Papa," Alain said. His father looked at him, as did the machtiern.

"You?" was his father's question. "You?"

Alain understood the question, the true question. *You? After all she's done to you? Why would you want to ease her pain?*

But he did not know the answer to other question, or believed he did not, so he only answered his father's words, nodding.

"Yes. Me."

five

A raven danced before the wobbly door when Alain reined in at the tiny cottage. The bird did not fly away but simply danced—black and ragged—like a mad mourner at a pauper's grave. It turned its head and showed one eye to the tall, young man on his huge horse. The eye flickered from onyx to moonstone and back.

"Be gone from this place," the raven said. The voice was made of gravel, but the words were clear. "I'll have nothing to do with ye, Evil Thing."

Alain snuffed and blinked through the dust raised by Reynald's hooves. His heart pounded in his breast as he prepared himself for the contest of wills that was to come.

"Mother?" he asked the bird. "Is that you?"

"Excrescent one! Filth! Go away!"

Alain's laugh was short and bitter. "That's you, all right," he said. "Do you know me?"

"Surely, I do," the raven grated. "Ye are the child of death. I can see ye plain. Go away from this place. I do not want ye here."

"You never did," Alain said. Anger pushed back his fear of the mad spirit that danced before him. He gritted his teeth and slid down from Reynald's back. Reynald pawed the stony hillside with a feathered foot and blew breath from massive lungs, misting the evening air. The raven capered and twirled twice before it stopped and showed Alain its other eye.

"Bastard Boy."

Leather reins creaked in Alain's grip and muscles bunched

along his forearm.   She knew just what words would rub him
wrong.

"Hush," he said through angry teeth.

"Unwanted pup," the raven taunted.

Alain knelt down and looked at the raven. He plucked at the
bloodstains that still colored his tunic. "Do you remember these,
Mother?" he asked through clenched teeth. Do you remember
how I came by these? Do you remember the last time you saw
me?" He brought forth all the remembered horrors of that awful
day. "Do you remember the scream? The sword? The blood?"

The spirit wailed and the bird collapsed in the dust, its eye
flickering between moonlight and deep-black night.   Alain
watched as the bird shuddered, then stood. Released from its
possession, the wild raven cawed and flew into the darkening
wood.

Picking up the trailing reins, Alain led Reynald to a tree that
had a few tufts of grass at its heavy roots. He tied the horse
loosely and walked toward the hut. The forest seemed pensive,
abnormally quiet, and brought to Alain's mind the image of a
hungry animal waiting to be fed, a wolf awaiting the quarry's
tiniest mistake.   In the boughs above the hut's domed roof
perched the starlings that had been in the wood since the night of
her death. For weeks they had swirling through the air at dawn
and dusk, filling the forest with their screes and whistles, but this
evening their throats were silent. They sat on every branch and
bough, fluffed their feathers, and stared down at Alain with
beaded eyes.

He walked up to the door of the hut.

"I'm here to send you on, Mother," he said to the shadowy
interior.   His voice was shaky and thin.   "Do you hear me,
Mother? I've come to lead you over."

The answer blasted through his mind, hot and vicious, laced
with hate. He saw the hunched and rag-draped form that had
been his mother, leaves still stuck in her wiry grey hair from a nap
she'd taken with her woodland spirits. She turned from the oven-
like hearth, the hot knife smoking in her hand. Her face was split
by a moss-toothed grin, but at the corners of her eyes Alain saw
lines of agony. Tears streaked down her dusty cheeks. Alain felt
the hemp cutting into his wrists and ankles and he felt the heat of
the fire-purged blade as it neared the pristine skin of his chest and

he heard his voice—so young, so young—saying "please, mama, please, mama, please," like the prayer of a dying man to an unresponsive god.

He returned from the vision to find himself curled up on the threshold, sweat cold on the back of his neck and fire running through the traceries that adorned his breast.

Payment for the deed, Boy.

Alain sat up and looked into the darkness of the cottage. The hearth was cold in the center of the room. He rose to his feet, one hand touching the decade-old scars that laced his chest. His breath grew short as the fire of his anger raged.

"I was a *child!*" The words were swallowed by the forest as if he had never spoken.

Child of Evil, Child of Pain, was the response.

"As if that's an answer," Alain said as he stepped across the threshold into the home of his early youth.

He turned at the door and made to drop his leather satchels in the corner between the door and the wall, to sit down in the place that for years had been his. He stopped, retreating from the spot.

Go ahead, boy. Welcome home.

Alain rejected his old place and stepped instead to the willow-wood cot that had been his mother's until a fortnight before.

Ah, came her wheezing thought. *Even better.* A vision of cracked lips, bony limbs, and sagging breasts lashed through his mind. Repulsed, frantic, he fell back away. He turned again, seeking a place to settle, but there was no spot, no clear place not contaminated by his memories or by the ravings of his mother's madness.

With a strong arm he overturned the hewn-log table that still held a collection of herbs and stones and feathers. Items flew across the room and the table crashed against the stonework foundation. He sat down in the neutral spot where the table had been and winced at her spectral laughter, the scent of her scattered herbs strong in the close air.

What do ye want, boy?

"I couldn't say," he told her sharply, arms on his knees and sand-colored locks falling to cover his eyes. "I should have let them come and burn you out."

Ah, sweet one, and why didn't ye?

Alain shook his head, shying away from the answer. He just

sat, staring at the ground between his feet. Bits of grass and leaves were scattered on the floor, and motes of dust floated in the last bars of sunlight. A long-leg spider silently tiptoed toward the cold clay hearth. He watched and waited, building his resolve. She had won the first fight. He would have to be stronger if he wanted to succeed and bring peace to his village.

Night stole into Dead Ox Wood on fox's feet, bringing a chill that crept up from the stony ground and into Alain's limbs. For an hour he sat, staring at the hearth in the fading twilight, the only sounds his own breathing, and the jingled step of Reynald outside the cottage door.

The clay hearth, nearly black with age and use, lay cold in the center of the room, its fire bed dark and sunken. The smoke hole stared coldly at the rafters. Twigs and branches lay bundled near the head of the cot, and there was tinder in plenty about the room, but Alain dared not start a fire in that ancient hearth.

That hearth had been hers and hers alone. He had never known his mother to stray far from her hut, not even to go to the village to trade. She preferred instead to let the steep mountainside weed out the merely curious from the truly lovelorn, the jealous, and the sickly who came to her for magicks and wards. The hearth was her heart, and Alain had never known it to be cold in all the days of his life.

He huddled in the corner facing the cold and empty hearth and waited for the night to deepen.

The cottage was dark. The moon had not yet risen and all was black. He wished for his mother's talents as he rummaged in his satchels. He found a candle and some tinder. Scraping flint to the dried grass, he made a flame and brought the candle to it. He set the candle on the floor and looked up to find a mouse perched neatly atop the hearth, washing its face with fastidious paws.

"Is that you?"

"Yes," it said with more thought than voice.

"Are you better, then? Do you know who I am?"

"Why are ye here, my bastard boy?"

"To send you over," he said.

The mouse ceased its cleaning and looked at Alain with cabochon eyes.

"But why?"

He knew where she was trying to lead him. She'd taught him

this way, tumbling questions down the levels of cause and effect, echoing back to him his own eternal curiosity.

"I didn't want them to burn you out," he said honestly.

"Why?" came the question again.

I know what you want, he said to himself. Forgiveness. Acceptance. He took a deep breath.

"Because," he said, "I feel guilty for killing you. Because at the end of it all, I can't say that I don't love you." There, he thought. That's the closest I can come to it.

"Ye stupid, worthless bastard," the mouse said. "I've wasted my time, my whole life." It shook its tiny head side to side. "And after all I've given ye."

"What?" Alain noticed only in passing her rejection of his answer. What he did hear, what rang in his ears, were her last two words.

"Given me?" His voice rose in pitch, then in volume. "*Given* me!" Memories swarmed his inner vision, images crisp and tortured. In his mind, hot blades seared his chest and legs, drawing raven wings and creeping vines in his tender flesh. Horsehairs were laid in open wounds, birthing welted scars. Sticks descended through moonlight, bringing stars and thumping pain. Long-nailed hands groped in his breeches. Mad, wild eyes glared as spittle-flecked lips poured hate and anger over his youthful heart. Ropes burned wrists. Words burned his soul. Pain ran hot and love ran cold, both accompanied by a mother's kiss. Alain cried out, a long vomitous sound built of the agony within him. When he opened his eyes, the mouse lay curled in a ball at the foot of the hearth.

"Given me," he said, breathless.

The mouse uncurled and sat panting, its sides shimmering with the rapidity of its breath. It turned with a mannerism that had been his mother's: a bold look, one paw clenched before its breast, the other extended. When it spoke, Alain could hear his mother's anguish, more than the creature's tiny voice could provide.

"I meant more for ye!"

It ran, a blur in the candlelight, leaping from hearth to floor, and disappeared through the crack beneath the door.

Alain blinked. Did she see what I saw? he wondered. Did I cast? Excitement at the possibility turned his anger to wonder.

He stood and stretched out the kinks his muscles had gained from so long on the cold ground.

Reynald's whinny came a moment before the hut crashed and jumped. Hooves as big as a man's head punched through the door. Alain jumped to the far side as the huge draft horse pounded his way through wood and thatch.

"*I meant more for ye!*" came his mother's words as the horse broke into the room. Reynald's bulk filled the space before the hearth, and Alain saw the terror in the animal's eyes, so close to the madness of his mother's.

"Reynald!" Alain shouted, trying to reach the animal beneath the possession. The horse cried out and reared, cracking timbers in the roof. Thatch and dirt fell. Huge, iron-shod hooves came down to crush the hearth itself. Alain leapt aside to escape, but Reynald reared again and a great hoof caught Alain in the chest. Lights burst behind his vision as he flew backward, and he landed on the remnants of the table he himself had tossed across the room. He heard his mother's words tumbling from the horse's lips, heard her insane screaming, and when he could focus he saw Reynald reared up and ready to crush him.

Sharpened by need, his mind dove down into the heart of the mountain. The barrier that had lain between him and the source of magic fell apart like a water-soaked leaf, and he found the dragon line waiting for him like an old and trusting friend. Power filled his mind and jolted his body. He pulled forth the magic, fashioned it like clay, and sent it flying.

Reynald was hurled backward, out of the hut. The backlash of force hit Alain full in the chest, knocking the wind from him. He lay there, stunned, both by the blow and by his actions. Then he heard his mother's moan.

His head pounded as he stood up, throbbing with each heartbeat. He limped around the shattered hearth. Beyond the wall, Reynald lay on his side, the sheen of sweat bright even in the starlight. The horse's breath was labored.

He knelt beside the horse. Reynald's eye rolled light and dark, dark and light.

"Son," said the voice from Reynald.

"Mother. I felt it," he said, squinting through a stabbing pain in his head. "The line. I felt it. It is full of warmth, like sunshine. All I had to do was reach in and pull it to me. I can cast, Mother.

I can cast."

"Ah," said the Delphine's voice from the horse's lips, echoing in Alain's mind. "Finally. Your father will be pleased."

Reynald's flank heaved with a huge, shuddering breath. Alain sensed the Delphine's spirit releasing Reynald, and the horse whinnied and rolled up onto his legs. Alain stepped back as Reynald stood. He grabbed the halter and held up his hand. The world around him swirled with power and spirits that he was blind to just a few moments before. He touched the ley line and the pain in his head flared, surprising him. He retreated and turned to the world of spirits, and with a word and a gesture, he touched the mind of the great beast and sent him a calming word.

"Quiet, old friend," he said to the horse, taking the reins in hand. "She is gone from you."

Alain looked out on a world that seemed so familiar and yet was so new. "Mother?" he asked the trees and sky.

The wood was empty. She was gone. Alain looked down the mountainside to the village, to his father, to Erol in his tavern, Betina and her growing child. He could sense them all, though only faintly.

He turned his gaze to the forest about him: the huge quivering horse at his side, the eerie darkness of the hut, the vague shapes of tree trunks viewed through morning mist, the stillness of branch and leaf. It was as if time was holding its breath, waiting.

Branches exploded as starlings burst into the dawning light. Reynald tugged and pranced as the air filled with fluttering wings and flights of song. Hundreds rose, more joined, became thousands. A dark cloud ascended until, broaching the ridge peak, they birds were kissed by the rising sun. Through the branches Alain could see them, high overhead, swooping and swirling, the morning light firing their plumage, turning somber black to brilliant green and glints of orange.

"Son," came a voice.

"Mother?"

An ineffable wave of sadness crashed over him. Sadness, sorrow, and a regret that brought tears to his eyes and clutched his heart with phantom hands.

"Mother," he said, knowing the emotions to be hers. The Delphine began to moan as she had on that first night. The

sadness in Alain's breast turned to grief. He fell to his knees and
held his head in his hands as the storm of emotions rose, rounding
the mournful compass through guilt and shame before coming
back to sorrow. The moan broadened, became a word, one he
had not heard his mother speak his entire life.

"Alain," she cried. "Oh, Alain. My son. What have I done to
ye?" The tide of emotions ebbed leaving Alain on hands and
knees, gasping for breath on the forest floor. He opened his eyes
and saw standing before him the shimmering form of a woman.

She was small and slender. Her long tresses, the color of
sunlit wheat, rose and fell, lifted by an unfelt breeze. The whole
of her shone with a light of summer and in her features Alain
recognized the face of the woman he had laid to rest not far from
where he knelt.

"Forgive me, my son," she said, "if you can, for there is much
of which I am guilty."

Alain forgot the pain in his skull, overwhelmed by the
apparition. At her bare feet there was neither the moss nor the
ferns of the deep forest. Instead, green grass grew, and small
flowers of periwinkle and white bloomed.

"Is it really you?" he asked in a whisper. "What has
happened?"

"I have crossed over," she told him with a smile. "As you bid
me. I am in the Summerland, where gods walk among the souls
of men." Her voice was strong and lovely, filled with the music of
youth. "My spirit has been healed, and I am whole once more.
Too late, though. Too late." Her brow furrowed and she seemed
about to turn away. "I have done you much harm. You and
Marrec both."

Alain rose to face his mother's spirit. Reynald stood close at
hand, calm now and undisturbed by the shining woman nearby.

"Papa?" Alain asked. "What harm have you done to Papa,
besides bewitching him into your bed?"

"I did worse to Marrec. I bewitched him to *believe* that he had
come to my bed. To hide my own shame."

Alain stared. The ghostly woman lowered her gaze.

"Marrec is not your father."

Alain thought back on Marrec's years of humiliation at the
hands of the villagers, humiliation heaped upon him for his union
with the Delphine. He thought, too, of the trips up the mountain,

first by Marrec, then by Alain himself, carrying a third of Marrec's
share of the produce he had gleaned from his work on Josselyn's
fields, all to fulfill a ruling imposed upon him for a crime—and a
shame—he did not own.

"His shame fed you," Alain said. "You kept him tied to a
village that shamed him. How could you do that? You ruined his
life! If it wasn't for Calin, Papa would have been rejected by
everyone, or did you bewitch Calin, too?"

"No," the Delphine said. "The steward's friendship is true."

Alain's heart began to pound in his chest as the truth settled in
upon him.

"And what of me? Life with you was torture. Papa was little
better. When I think of the times I was beaten and lashed by a
man not even my father." Alain's anger crashed in upon itself like
a burned-out house. He fell once more to his knees. The futility
and waste of his life stood open to the sky.

"Why?" was the only word he could speak. "Why?"

The Delphine stepped forward. Sunlight preceded her, and
where her feet stepped, grass grew. Her light touched his head,
his shoulders, his back, warming him. He felt a hand stroke his
hair, loving and motherly. Her gentle touch infused him, filling
him as a lantern's light filled a dark room, and Alain felt the angry
hardness that had encased his heart for so many years suddenly
melt away. He looked up into his mother's face, a face that had
been hidden his whole life by an obscuring madness, and
recognized the truth of her love.

"Why did you do it?"

"Shall I show ye?" she asked him. The light and the blueness
of her eyes, so unlike his own, filled his sight, became a field of
azure, a summer sky clear and vast. A bird soared through and
down into the branches of a tree, and suddenly Alain was in
another time.

He was still in the Dead Ox Wood, but behind him, the hut
was whole and above him, the sun shone bright in a cloudless sky.
Nearby stood a young woman, the Delphine from decades past.
He gaped at her like a gigged frog. The vitality of the vision—
unlike any of the nightmarish sending of the past weeks—shocked
Alain into stillness. He could feel the gentle breeze on his face,
could taste the dust in the late summer air. Each strand of the
young Delphine's hair was visible in sharp detail. He tried to take

a step toward her but found he was unable to do more than turn.

"I can't move," he said.

Wait, came his mother's words from beyond the vision. *He comes.*

Horses, at least seven of them, came up through the trees of the Dead Ox Wood, their breath hard from the climb. Their riders drew up in the dappled sun; fierce men atop well-appointed steeds. The men were armed with sword and bow, and their hair was long and curled in the manner of the Franks. One held his sword at ready and green-leafed sunlight play along its edge. Alain looked to the woman near him. She smiled and inclined her head to the warrior.

Such brave men. So fearful of a tiny witchwoman.

Alain did not know if he heard the thoughts of his mother's spirit, or of the young woman in the vision; perhaps it was both.

Another man rode up. His clothes of green and black were fine and new, his black hair long and combed. He maneuvered his horse between the mounts of the nervous soldiers and reined in ahead of them.

"Who is this?" Alain asked of the voice. "He looks important."

Yes, his mother responded. *Very important.*

The nobleman in green slid off his horse, landing with grace and strength. The Delphine knelt and bowed her head as he stepped toward her.

"My lord," she said, speaking not in the Old Tongue but in Brezhoneg, the language of the Briezh lands.

The man reached down and touched her arm, urging her to her feet.

"Delphine," the noble said, and smiled with white, even teeth.

Recognition flooded Alain's mind and the vision went dark.

"I've seen him before. Just today in a dream. He tried to kill you."

No, and Alain heard a hardness in his mother's voice. *To kill was not his purpose.*

The vision brightened once more. Alain found himself squatting in his customary place behind the door of the hut. He peered around the door and saw the Delphine sitting before her hearth, steeping leaves in honeyed wine. The nobleman sat on a stool beside her. Alain smelled the smoke that hung in the room and felt his throat constrict with sudden grief.

"I may have hated this place," he said to the unseen voice, "but it was home." He felt rather than heard his mother's sad agreement. "But who is this man? What does he want here?"

He is Guihomarc.

"The Count Vannes?"

Aye, and he wants my talent.

Alain knew of Lord Guihomarc, count of the city of Vannes. He ruled most of Morbihan, including Alain's town of Belvanetes, but Guihomarc had been a distant lord, never present himself, always working through surrogates such as his machtiern. Never before had Alain seen a face to put with the title. To learn that this remote noble had dealings with his mother confused Alain. Who *was* his mother, to attract such attention?

Next to the count, the young Delphine dipped a dried flower in the infusion and spoke to the forest spirits in the Old Tongue. Alain sensed their awareness and felt them draw near. The flower freshened, renewed as the Delphine channeled a tiny bit of the forest's presence into the bloom.

She turned to her companion and laughed at the look of disbelief on his face.

"You try," she bade him.

He was not able to master the subtleties of earth-bound magicks, his mother said as Guihomarc dipped a dried bud into the brew. He held it before him and called just as the Delphine had done. With his new-found abilities, Alain could tell that the count saw the words of the Old Tongue as nothing more than that—mere words—and not as the method of attunement that they truly were. The spirits did not respond to his call, and the flower only dripped honeyed wine down the count's fingers.

Guihomarc tried again, again to fail.

"Hunh," he said with a snarl, and beetled his brow. Alain heard the hum of the ley line deep in the mountain and the dried bloom burst into crackling flame.

He had a tremendous command of the lines, though.

"You are holding something back," the count growled at the Delphine. All good humor fled from the young witch's cheeks and she held up an arm in defense.

The count's first blow knocked the cup from the hearth. Wine formed a steaming arc across wall and floor.

"You dare toy with me?"

The second blow was for the Delphine. As was the third. Unable to move, Alain was impotent to act, and though he knew he was seeing events from before his birth, still he wanted to change the outcome. Frustration built to anger, and Alain closed his eyes as the count's hands reached out to throttle the young woman.

When he opened his eyes again, the vision had shifted. It was night and he stood once more in the forest. The Delphine lay on the ground, her arms and legs spread wide and tied by leather strips to stakes in the ground.

Two of the count's men stood nearby, each holding a smoking torch. Their eyes glanced to the woman on the ground, then away. They were even more fearful of her now than they had been when they first arrived.

The count walked into the circle of light and past the two guardsmen. He stood over the Delphine. She looked up at him, her face purpled and bloodied by his blows.

"Guihomarc," she pleaded, but he waved a hand and her jaw froze shut and the tendons of her neck stood out as she strained to speak.

"No words for you, or any casting. Besides, there is nothing you can say that will change my mind," the count said to her. "For months I have tried to learn your earth magic and become the Fair One that links the worlds of Fey and Men. But you have thwarted me, keeping your secrets hidden from my talent." He walked around her as he spoke. "So, though I cannot link the worlds myself, there may yet be another way."

The Delphine struggled against the leather that bound her limbs. The muscles of her neck were taut and strained. Her eyes were wide, searching the face of the man standing over her and the darkness beyond the torchlight. The sense of impending danger was strong, and Alain shut his eyes, aching to do something, to free her, to stop him, anything to spare himself the experience of watching what he was sure to come.

"I do not wish to see this," he said aloud, and his mother's thought answered.

To understand the end, you must see the beginning. Watch.

Alain looked once more.

On his knees between the Delphine's legs, Guihomarc untied

his breeches. The Delphine struggled against her bonds. Without a word of warning the count leaned forward and struck her a backhanded blow across the face. When she looked back Alain saw fresh blood running from her nose and from a cut below her eye. There was fear in her eyes, and hatred, too, but she no longer struggled. The count lowered himself onto the Delphine.

"Stop him! He can't do this!" Alain yelled. The two guards looked back at what was happening and turned away quickly. "Stop him," Alain shouted at the count's men, but they did nothing. Alain realized that, even if they could hear him, they were too intent on ignoring the crime taking place behind them. Their presence here, witness to the count's act of rape, placed their own lives at risk, for even the rape of a poor witch woman with no family was a transgression of law, Briezh and Frankish both. "I don't want to know this!"

Alain's rage nauseated him. Revulsion and frustration tore at his guts, but all he could do was stand and grit his teeth.

And then it was over. Alain saw tears glisten on his mother's cheeks, mingling with blood. Guihomarc stood up from the Delphine's still form.

Alain's wave of ire crashed down, flowing away, leaving simple resignation. "My father," he said bitterly.

I am sorry, his mother said. *But, yes.*

"Will you take me from here now?"

No, she said. *There is more you need to see.*

Guihomarc raised his arms and closed his eyes. From the heart of the mountain, there came the song of a two-toned chord. The ley line sang. Alain heard it, as did the woman on the ground. The guards, unattuned to the power of the lines, remained oblivious, concerned only with their feigned ignorance of their lord's activity.

To either side of the Delphine there formed a dim violet glow that grew in intensity, shifting to a blue that was first deep, then light. Within each circle of twilight stood a man. One of the guards saw the light and turned. Startled by the apparitions, he went for his sword but a raised hand from the count kept the sword in its scabbard. Alain hardly noticed the exchange between lord and guards. His attention was drawn to the two arrivals.

The mysterious men were both tall and slender. Their faces were clean-shaven, their long dark hair pulled back. The cloth of their simple garments, bound at the right shoulder, hung in luxurious drapings that reached to their unshod feet. Wide, fair brows narrowed to high-boned cheeks and to delicate chins. Their lips were thin and their large, wide-set eyes—Alain could only stare at their eyes—were of the deepest black; not like the night sky, not like a polished onyx stone, but black like the absence of all light and substance. No reflection marred their surface, nor any hint of emotion.

"By all the gods," Alain murmured. "Fair Folk."

Aye, his mother responded. *Fey. From beyond the Veil.*

"I've never seen their kind. I never even believed they existed." He looked at the count. "What can he want with them?"

As if in answer, Guihomarc spoke to the visitors.

"Lord Rill. Lord Vert. My grateful thanks for answering my call."

"Greetings to you, Guihomarc of Vannes," said the one called Rill. His voice was deep and sonorous, his diction precise. "Why have you called for us?"

Guihomarc pointed to the woman at his feet.

"I wish that my seed so recently sown shall take root in this woman's womb. I wish, too, that she shall not rip out what I have planted. To ensure these two things is beyond my skill. I require aid from beyond the Veil. Will you grant me this?"

"To what end is this to be done, that it concerns the Circle of Merddyn?" Rill asked.

"The woman is strong with earth magic, and I am a master of the lines. I believe that our progeny—"

"You dare?" said the other Fey lord. "You even *presume* to dare?"

Lord Rill held up a hand for silence. A cold and tooth-filled smile crept onto Rill's face, and Alain shivered, suddenly thankful that he did not stand before Lord Rill himself. "He does, indeed, Vert. He dares. So, Count Vannes, you believe you can father the Fair One, the Destroyer of Worlds, and hasten The Return."

Guihomarc bowed slightly. "Every prophecy must have its agent of fulfillment. I dream that I may do that service for the Circle."

"And reap the rewards of our gratitude when The Return comes," Vert said, teeth bared.

The count shrugged. "I do not think that unreasonable, Lord Vert, do you?" He turned to Lord Rill. "Will you assist me?"

Rill looked down at the bound woman on the ground. "You have been of service to us in the past, Guihomarc, and the Circle of Merddyn is well-disposed to return the favor. Mark me, though. To do as you request will ravage this creature's mind, perhaps beyond all healing. Do you truly wish this thing, mindful of the damage it may do?"

"Aye," Guihomarc said with a firm nod. "The witch is spent. I can get no more from her, save the babe. Once born, I can foster it if need be."

The two Fey exchanged a glance, then nodded in unison.

"Aye, and well. It shall be done."

The vision went dark, and Alain found himself back in the dawning sun, Reynald beside him.

The shining spirit of the Delphine was gone.

six

Guihomarc sat up in bed, shocked awake. The discordant tones of the ley line reverberated through his head like notes from an ill-tuned cittern.

"Ach!" he muttered, rubbing his temples. "Who is that?"

"My lord?" asked a sleepy voice beside him. The woman in his bed rolled over and came up on one elbow, a dim form in the darkness. "Is something wrong?"

The count patted her bare shoulder. "It's nothing." He looked and saw the barest of pale dawn light showing through the cracks in the shuttered windows. "It is early yet," he said gently. "Go back to sleep, girl." He looked back and saw that his words were unneeded. His bedmate had already dropped her head back to the cushions.

Guihomarc grabbed his tunic from the foot of the bed and pulled it on. Stepping out into the cold, his feet shied from the cold floor. He reached back for a pelt from among the coverings and threw it around his shoulders. The wolf skin was still warm from the bedclothes and the fur was soft against his neck and arms.

A thin skin of ice had formed on the water in the basin near the window. He broke through with one hand and splashed his face with the frigid water. The cold felt good and cleared from his eyes the last remnants of his fleeing slumber. He listened again for the lines as he moved to the shutter and cracked it open.

The sour song of the ill-struck line continued to ring as he looked out into the deep blue of earliest dawn. A drizzling mist from the Cornish coast shrouded the walls of the inner keep, hiding sky, courtyard, even rooftops from view. The line sounded again, a slightly finer note this time, a bit softer, a bit gentler. Guihomarc did not recognize the signature.

"Who are you?" he asked the ethereal player.

He closed the shutter, grabbed leggings and boots, and went to the door. When he opened it, a young woman stood on the other side, hand raised and about to tap. Guihomarc noted that her hair, usually pulled back and bound in the Cornish style by a thin bit of leather, now hung loose and rumpled about her face.

"Ah, Bronwyn" the count said with a laugh. "It woke you, too, eh?"

"Shh," the dark-haired woman said with a finger to her lips. "Ardath may grow jealous to know I'm here at this hour."

"Hmm," Guihomarc said with a glance toward the rumpled pile of bedding. "It wouldn't matter. I'm growing tired of her. She's becoming accustomed to my attentions. I do so tire of them when they become accustomed to my attentions. Still...." He stepped out into the corridor and closed the door behind him. "No use bringing her wrath down upon your tousled head." He took Bronwyn's hand in his. "Come," he said. "Let us see who our new minstrel is."

Guihomarc's keep stood on a bluff a few miles upstream from the mouth of the Sid on the southern coast of Cornwall. The south tower along the outer palisade was set aside for his private use. As he and Bronwyn climbed to the sparsely furnished tower room, serving men descended, crowding the narrow stair. When the pair entered, warm light flickered from a hastily laid fire, and a pitcher of wine sat next to silver cups on the lone table.

Guihomarc motioned to one of the two fireside chairs, and Bronwyn sat. He went to the window and behind him heard Bronwyn pour two cups of wine. He pushed open a shutter.

The scent of salt from the coast was stronger on this, the windward side of the keep. Cries of gulls carried through the mist.

"Who would be casting at this hour? And with such awkwardness?"

Bronwyn came up beside him, handed the count a filled cup. "Don't you know?" she asked. "It is he."

Guihomarc turned. "Who? The boy?"

"Surely, it is."

"Don't be daft." He closed the shutter and latched it safe. He walked to the fire and stared into his cup, the wine black in the dim light. "The boy is a lost cause. I'd have heard from him years ago if he was ever to show talent." He shrugged the pelt closer about his shoulders and wished for a measure of the wolf's brashness and courage in the face of the unknown.

"No," he continued. "It is not him. It is some boy who has stumbled upon his skill." He sipped the wine and sat cross-legged on the hearthstones. "Let's find out. You will watch?" he asked.

The dark-haired woman smiled a mischievous smile. "Fear not, my lord," she said, and from within the folds of her robe she produced a thin iron dagger. "I shall be ever at your side."

The count smiled in return. "It is a shame that I let you spurn me. We would have been formidable." He clasped his hands in his lap, closed his eyes, and took a deep breath. "With you at my side, we would be at court in Orleans now instead of here in this benighted moss-pot. Why was it again you refused to come to my bed?"

"You would not take me to wife, my lord."

Guihomarc's breathing slowed and became deeper. "Ah," he said, his voice dreamy, slow and serene. "Yes. And yet we remain friends." His bearded chin dipped down toward his chest. "How fiendishly feminine of you."

Bronwyn laughed quietly. "You'd best leave off that and look to the task at hand."

"Yes, Bronwyn," the count said with a deep, sighing breath. "Don't worry. I'm almost there." He took another slow breath and let his fingers relax, hands releasing one another. In the darkness behind his eyelids, Guihomarc saw the colors begin to pulse. The sounds of the fire faded, as did the tannic taste of the wine. The dark colors built, pushing aside other senses until even the faint, flowered scent of Bronwyn's velvet robe was washed away by a rhythmic throb of dark blue, deep violet, and a red the color of pulsing blood.

The colors darkened and began to break apart. Guihomarc was alone, bodiless, motionless in a swirl of dying colors.

All went black.

Where are you?

Light and sound answered: a blue-green light bloomed below

him—as if the sea had swallowed the moon—and a plucked note, a tapping of the ley line, sounded in his skull. Each note thrummed with an increased confidence, a surer, more delicate hand.

Who?

With a thought, he swept down to the light. The light lengthened as he neared it, becoming a field, a path, a vibrating string. His mind sang in harmony as he moved along it, searching for the source.

Other lines crossed over and fed into the one Guihomarc traveled, each singing its own tune, but they remained only echoes of the song he followed. An ethereal landscape passed beneath him, built of shadow mountains and vague, auroral plains. The temptation to fly off and explore the unknown was strong, but Guihomarc knew the dangers of such wanderings, and kept to the ley line below him.

The tune strengthened, the light grew. The ghostly panorama became imbued with scattering light and achieved a threshold of solidity. Guihomarc searched the land beneath him and knew it. As his view sped forth toward the phantom Dead Ox Wood, he laughed, his surprise and excitement billowing out in gales.

The final junction swept past, and Guihomarc flew up into the Wood. Trees flashed by, a stream, a hut, a giant horse, a boy, a face, and then again, blackness.

Guihomarc blinked in the sudden firelight, a grin fastened to his face. Bronwyn knelt at his side.

"What?" she asked, anxious. The count regarded her, still grinning.

"You were right," he said, his breath suddenly short. "It *is* he."

"You are sure?"

Guihomarc nodded. "Indeed, it is Marrec's ward. I had my machtiern point him out to me once. A fine, tall man he's become, eighteen or so, fair of hair like his mother, but with dark and haunted eyes. He sat there near the hut of which I've told you, facing the vale below Dead Ox Wood, calmly lighting and re-lighting the end of a twig, each time with more deftness and confidence." He slapped his thighs and laughed, a short barking sound. "Can you believe it?"

Bronwyn did not answer at once, and Guihomarc looked into

her face. She still knelt beside him, sitting on her heels. The dagger was still in her hand, her fingers feeling its point. Her eyes were hooded as she turned to him, and Guihomarc wondered if he had erred in trusting this most dangerous woman. Beautiful, young, and powerful, even if she had not come with Rill's recommendation, she was someone Guihomarc would want as an ally.

"Yes," she said at last, a faint smile creeping across her face. "I can believe it. But only of you." The dagger disappeared up her sleeve and she stood. Guihomarc found that he had been holding his breath. He let it out slowly, relieved at the distance between himself and the dark Bronwyn. He remembered the real reason he had remained friends with her after she rejected him: she was too dangerous as an enemy. The count stood, regaining his composure.

"You seem disturbed by this news," he said. He splashed fresh wine into his cup and relaxed into a chair, feigning a calm he did not feel.

The pale woman by the fire shook her head slowly. "No," she said, staring into the low-burning flames. "Not disturbed. I am only thinking of what must now be done." She bent and threw another log onto the coals. "Your plans have lain sleeping for years. Surely you, too, are thinking of what you must now do?"

The count regarded her intently. Like most folk of the old Briezh bloodlines, she was tall and fair-skinned. Her dark, straight hair and deep brown eyes, however, told of an inconstant ancestry. "At times, my dear, I think that you and I might perhaps share a Frankish progenitor, so like a sister do you seem. At others—such as now—you seem to have sprouted from some ruthless Roman stalk, or even something else, something not of this world."

Bronwyn's smile died.

"I fear I shall never understand you," the count said.

Bronwyn looked back into the flames and tried to look demure. "My lord should not trouble himself with trying to understand me."

"I'm not so sure," Guihomarc said, trying to keep his tone casual, warm. "I suddenly think that it might be quite important for me to understand you. But, in answer to your question, no, I had not thought that far ahead."

Bronwyn turned and Guihomarc saw the calculation in her eyes, the briefest flash before she smiled, broadly.

"Ach, you know how I get sometimes," she said circling her hand about her head. "Always thinking, always planning. The mind never stops." She took the pitcher of wine and her cup.

"A toast," she said, refilling for them both and raising her cup. "To your son."

Guihomarc touched his cup to hers.

"To Alain," he said.

seven

Alain strummed the line and fed power into the end of the twig. It burst into flame, a tiny sunrise in his hand, astonishing him no matter how many times he did it. He blew it out and smoke spiraled upward, tickling his nose. The pain returned with each casting, but he could not leave it alone. Even the agonizing truth of his heritage failed to douse the joy he felt at his new-found abilities. He found that casting was bearable if he drew only a touch of power, but too often he grabbed too much, and his vision darkened with the pain. He sat on the granite outcropping, out on the edge of the ridge, and looked out over the valley of his home.

A trio of geese, returning from their winter homes, flew low over the treetops and down into the vale. Alain watched them, heard their plaintive calls echoing off the rocky cliffside. They glided on recurve wings toward the river and its tasty, green water grasses.

"How far have you three come?" he wondered aloud. "And where will you go?"

The clean light of morning graced the huts and houses of his village. Women washed clothing on the rocks of the river bed. Men worked in fields green with new growth.

"I can see my whole world." He thought a moment and shook his head, negating his words. That was no longer true.

Behind him, over the ridge, palisades surrounded the city and the villa of the Count Vannes. Alain knew his world now extended at least that far, perhaps farther now that Guihomarc had once more abandoned his county to Viking raiders.

His mind reeled, exhilarated by new thoughts and new vistas. Imaginings of distant lands and powerful lords tempted him, called him. He reached down with his mind once more and plucked the ley line. Siphoning off a handful of power, he honed it, and set it to the end of the charred twig. The blackened wood sparked and ignited in cheerful flame.

Power, he thought, and imagined all the control he could now wield, the places he could now go. "The bastard boy can be a lord," he said, staring at the flame he had created. "But is that what I want?"

His gaze moved out beyond the twig to take in the village, and a smile graced his face. No, what he wanted wasn't to rule men and control their lives. What he wanted was to marry Josselyn, to be respected, and to live peacefully in the place of his birth.

He stood, brushed the dust from his seat and legs, and went to get Reynald.

It was noonday when he finally made it back down the mountain. He had not hurried, and had actually walked part of the way, Reynald keeping slow pace behind him.

He turned his face up into the shining sun and grinned into the light. With a deep breath, he smelled the aroma of warm grass and clean air. He felt no hurry, no impetus driving him home to do his father's bidding. The knowledge of his noble blood did nothing for him, for he did not feel like a count's son. He felt like a ploughman's son, but one given a gift that he could use to help himself and his loved ones. The presence of that gift relieved him, and freed him from care. He rode across the river ford, Reynald's hooves making hollow barrel sounds in the pebbled bed.

"The old soldier isn't even my father," he said to Reynald as they walked. "I share as much blood with you as I do with him." He patted the horse's neck.

At the village outskirt, Reynald pressed the pace, eager to be home. Alain let him have his head, and soon the horse was running through the heart of the village. Alain began to laugh, the tension of the last weeks—the raid, Marrec's injury, the Delphine's death, and fortnight of haunting—all ebbed away. The past fell away, sloughing off like a snake's crusty skin, leaving him with a feeling of renewal that bubbled out from his soul in laughter. His joy seemed to infect Reynald, for the more he laughed, the faster the horse ran until finally they were loping across the land, Alain holding on to Reynald's mane in hysterical glee.

Finally they approached the homestead and Alain feared the horse would run headlong into the stable.

"Hold up," he said, tugging on the bridle. Reynald pulled up in front of the low stable door and Alain jumped down, letting the horse walk on inside to find stall and hay.

Alain walked toward the household, eager to share the news of the Delphine's crossing and show off his new talents. His feet slowed, however, when he thought of his other news, his mother's revelations concerning his parentage.

"Poor Papa," he muttered to himself. "How will I tell him the news? Or should I tell him at all?" He considered it.

After all, he thought, who needs to know?

The gate opened and Josselyn stumbled out. Alain grinned and waved, but there was terror in her eyes. Barely keeping her feet, she ran across the turnip field.

"Go back," she shouted. "Go back to the Wood."

Alain stopped at the edge of the field, confused. Josselyn met him there and clutched at his arms. Wisps of hair had escaped her braid and her eyes were wide and reddened.

"What's wrong? What is it?"

"It is Marrec," she answered breathlessly. "The sendings. Last night. After the Delphine crossed over."

Alain held his frightened friend at arm's length. "You saw them here as well?"

"Yes. Just like before. And he's been drinking since."

A bellow rose from beyond the whitewashed walls.

"Go," Josselyn urged. "Now!" She pushed at him, turning him back toward the river and the mountain. Alain shrugged off her hands.

"No," he said, and stepped around her. "I'll talk to him."

"But he means to kill you."

By the tears in her eyes and the desperation in her voice Alain knew she was not exaggerating.

"Don't worry," he said to her. "It won't be the first time Papa has visited me, drunk and vicious."

Marrec burst through the open gateway, Calin close behind and trying to hold him back. Alain felt a chill as he saw his Viking sword in Marrec's hand.

"Where are you, Bastard?" came the drunken roar. Calin tried once more to restrain him but Marrec swung a backhanded fist and the old steward went down. Marrec spied Josselyn with Alain at the edge of the field and pointed with the sword. "Leave off from him, girl," he shouted as he walked toward them. "I spent nigh on twenty years fostering another man's shame. It is time to end it."

Josselyn held tightly to Alain's arm. "He'll not harm you with me by your side," she whispered into his ear. Alain pushed her away.

"You don't know that, and I won't risk it."

"Then run!"

"*No!*"

Josselyn jumped at the violence in his voice. Tears ran down her cheeks and her lip trembled. She stepped back away.

Alain faced the oncoming Marrec.

"Please, Papa, stop where you are."

"Don't you call me that, Bastard Boy." Marrec stopped. Ten paces of dusty path separated the two. The old man's face twisted in a grimace of turmoil. "Don't you dare call me that." He covered his eyes with his arm and the tip of the longsword dipped to touch the dark earth. "I'm not your father," he said between sobs. "I'm no man's father."

"You're the only father I've known," Alain said, wanting to be believed.

Marrec looked at Alain and the sword rose again. Tears rode cleanly through the dust on the ploughman's cheeks. "I have no son. I have only shame and ridicule and eighteen years' service to a witch and a lie." He spat into the dust. "Well, I'll have my vengeance, I will. And if not on her, then on you." He stepped forward.

"Stay back, Papa," he said, trying to reason with him. "If not because I'm your son, then because I am the Count's."

"The Count's bastard, you mean."

"All the same," Alain said, but Marrec came on, sword raised to strike. Alain felt for the ley line. It was not there. Panic flashed through his body, running cold and fast. He had misjudged, expecting the line to be as close as it had in the Wood. He searched again, quickly, deeper, farther. He heard Josselyn scream just as he found it, tapped it, and sent a shield against the descending blade.

The sword rang as it struck hardened air. Marrec howled as the blade shattered in his hand. The pieces fell to the ground and Marrec clutched his forearm. A blind, drunken hatred clouded his features. Alain stepped back, pained by the power of his casting.

"I'm sorry, Papa," he said, instinctively. "I didn't mean to hurt you."

Marrec stood, feet apart, crouching, cradling his nerveless arm, weaving slightly from wine and the blow. His breath came in growling gasps that moved the spittle hanging from his lip.

"You, too?" he asked with a voice like a maddened dog. "A witch, like that mare who begot you?" He lunged.

Fearful of his own power, Alain tried to fashion a gentler force but had neither knowledge nor time. Marrec crashed into him and they both went down.

They hit the ground hard and Alain lost his breath. Marrec pushed himself up and swung his fist back and forth. Alain, gasping for breath, tried to ward off the blows. One arm was pinned beneath the ploughman's knee. He reached for the line but could not find it, each ringing blow shattering his focus. He tried to strike at Marrec, but from his place on the ground, his blows were weak and useless.

Marrec's blows began to take their toll. Alain saw Josselyn come at Marrec but the big man pushed her aside. Alain's vision began to dim. A weight lifted from his chest and he became aware of more blows, to his stomach and back. He had the impression of others nearby, and of much shouting. He reached out for the line seeking solace, seeking escape, but found nothing. Finally, he was aware only of the taste of blood and the aroma of crushed turnip greens, and knew no more.

eight

The light rang in Alain's head like a huge, painful bell. Hands opened shutters, letting in the awful sun. He squinted against the light, but that hurt even more and he could only lay there, agony assaulting his eyelids from beyond the window. Eventually, the pain receded to an unbearable throb and he opened his eyes.

He was in a small room in the servants' wing of Josselyn's villa. Sunlight slanted in, filling the room with early morning, rejuvenating the cracked and worn floortiles with its glare. He lay on a straw pallet on a low frame. It smelled of mice and creaked as he moved his head to see the rest of the room. Another bed took up the remaining space in the small room, and on it laid Josselyn, skirts tangled in her legs, her hair undone, one hand under her cheek. Alain's cot creaked again and Josselyn blinked. She saw him, blinked again, and a smile broke across her face like a wave rushing a beach.

"You're awake," she said, up and at his side in a moment. She clasped his hand in hers and held it against her breast. She reached out and stroked his hair with a gentle hand. "How do you feel?"

Alain was flustered by her ministrations. He could not form an answer to her question. All he could think of was the closeness of her face and the hand she held tightly against the warmth of her bodice. A tiny furrow creased her brow and she touched first his one cheek, then the other, then his forehead.

"You're flushed," she said, "and quite warm. You've a fever."

Alain looked toward the wall, feeling his cheeks burn all the more for her notice of it. "Perhaps," he said quietly. "I do feel a bit warm." His head still pounded and his stomach was sour. He turned back to Josselyn. "What happened?" he asked. "How long have I been here?"

"A day and a night. Though Calin says the last has been sleep and not insensibility. We were loath to wake you. Oh! But you'll be famished! Do you want some broth?"

Alain nodded.

"Good," she said and touched his cheek again. "I'll be right back."

Alain breathed a deep sigh as she left. He turned his attention to his injuries. His face felt swollen along one side of his jaw and there was a raised cut along his cheekbone. As he moved, he saw bruises covering his forearms. Checking beneath the blanket, he discovered that the bruises extended down the length of his scarred torso. Marrec had been thorough.

He spied his clothing at the foot of the bed. After two attempts and with his head swimming, he sat up. The tunic had been rinsed and the tear had been mended, but faint stains still showed on the yoke and front, dark brown spatters against the tan fabric. He grunted against the fiery soreness in his limbs and body, and slowly he maneuvered the shirt over his head. He welcomed the pain, though, as it drove away the nausea. Breathing heavily, his nakedness covered, he rested, leaning back against the wall.

Slow steps sounded on the tiles of the next room and Alain looked up through fallen locks to see Marrec standing at the door. A shock of fear lanced through his heart. He could not run, could not even stand at this point. But Marrec did not move from the threshold.

He stood in the doorway and looked at the floor tiles. His eyes were still red-rimmed and his face was pallid. The scar from the Viking's sword stood out, red and angry across his face and neck. A glossy shine of sweat covered his brow. Alain realized that Marrec felt little better than he did. That fact alleviated his fear.

"What do you want?" Alain asked, his speech thick from the swelling of his jaw and lip. Marrec did not speak right away, did not look up at the youth who had been his son until a few nights before.

"I've...come to take my leave of you," he said. His voice held a tremor that Alain could not fathom.

"Where are you going?"

"I...don't know yet," the old man said. "West. To Osismi lands, perhaps. To Kemperle. Maybe to Brest. I have a sister's son in Brest."

Alain heard pain in Marrec's voice and felt his own heart twist at the news.

"But there's nothing but boats and fish salters in Brest," Alain said. "What's a ploughman going to do there?"

"I don't know. I may go east. To the Frankish March. Always a place for an old soldier along the March."

Silence lengthened.

Don't go, Alain wanted to say. *I don't know who I am without my father near.* But Marrec wasn't his father, no matter how much he seemed one to Alain, and the shame he suffered for so many years was now compounded by the lie he'd lived. Marrec couldn't stay and endure it.

"I'll go with you," Alain said.

Marrec looked up from the tiles, surprise clear on his face. He blinked, his expression twisted, and Alain regretted the offer.

"I'm sorry," Alain said.

Marrec looked up at the rafter beams, his eyes bright with reflected sunlight and tears. His grizzled jaw worked back and forth beneath his bushy mustache.

"You're a man now, a man of your own. You're no longer the boy of a fortnight ago."

"But, Papa—"

Marrec went on as if Alain had not spoken. "You'll do fine," he said. "Better off without me." He looked out the window and then, finally then, gazed at Alain with a look that was part man-to-man, not devoid of father-to-son. Alain found the ploughman's regard too much to bear, and himself looked away.

"Epona watch over ye, boy," Marrec said. Alain heard the scuff of a foot. When he looked up, Marrec was gone.

By the time Alain pulled himself up and limped to the window, Marrec was walking away from the compound. The servant's gate hung open, swinging slightly.

"Papa," he said, but his voice was weak and did not carry. "*Papa*," he yelled, and heard his raspy voice echo off the gleaming walls. From beyond the open gate came the jingle of harness and a horse's familiar whicker.

"Reynald!" Alain shouted. Reynald answered, a whinny and the draw of a shod hoof along dirt and gravel. Then came the murmur of Marrec's command to the great horse. "*Papa!*" The fading sound of Reynald's hooves along the dusty path was the only response.

Jaw set, Alain stood at the window. Grief piled upon grief and loss piled upon loss. What had he done to deserve this fate? What gods had he displeased? What crimes had he done?

Something touched his hand and he looked down to see a drop of water rolling off between bruised knuckles. Another fell, and the realization that he was weeping hit him fully. Confusion, anger, fear, and frustration warred within his breast. He knelt, then sat. He pulled his knees in close and, with gritted teeth, gave himself up to his tears.

After another day's rest Calin pronounced Alain fit enough.

"Fit enough for what?" Josselyn inquired from her seat at the garden window. Alain struggled with his tunic and said nothing. Calin handed the stained linen bandages to the maidservant.

"Fit enough to move on," the steward said coldly. Josselyn turned from the garden view and looked at her steward, eyes flashing in the light from the evening lamps.

"Calin," she said in a low, even tone.

"S'truth, Mistress," Calin said without concern for her warning. "He's fit enough to move on. And we can't have him here any longer."

"Alain can stay on with the household, just as Marrec did."

"He can do nothing as Marrec did."

"*Calin.*" The maid jumped and the old man became still. Josselyn walked up to him. He bowed his head in respectful subjugation and looked at the floor.

"Your pardon, Mistress," he said. "He cannot. The folk of the village—"

"Of the village?"

"They do not want him here."

Josselyn stared. "Who says this? Erol? Faustin?"

Calin spoke to the tiles. "All, Mistress. And the machtiern, too."

"But Alain is no different than he was before."

"Aye," Calin said. "A bastard then and a bastard now."

"Except that now," Alain said, speaking for the first time, "I am not the bastard of Calin's beloved friend, but of an absent count who's done none of us any good."

Calin nodded and hooked a thumb toward Alain. "Aye. He doesn't even have a decent ploughman's blood in him."

Josselyn took a step closer to her steward. "But he *is* the son of a count."

"Your pardon, Mistress, but people say that if ye go to Vannes and throw a stick into the air, it could hardly come down without hitting one o'the count's whores or one of his bastards."

Alain blushed at hearing such frank speech in Josselyn's presence. The maid hid a smile behind her hand. Josselyn, however, was unabashed. Hands on her hips, the mistress of the manorhouse stood before her steward. Alain watched her stand toe to toe with the old man, her tininess accentuated by the steward's lean height and cowed stance. The maid's smile died.

"And yet," Josselyn said, speaking up into Calin's downcast face, "were I to invite every one of those whores and bastards to sup with me in my house, it is not the place of my serving man to chide me for doing so." Calin ducked his head even farther and wrung his hands. She turned her back on him. "Leave us."

Alain saw Josselyn's hands shake as Calin and the maid left the room and closed the door behind them. She stood there a moment more, the only sounds the tremor of her ragged breath and the filtered song of swallows arcing through the early evening air. Alain stood—much easier now than the day before.

"Josée."

At the sound of her name, the mistress of the estate disappeared, leaving in her place Alain's childhood love. She ran to him and buried her face and her sobs in the fabric of his tunic. Her tears touched off a fire in Alain's body, a fire fed by the embrace of her arms and the smell of lavender-water in her hair. He fought it, resisted it, but found his arms enfolding her just the same. Her sobs lessened though her trembling did not.

"Nothing has happened the way I hoped," she said. Alain looked down and found her gazing up at him. Her eyes, filled with grey and blurring tears, did not waver. Her lips parted and her hand pulled at his shoulder.

"Alain," she breathed. "Love me this night. Make one thing

happen the way I had hoped."

Resistance crumbled. They kissed and Alain felt years of friendship and longing well up and flare. He held her to him, returning her kiss, her embrace, her passion. They fell to the rough servant's bed. Josselyn's hands reached beneath his unbelted tunic, touching him. Alain fumbled with the ties of her bodice and blouse. She aided him, removing blouse and tunic alike, until they both lay unclothed in the last shafts of evening sunlight slanting through the garden window.

Alain hesitated, suddenly shy, afraid of soiling her beauty with his marred flesh. Josselyn reached out a finger and, looking up at him briefly, traced the scars that laced his chest. He shivered beneath her touch. Then she took Alain's hand in hers and brought it to her breast. Her skin was so soft he could barely feel it with his callused hands. Then they were together, coupling in tear-filled fervor. There was no laughter between them, no words spoken. They loved in desperate earnest, filling each other's need and after, they let their tears flow without embarrassment.

"Josée," he said as they lay in each other's arms. "Do you know that I love you?"

"Of course," she said, "and am sorry for it."

"What?" He sat up. "Why?"

She caressed his arm, his hand. "Because Calin is right. You must go."

Alain's stomach clenched like a fist within him. "Again, why? Because he says so? Because your neighbors say so? Who rules this house?"

Her caressing hand gripped his wrist and her eyes looked sternly into his. "I am mistress here. None else. If you leave, it is because I say it and no one else."

Alain paused, regarding her as his last hopes for dreams fulfilled slunk away. "I have been a fool," he said. "You do not love me."

"I do," she said. "Believe me that I do." Her hand went soft along his arm once more. "But my villa is here, my lands are here. I must live with these people."

Alain took her hand in his. "Then let us marry. Bastard or not, I *am* the count's son, and I have found my talent. There is power in that."

She touched the fading bruises along his ribs. "What good has being the count's bastard brought you? And what power did the Delphine's talent bring to her?" She shook her head slowly. "Besides, if what Calin says is true, it would take years to build the goodwill of the villagers. My needs are more . . . immediate, if I am to keep my father's lands." Her mouth was sad as she spoke. "I need a quick solution, Alain. What I need to do would drive you from me, even were I to bid you stay."

Alain released her hand. Josselyn touched his cheek and turned his face to her. "Alain," she said, and her brow knit a little ridge. "It has nothing to do with what I feel for you. It has nothing to do with what we've just shared. It is simply that you cannot give me what I need to keep this land."

He said nothing, only stared back at her, his body cold with the meaning of her words. She looked out the window as she spoke, emotion coloring her voice. "I've learned more in these past weeks than I ever wanted to learn. Father left us near destitution. The last of our worth was taken in the raid, and now our debts far outweigh our income. I thought he was fighting to save me, but it was for more than that. It was for this whole place." Her arms went wide, denoting all. "It was for our home." Her hands dropped into her naked lap and her shoulders slumped. Her hair spilled forward, covering her breasts. "If only I had died in the raid with him."

Alain reached out and pulled her close. "Hush," he said, stroking her hair. His body stirred at the touch of her skin against his. Josselyn noticed. She touched his growing member and whispered in his ear.

"Be husband to me this night," she said, "for tomorrow you must go and I must find another to play the role."

With an aching heart, Alain complied.

Alain sat on the rock wall in the garden, waiting. On the flagstones at his feet was a cloak and a sack that held a few loaves, some smoked fish, and a small knife. Dew still dazzled on the tips of the herbs that grew behind him. He reached over, plucked a few leaves of lavender, and crushed them beneath his nose. The pungent scent revived the memory of the night before. Of Josselyn.

His throat tightened and he dropped the crushed leaves to the ground. He wiped his fingers on his leggings, but still the fragrance—and the aching memory—lingered.

"Mistake," he said to himself.

"Do you think so?"

Alain jumped up and turned to find Josselyn at the garden window. "How long have you been there?"

"Not long," she said and swung first one leg and then the other over the sill. Alain saw her bare feet, glimpsed the length of her calf as she moved, and longed to touch her and hold her closely. She hopped down, knee-deep in lavender and herbs.

"Do you really think we made a mistake?"

"Yes," he said without hesitation, face dour. Josselyn tilted her head and looked up into his face, teeth bright in a quirky grin.

"Really?"

"Josée!" he said, fighting laughter. "Please, can't you see...?" Josselyn giggled and hid her mouth with her hand. Alain looked at the ground, a smile on his lips. "Can't you see I'm miserable?" They both broke into laughter then, but too quickly it fled. Alain's heart filled with the deep ache of longing.

"Yes," he said, sitting on the hard stone wall. "It was a mistake. I wish it had never happened."

"Oh, no, Alain. No. Don't wish that." She knelt on the ground before him and clutched at his knees. "It was the only thing that we've done, not because we were told to, not because we had to, but because we wanted to. It was for us and us alone. And it was wonderful, Alain. It cannot have been a mistake."

"But it is a memory that will bring only pain. Don't you see that?" He clasped her hands in his. "It only makes parting from you all the more difficult. It has only made me love you more."

She smiled up at him. "Then we have succeeded in making something good out of this terrible mess we're in. Carry that with you, not the pain. Carry that and the knowledge that I love you as well."

Alain pursed his lips to keep his feelings in check.

"Promise me," she bid him. "Promise me to remember last night with happiness."

Alain nodded and Josselyn rose.

"I've brought something for you." She went back up to the window and reached inside. From within she withdrew a long, cloth-covered object. Alain recognized the long, thin length and began to shake his head.

"No," he said.

"Yes," she said, removing the cloth and handing him her father's sword. "I will allow no other man to have it."

Alain looked at the bright weapon in her tiny hands. He thought of Jessup, lying on the trestled plank in the kitchen, the smell of death and lively bread all about, the sword at his side, its white edge stained red with blood. If Alain did not take it, the sword with which Jessup had defended his home would go to the next lord of the manor.

"I know your meaning," Alain said. He took the weapon in its thick linen covering and wrapped it into his rolled cloak.

"Father liked you well," she told him. "Better than any other did. Eventually, I think he might have given it to you himself."

Alain reached beneath the collar of his tunic and removed the snakestones that hung about his neck. He rolled the blue and white beads between his fingertips. "I know they are not thought proper by your Christian god, but they are all I have." He opened his mind and heard the faint earthsong the stones played. "There is some power in them. They will help keep you safe." There were tears in Josselyn's eyes when she took them from his outstretched hand.

Alain shouldered his cloak and satchel. He turned to go. At the garden gate he turned. Josselyn stood in the center of the garden, surrounded by flowers and greenery. Swallows flew from the eaves and back, circling her. In her hand she held the snakestones. She lifted the cord over her head and settled the stones on her blousefront. Behind her at the door to the house, Alain saw Calin and the other servants. Calin's face was stern and set. He bade Alain no goodbye.

Alain drew himself up and faced the remnants of the only family he had ever known.

"When next you see me," he said to them, "I shall be a great man."

Calin puffed air through thin lips and went inside the house. The maidservants lingered a moment more, disappearing only at Calin's barked order. Josselyn remained.

"I have no doubt," she said.

Alain turned before the tears in his eyes wetted his cheeks. He closed the garden gate and walked away from the old manor.

At the edge of the turnip field, he met the river path and

turned east toward the village and the city of Vannes. From the water's edge there came a furious flapping. Three geese sped out from the shore, honking alarm, flapping so deeply that their wingtips touched the water. At mid-river, their webbed feet slapping the water's surface and they rose into the air. They flew in a lazy curve, circling Alain. He watched them lift themselves farther into the sky, turning as they flew around him. When they straightened out and struck their course, Alain was facing west. Away from the village. Away from Vannes.

He looked down the westward road that led to the standing stones of Carnac, to the crossroads at Lorient, and, eventually, to Brest and the ships that plied the sea between Finistére and Cornwall.

It seemed as good a direction as any.

He began to walk.

nine

The muscles in her breast burned with exertion. The flight and ascent had been sudden and rapid. A tilt of her head brought the youth back in view, beneath her wing and far behind her.

But he was walking west, and that was what she wanted.

Nearly a hundred leagues away, Bronwyn smiled. She stayed with the goose, enjoying the freedom of flight, the near-effortless soaring as she rode the ripple of wind that spilled from the wingtip of the leader. As the trio rowed the air past a tree-covered hillside, she looked back once more.

The lonely figure, head up, sandy hair blowing in the crystal breeze, walked on. The land curved beneath her and the figure was lost from view.

Bronwyn left the bird and silently retreated along the lines. She felt the warmth of the sun on her face. Opening her eyes, she inspected the glade.

The ancient standing stone towered above her, a tall, granite sentinel marking the intersection of two major ley lines. She breathed deeply of the moist air, smelling the rich scents of forest and sun-lit grass that the gentle breeze presented. The temptation to relax, to enjoy the lingering illusion of freedom and winged flight, was great. Succumbing for the moment, she leaned back against the standing stone and stretched out her arms. She felt the breeze move the sun-warmed hairs on her arms and pretended that the rustling of leaves in the oaks surrounding the glade was the sound of the wind through the feathers of her outstretched wings. It was a moment of indulgence, luxurious, a bit of play.

She ignored her duties willfully, holding on to the illusion. She imagined the land as she had seen it through the goose's eyes, passing beneath her, effortless.

The tiny urgencies of sparrows broke through her reverie and brought her back to the glade. Bronwyn looked around her, but found no intruder. The squabbling sparrows burst from among the flowers of a dogwood and zigzagged across the glade. She looked more closely at the darkness beneath the dogwood's boughs. From between the fronds of ferns came the glitter of two eyes and the ghostly image of lime-whitened hair above an open-mouthed face.

"A visitor." The glade had been a safe haven for Bronwyn, a place of solitude and peace. The townsfolk disliked the spot, and the barbarous locals of Clan Garw avoided it altogether, though it seemed that one of them had grown brave enough to overcome his superstitious fears. Legends of ghosts and spirits surrounded the place. Evidence of rites from before the days of Rome lay in the tumbled altar stones that rested, lichen-clad, among the tall, seed-heavy grass and fragrant rose brambles.

"If I had more time," she said to the hidden observer, "I'd give you a tale to tell your grandchildren, but as it is...." She rose, drew a touch of power from the intersection beneath the standing stone, and sent it swirling toward the clansman. The dogwood above him shuddered and dropped a snowdrift of white petals. The clansman yelped and ducked down, diving back into the underbrush.

"Good enough," she said to herself with a smile. She threw her cloak across her shoulders and, with a long backward glance toward the darkness beneath the dogwood, walked away into the forest.

She arrived at the keep on its lonely hill before the sun had crested the sky. The lime-washed stone of the keep's eastern curtain shone brilliant white in the clear day of lengthening summer.

At the gate to the keep, she walked through unchallenged, as did everyone. Discipline was lax in Guihomarc's forces, and regardless how many times she pointed it out, the advice always went unheeded. "What is to fear?" he always said. "An attack by the barbarians in the woods?" And so Bronwyn walked up to the gate at Sidmouth keep with no more than a glance from the sentries.

Washer-women, massive baskets of clothing and linens balanced atop their heads, gossiped on their way down to the river Sid. A herdsman haggled with the cook above the heads of bleating sheep. Boys and girls carried bushels of greens and vegetables toward the kitchen and two men shouldered a heavy, rough-sawn timber toward the carpenter's bay.

Beyond the gate was bedlam. Pigs and goats kicked up a ruckus from their pens near the eastern tower. Children ran across the yard, chasing one another in mock battles. Outside the kitchens, merchants and peddlers thronged Boduos, the count's steward, as he attempted to provision the count's table and house. Chickens squawked underfoot. Soldiers in the count's green and black laughed at jokes near the stablery, and above it all was the rhythmic pulse of hammer on anvil, adz on fragrant wood.

Bronwyn picked up her skirts and squelched her way through the muck of the inner yard.

"Boduos," she shouted. She waved and caught the steward's eye. *Where is he?* she mouthed.

The tall man wiped sweat from his brow and pointed up at the southern tower. Then he puffed air and fanned his face before returning himself to the attentions of merchants. Bronwyn laughed at his exaggerated distress and crossed the yard.

Here, too, she entered unimpeded, though liveried horsemen sat on stools rolling dice on an upturned hogshead. She took the stairs, one at a time, quietly. It was only at the top of the stair that any guard took notice of her, and he, she thought, only because of the narrowness of the passage.

The man regarded her steadily, suspiciously. "My lady," he eventually said.

"Is he within?"

"Aye," the guard said with a nod.

"Alone?"

Another nod. The man did not otherwise move. Bronwyn let a moment pass.

"And may I go in?"

"Yes, Mistress." Still the guard made no motion to open the door for her. He stared at her, a slight scowl rumpling his features. Bronwyn recognized the reaction. It followed her wherever she went, had kept her moving for most of her life.

And she hated it.

She took a deep breath to calm herself. The curiosity of the clansman at the grove was one thing. This was another matter entirely. This was nothing but ignorant prejudice.

Her next step was not toward the door, but toward the guard. His eyes widened the merest bit. Bronwyn noticed. With a lazy finger she traced the seam of his sleeve from shoulder to elbow. She looked up at the man's face. His state was obvious.

"You're afraid of me, aren't you?"

The guard shook his head. "No, Mistress."

"Oh, yes you are," she said with a little shake of her head. "Absolutely...petrified."

"No, Mistress. I do not fear you."

"Oh, come now," she said, her smile broad. She placed her palm on his chest and gave it a playful shove. "Of course you are." The man flattened himself against the wall. The odor of fear rose from him like heat off a bed of coals. Bronwyn reached toward him as she spoke, touching him, adjusting his collar, removing imagined dust from his tunic and cloak. "I'm sure you've heard all the stories by now. A young woman, alone, walking the roads of the world, arriving on your master's doorstep with neither baggage nor servant." She laughed. "Why, such a woman could really only be one of two things, don't you think?" With each contact the guard tried to press himself farther into the stone at his back.

"And of those two things," she continued mercilessly, "which is it you think I am?" From the ley line beyond the keep she pulled a touch of power and fashioned a transparent mask. "Surely you don't think me a whore. I can't imagine such a stalwart fellow being afraid of a whore." She shifted the mask. Her eyes flashed red and the lines of her face deepened and sagged. The sweating guard closed his eyes. She gave him a tiny slap on the cheek and he looked at her again, eyes wide.

"You must think me that other thing," she said through sharpened teeth. "Tell me, do you think me a demon?"

The door opened.

"Bronwyn," Guihomarc said, face stern. "Leave him be."

The demonic mask snarled up at the guard, then disappeared, revealing Bronwyn's smirking face. She tsked at them.

"So serious, Guihomarc. We were just getting better

acquainted." She stepped to the door and the shrinking soldier let out a long-held breath. At the door she stopped and, with her most coquettish demeanor, delivered her parting thrust.

"Come to me tonight, when the moon is risen, and we can finish our chat." She closed the door and listened. There was a clumping clatter as the guard abandoned his post two stairs at a time. Shouts and curses from below told of a dice game interrupted. The commotion continued out into the yard as the guard went in search, she supposed, of a place to empty either his stomach or his bowels. She leaned back against the door and laughed; a velvet contralto cascade.

"You shouldn't have done that," Guihomarc said. Parchment, quill, coins, and a stick of wax covered half the table before him. His expression had not changed.

"Oh, come, my count. Don't begrudge me the simple joys I can find in this place. It was only a little jest."

"It just makes my job the harder," he said. "Getting the locals to accept sorcery was difficult enough during my younger days. Now the Christians have made it nearly impossible." He stood and paced to the hearth. "He who was once a mage is now a witch. What was sorcery is now concourse with the devil. The world has become intolerant and 'little jests' like that one of yours only make it harder to keep loyal men loyal. Ouen will probably leave my service now, fearing for his immortal soul."

"Witchcraft. Bah." Bronwyn poured herself a cup of wine from the pitcher near the window. "Their hero was just as much a sorcerer as you or I. More so, in fact. *I* haven't raised anyone from the dead lately, have you?"

"That's not my point."

"No," Bronwyn retorted. "Your point is that your men run from our magic, because they fear they will suffer eternal damnation. My point is that you know that that is not the way things are."

"Do I?"

"Of course. Why, you have told me yourself. Summerland exists, where the Fair Folk live and the old gods still rule. Do you deny this now?"

The count met her gaze for a long moment across the table, then looked away.

"No," he said. "I don't deny it."

"Then you know that it is not as the Christians say."

Guihomarc looked at her again, a quizzical smile on his face. "But what if it is? What if both are true?"

Bronwyn regarded him, cup halfway to her lips. "Both?" she asked.

Guihomarc nodded. "Both. We know of a world beyond this one. What if the Christians have found another?"

"With their heaven and hell?" Bronwyn laughed. "Then I choose Summerland and another turn on the Wheel."

Guihomarc leaned across the table. His voice was silken. "What if you are not the one who makes the choice?"

Bronwyn realized that her jaw hung open and closed it. She put down the cup of wine untasted.

"I do not care for this conversation, my lord," she said. "With your permission?" She turned and walked to the door.

"Was there some reason you came to see me?" the count asked.

"Oh, yes. Your son is on his way. You may want to send escorts soon."

Guihomarc sat down and began gathering together the loose pieces of parchment. "I've already done that. I put my seal on papers for the harbormaster at Sidmouth this morning."

"What?" Bronwyn's heart stumbled within her breast before it kicked itself into a run. "I mean, so soon?"

Guihomarc looked up from his task. "Naturally. The boy is an unknown quantity. Who knows what he will do, where he will go, or how fast he will learn."

"Ah," she said from the doorway. "Of course." She moved to leave and then stepped back. "I also came to beg leave of you, my lord. My business dealings call me back to the south. And it's just as well. I fear I have overstayed my welcome."

"Certainly not *my* welcome."

"No, my lord. But with your people." She crooked a thumb toward the vacant guard post outside the door. "And with your men. I think it best that I be on my way."

Guihomarc walked over to her. Ring-studded fingers reached toward her, and he caressed her cheek with a gentle hand. "Sweet one, forgive me. I did not mean to offend you with harsh talk of witchcraft and sin."

Bronwyn smiled. She took his hand in hers. "On my word,

dear Count, I took no offense. My choice to leave has nothing to do with our discussion. Please believe me. It is business that calls me away."

Guihomarc sighed. "Very well." He returned to the table. "Will I be able to contact you?"

Quietly, Bronwyn said, "No, my lord."

Guihomarc shook his head. "How do you block me like that? I've never been able to do that."

"How I maintain my privacy will remain my secret, I'm afraid."

"Ever the woman of mystery."

"Anything less would disappoint you, my lord. A few weeks, a few months—"

"A few years?"

"We shall meet again."

"I look forward to the day. Goodbye, Bronwyn."

"Keep well, Guihomarc."

She closed the door behind her and walked down the stairs, past the silent, staring guards in the lower room and out into the bustle and reek of the yard.

ten

"What news, friend?"

Alain looked up from his hoeing and saw a man sitting atop a light horse. He looked to the right and left before deciding that the stranger was speaking to him and not to any of the other men and women who labored in the field beside him.

"News?" He pointed toward the somnolent village on the hillside. "The tavern keeper's wife had her first babe last week. A son, much to their pleasure." As Alain related the small bits of local news and gossip that were the lifeblood of Briezh society, he felt a sudden elation. It was more than the simple joy of conversation. It was, he realized, that it was so normal. So much of the everyday had been denied him by family and the villagers of his home that it often caught him unawares when he was suddenly able to partake of them.

As he related the story of the abbot's mare breaking free and pounding its way through the midwife's vegetable garden, it struck him odd how here, only a few days' walk from his old home, he should be able to live a life that was so different, so pleasantly different from the one he had always known. It gave him hope for his future, and for the new and barely-formed goals he was setting for himself.

"I thank you, my friend," the man said when Alain had done. "Forgive me, though, for I cannot recall your name. I thought I knew the names of all who worked on my land. How are you called?"

Alain blanched. "Your land?" He noticed for the first time the handiwork on the pommel of the landlord's saddle, the sword that lay tucked under his rolled blanket, and the gold signet ring on his right index finger. Alain ran through all the stories he had related, searching for any that might have been disrespectful of Master Erispoë or his household.

"Master Erispoë, your pardon. I meant no offense by being so familiar." He straightened and bowed to the man on the horse. "I am called Alain. I have been here less than a fortnight, working for a few coins to take me on my way."

"Ah, a fellow traveler." Erispoë seemed pleased. "Then I bid you welcome to my household, for whatever time you are with us. I am a merchant, as you may have learned, and am on the road much myself. Dine with me this night, and we will share tales of our travels."

Alain shrugged. "Tales of my travels are small in number, my lord. I have not been on the road very long."

"Then you shall regale me with stories of where you are going and why. Come to the house an hour before sunset."

"I would be honored, Master Erispoë."

"Good," the man said. "Till tonight, Alain."

Alain bowed again as Erispoë *tch*ed to his horse and made his way on down the path toward the village. Alain looked up at the sky where the sun blazed brightly in its bed of shining clouds.

Dinner at the landlord's table! He grinned and shook his head. Not even Jessup had shown him that much favor.

"I *will* regale him with stories," he said. "Erispoë is a worldly man. He will see that I am more than a simple ploughman's son."

"Alain," came the creaky voice of the lead farmhand. "Quit jabbering to the spirits and get back to work. We need to finish this field today."

Alain waved at the rotund old farmhand and nodded. He returned to hoeing the weeds out from amid the turnips. His thoughts, however, ran about, racing up and down the furrows like gleeful children.

At an hour before sunset his hair was still wet and his skin still tingled from his scrub at the creek. His chin and cheeks sported a few nicks from the blade, but shaving them made his new-grown moustache appear thicker and made him look less like the boy he had left behind.

Alain left the low-roofed cottage where he bedded down with

ten other hands, three dogs, and four goats. The conditions within were cramped, but the closeness of others warmed the nights when the coastal wind ripped through cracks in the thatched roof and mud-daubed sidings. His invitation from the master had won him no advantage with his fellow servants, and the lead farmhand even smirked at some jest only he knew.

He walked the short distance to the main house, but paused at the gate and glanced to the southwest. The ridgeline, dark and heavy with trees, rippled in slow, ponderous waves under the chill wind. Four such ridges lay between him and the village of Belvanetes, between him and his home.

Between me and Josselyn, he thought.

"How are you, Josée?" he asked the distances. "All is well, I hope." Then he took a deep breath. He had never spent time with a landed gentleman, at least not as a guest of his household, and the prospect made him nervous. But it was just such a life that he now envisioned for himself, and if he was to succeed, he would have to learn the ways of those who ruled. He entered the gate in the low fence that separated the landlord's home from the fields.

"Alain," said Erispoë from a wooden bench in the garden. "Welcome." He stood and Alain noticed that the landlord was a short man, but well-formed. He wore a loosely belted cotton tunic in the Roman style, and his breeches were of pale linen. His upper arms were thick, formed by hard labor, and his hand, when he clasped Alain's, was wide and strong. His face was handsome, tan, and seamed at the corners of his blue eyes. Alain imagined his host riding year after year between the coast of Bretagne and the towers of Rome, squinting into wind and sun.

Here is a man who has seen much, Alain thought as he was ushered inside the house.

Erispoë's wife was a tall, dark, morose woman; a contrast to each and every of her husband's aspects. She did not greet her guest, only nodded. Alain put her treatment of him to the differences in their standings and thought no more on it.

He was offered a place on one of the four simple couches that squared off the large central room near the hearth. Erispoë's two sons entered and Alain thought again about his hostess. What he had taken for coldness might be outright resentment at having lost her seat at the family dinner.

Alain had never eaten in the Roman style before and began to worry. He knew little of this family, and childhood stories of the barbarities of the Roman cities filled the back of his brain. There was no table, no benches, only the low, uninviting couches strewn with pillows. He looked to his host for guidance, and followed suit after watching Erispoë and his two sons recline.

The boys were a handful of years younger than Alain and, though they tended toward obesity, resembled their mother in appearance and demeanor. Erispoë did not introduce them and they lay, chins on elbowed forearms, sullen and unspeaking. They regarded Alain dully, without emotion or expression. Their stare made Alain uneasy, and he turned to Erispoë.

"Was your trip a long one, Master?"

"Ah, no," Erispoë said. "This was only a short one. To Nantes. I went to prepare the way for a shipment of *garum* headed for Rome."

Alain's stomach did a small dance. Oh, gods! he groaned inwardly. He despised the salted fish paste, and prayed desperately to the white goddess. Please, Epona, no *garum* tonight!

Erispoë went on about the price of *garum* and the troubles of bringing it from the vats in Brest all the way to Rome and Alain smiled and tried to look interested. His anxiety about the evening rose considerably.

When Erispoë's wife and a serving maid brought out bowls of rose-scented water, Alain breathed a nearly audible sigh. He dipped his hands and gave thanks to Epona and Lugh, the god of the sure hand.

At least this man is civilized, he thought to himself.

The serving girl brought Alain a glazed ceramic goblet and filled it with a deep, dark wine. Then she brought a wooden platter of heavy bread and *pulmentum*, a rough paste of beans and vegetables. Alain fell to with a passion, for it was the first decent food he had seen since leaving Belvanetes.

Except for Erispoë, who spoke constantly as they ate, the only spot of life in the house was the serving girl. Thin, with a quick smile and hair like the sun through fall leaves, she paid close attention to her guest's needs. Alain never tasted his wine more than twice but that she was there to refill his goblet.

"You would find it amazing," Erispoë was saying, "how much a few weeks bad weather can affect the price of *garum*. Why, only last year my profits shrank to a quarter of their previous amount, simply because of a few weeks of storms."

Alain took extra sips from his wine, just to bring the serving maid near. By the time she served him a platter layered with strips of grilled lamb, the wine had quite gone to his head. He smiled at her freckles as the scents of cumin and nutmeg swirled up from the dish. She said nothing, but her grey-eyed gaze caught his for a moment and held him, transfixed. She stepped back and went to the kitchen, leaving Alain wondering why he was suddenly thinking of Josselyn.

"But what of you?" asked the host from around a mouthful of sauce-daubed bread. "You've let me go on too long about my travels. Where is it you are going?"

Alain took another sip of wine and, with all solemnity, told his host, "I am the son of Guihomarc, Count Vannes, and I have struck out on my own to make my rightful place in the world."

Erispoë stopped chewing. His slack-jawed sons stared. From beyond the doorway came the sound of a wooden spoon hitting the tiled floor.

Alain went over the words he had spoken but, no, he had said them just as he had practiced them. Why, then, he puzzled, did they all look so stunned?

Finally, Erispoë coughed, coughed again, and swallowed his mouthful of half-chewed bread.

"Your pardon," the landlord said. "I have met many people in my travels between here and Rome, but never would I have guessed that one of the workers in my field was the disenfranchised son of a great count." The two boys sputtered with suppressed laughter. Alain felt the color rush to his cheeks.

"You do not believe me?"

Erispoë raised a hand. "No, no, I assure you. It is not that." He swept a hard glare across his sons and they fell silent. "It is only that it is so unexpected a tale." He raised a hand, and shrugged. "I had expected you to be running from some girl's irate father, or to be the youngest son off to seek some land of your own. Most anything else. You must admit, Alain. Your story is not a common one."

Alain regarded his host steadily. "I am not a common man."

Erispoë smiled, though Alain could not read the meaning of it.

"Yes," Erispoë said as the plates were picked up by quick-moving servants. Alain noted that the serving girl did not look at him as she took his platter. "You are, indeed, not a common man. That much is clear." Erispoë stood.

With a gesture he dismissed his two sons. Silently, they fled. His cup in one hand, the landlord snagged the wine pitcher with the other and crossed to Alain's couch. Alain made to sit up but Erispoë bid him stay. He sat on the edge of Alain's couch and poured, first for Alain, then for himself, emptying the pitcher.

Goblets clinked and were brought to lips in a silent toast, to what, Alain did not know.

"Tell me," Erispoë said, leaning over his guest. "Just how uncommon a man are you?"

Alain was confused by his host's sudden change in manner. His voice was low, his wide eyes were now half-lidded. "I do not think I understand your question."

From the ley line out near the coast emanated a trilled note like a shepherd's flute played in the distance. Alain was startled out of his tipsy state into alertness.

Erispoë chuckled. "Let me tell you what I think," he said. "I think you are a young man, alone in the world, and that you have a secret—a secret you are afraid to share with anyone, lest they dub you a witch, or worse. Am I on the right road?"

Slowly, Alain nodded. "How did you know?"

"I heard you," his host said, and chuckled again. "All the way from Nantes, I heard you, such a noise you made along the lines. I hastened back home, hoping to find you."

"Hoping to find *me*?"

"Yes," he said. "There is much we can do for one another."

Alain grew fearful, unsure of the landlord's game. "Such as?"

"You needn't be afraid, anymore. I can protect you, and I can instruct you. You would be safe from harm, and live here, in this house, as my protégé."

"And what is it that I could do for you?"

Erispoë put a hand on Alain's thigh. "I would benefit from your presence, as well. With our combined talents, we could expand my business, increase my lands. And I could use a companion in my journeys to Rennes and Nantes. Even occasionally to Rome. You could see a lot of the world." The hand that rested calmly on Alain's thigh began to move, a slow quest upward.

Suddenly, Alain caught the secondary drift of the conversation. "Oh, Master Erispoë," he said, apologetic. "I am sorry, but I don't think I can help you in that other way." He rolled toward the far side of the couch, but hands on shoulder and thigh held him fast.

Erispoë's face was very close. "I think you can," he said. His voice was still soft and gentle, in conflict with the strong arms that pushed Alain down into the cushions. "Considering the secret you keep, I think you had better. The folk of my village are fearful of mages. If they learned of your talents..."

A song of fear played in the back of Alain's mind, joined by a harmony of anger. The questing hand groped higher, beneath tunic and breeches, and memories of the Delphine's sins rang out in his mind, pealing with rage.

Red wine splashed blue eyes. Erispoë howled and Alain rolled away. The ley line whistled and Alain felt his arm gripped by an unseen hand.

The blow across his face would have tumbled him to the floor if not for that ethereal hand. It held on to him, dangling him like a doll. His host's physical hand pulled back for another fisted blow. It fell, struck, was repeated. Finally, after the fourth one, the magic released him and Alain was allowed to fall.

But he did not.

Alain was no stranger to beatings, only to beatings by strangers. He had not expected violence, but once it had visited him, he was ready. He landed in a crouch and from there, leapt.

His head struck Erispoë between ribs and gut. Air whooshed out of the shorter man as he fell backward. Alain regained his feet and dabbed at his nose. Blood smeared but did not flow. He pointed down at Erispoë.

"You are not my mother. You are not my father. And you are not my owner. I am a free man, beholden to none."

He turned and faced the atrium where frightened faces—the wife, sons, and maid—stared out at him. He watched them as he approached, saw their eyes widen. Alain heard the line shrill another note.

By the time the maid shouted her warning, he was ready.

The line reverberated as Alain whirled, a dark sphere of deadly force in his hands and his vision tinged with murderous blackness. Erispoë, his white tunic stained purple, his teeth bared, sent the ceramic pitcher on a thrust of power to smash Alain's head. But the pitcher hung in the air between them, motionless. The maid's shout still rang in his ears, the line still rang in his head, his desire to destroy still rang in his breast; yet nothing moved.

A droplet of wine elongated and broke away from the lip of the pitcher. Alain watched as it fell with a dreamy, feather-weight quality, as if it were reluctant to reach the ground. The tiny, burgundy ball dropped through air turned honeyed and thick. Alain realized that the attack had not ceased, only slowed, or perhaps he himself had sped up. He did not know which. A breeze blew over the inner fields of his mind, and there was the touch of a breath on his neck. Something, someone, was with him.

Mercy.

The single word whispered like a wind, and his blood chilled as he looked at the ball of death that crackled in his hand and realized what he had been about to do.

Slowly, the pitcher flew toward him. Alain—his own movements curiously slowed—divided the ball into two parts, changing their purpose and shape. The air snapped and fizzed between his hands. The sections of the ball swirled from sardonyx to malachite.

He ducked and lunged, slowed by the syrup of time. The pitcher sailed over him, and with one hand extended, he threw power and struck Erispoë a dream-time blow in the chest.

Time sped up. A light flashed. Erispoë flew backward across the room. He crashed into one of the couches, toppling it. The pitcher hit the doorpost and shattered. Erispoë lay amid the wreckage, moaned, and did not move.

Alain turned.

Four faces still stared from the doorway. At his glance, three of them fled. Only the wife remained, trembling fingers before pale blue lips. She fell to her knees and looked up at the young man who stood before her: tall, imperious, an emerald ball of whirling power sizzling in his right hand. She looked into his eyes for a long moment. Then her gaze dropped.

"Do not kill us, my lord. I beg you. Do not kill us."

Her words echoed through his soul, and the battle between his anger's desire and one whispered word still raged within him.

"Kill you?" he asked. He looked over his shoulder to where

the fallen Erispoë still lay. "What of your husband?"

The frail woman looked up at him once more. "He is not a bad man, my lord. Spare him. Please."

Alain reached out with the ball of power, extending his will. Erispoë moaned as he was lifted by an invisible hand and carried to a couch. Alain laid Erispoë's head back onto the pillows. Then he shook out the ethereal tether and let the power flow back to the line.

The woman kneeling in the doorway gaped. She looked from Alain to her husband and back again.

"I did not come here to kill," he told her, taking her hand and bidding her rise. He walked her over to her insensible spouse. "I did not even want to harm. I just...." He looked down at Erispoë, at the scrape on his brow, the purpling bruise on his jaw. Alain touched the soreness of his own face and sought the anger that had nearly killed this man.

It was gone. What had burned bright and hot in the forefront of his brain he could not now even feel. That a violence of such potential lived within his breast disturbed him, especially in light of his new talents. Does one come with the other, he wondered? He regarded the man before him.

"But I might have killed him," he murmured, watching the slow rise and fall of the unconscious man's breast. "I would have, but for...." The memory of the moment was clear: the world holding its breath, the pitcher hovering, Erispoë's injured rage, and—deep, deep within—Alain's sense of another at his back, an overseeing spirit. He turned and went to the door.

"My lord?"

He stopped.

"Are you man, or are you demon?"

"Forgive me," Alain said without turning, "but I do not know."

The creekbed mumbled; a conversation between water and slick rocks. Alain listened to it, adding his own comments as he washed grease from his hands and wine from his tunic.

He made a bowl of his fingers and brought cool water to his face. Dried blood washed away. The swelling remained. Pain stabbed through his skull, more than the beating could have earned him. Casting came with a price.

The spirits of the wood spoke among themselves. Trees, water, and rocks. Night birds and phosphorescent witchwood. Alain, his fingers numb from the cold water, listened.

They spoke of summer, of fruit and seed, of the music of wind through branches and the fledging of young. It was a quiet speech, reaching Alain only in images and impressions. Small fry slept beneath the water's surface in the depths of the pool, and frogs called to one another, dreaming of motion and sated bellies.

Alain felt both at one with the natural world around him and apart from it. He could see it, hear it, smell it. He could sense its mind, its yearnings. Yet, he was alone, separate.

So, too, were his feelings regarding the people of the land and villages around him. If he wished, he could feel their desires and hopes in nebulous, dreamlike stirrings.

Right now, all he sensed was their fear, and their building thirst for vengeance.

He stood, straightening sore limbs and stretching a cramped back. The damp tunic lay cold and limp on his shoulders and chest. Overhead, clouds obscured the stars and the moon was dark. Anger was brewing all about him. It would not be long before the storm of hatred broke.

A few paces upstream, from a crevice covered by the curling fall of water, he retrieved his cached treasures: Jessup's sword, wrapped in a length of oiled canvas, and a small leather pouch in which he had stashed the few pieces of coin he had been able to earn since leaving his home. He lifted the loop of rope he used as a baldric and settled it on his shoulder. The pouch he tied to his belt. In the distance, he heard the sound of voices. He sought the line and was rewarded by a jab of pain that caused his vision to blur and double. Earth magic would have to do.

"Spirits," he whispered, using the Old Tongue, "come ye near. I have need of thee." His mother's teachings, pounded into his mind by numberless repetition, came to him without conscious thought.

At the foot of a tree, he knelt. He brushed away the litter of leaves and twigs from a place between splayed roots and uncovered the pale green glow of decaying witchwood.

More voices joined the first few. They came from a new direction now, from near the farmhands' huts. Alain heard hard anger in the voices, an armor to cover their fears. Dogs barked, excited by the stormy emotions around them.

This is folly, he thought, wondering at his own actions. I should flee. I should run up into the hills and keep to the ridges all the way to Finistére.

But he did not. A feeling had descended upon him, and it bade him stay. He puzzled at it, for it was neither anger nor fear. It was calmness, serenity, as if the powers of the earth stood by his side in silent counsel.

He loosened and lifted the witchwood gingerly and was rewarded with a squarish chunk that filled his hand and shone with a pale green light that shied from his direct gaze, seeming stronger when he caught it from the corner of his eye. He pulled his sword from its scabbard and briefly touched the edge to the back of his hand.

A thin line of blood welled, formed a droplet black and shiny in the dimness. He let the droplet fall into the hole left by the wood he had taken. Then he drew the blooded blade across the glowing wood as if across a whetstone, first one edge, then the other. As he did, the faint light disappeared from the wood in his hand until the piece went dark and crumbled away to nothing.

The dogs were close now. He heard their baying and knew them—Hep, Clip, and Montrice—who last night had lain close to his warmth and tonight would dutifully tear out his throat. The yellow light of torches chased away the blue of night that clung beneath the trees. They were coming for him. Alain wondered if they were led by the landlord's sons, or perhaps by a recovered Erispoë. He walked up the path to meet them.

The dogs came on first, two shaggy shepherds and one hunting hound. Holding their leads was Erispoë and behind him came a handful of men with torches and sickles. Alain took a deep breath and called again to the spirits that surrounded him.

"Please, may my talent run true."

He stepped out of the shadows of the trees and into a clearing. A howl rose from men and dogs as one. Erispoë released the hounds and they came snarling on.

The same word that had calmed Reynald back in Dead Ox Wood stopped the dogs in their tracks. They stepped forward and back, looking from Alain to their master, unsure and confused. Another word sent them running and Alain laughed at the gawking faces of landlord and men. He raised the sword, blade before him and level with the ground. He called on witchwood and blood, firing them to new life.

The sword burst into a green radiance that blinded without heat. Several men ran, dropping their torches as they fled. Alain felt the power of the earth surge within him. He felt he could fly, run with the wind, he sensed the trees, the life in the ground, his blood pounded like hooves on an open plain, he saw with preternatural clarity the sweat on his former host's face, and the tremulous contraction of his pupils in the flare of light. He pointed the sword at Erispoë and his remaining servants.

"Run."

They did.

Alain retrieved one of the burning torches and doused the rest in the dirt. He kicked out the leaves that smoldered where the torches had fallen. Then, witchfire in one hand, torch in the other, he went to the huts.

No one bothered him as he collected his remaining things. Only the three dogs came near him, sniffing at his heels with tucked tails. He let them, knowing they would do him no harm. Outside, he saw Erispoë, his family, and his servants standing in a crowd at the garden's rough-wood fence. They watched him in silence. Fearful eyes reflected torchlight.

Alain scabbarded his sword and dropped the torch to hiss in a bucket at the hut's doorstep. Then he shooed the dogs back toward the house and struck out into the night.

Guihomarc listened to the reverberating lines and stared into the fire. He stood, poured himself a cup of wine, and drank it in two large gulps.

"He's growing too strong too fast," he muttered. "And moving too slowly. Damn."

He seated himself again before the crackling feathers of flame. Staring into the coals, he smelled the sweet smoke, saw drafted air ripple across the embers in waves of orange and red. The traceries of heat and fire persisted in his vision as he closed his eyes and sought the lines. The remembered glow became a lacework, fired to bright heat through red to orange and yellow. The lacework flared white, became a web in sunlight, and to this web Guihomarc stretched his mind.

He sang to it a song both small and blue yet ringing of white

lines that curled just so—down a bit here, up a bit there. The web
embraced the song and carried it away. A moment passed and
then he heard an echo, faint and smelling of thyme. One of the
strands glowed brighter in the ethereal darkness.

Guihomarc flew down to the nexus and up along the glowing
line. He sang his tune again and heard the echo, closer, warmer.
At the proper point he sheared off from the line and headed
toward the warmth, the scent, the parried song.

Pouldou.

The man Pouldou came awake in an instant, clutching his
sword with one hand and the other gripping the inlayed
snakestone he wore around his neck. His face was warm from the
campfire and from sleep. His comrade placed another branch on
the fire and looked across through aromatic smoke.

"Bad dream?"

"It's the master."

"Same thing."

"Hush, he'll hear you."

Pouldou.

Pouldou raked a dirty hand through his hair and cleared his
eyes of sleep.

"Yes, m'lord?"

Guihomarc pushed across the miles, giving his instructions in
words laden with emotion. Pouldou would get only images,
feelings; it was all that could be forced through to the unattuned.
It was no easy task, sending to waking men. Guihomarc found it
much easier to enter a man's dreams and press his images there,
but a man can ignore his dreams, misinterpret them, even forget
them. This was too important.

The web shimmered with the strength of his message.
Guihomarc saw Pouldou's face wrinkle in concentration, heavy
features folded like a crumpling rug.

"Hurry?" Pouldou asked the air. "Going to ground? You
mean he might head for the hills?"

Yes.

"Ach. We'll never find him up there. Where is he now?"

Guihomarc sent more. He sent an image of the old Roman
road, the rising sun straight ahead, the curling slate of the sea to
the right hand. He built a town, off to the left, nestled in a valley's
folded arms, and sent a word: *Border.*

"Border town, north of the old road. Kemperle."

Yes, and then, *Caution*.

"Be wary. Aye, m'lord."

Guihomarc released the contact and retreated, moving northward along the lines that laced the other world, threads in the Veil between Summerland and the Lands of Men.

He opened his eyes. The candle had gone out and the fire had burnt low. Sweat soaked his hair, neck, and back, chilling him. He sighed.

A sheepskin vest lay on the nearby chair. He pulled it over and shrugged it on. The room was cold, dark, and nearly empty.

"Why do I live like this?" he wondered.

He thought of trying to reach Bronwyn but knew it would prove futile. In the five years he had known her, he had never been able to penetrate her wall of silence. Contact came at her desiring, not his. She was, to him, like a wild cat that laps milk from the milking bucket: beautiful and alluring, never to be trusted, never to be controlled.

Guihomarc smiled to himself. *I have some secrets, too.*

Logs snapped and settled in the hearth, throwing fireflies up the flue and waking the bedded coals. Guihomarc poured another glass of wine and thought of sleep.

Eventually, near dawn, it came for a visit.

eleven

The last miles were miserable. For most of the day, a storm had lain offshore like a wounded boar in a thicket, rumbling and casting baleful looks landward from the waters beyond the Ile de Groix. As the sun prepared to set, the storm turned and ran for land, catching Alain alone on the road, miles from town.

The gloom deepened and rain burst from the sky. Alain ran for the trees and huddled beneath their spreading, wooden arms. Within minutes, the downpour had penetrated even the thickest of the leafy protection. He muttered a curse and kicked the heavy bole of the broad-limbed chestnut.

He'd avoided towns, passing by Auray, Carnac, and even the city of Lorient in his desire to put some distance between himself and the events at Erispoë's manor. He viewed every person he met as a threat, and was sure every town harbored a mage eager to kill or control him. But his suspicions had kept him hungry, lonely, and now they had caused his utter drenching by the storm. Surely not *everyone* was after him.

The wind threw slanting sheets under the boughs. Branches shook themselves like wet dogs. Alain wiped rain from his brow with a dripping hand and wound his cloak tighter about his neck. There was no cover to be had.

He picked up and went back down to the road.

The coastal wind turned frigid and sharp as he walked, but the terrain of Finistére was hilly, much more so than the coastal *landes* of his home back in Morbihan. Here, the hills confused the weather's onslaught, forcing it to whip and gyre between dale and hillock, making it unpredictable and nearly impossible to avoid.

He rounded a bend in the road where trees stood on either side and the rain could not hit him from right or left but only fall straight down. Fat drops burst on his head and shoulders. They spattered on leaves and smacked in puddles with the hiss and crackle of a green-wood fire. From the edge of the trees, Alain saw a crossroads a stone's throw ahead. In the center of the crossroads was a lump, grey and shapeless.

Alain approached and, in the failing light, descried the outline of a bull's hide laid flat in the roadway and staked down at each corner. The hide was fresh, and lay flesh side up, dark rain gathering in bloody pools. In the center of the hide was a pile of ragged cloth and hair. Alain stopped, seeing bony arms and hands stretched out wide. He felt for the reassuring weight of the sword beneath his cloak.

The clothing moved and the hair lifted, uncovering a skeletal face beneath a beard and filthy locks. Alain stepped back, but the gaze of robin's egg eyes kept him from retreating farther from the mystic in the roadway. Lips parted—revealing darkness—then curled in a satyric smile. The seer blinked through rivulets of rain.

"A callow stripling!" he hissed, his voice as sibilant as the falling rain. "We are sent a stripling lad. Sooth, sooth. All the better."

Alain had a healthy respect for eremites, woodsmen who shunned the world of towns and men for reclusion and solitude. The Delphine had been one, after a fashion, though she had been isolated by violence rather than religious choice. The result was nevertheless similar: insanity and unpredictability. Alain looked about the roadway. He was alone with the mad hermit.

"Can I help you, Old One?"

The mystic's eyes swam and wobbled. "Help you. Help you." His fingers plucked at the bits of flesh that clung to the untanned hide. Crossroads were places of power, and the hermit had laid out the bloody skin to force demons to the surface, that they might be contacted. The hermit's gaze spiraled in and locked on Alain. The ancient face settled into old lines and a look of lucidity returned. "Men bring death; women, life," he said, his voice strong and chanting. "Love is banish'd, and lust rebuilds the world."

Alain jumped as a ley line sounded, a distant thunder inside his mind. He had not touched the lines. The mystic, he wondered, a mage as well as a hermit? Other lines joined the first and their dolorous harmonies surrounded the crossroads. Fear gripped him, for a great power moved in the darkness around him, lurking, and he did not know which way to run.

"What do you mean, Old One?"

The voice that issued from the hermit's mouth was suddenly not his own, but a woman's. "Take care, Fair One. Violence is inescapable." Alain's heart thumped in his chest and the hair on his neck rose despite the rain. The hermit's eyes rolled and Alain remembered Reynald, possessed by the spirit of his mad mother. He backed away and looked to his right.

A light winked through the rain and he saw atop the hill the hunched and huddled shoulders of thatched roofs.

"There?" he asked, pointing to the village on the hillside. "Are you saying I should stay away from there? What do you mean?"

"Towns are dangerous," said the hermit, his voice his own once more. "And violence is inescapable. The scarred man will avoid further pain. Thus play out the words to the son."

"Scarred man?" The hermit was probably raving, Alain knew, and yet it was clear that his words were for him.

Fair One. Scarred man. Words to the son.

"Who's son?" he wondered. The Delphine's? Or Guihomarc's?

The sky broke open, spilled light and threw thunder. The flash illuminated the old man's face in harsh lines and deep creases. His eyes, so blue, seemed ready to pop from his head.

"Who's son?" he asked, speaking louder through the intensifying rain. "Where is the danger?"

But the mystic was lost to him, staring unblinkingly up into the rain, saying, "Ye gods. Ye gods."

Alain stepped around him, keeping away from the hide and the spirits that possessed the hermit. He looked to the north. The village beckoned. There would be warm food and a fire to eat it by at the traveler's inn. Yet if danger lay in wait, it could easily lay that way.

The mystic, lucid once more, had stopped babbling. He sat in the raging downpour, looking at Alain with calm, clear eyes. As the man fell silent, so had the music of the lines. The only sound was that of the falling rain.

"Towns are dangerous, eh? Well, you don't have to tell me that. But I can't avoid them much longer." He looked toward the village—so close—and then at the man sitting at the crossroads. He felt the rain patter onto his scalp, seep through his clothes, soaking him.

"But this one or the next, it hardly makes a difference to me now. I'll take your counsel, Old One. My thanks." He settled the strap of his sodden load on his shoulder and started walking again. He did not take the north fork toward Kemperle, but continued westward, along the coast.

When he reached the fishing town of Manech, Alain did not hesitate. He headed straight for the building along the roadway with the sign of the Boat and Anchor. Wind swirled in through the open door as he entered. Men covered steaming cups and yelled, "Shut the door," with varying levels of politeness and profanity.

He ducked inside and pushed the heavy door to. The wind was banished as the bar fell home.

"Ah, another traveler driven in by the storm," boomed a voice from across the room. The tavern-master leaned against the galley doorway at the far side of the room. "That makes six. What did I tell you?" He slapped at a patron with a rag as he stepped away from the galley and into the common room.

A huge man of immense girth, his arms looked like they could lift an ox. His thick black beard challenged a pate as hairless as an egg. Alain wondered how the two extremes could live on the same head. Across the man's baldness and down across one eye lay a patch of skin the color of wine-stained linen. The tavern-master walked between long tables with a broad, crooked-toothed smile, touching shoulders and checking on appetites. Eventually, he came up to Alain. The big man pulled him into the crook of his arm, gave his shoulder a fatherly squeeze, and said, "So, my little wet wren. Let's see if we can't find you a place by the fire."

Alain liked him immediately.

His voice was deep and sounded as if it had rolled about for a time within his huge chest before finally bubbling to the surface in the form of words.

"I am called Hector," he said as he led the way toward the fire, "and I am Greek." They stopped at the hearth. "You are called...?"

"Alain."

"And you are...?"

"Poor."

Hector stopped and stared as if he were unsure what Alain had said. Then he laughed, a hearty, growling thing that grew to fill the room.

"Well, then, you shall be my good deed for today."

"I do have some coin," Alain protested.

"And I have a tavern full of travelers and fishermen sitting out the storm. Make room, Bitoire." He slapped his rag and a bull-necked man scooted a bit down the bench. Hector pressed Alain into the newly-made vacancy.

"Bitoire, Bertrand, and Salomon," he said, pointing to the bull-necked man and the two men sitting opposite. He tapped Alain's soggy shoulder and told them, "This is Alain." Then he left, leaving Alain sitting at the end of the bench, rain still dripping from his hair and his clothes, the sullen faces of three thick-thewed men staring at him as they slurped their chowder.

Salomon, a ropey old man with one eye gone as white as the hair on his head, dipped bread in the pasty stew of barley and fish and stared at Alain with his brown eye. Bitoire and Bertrand ignored Alain completely. Silence set up housekeeping on the table between the foursome and made no motion to leave. Finally Alain spoke.

"Salomon," he said and the one eye narrowed. "Sir, I mean. What news?"

Salomon bit into chowder-softened bread with sparse teeth, wiped a rough knuckle along the dribble that escaped toward his beard. Alain felt like a worm beneath a robin's one-eyed gaze. He sat, waiting for the robin to strike.

The gaze broke and Salomon dipped his bread again.

"Naught new since storm broke." His few words were thick with age and toothlessness.

"Fisherman?"

The grey head nodded. "Aye."

"Father?"

"Aye. He, too."

Alain tapped his chest. "Ploughman raised me."

Salomon grimaced. "Pfagh."

"Was an old soldier, too."

"Oh, aye?"

"Aye. Jengland-Breslé."

"Don't say."

"I saw that day," said Bertrand, leaning in.

The four continued on in fragmented conversation until Hector returned with a full bowl and a half-loaf of bread. Alain set upon the food. Salomon produced a few coins and asked for wine. Hector went away smiling.

After two bowls of the thick chowder spiced with thyme and another half loaf of the heavy brown bread, Alain sat back. Bitoire was recounting the damage one of his nets suffered already, so early in the season. Alain stretched and yawned. Coals in the hearth glowed at his side.

Warm for the first time in days, he sipped at his wine and sighed. Exhaustion plucked at his muscles and the wine freed his spirit. His stomach was full and the trials of the road seemed very far away. The tavern had grown quieter, most of the locals having left for their homes.

This is another place I might stay, he thought to himself. *I could fit right in.*

"So. What of you?" Bitoire leaned over and filled Alain's cup. "We've talked of ourselves while fire's burnt low. What of you?"

The men around him grew quiet, waiting to hear the traveler's tale. Alain saw in their eyes an eagerness, a hungering after things new and unusual. Their lives were small, settled, sedate. By choice or by necessity, they would live out the rest of their lives in this town near the sea. Alain realized that no, even were he to lie to them about his beginnings, he could never fit in with them. The scars on his chest, the vines on his legs, the burning talent in his heart; these things separated him from common men. No matter where he went or what he did, he would always be a marked man, in more than one sense.

But beyond that, Alain realized that he did not want to hide his past from these men. He was who he was, and not a small part of that identity had been embedded in his flesh by a lunatic mother.

The faces before him were eager, awaiting a tale of romance and danger.

Why did you leave your home?

What do you seek?

The questions were written on their faces and in their twinkling, wine-lit eyes. So, too, were the answers they desired.

"Come, young one," Salomon urged. "What placed your foot upon the road?"

"It is not a pretty tale," Alain told them. "Are you sure you want to hear it?"

"Oh, aye," they all said at once.

Alain wrinkled his face into a squint. "Very well," he said. "But you must hear me out for—fantastic as it will sound—I swear that all is true. Agreed?"

Nods all around. Alain sipped his cup and began.

"I am accursed."

Alain wove his tale well into the night. Hector brought pitcher after pitcher of cider and wine. Each time he set one down he had a wink and a smile for Alain. Men from other tables came closer to join the group gathered around the hearth, and in the corners of the room, Alain saw conversations slow as people listened. He pridefully embellished only little and, when met with disbelief or skepticism, he produced Jessup's sword or showed them the cut on his cheek left by Erispoë's signet ring. Their fascination shone from their firelit eyes, encouraging him in his tale. He told them all, but scrupulously avoided any mention of his talent with magic, and though it made some portions of his tale less believable, he felt it safer to be called a liar than risk being labeled a witch.

He wrapped up the tale, finishing his story with the mad hermit at the crossroads and his last miles from Kemperle to Manech, and the group before him pounded the table and toasted him with the last of the wine.

"A fine telling, lad," said Hector with a friendly slap of his rag. "They'll be retelling that tale for months. Here. You brought me good business tonight. Take this." He placed some coin in Alain's hand. "And you've my leave to stay the night in the stable, if you wish."

Alain looked at the coin in his hand. For a night of storytelling! He would have had to work a week in the fields to earn half what Hector had just given him.

"Thank you," he said, looking up at the big man. Hector beamed.

"Feel free to stay on a while. Others will want to hear that tale. And any others you come up with."

Bitoire and Bernard clasped Alain's hand as they prepared to leave. Salomon stopped by, as well.

"Will you be here on the morrow night?" he asked.

"I...I'm not sure," he told the old man. He thought he saw disappointment in the craggy visage. "I may be."

"Good," Salomon said. "My cousin should hear that tale."

Alain clasped Salomon's hand. "It would be my pleasure."

He followed the old men out, leaving only a few people behind in the tavern. He was tired, and a little woozy with all the wine. Sleep would be good, he thought. He lurched toward the small stable behind the tavern.

The rain had lessened, but still fell in a mild drizzle. Alain stopped and stood a moment. The mist kissed his face, cooling the fingerprints left by wine and fire.

The tavern door opened. Alain turned as two men walked out. They looked around and saw Alain. He recognized them as the pair that came in very late and had taken a seat near the back wall. They started his way, and Alain grinned, immodestly expecting more praise for his performance.

The two, one thin, one wide, walked up to him directly. Without a word, the wide one hit him in the gut with a fist of stone. Alain doubled over and fell to his knees. Breath gone, he tried to rise, but a blow to his back from the same granite hand drove him down into the mud of the tavern yard. Foul water filled his mouth. All he could see was the ground and the wide man's leather boots.

A blade sang free. A hand grabbed at his leg and Alain rolled and kicked. The thin man dropped, holding his knee. Alain tried again to rise but the wide man knelt and grabbed him by the hair. In his hand, Alain saw a dagger.

Alain reached for a line. Far off, one thrummed. He pulled from it and cast a blow at the face that hung upside-down above his own.

From beneath the man's collar, an azure flash burned forth like a burst of daylight. Alain felt his grasp on the magic slip. The blow he fashioned twisted and spun. It broke against the blue light and careened away to strike the underside of the thatch that roofed the stable. Light sparked and flame bloomed in thatch and wood. Alain looked back at the man who held him.

The face above him grinned. A phlegmy laugh told of recent fish and wine. The dagger blade lay cold against his neck.

"By Bibé's teats, ye scrawny lad," the wide man said, his accent broad and harsh-edged. "Yer life is t'be hard enough withal. Don't be complicating things. That's a good 'un."

The thin man had risen again. He stepped forward and without preamble kicked Alain in the side. Then he drew a blade of his own.

"Take care," the wide man. "It took us all night to track 'im here. I don't want 'im killed."

The other man seethed with anger, but decided to follow his companion's advice. He stood back a pace and nursed his wounded his knee.

"All right, lad," the wide man said with a look at the burning stable. "Time we got going. You'll have brought every head down upon us 'fore long." He grabbed Alain by the collar and dragged him to his feet, but Alain was not going to acquiesce.

"Hector!" Alain shouted. "Fire!"

"Shut him up!" the thin man said, dancing back and forth as he glanced toward the tavern door. The wide man clamped a choking arm around Alain's neck, but it was too late. Alain's call had been heard.

"What's this!" bellowed a voice. Hector appeared at the tavern door, lantern in hand. He saw the burning stable, saw Alain beset by two men. "What are you doing?" he shouted as he ran to Alain's aid.

The strangling arm denied Alain any chance to shout further warning, and when the thin man turned, Hector met not a fist but a blade. The dagger took him through the ribs, and the tavern-master fell forward, dead before he hit the ground. Alain struggled to cry out, in anguish and in anger, but the wide man's grip denied him.

"Let him breathe, at least," the thin man said.

The grip around Alain's his neck relented and he was able to take in a gasping breath and spit it out in an anguished moan.

"What do you want?" he asked through a jaw clamped shut by the arm around his neck. "I don't have much money—"

"We don't want yer coin," the man behind him said as the thin man smiled, staring with hooded eyes.

"Naw," said the long-featured face. "We're here to take you home."

"Home?"

"Aye. Home. Home to yer—"

The thin man jerked and his eyes popped open. His lips moved, but there was no sound. A shadow stepped back from behind him as he folded up; knees, rump, and face hitting the ground in quick succession. The cloaked and hooded figure crouched, a narrow blade in hand.

"What in the..." The dead man's wide companion tightened his grip on Alain's neck, holding him like a shield. He brought his own dagger up to Alain's throat and Alain felt it bite. The blade of the hooded figure was held up, flat and level in an open palm, shoulder-high. The shadow took a step.

"Stop where ye are," the wide man warned. "You're here for this one, I'll wager. One more step, and the only way you'll get him is cold and breathless."

The cloaked figure did not move. Alain heard the ley line ring with far off bells.

A mage!

Fearing that this mage's blow would be turned aside as had his own, Alain shifted to the side but the wide man held him firm. The line chimed. Alain winced.

The blade in the mage's hand rose, hovered, and flew, too fast to dodge. It clipped Alain's collar and shot home with a thunk that threw the wide man's head backward. The arm at his neck dropped and his attacker fell without uttering a word. Alain stood there, facing the cloaked figure, trying to decide what to do.

The figure threw back the hood and revealed a woman's features in the clouded moonlight. She stepped toward him. Alain retreated, but he was not her goal. She knelt at the wide man's body and rolled it over. The hilt of her dagger protruded from beneath the man's chin.

"Daggers," she said. "So many daggers." She pulled her blade free and snatched up the one in the dead man's hand. "Everyone has a dagger these days. You, get that one." She pointed to the one near the thin man. "Every time I turn around, someone's pulling a dagger."

Alain leaned over and picked up the dead man's blade. The man's eyes were still open, staring upward into the night, and

Alain tried to ignore the sight.

"Violence is inescapable," he said to himself, thinking of the soothsayer at the crossroads. In the stable, horses began to whinny and scream as the flames spread along the roofline.

"Come," said the woman, beckoning. "Come quickly. We must leave this place."

"With you?"

"Yes, with me. Now! Come."

"I don't think so," he said, backing away from her. "Help!" he shouted over his shoulder, and then, "Stay away from me," he said to the woman.

"You idiot. I just save your life."

"You just killed two men. Help! Fire!"

"And how will you explain all this, with a bloody blade in your hand?"

Alain stopped, staring at the dagger he held. "Oh, gods."

The fire, his shouts, and the screams of horses brought people running. They poured into the stableyard but stopped short when they saw Alain and the woman standing over the bodies of three men.

The woman, hood once more obscuring her features, ran forward and grabbed Alain by the arm. She retreated, pulling him along with her. Several men from the crowd chased after them.

Alain heard the ley lines chime a far-off chord. His companion stopped and turned, arm leveled. He shouted as magic left her hand. A wall of steam shot up from the mud and two men fell back howling in surprise and pain. Three others ran past the first.

Bells rang another chord and Alain shouted. "Don't hurt them!" He pulled power from the line himself, a strumming of urgent strings. As the woman threw her power, Alain built a wall. Her magic hit his with a coruscation of blue fire that spread out, contracted, and exploded backward. The concussion of thunder that followed knocked them all to the ground.

Alain got to his feet, head in agony. He saw townsmen rising as well. The woman remained on the ground, unconscious from the blast.

It didn't matter what he did, now. To stay meant death. To flee gave him a chance at life. He reasoned that he might as well do what needed to be done in the time he had.

"Stand back!" he yelled, and the men did as he commanded.

He looked up at the burgeoning flames. Another horse bellowed in fright. He could hear them pounding on the doors and stalls. Through blinding pain, Alain made silent music with the lines. With giant unseen hands, he skimmed water and mud from puddles in the stableyard. A mass of sludge hung in mid-air. Thin lines of crackling light writhed between it and his cupped hands. The liquid rose, sloshed as it traveled. It passed over the flaming thatch, and Alain dumped the contents. Flame hissed and smoke rose. When he was done, the thatch was a ruin, but the building and the horses were safe.

As the light retreated, flickered, vanished, Alain swayed and felt the world tilt. He hit the ground on one knee and clutched at the pain in his head. The villagers who had come to his call now shrank from his presence. He rose to his feet, grimacing at the pain in his head.

The woman still lay unconscious at his feet. Alain looked from her to the townsfolk. He considered warning them, but thought better of it. After all, she *had* saved him from two attackers. He didn't think she intended the townsfolk any harm.

He picked up his bundle from the puddle in which it lay and slipped the thin man's dagger into his belt. Then he ran off into the dawning mist, his head pounding with each stride.

By noon he was sitting in a small clearing on a hillside. Above him, linden whispered to aspen. His belongings, rinsed in cold clear water from the creek, had dried in the strengthening sunlight. He made no fire, for the entire world was still soggy, and he wanted no smoke to mark his resting place for searching eyes.

He sat on one boulder and leaned back against another. Relishing the two-sided warmth of the sun and the sun-warmed rock, he watched the play of sunlight beating red and blue through his eyelids.

The pain in his head had left him an hour before, burning off along with the last of the clouds and drizzle that had chilled him through the night, but another pain had remained. Grief, it seemed, followed in his wake. From Belvanetes, to Erispoë's manor, to Hector's tavern, all he brought was destruction. Though he had been lighthearted when he called himself accursed down at Hector's tavern, he wondered if it might actually be true.

He was beset by mages that wanted to control him, and men who wanted to capture him, and the things that Alain wanted for himself—freedom, peace, and comfort—played no part in the minds of others. He was alone and scared and at a complete loss for a plan.

He sighed. "So much for being the master of my own fate," he muttered to himself.

At least now he was warm and dry. His physical comfort was nearly complete, and would have been so but for the hunger that gnawed at his innards. There was also the unsettling conviction that he was being watched. He lay a hand on the pommel of the dagger in his belt and listened to the forest. He heard only water, leaves, birds, and, somewhere in the distant wood, the high-pitched bark of a vixen to her cubs.

"Head still hurt?"

Alain yelped and rolled off the rock, drawing the thin-bladed dagger. His breath shook and his heart rattled in his chest as he looked for the speaker.

She was perched on the rock above where he had been sitting, the woman from the night before. In the full light of the sun he saw that her hair was glossy black, her skin fair, her eyes the brown of acorns in autumn. She was a handful of years older than he and was quite beautiful, a fact that he had missed the previous evening. She wore a long ruddy dress, vested overshirt, and boots. At her side were a satchel and her cloak.

She squatted atop the boulder, eyebrows lifted in a questioning gaze. She looked to the dagger in his hand, then back at him. She showed her hands. Empty. Her eyebrows lifted a touch more.

Alain listened for the lines, but they lay silent in the deep earth. Lips drawn in a tight line, he sighed and put the blade back in his belt.

"What do you want?" he asked.

"To talk," she said.

"Why?"

"That was quite a tale you spun last night. How much of it was true?"

"All of it."

"Ah. Well. It seems you left out some rather salient points."

"I thought it wise."

"It probably was."

"What do you want?"

The woman cocked her head and wrinkled her brow. "You don't trust me, do you?" she asked.

"Why should I? After last night?"

"Last night, my friend, I saved your scrawny hide from two hired knives." She slid down from the boulder and onto the lower rock. Alain took a backward step. "And then, to thank me, you knocked me silly and left me to drown in a puddle."

"Hmph. Another reason not to trust you."

"And what is that?"

"You might be here for revenge."

"Hoo!" She leaned back and grinned. "You *are* a tough nut." She laughed, and leaned back against the boulder. Then her laugh died, and with it all trace of humor fled from her face. "Listen, my friend," she said, pointing at him. "Listen well. I do not play games with revenge. Trust me in this. If I had wanted you dead, you would be so. On this matter you have my solemn word."

Alain shifted his stance and stood a bit straighter. He regarded this strange woman, so unlike any other he had known.

"Who *are* you?" he asked.

She smiled and the specter of death departed. She stepped off the rock and extended her hand.

"My name is Bronwyn."

Alain regarded her offered hand. A silver ring banded her thumb, and another on her long finger carried a heavy garnet. They were not working hands, but fine-boned and womanly. He reached out and grasped it, and was surprised by the strength within it.

Bronwyn shook his hand once, then stepped back up onto the rock. She reached for her satchel. "You're as skittish as one of the goddess's own fillies," she said. The cloth bag flopped open. Within, Alain spied a large round of traveler's bread and the rinded heel of a hard cheese. She pulled out the bread and wrenched off a small chunk. She sat down, leaning against the boulder and held out the chunk of bread.

"Hungry?" she asked. "Come. Sit. Eat."

Alain refused food from someone he did not trust. He squatted down opposite her. "How did you find me?"

Bronwyn shrugged and took a bite of the bread herself. "It wasn't difficult," she said, chewing. "A lone man, crashing about in the forest like a blind beggar in a marketplace. The forest told me, though I could have found you without help."

"The forest?"

She nodded. "Aye. It is a simple thing. Every bird and hare in half a league knows where you are."

"You talk to them?"

She squinted at him, as if trying to make him out from a great distance.

"You really don't know anything about your gifts, do you?"

Alain drew himself up and looked at her squarely. "I know enough to protect myself. I bested you, didn't I?"

"Aye, and got your friend killed and nearly burnt down his stable in the doing. Hmm. I thought perhaps you had been caught off-guard, that those two thugs had rattled you. I'd never dreamed...." Her voice trailed off. "However have you survived until now?"

Alain disliked her reminding him of what he had cost poor Hector, and he fidgeted beneath her frank regard. "What do you want from me?" he asked, his voice rising. He began to pace, four steps this way, five steps that, wider and faster as the words spilled from his mouth.

"I mean, I've done nothing to you, well, not intentionally anyway. Besides, what was I to think? You come out of nowhere, you kill two men in the time it takes to draw breath—"

"Alain—"

"You throw magic around, scaring the locals. Then you follow me up here, and scare *me* out of my wits. What was I to think? I thought you wanted me dead. It's been a common thread in my life lately—"

"*Alain.*" Bronwyn rose and stood before him, eyes filled with confused concern. He stopped in his pacing, surprised by the passion in his breast, the pain in his heart. His eyes were full, brimming. His calves shivered, his breath trembled. His guts roiled in Gordian knots. He swallowed, tasted bile, and let a long, fragile breath pass into and out of him, like the wind's invisible stirring of the surface of a silent lake.

"I'm sorry," he told her.

"It's all right." She reached out to touch his shoulder. He did not allow himself to flinch, did not retreat though it was what his instinct told him to do. Her touch was gentle, and it battered at his delicate resolve. He withstood it.

"I am not here to harm you," she told him. "By Epona and all the gods, I swear it."

He stared at her. The breeze awakened, lifting branches and smelling of salt and low tide. A cloud rolled across the face of the sun and he shivered.

"Why are you here?"

She smiled. "Build us a fire while I tell you."

By the time he had gathered enough wood for a fire, the sun was well on its way toward its home beyond the western edge of the world. The wind had continued its chill course in from the ocean. As Alain began to lay pieces of wood in the lee of the large stone, Bronwyn produced a strip of leather upon which was a single blue bead.

"Do you know what this is?"

He took it from her. White clay inlay spiraled and circled the bead. "Aye," he said. "A snakestone. My mother wore several on a necklace of boar's teeth. She wore them for protection."

"So did the man who owned this one. I took it from the neck of one of your attackers."

Alain remembered the flash of blue daylight as he cast against the wide man with the knife. He remembered how the power from the lines had twisted and squirmed beneath his wavering control. He looked at the small bead in his hand.

"It stopped me. But you got past it. How?"

She held out her hand, turned her palm up, then down. When she turned it up again, she held a dagger. It was little more than a handled skewer. She flipped it in her hand, pommel to blade, blade to pommel.

"The blade was moved by magic, but was not *of* magic. The stone repels only power, not material. By the time my blade struck home...." She tossed the blade in the air. It made three lazy rolls and buried its tip a finger-length in the earth. "...It was just a piece of flying iron."

"Hunh." Alain's mouth gave a lopsided smile. "Clever. But what were you doing out there in the first place?"

"After you left the tavern, the two knives got up and followed. It didn't take a wizard to scry their purpose."

Alain placed a few more sticks on the others. "But why did you care? You could have gotten killed."

"I've been looking for you."

"Heh," he said bitterly. "I've suddenly grown very popular. How did you know I was the one you were looking for?"

"Well, I listened to your tale in Hector's and thought it might be you. I wasn't sure until we were outside."

"When I cast."

"Aye," she said. "There are many mages in the world, but not so many that we don't know one another. We all play the lines in our own particular fashion, and when a new player sounds his first notes—especially when they are as loud as yours have been—the rest of us become curious."

"More than curious, I'd say."

She smiled gently. "For some, yes. More than curious. Competitive. Even frightened."

He sat back on his haunches. "The other men.... They were looking for me, too. But they weren't mages."

"Aye, but the man who sent them is. The man who sent them sees you as a rival. To him, magic is power, and power not under his control is a threat. He is like most of the others: vain, insecure, and afraid of losing his grasp on what he has as he reaches for more." She retrieved the dagger from its earthen sheath. A few deft movements and it disappeared. "I, on the other hand, see you as a possible colleague, and do not presume to know your intentions."

"The men who attacked me," Alain said. "You speak as if you know who sent them." The air had grown chill. The unlit fire lay before him, but he paid neither it nor the cold any mind. His attention was on Bronwyn.

"I do," she said. She reached deep into her bag and pulled forth a piece of paper. "I found this on one of them." She held it out. The wind caught at it and made it flap like a bird resisting her grasp.

"I do not read," he told her.

"You don't have to."

Alain took the note and inspected it. Four rows of fine-lined characters—tall and hooked—filled the upper half of the small parchment. The scrawlings made no sense to Alain, but he recognized them as writing and not design or decoration. The lower half of the page, however, was a puzzle. Written there was a large, intricate group of loops and lines, the purpose of which

Alain could not divine. Next to it, however, and slightly below, was a large blob of green wax, about two fingers broad, into which had been pressed an insignia. He turned to the evening sun and tilted the seal to highlight its relief.

A vine-bordered square surrounded a shield with a crown above an open hand. He recognized it at once, having seen it in the autumn and spring when tithes were due and having missed its presence in summer, when Vikings raided the coast. It was the sigil of Guihomarc, the Count Vannes.

He ground his teeth and tossed her the note. It landed at her feet and lay flapping, a wounded bird in the wind, pinned to earth by the heavy wax seal. Bronwyn picked it up.

"You don't seem surprised to learn your father is a mage."

Alain turned back to the unlit fire. "The Delphine told me."

"Ah. Another detail you neglected to tell the crowd last night."

Alain stared at the stack of sticks and twigs. The wood still glistened with moisture where the bark had cracked away. The boulder against which they lay provided some protection from the wind, but not much. If he drew from the lines, he could start the wood burning, but not keep it alight, not without pulling again and again from the source until the wood was hot and burning on its own.

"If Guihomarc heard me pull from the lines in Dead Ox Wood, he'll certainly hear me here."

"True," Bronwyn said. "Unless you pull with delicacy and skill. It does fade with distance. Perhaps I should—"

Alain raised a hand and shook his head. He leaned forward to touch the tent of stacked wood and closed his eyes.

Clouded images of light and green shadow filled his mind, memories of the wood beneath his hands, fading dreams of life. He focused on the visions, added to them the memory of the warmth of the sun, of heat, of light. He called to them, and breathed in the scented wind that slipped up from the valley. He spoke to the spirits of the world around him, and felt their acceptance of his desires. The dream of sunlight and warmth ran home to the heart of the wood, was gathered, was loved.

Alain felt the heat begin to radiate and touch his fingers with feathers of remembered light. His hands retreated, drawing out the heat, urging it, coaxing it. There came a low hiss and he opened his eyes. Steam lifted from the wood in lazy tendrils. He smelled smoke, saw flame, and released the wood from his control. The flames hesitated, unsure as the spirit dream faded, but the fire took hold and grew, full of hisses and pops.

Bronwyn watched him, watched his hands, her head tilted first one way, then the other, like a robin in a newly-turned field.

"The lines are silent. You couldn't possibly have...." A smile lifted one corner of her lips. "Earth magic. You can call the spirits."

He nodded.

She grinned and came to warm herself by the growing fire.

"I had come to see if you wanted to learn from me. Now it looks like I might be able to learn from you as well. What do you think, friend? Shall we be partners?"

He put some heftier sticks on the fire. "Perhaps. But it seems that you have not been completely truthful with me." Bronwyn started to speak but Alain pressed on. "I know, I know. My story at the tavern. But I only left certain details out of my tale. You, on the other hand, have lied to me. Either that or you are not as clever as you appear. I don't want a colleague who is dim, or one who is a liar."

The woman's ivory skin had gone alabaster with smudges of high color on her cheeks.

"You see," Alain continued, "I know those men were not here to kill me. You should have guessed it, too."

"How do you know they weren't?" she asked, stiff-jawed.

"First, they told me so. You wouldn't have believed them, of course, so I'll discount that. But then there is the fact that they did not kill me right away. Even if they weren't sure if I was their target when we were all in the tavern, they would have been sure once my casting was thwarted by the snakestone."

Bronwyn still stared at him, eyes grim. "Perhaps they did not want to kill you in so public a place."

"Possible," he admitted. "But if so, then why kill Hector? No. Their task was to bring me to him. Guihomarc sent them here to find me and take me to him." He looked at her with sudden wariness. "Perhaps he sent you as well."

"Sent me?" she said. "I killed those two men. Why would I kill them if we were all working for Guihomarc?"

"I've seen crueler things," Alain said.

Bronwyn looked away. She spoke to him across her shoulder. "What makes you think he wants you?" She turned back and eyed him evenly. "Why is the Count Vannes interested in a crazy witch's bastard?"

The words slapped and stung. Shame flushed his face and fury boiled up in response. "Because after he raped that crazy witch, he made a pact with the Fey to see that I lived. They spoke of prophecies and made promises. Why would Guihomarc do that, if in the end he only wanted me dead?"

Bronwyn glanced to the fire. Alain looked, too, and stepped back from the heat. Flames reached up to the height of a tall man and the wood shed its ashy coat to show a white-hot glow. Alain looked within and found the spirit of the wood still tied to his own through nebulous traceries. He calmed it and sent it to sleep once more. The fire dropped down. He withdrew once more but found the spirits of the wood and the forest around him still bound to his soul. He blanked his mind, thought of darkness and void, of emptiness, and felt the connections finally drop away. He opened his eyes to find the coals nearly out and Bronwyn staring at him.

"The spirits respond to your emotions." Her voice was a whisper.

Alain shook his head. "I had not released them. I am still learning what my mother knew without thinking. Bits and pieces of her manner and teachings fall into place as I use my talent."

Bronwyn was silent a moment. "About this pact," she prompted him.

"I wish I'd not told you."

"Who told you of it?"

"My mother."

"No offense, but, your crazy mother?"

"She had crossed over to the Summerland and been healed when she told me. I have no reason to doubt her."

They sat there on opposite sides of the fire, the sky growing dark above them. A cricket sounded a tentative note, small and timid on the windy hillside. The note repeated and was joined by another a few yards away. The tiny duo filled the space beyond the fire with their homespun song. Alain felt his temper abate and saw Bronwyn's shoulders relax beneath the fabric of her cloak.

"You know him," he said after a while. "And better than you

have let me believe." She looked away again, but not completely as she had before. "You know his purpose, too. Am I right?"

She sighed and a crease divided her brow. "Aye," was all she said.

"What does he want?"

"To control you."

"Same as you," Alain laughed. "Same as everyone. My mother, Papa, Erispoë, you. Even Josée."

"You think I want to control you?"

He nodded. "You want to use me against him. I don't know why, but I feel your purposes are definitely at odds with his."

"All right," she said. "True enough. I have old scores I want to settle. But what of you? What are your intentions?"

Sparks spiraled as another branch was laid on. They swirled, a cloud of elemental gnats ascending to join the awakening stars.

"Guihomarc destroyed my mother's mind, destroyed the lives of three people. But he sired me with a reason. He is my father, and I am his son. Perhaps more so than I wish." He watched the rising cinders disappear up into the night. "My intentions? Nothing. I have no intentions. I just want to live and be happy. Is that so much to ask? A home, a wife, a family?"

"Not much of a goal. It seems a waste of your talents."

"They're mine to waste, aren't they? And small goal or not, it's worlds away from where I grew up."

She frowned, dissatisfied. "But there is a destiny that surrounds you. Can't you see that?"

"I don't want a destiny," Alain said. "I want a life."

She sat back. "You don't get to choose."

"Who says I don't?" He looked at the woman across the fire. Flames flickered in her eyes. "Still interested in a partnership?"

She shrugged, non-committal. "I suppose I might still learn a thing or two from—" Her eyes went wide and her spine stiffened.

"What is it?" he asked.

She did not respond but sat frozen, staring into the approaching gloom of night. From far off, Alain heard the first tones of a stirring ley line. A single tenuous note, soft, but growing.

"Bronwyn! What is it?"

She began to search around her, on the ground, in the satchel. "The stone. Where is the stone?"

"What stone?" Other ethereal voices joined the first, still far off, like a hymn heard across a windy valley.

"The snakestone! Where is it?"

"I have it." He tucked thumb and finger into his belt pouch and pulled out the small glassy bead.

"Give it to me." She clutched it in her hand and gripped it tightly, her eyes squeezed shut and lips pulled back to show clenched teeth.

Alain sat, alarmed by her urgency. Though he was unaware of the dangers that seemed to surround him, now that he had discovered his talent, he was intensely aware that he must not disturb her. He listened to the lines around him, several off in the hills with voices of shepherd's song and one long line down along the coast singing sweet and high like a young maid at Samhain.

"Stop it," Bronwyn hissed. "Don't listen. Don't listen to them. Forget them. Think of the sea. Think of the wind. Think of anything, just don't listen to the lines." Her hands were pale, gripping the snakestone and each other. Her face was a grimace of concentration.

Alain shut his eyes. He thought of the one thing furthest removed from magic and the lines. He thought of Josée. He thought of her smiling face and frosted eyes, eyes like the sky on a wintry day; all clouds and hard light. He thought of her lips and her mouth. He thought of her naked breasts and of the night he shared with her. He felt an ache in his heart, a place that she had for so long filled, now empty and hollow. He missed her, longed for her.

"It's all right, now."

He opened his eyes. Bronwyn had not moved, but was visibly more at ease. Still, trouble tugged at the corners of her mouth.

"What was that all about?" he asked.

She swung the snakestone on its leather tie, letting it wrap itself around her finger, first one direction, then unwinding and wrapping itself in the other. "That was your father."

"Guihomarc?"

"Aye. Searching for the man who wore this stone." The snakestone widened its orbit around her finger and spiraled in once more.

"How do you know?"

"Did you hear the lines at all?"

Alain shrugged. "What? Before you yelled at me?"

She ignored his petulance. "Yes. What did they sound like?"

He thought back. "Like voices. Like singing."

Bronwyn nodded. "That is Guihomarc. When he plays the lines, they sing for him; with his voice and with the voice of the seeress who taught him. No one else alive makes the lines sound like that."

"And he was searching for the stone?"

"And the man. The stone can guide, like a beacon. It leads him to the man so that he can speak to him."

"Speak? Across such distance?" You can do that?"

Again she nodded. "It is easier between mages who are already attuned to the lines. It is quite difficult with regular folk. The stone helps."

Alain thought for a moment. "Sendings," he said.

"What?"

"Sendings. We called them sendings. Once in a while, when her madness was great, and then for weeks after her death, the Delphine would send down visions among the villagers. They came usually at night, like dreams or nightmares."

"It sounds similar. But she did not know line magic."

"No, she didn't," he agreed. "Unless she touched upon them in her madness." He sighed. "I'm beginning to understand how little I know of all this, and how much there is to learn. But wait. What about Guihomarc? Won't he know something is wrong?"

"Soon. Not yet. He will only think that his man was occupied and did not hear the call. Eventually, though, he will suspect trouble and take some action. We must be wary of him."

"Why not just break the stone?"

She shook her head. "To break it would alert Guihomarc immediately. He would hear it crack, even in his sleep."

She clasped her hands and lifted her arms to stretch and yawn. The outline of her body was well-formed and Alain felt a flush of embarrassment as he caught himself ogling. Bronwyn did not seem to notice.

"For now," she said beneath another yawn, "I suggest we eat and sleep." She pulled the bread and cheese from her satchel. "This will have to last us a while. This and what we can forage. We can't go back to Manech, and word of the killings will quickly travel the coast. We'll have to go to the hills, over the Montagnes

Noires. I'd prefer that, anyway; I know the region well."

"And the stone?"

"We'll keep it for a time. It may buy us a few days, enough to cross the mountains. After that we'll shatter it. Guihomarc will know, but he will have guessed something was wrong by then anyway."

Alain regarded her for a long moment. "I'm going to have to trust you, aren't I?"

"Ach," she said with a shrug. "No. You don't have to." She ripped off a piece of bread and tossed it to him. From beneath her hemline she produced a blade, different than the one he'd seen in her hand earlier. She began shaving slices off the round of cheese. "I'd suggest it, though," she said, and winked.

Alain sniffed at the bread and ate. He laid more wood on the fire. It crackled and snapped as the flames bit into the new fuel. To the west, the sun was long set, with only a haze of azure left, a memory of the day that had sailed far out to sea. The bread, sweet and spiced with rosemary, tasted of summer hillsides and warmth.

He felt his muscles begin to untie themselves. Tradition protected the peace between those who shared a meal, and when Bronwyn offered him cheese, he took it gladly.

twelve

Guihomarc couldn't sleep. His mind was awash with possibilities, contingencies, strategies. He'd not slept in two days, having spent the time coursing across the lines in search of information, and meeting with late-night arrivals in the hall below. Now, when sleep was what he wanted most, it was furthest from him. He lay under the heavy coverings and stared into the darkness of the bedchamber. He was cold, too, and wished vainly that he had not sent Ardath away for the evening.

Still, he thought as he rolled over, it is better to be restless alone than to deal with the prattling concern of a kitchen maid.

He had been anxious and short-tempered since his casting earlier that evening. True, sending to men was difficult, and Pouldou was a challenge under the best of conditions. "Probably wenching," he muttered, but still there lay, deep in his heart, a germination of doubt.

In the yard beyond the shuttered window, he heard the quiet words of watchmen changing guard. It was late, very late.

"Ach!" he growled and kicked off the covers, abandoning hope of sleep. "I can't just lie about and do nothing." He thought of sending for Ardath but decided against it. His mood was too foul and she bruised too easily. He paced across the floor, fur-lined bed-coverings heavy upon his shoulders. He went to the shutter and pushed it open. Outside the window, the night lay deep and dawn was ages away. The moon commanded the sky, accompanied by one star, bright and ruddy.

It would not do to call to Pouldou again, not now. All he would get would be a jumble of dreamscapes and nightmares.

The sea lofted its scent to the onshore breeze and Guihomarc breathed it in, closing his eyes.

"Oh, how I miss you," he said to the sea and the far-off shore of his homeland. It chafed at him, this forced abandonment of the coasts of his youth.

"A necessary evil," he told himself. "Soon it will be over. Soon. The boy changes everything." Up in the sky the red star gave a conspiratorial wink and Guihomarc lifted an eyebrow.

"A sign? That's not much of a sign." The star did not waver again. Guihomarc humphed and closed the shutter, leaving the star, the cold, and the pristine moonlight to the night.

At the hearth, he squatted and threw on some wood. The merest touch of power awakened the sleeping coals. He brought a chair in close and sat, staring into the flames. He considered food or wine, but it was only reflex. He was neither hungry nor thirsty. So, he just sat and stared, his ill-defined discontent rubbing against his soul like a hempen rope against his skin: rough and irritating but without genuine pain.

The fire, with its crackle and flutter, helped to cheer his mood. It was a calming thing, and he let it relax him, gazing into its depths, seeking solace from his doubts.

His mind began to drift and wander the happy pathways of near-sleep. He drifted down, beyond the flicker and play of the firelight. Drawn to their familiar song, he fell down to the lines.

Colored light sketched artists' outlines all about him as the nether-world took shape. An awesome web of intricate beauty covered the world. Fiery lines, broad and narrow, stretched out like cracks in the glaze of an ancient urn. He yearned to see through those cracks, to travel beyond the glaze that separated this world from the next, but that lay beyond his capacity. Between this world and the Summerland lay the Veil, the barrier the gods drew across the void as they relinquished their control over the lands of Men. Now the two worlds were separate, and where they touched, the Veil, the lines, and power.

Familiar landmarks passed on either side as he drifted along on the currents: the trefoil junction of Mont Saint-Michel, the hundred-petaled bloom of Carnac. Without meaning to, he found himself at the crossroads near Kemperle and he thought idly of the two men who sought a boy on his behalf.

A son, he said to himself. Of all the pleasures of my life, none has included a son. I've fathered plenty, but raised none. What does that say about me?

As he traveled the line-world, the doubts that had only nagged at him earlier began to pound on the doors of his exhausted mind. There had been the forceful ringing of the lines the night before, followed by Pouldou's sudden silence, all compounded by his own sense of unease. He could ignore it no longer.

Alain, he sent, and felt a response. *Alain.*

The lines carried him forward, bringing him to a place where he saw something he had never before seen. He saw tendrils, rootlets of power reaching out from the lines themselves. They grew and shifted as he traveled along them, lines Guihomarc had always thought fixed and immutable.

What is this? he wondered.

As his mind slowly coursed the thin, bright line, he saw others closing in on a central point of light. It was toward this light that he was being led. Movement along the new, tender lines was slow and full of resistance. Finally, he could travel no closer.

Alain?

The thin strands shimmered, his question rippling down to their center. As the pulse of his question reached the nexus, another pulse of faint brightness expanded. When it reached him, the question was, *Father?*

His own pleasure at receiving that question came as a surprise, and his joy flowed toward his son before he could think about it.

A wave of light stood up. It rushed outward in all directions. The tiny lines that had so earnestly reached for the glowing center now flared and burned as the wave passed over them. Guihomarc tried to flee, but traversing the smaller threads was torturously slow. The oncoming crush of power was not so restricted, passing over space and line alike, leaving emptiness in its wake. He could not escape.

He pulled power from the lines around him. The light crashed into him just as his defense had formed. Blinding pain fired his mind. His vision contorted as he was thrust backward, up and out of the nether-world of the dragon lines. He saw fire and darkness. His voice cried out. He tasted blood.

When he opened his eyes, he saw the hearth with its low-burning fire. He lay on his side on the floor. He was threaded with pain as if the traceries of the ley lines had been burned into every inch of his flesh, his mind. He could not move.

A fist pounded on the door. Voices rose beyond it. As shoulders were put to the door, he thought of his son, of the power he had shown, a power greater than he had ever seen, greater than he had ever dreamed.

Come to me, Alain, he sent, and closed his eyes,

Bronwyn came awake. "What? What is it?"

Alain stood in the last of the firelight, hands to his temples, his eyes wide. She had come awake at his shout and the cacophony loosed by the ley lines. While the echoes of his shout had faded, the lines still murmured, an unhappy booming like ancient thunder.

"Alain, what happened?" getting to her feet, but he did not respond, just staring off into space, eyes searching the darkness beyond the fire. She realized that he couldn't hear her and she stepped forward into his line of sight.

"Alain," she said again, waving her arm. His eyes met hers and she saw the fear in his face. "It's all right," she said slowly and with exaggerated diction. "Keep calm. Whatever it was, it is gone now."

The wild look left his eyes and he looked merely frightened instead of crazed. He took a deep breath and let it out slowly. Pain crossed his brow and she grabbed him as he stumbled. She held him up and led him back to the fire, feeding it the last few branches and a bit of power to revive it. No need for silence now, she thought. Not after that.

She threw her cloak and her arm around Alain's shoulders as the chills she knew would come set him shivering.

"Can you hear me yet?"

He nodded. His teeth began to chatter.

"Good," she told him. "The chills will fade, too, as will the pain, though that will take longer. I dare say you've had some experience with that. The pain lessens with practice, but pulling that much power always takes its toll." She rubbed his shoulder and pulled him close. He resisted the slightest bit before yielding to her comfort.

"What happened?" she asked him.

His words came stiltingly, hampered by his trembling. "It...was him."

"Guihomarc?" He gave what she took to be a nod. "How do you know it was him?"

"I saw...his face and...heard the song." The worst of his shivers had passed, but he did not attempt to leave her embrace. She held him close, pleased to have him near.

"I was dreaming," he said. "I was a great tree in the forest. Someone called my name. I thought it might be him. Then everything was dark and I was floating in the night sky and he was there, floating there with me, closing in on me." A final tremor passed through his body. "I got scared and pushed him away."

"With magic."

"No," he said, earnest. "That's just it. I pushed at him with my hands. I did not try to cast."

"Ach. Well, you did. And with quite a horrid clang, too." She rubbed his shoulder and neck slowly, to comfort rather than warm him. "Guihomarc will be hurting. I wouldn't want to have been on the far side of that amount of power. How is your head?"

"Ach, it hurts. I see spots."

"Keep your eyes closed. Here. Lie back." She made him lie with his head in her lap. She pulled their cloaks close and poked at the fire. With gentle fingers, she bid his eyes close and placed a cool palm on his forehead. His breathing calmed and lost its ragged edge. "There's a lot you need to know about your talent. We should start on it today, if you're able."

He looked up at her through pain-framed eyes. "Why are you being so kind to me?"

She gazed down upon his gentle features. Her fingers caressed his brow, touched the smooth skin of cheek above the rough featherings of week-old beard.

"For all your trials, you are still a good man, aren't you? I'm a few years older than you, but I haven't seen half the sorrows you have."

"You seem so confident," he said.

"I've had my talent for years. You've had yours for a few weeks. I had a teacher who showed me the way to mastery. You had a mad mother who tortured and ridiculed you. It's a wonder you are sane."

"That doesn't answer my question. Why are you being so kind?"

She chuckled and a weak smile crossed his lips. "You can do things I have never seen done—earth magic, dream casting. I'm being kind because I want to learn from you. But before you can teach me, I must teach you." She pulled a lock of hair away from his eyes. "Besides," she said, "I rather like you."

His whole body tensed. She said nothing, but just put a hand across his gaze. "Sleep," she said. "We'll start in the morning."

Eventually she felt him relax once more.

He was different from every other mage she had ever met, and unlike any man she'd ever known. He was honest and pure, but unvarnished and wounded to his very core.

How have you survived intact? she asked him silently. What saved that kind heart of yours from being ravaged? You soak up love like a sponge, but you radiate it back without knowing it. You want to trust, but are so afraid, and so alone. Like me.

Bronwyn heard him slip into sleep, and she closed her eyes. The line-world opened up below her, and what she saw made her pulse race. The coastal line lay off to the south, and the double lines of her valley home glowed in the north beyond the ridge, but between them, in an area where there had been no lines, there was now a webwork of traceries. A thin questing line spun out from the coastal line and curled toward them, splitting apart and forking like rootlets in a garden, surrounding the place where Alain lay.

A line-weaver.

She left the lines and opened her eyes, staring down at the man who slept with his head in her lap. Had Guihomarc done it? In his massive, egotistical vanity, had he actually sired the Fair One? Line mage, earth mage, and a weaver, too?

She suddenly became very afraid for this man. And for herself, too.

Quietly, gently, she laid his head down and curled up behind him. To share the warmth, she told herself. She knew, though, in her heart, that there were other, less rational reasons for wanting to be close. She only hoped that her heart could bear it if her fears turned into reality.

Dawn brought the sun, but the sea sent an army of clouds to form a ceiling of grey that let in only the feeblest of the morning's weak light.

Alain was awake and he was cold, but he did not move. He

did not wish to. He lay on his back, his cloak strewn to one side. Beside him, curled up alongside, one hand on his chest and her head pillowed on the shoulder of his outstretched arm, lay Bronwyn. Her dark hair had pulled loose from its tie and her lips were parted, shaping a vague circle and revealing a glimpse of slightly uneven teeth.

She seemed younger to Alain, and less beautiful in repose. Gone was the fire, the hint of mischief, the mind behind the eyes that so expressed itself in her features. Of course, he admitted, gone too was the hint of danger, and the threat of death he had seen the day before. She seemed safer and more innocent in her slumber.

His gaze was drawn once more to the swelling curve of her breast. He could feel the rounded subtleness where it lay against his chest, and he watched it rise and fall with her breathing. Unconsciously, he compared her to Josselyn. In both form and character, he had to admit that Josselyn was still a girl, and that Bronwyn...Bronwyn was a woman.

Her eyes were open. Her teeth tugged at her lower lip and she smiled.

"How do you feel?" she asked.

"I, ah...I am well," he said. "And you?" She laughed at his confusion and rose to her feet.

"Come along," she said, extending her hand down to him. "We can breakfast as we walk."

They washed their faces in the clearness of a nearby stream and headed up to the ridgeline. The clouds seemed low enough to touch, butting up against the heights, hiding peaks and wooded slopes behind a sky smudged grey with the soot of hearthfires. Alain and Bronwyn climbed the hillside, the clouds above their heads slowly transforming into a surrounding fog.

They picked berries to supplement the last of the bread and cheese Bronwyn carried. They ate as they hiked, picking as they went, traveling mostly in silence. Thus was Alain surprised when, climbing higher into the shroud of grey, his fingers stained red with the juice of a hundred berries, his mouth absently chewing the last crust of tough bread, Bronwyn asked him, "Who is Josée?"

He stumbled and choked on a breadcrumb that went the wrong way. After much back-pounding and a coughing fit that brought tears to his eyes, he regained his composure and his voice. He looked up at her. "What?" he asked.

"Who is Josée?"

"She is...a friend. I knew her back home, in Belvanetes."

"Ahhh," Bronwyn said with interest. "Josselyn. The landlord's daughter from your tale."

Alain recalled the frankness of his portrayal of her at Hector's. "I may have...embellished that part a bit," he said. "We parted only friends."

"Oh, I don't doubt it," she said with a laugh that meant that she did, indeed, doubt it. "Do you miss her?"

"Yes," he said. Though not as much as I thought I would, he wanted to add.

Bronwyn had been leading them up a steep slope to which there seemed to be no lessening. "Do you know where you are going?" She had taken a lead on him and was nearly lost in the moving fog.

"Indeed," came her response from out of the mist. "I walked these hills as a girl. We are among old friends." They trudged on another minute or two, Bronwyn silent up ahead in the fog, Alain crashing through dew-sodden undergrowth with the grace of a bull in rut. "Would you like to see her?"

"What?" he shouted. She was lost to him in the threading mists that wafted between the trees. "See who?"

The answer crept down out of the fog. "Josée. See Josée. See how she is getting along without you."

"Well, yes, of course I would, but—" It was like following a ghost, maddening and futile. No sooner did he think he was gaining on her then her voice seemed even farther away. "Where are you?"

"Up here. Keep on climbing. You are almost to the top. Careful, though. It gets a bit steep."

Bronwyn's idea of "a bit steep" turned out to be nearly vertical in Alain's estimation. He clambered his way up a wall of bracken and sedge, around trees that were forced to lean out away from the hillside, turning to grow straight before their own weight pulled them down. Then the trees thinned and the wind freshened at his back, urging him on.

"Are you still up there?" he called.

"Right here," she said, suddenly above him. He looked up

and saw her standing on a rock a few feet above his head. Beyond her, he saw branches swaying. Beyond them, he saw blue sky.

He took her hand. She pulled him up the last few steps and into the full light of the sun. The ridge top was flat for a stone's throw before it sloped down toward the far side. Alain walked forward a few paces, entranced by the view.

The sun shone in a hard blue sky, a circle of brilliance two hand-breadths above the horizon. The horizon, a craggy line of mountains, taller yet than the ones they walked, divided heaven from earth, bright blue from dark green. Between the far peaks and their own lay a crooked valley piled high with puffed lamb's wool clouds. From their side, streamers of mist trailed through the lower passes, flapping in the constant wind like the pennons of a ghostly army holding the high ground. In the air below them, silhouetted by sunlight bouncing up from the heads of clouds, a hawk stretched her wings and soared the currents of air. The rushing course of wind through coniferous boughs filled the scene with a sound like waves upon a shore.

"You once lived up here?"

She pointed down into the woolen valley. "Down there. I came up here often, though. Come. I'll show you my favorite spot."

They walked along the ridgeline a while before stepping down on the inland slope. She led them down deer trails into thick growth, lush and green. The air was still on this side of the mountains and when, a few moments later, they stepped out onto an outcropping of quartz-veined granite, the world was nearly silent. As the sounds of their passage faded into memory, the forest that stood behind them and that covered the slopes beneath them, awakened.

Far off, Alain heard the sound of rushing water. Nearer, wrens began to call, their cheerful song echoing in sharp repartee.

"I would come here to be alone," she said. "It is a safe place."

"Safe from what?"

"You'll see what I mean. Let's find Josée."

She sat him down on the hard granite and he was reminded of the outcrop back at Dead Ox Wood. The stone was cold despite the sun's attentions. His leggings, still damp from a night in the hills and a scrabbling climb through the undergrowth, clung to him in clammy folds.

"Quit fidgeting," she scolded. She sat cross-legged in front of him, palms on her knees. "Now, there are two ways to travel the lines; by sight and by talisman. A talisman will draw you to your target. It will also keep you on course and thus shorten your journey, but we don't have one so we must go the long way. Close your eyes and listen for the lines."

Alain did so. The lines lay silent, deep down in the valley. His sensitivity to their whereabouts had increased dramatically in the past weeks. He reached out with his mind to pluck one.

"Don't touch them," Bronwyn's voice warned him. "Just listen."

"But they're not making a sound."

"Listen harder."

He did, and heard nothing. He stole a peek through squinted lids and saw her watching his every move. He sighed and tried again.

The lines were there, but he heard nothing. The old frustration began to play within him, the one that had tormented him when he couldn't feel the lines at all. He breathed deeply, quashing it. Bronwyn would not ask something she herself could not do, he reasoned.

He listened.

Birdsong shimmered in the forest below him. Wind played quietly in the boughs above. The sound of the stream that tumbled through some hidden cataract lay beneath it all. The lines filled his mind, the sound of water filled his ears. On his face lay the warmth of the sun and, as he breathed a contented sigh, the glow expanded, engulfing him.

The darkness behind his eyelids took on a quality of depth. He floated high above an endless plain. He became aware of a sound; a dim, wide, open sound that reminded him of the ringing that followed one of Marrec's beatings. His heart leapt in response.

"Settle," Bronwyn chided, and her voice came from within as well as from without. It was as if there were two of her. He took another deep breath. The ringing resolved itself and, though similar to the aftereffects of Marrec's temper, Alain found it to be much more pleasant.

It was as if the air had learned to sing, and the glassy tones of its subtle song filled him.

Good, came the voice, now only from within this strange world. *Do you see the lines?*

He looked down onto the black plain. Ahead and far below, he saw two pale threads of light. He turned around toward what he thought would be the coast, and saw another, much stronger line.

Yes, came his thought, and "Yes," he felt his body say a half-moment later. He tried to isolate the former, and *I see them* said his inner voice.

Good. We will travel the coastal line, but stay alert. The lines are seductive and it is easy to fall under their spell. He felt her move away from him, though he could see nothing of her. Still, he knew she was on her way down to the line. He wanted to follow, and the desire made it so.

There was the sensation of being stretched, of inhabiting two places simultaneously. It at once frightened and exhilarated him. Then he let go of the memory of where he sat, up on a mountaintop, and concentrated on where he was and where he wanted to go. At once, he was combined and free.

He flew.

He flew toward the line, sensing Bronwyn up ahead. The freedom birthed an elation so intoxicating that he wanted to shout with glee. He zipped past Bronwyn's presence and flashed down to the line. He turned to the left and pressed onward along it. It grew beneath him.

Alain, he heard her send to him and he sent back a triumphant billowing of joy that used no words. He was the wind! He was brightness! He was thought!

His sense of speed increased. Lines coursed off and merged into the one he traveled with greater and greater rapidity. *Where do they all go?* he asked. Some were hued light blue or mallard green, some curled and swept off in directions that bore no resemblance to any earthly landscape, but all pulsed with the thrum of power, the rhythm of the song, the heartbeat of the Dragon.

Colors raced past, so fast that Alain couldn't even slow enough to discern one from the other. He felt himself being pulled along, as if his speed was building on itself. The lines began to blur, and his grasp on the world began to slip. Control leaked away from him and he felt himself shunted through junctions and spun through curves.

Bronwyn!

Bells rang, chimed, and reverberated, pitched high and low in odd sonorities. He hit a sudden wall, power sparking all about him. His speed fought against it, but his spirit latched on, pulling power from a line made suddenly visible by Bronwyn's aid. He fed power into the wall, and used it to slow and finally to stop.

Bronwyn—or the sense of her—glided up to him.

You are almost too strong, she sent to him. *Look.*

He did look, expanding his view, and saw a massive network of lines. Colors gathered in swaths like threads in a tapestry.

Where are we?

Nearly to the end of the world, she sent to him. *Come.*

She drew him along, guiding him, and he followed meekly. As they traveled, he saw bright spots like glowing seeds.

What are those? he asked.

Other mages, she sent.

So many, he said, filled with wonder. There were hundreds of them scattered along the lines, perhaps thousands, each limned in a different colored light. He turned toward Bronwyn to see what her color was, but could not find her. He looked in all directions, but she was not visible. Then he saw, against the background of glowing lines, a sphere of darkness where her light should have been.

Your light has no color. How do you do that?

He sensed the echo of her laughter. *You'll have to allow me a few secrets of my own.*

She brought him back along the twisting trail of lines, teaching him how to sense where his body was, and how to see the land above the line. He saw ghostly cities and pyramids of translucent stone. Insubstantial armies rode across invisible steppes, and mountains of mist rolled across the world. Everywhere he looked, he saw the glimmering seeds of mages, and from every light came the music of their casting.

Eventually, they passed over the Frankish March and arrived back in the lands of the Briezh.

I did not think the world was that large, he sent.

That large, and larger, she told him. *You must be careful here.*

They came back to the place where they had begun, and Alan was ready to return to his body. Bronwyn pushed him back to the lines.

We came for a lesson, she sent.

They traveled slowly down the brightness of the coastal line. Then Bronwyn nudged and they turned onto a smaller line. Soon, there formed in the distance before them a haze of light.

There lies Carnac.

Alain remembered the place he had passed through a few weeks before. A small village, it held low onto the thin soil of the coastal hillside like a stunted pine. The people of Carnac had been dour and taciturn, but most memorable had been the multitude of standing stones on Carnac Plain.

Like ranks of petrified soldiers awaiting long-dead orders, they commanded the plain to the west of the hamlet. The power of the place had been awesome and he had avoided it, afraid of it as a child is of the fire after having first been burned.

Here, in the world of lines that lay beneath his own, was the source of that power.

The line they traveled sloped upward and the haze that had continued to build now fractured and drew apart. A hundred lines crawled up from the dark depths below them. They wove themselves together in a quilt of power that spread out across the vastness. The two travelers slowed as they approached. Their own path entered the patterned maze of lines and junctions in a place not too far before them.

Our path lies through this. Take care in crossing.

They entered the shimmering weave of lines. Alain felt the pull of the many paths around him, but he banished them from his mind and fixed his gaze on the one line that would lead them across the pattern. The place was loud with the ethereal song of lines, descant harmonies vying with the rumbling tones of deep-seated power.

They crossed slowly, calmly. Bronwyn radiated serene confidence and focus. Alain followed her apace, afraid of another misadventure. He felt the buffeting of the lines' call, felt their song fill his blood. The draw was strong and, with so many, impossible for him to ignore.

Is this the only way? he sent to her.

No, she replied. *But you must learn how to control your path.*

She led onward. Alain followed, trying to deny the resonance that cried out within him. He hesitated, but then pressed ahead, trusting that Bronwyn would not lead him into danger. With every joining, every meeting and parting of paths, he felt himself drawn, stretched, pulled. They were too numerous to be ignored, and he could not defend his mind from them all. He tried to shield himself, but their call broke through. In desperate response, he withdrew, pulling himself deeper into the line he traveled. The line itself became his shield, its one song drowning out all others. It surrounded him, and he was swallowed by its light and power. Finally, he felt the lodestone pull lessen, and emerged to find himself on the far side.

Bronwyn, he called.

Here, she responded, coming up to meet him. She vibrated with fading concern and growing amazement. *Come along,* she sent. *We are almost there.*

The path was much easier here, again with only one line for him to follow, and they traveled quickly.

Now, she said. *Lift your mind up out of the lines.*

He did as he had learned just a short time before, and a vision of a river valley imposed itself upon his view of the ley lines. The bright path of the line shone deep along the lazy curves of the river. Ridges of ghostly hills rode high along his left hand. To his right, stands of ancient chestnut rose in sinister clouds.

I know this place, he said, seeing the long dark ridge of Dead Ox Wood lift up out of the vaporous landscape. *Stop! Stop. We are here.*

The valley slowed and halted beneath him. He looked left. The hills had receded and meadows opened wide their beckoning arms. He saw the old river path he had walked, first with the house servants on their way to wash or collect water, then alone during his years under Marrec's hand. In the distance, he could see men in the fields, the burnt-out shell of his former home, and the gleaming walls of Josselyn's villa. Bittersweet memories filled his heart at the sight and he sent his desire toward the villa, but he did not move from the line.

We need assistance, Bronwyn said, *before we can leave the line.*

Assistance? What kind?

Without a talisman to draw us off the line, we need the help of someone. Or something.

Alain saw a woman coming toward the river. A pole rested across her shoulders and waterjugs hung from each end. The woman's face was lined with age, her eyes drooped with sorrow, and her hair was pulled back in a taut greyness.

Look, he said, recognizing Josselyn's housekeeper. *It is Judica. Could she help us?*

Possibly. It is easier, though—and safer, too—to avoid enlisting the help of people. Follow.

She led them a bit upstream, to where a willow leaned its lace over the water. Swallows dropped on scimitar wings to race their reflections in the river's twinkling surface.

Take one, Bronwyn said and in an instant was gone. Alain searched the non-land for her but felt himself alone. He reached back up to the ghost-image of his home, reached out to a swallow's passing blur and grabbed at it.

The world became solid around him. Sunlight flashed off green water. His heart fluttered within his breast and sky and earth wheeled as he carved his wingtips through the substantial air.

Alain. She was nearby, curving a path past him. A flip of her tail took her up and out across the fields. Alain followed.

The fields Marrec had turned under were now green with new growth. The planted lines, however, pulled by another hand than his foster father's, were irregular and crooked. A sense of obscure pride filled Alain as he flew on toward the villa.

The slanted tiles were warm beneath his feet as he perched on the eaves, Bronwyn at his side. They looked down on the main house's inner garden, its puzzle of rose and lavender, bean and garlic, happy in the sunlight. Alain remembered his last visit to this garden, months before, and wondered at the wisdom of coming here. He was not going to find joy here, today.

The kitchen door opened and a woman emerged. Alain lost his footing as he saw her. His wings flailed the air and he landed clumsily in a patch of lavender. Bees snarled around him, and he struggled against the enclosing branches. Suddenly his wings were pinned, and he was lifted free of the fragrant bush.

"You must be a new one," Josselyn said, her face huge above him. She straightened, holding the tiny bird gently in her hand. Alain was too frightened to move. She placed him on one of the stone benches and he stood there looking up at her.

"Go on," she said with a shooing hand. "Go on, you silly thing. Your friend is calling you."

Bronwyn was indeed calling him, a constant chirping from the eave. But Alain was content to stay where he was. She was still beautiful, perhaps more so he thought. She was bedecked in silver and bronze that glinted hot and cold in the summer sun from neck, wrist, ear, and hand. Carved bone held up her braided hair, and the fabric of her dress was threaded with indigo and red. She had taken her place as mistress of the house.

A maid came out of the kitchens. "Mistress," she said. "Master Charles sends word that he'll be coming home tonight. He's finished his business with his father and he should be back by sundown."

A spectral bolt shot through Alain. You have married? he asked her silently. So soon? And to Charles, son of Robert the machtiern? You told me you would marry. I just did not believe...so soon.

Josselyn smiled, nodded, and the maid departed. She pushed a few strands of hair back from her face. While her visage had not overtly changed, her eyes had gone a cold, wintry grey. No longer the grey of fall skies and Bretland wool, now they were the color of the sea lying chill beneath a coming storm. Alain had not seen the look before, and did not know what it meant.

Josée, he sent to her, and saw worry touched her brow.

She sat down, delicately and with great poise, on the rock wall where they had said their goodbyes. She looked again to her small charge. As she leaned forward, there slipped from beneath the collar of her bodice a flash of blue and white, vulgar and crude in comparison to the fine metals that decorated her breast. The snakestones clinked quietly as she tucked them back beneath her collar.

"Go on, little one. Back to mother." She smiled a warm smile and ran a hand across her belly. "Mother is worried."

From the eave came another stream of warbles, and Alain looked up. *Yes*, he sent to Bronwyn. *Let us go.*

With a final look back at the woman he no longer knew, he walked to the edge of the bench and hopped down. A whoosh of wings and a word from Bronwyn reminded him that he was still a swallow. He spread his curving wings and pulled himself skyward. In a few moments, they were back at the river's edge, following the ley line home.

That life is gone, he thought to himself. And Josée is gone with it.

As his old life dropped away, he was freed to move ahead on

the new path he'd discovered. The loss, however, of old dreams and old hopes, was sharp and raw. When he and Bronwyn returned to their rocky perch, the bright sun brought tears to his eyes. But his tears did not stop, not when Bronwyn's arms embraced him, and not when he kissed her out of sheer hunger for affection and the desire to dispel the loneliness that tormented his soul. She returned his kiss, and held him tightly, until his grief had subsided, and the sun had crept a bit farther up into the sky.

thirteen

What did you expect her to do?

Alain gritted his teeth, concentrating on Bronwyn's sending while he tried to follow her down the mud-slick path.

"I don't know—"

No. Not with your voice.

She had been drilling him all day; for hours up on the ridgeline, and then for hours more as they wended their way down from the heights. She'd made him practice until he could touch the lines with only the barest sound. She'd tutored him in how to manipulate everything from stones to the air itself. She threw techniques and tips at him in profusion, but he could only field the smallest portion of them. It was a deluge, and now she was making him talk without talking!

"I—" *I don't know what I expected,* he sent, though he didn't know if she could hear him. *She told me she would marry. She had to, in order to keep her father's lands. I guess I just never really thought that she would.*

The forest was dense and heavy. It blocked out the sky above them and closed in on all sides, making passage difficult along the nearly indiscernible deer-trails. All Alain could see at any one time was Bronwyn a few paces ahead, the trail a few paces back, and then nothing but the impenetrable depths of greenery. The scent of moisture and mulch was thick as they tramped between moss-covered stones and trees.

I am sorry, Bronwyn sent. *It is never easy when friends grow apart.*

Alain silently agreed. Now, if they would only get to where they were going! His feet were soaked through. The descent was endless—a forever downward stumbling—and he was once more shivering with cold. A stoat shouted from the underbrush, and nearly cost him his footing.

"You'd think there would be an easier way to get where we're going."

There is, she sent, *but the lines would ring for days with the power. You are far from ready to attempt it.*

"Oh?" he said, bristling. "What about last night? I handled myself pretty well then. And if I can handle him, it should be a simple—"

Bronwyn stopped and turned. Her jaw was set and her finger pointed at his chest like one of her daggers.

"If that *was* Guihomarc you met in your dream, and *if* you forced him back, then either you were lucky, or you caught him by surprise, or both." She took a long, deep breath, and continued more calmly.

"Understand this. Your father is powerful, crafty, and ruthless. He is seeking you, and you'll have to deal with that sooner or later. But to tempt him, to give him a way to find you without question, where he is practiced and you are still green, is to invite disaster in to supper."

She planted her feet on the slippery path and looked up at him with gritted teeth. "Do not—do *not* mistake your power for strength. They are not the same thing."

Alain stood on the trail, his face red with humiliation. His fists pulsed at his sides. "Don't treat me like a child," he said.

Slowly, she whispered, "Then do not act like one."

Untuned strings stirred and rattled as Alain touched the lines with an angry mind. He formed a hot-handed slap, aimed for her cheek, but a silver bell rang high and clear and Alain felt his feet go out from under him.

He hit the mud and slid downhill. Bronwyn stepped lightly aside as he slipped past her down the steep mountainside. He crashed through ferns and over ivy. His sodden feet and muddy hands could gain no hold. He tumbled, rolled, and spun, grunting with each bounce and jar. A tree trunk presented itself and he hit it with a great *woof* of air.

For several heartbeats the forest around him was silent. Nothing stirred. Even the branches above seemed to hold their breath. Then, somewhere uphill, a raven voiced a rattling call.

Nearer, a tomtit peeped and fluttered unseen. Alain moved and twigs cracked beneath him, poking him, prodding him to rise. He sat up, albeit slowly, and looked up the sloping mountainside. The forest had closed in behind him. There was no evidence of his passage, of the trail, or of his companion.

"Bronwyn?" He coughed. "Bronwyn?"

Silence.

A sound came from off to his left. "Do you live?"

He grunted as he tried to rise. He slipped and fell again. "Yes," he said, petulant.

"Are you still angry?" Her voice came from below him now.

He sighed. "Yes. But not with you." The undergrowth crackled and she appeared from around a tree.

"You fly too easily to anger," she said. "If you wish to survive as a mage, you must learn to never cast in anger. The coolest temper will always prevail. And between the two of us, there must be a pact never to do so. If we are to learn from each other, we must have safety and trust. Are we agreed?"

Alain nodded. "Agreed."

"Good." She beckoned to him. "Slide down toward me." He scooted down the slope, got to his feet, stepped around an elderberry bush and down onto the trail beside her.

She looked him up and down, touching at the rents his clothing had earned in his fall. She clucked her tongue at leaves in his hair and mud and dirt that smudged his legs, arms, torso, face. He stood before her and observed her wordless fussing. She realized he was watching her intently and smiled. She reached out and touched his cheek.

"Come. Let's go meet Mother Marmie."

The trail became a track, became a path, leveled out, and eventually showed signs of passage by creatures other than deer and rabbit. The sound of falling water intensified as they approached the valley floor, quiet thunder filling the air. When Alain stopped, he could feel the rumble come up through the ground and into his feet, but the waterfall itself remained hidden.

Signs of habitation emerged: woodchips strewn at the base of a stump, the recurring tang of smoke that wafted in the moist air, and the sight of footprints in the soft earth of the widening path. There appeared between the towering pillars of rough-trunked pines the rounded hump of a thatched roof. Smoke escaped from an open triangle beneath the eaves carrying with it the scent of stewing meat and toasting hearthcakes. Alain's stomach grumbled as his hunger let its true size be known.

"Marmieee!" his companion hallooed through cupped hands. Her call rang in the air and a small, questioning voice was heard from within the cottage. "Mother Marmie," Bronwyn called again.

A face, wide-eyed and with a thin-lipped mouth that said "Oh?" popped out from around the low corner of the thatched roofline. When she saw Bronwyn, she broke into a toothy grin.

"Ha-haa   aa," the old woman laughed as she ran around the corner. She was tall, bony, and gangly as a yearling foal. She ran up the path in great bounding strides that spoke of a youth and vibrancy that belied her grey hair and wrinkled skin.

Bronwyn ran down the last of the path to meet her. Alain lagged behind, feeling like an interloper at a private reunion.

"Ach, my bonnie girl. You fetch my heart, lass, you do." Half a head taller than Bronwyn and nearly as tall as Alain, the old woman wrapped Bronwyn in her arms and held her tightly. Then she caught sight of Alain. "Who is the filthy one?" she said into Bronwyn's ear.

Bronwyn, an arm around the old woman's waist, beckoned Alain closer. He walked down to them.

"This is Alain," she said. "He and I are traveling together." The woman glanced at her with an unspoken question that made Alain blush and Bronwyn smile. "I'll explain later." Then to Alain she said, "This is Marmohec who raised me, and who taught me the lines."

Alain stopped mid-bow and looked up. Marmohec nodded.

"'Tis true," she said. Then she smiled again and threw her arms around Bronwyn. "I've a rabbit in the pot and—oh! The cakes!" She turned and fled for the house. Bronwyn and Alain followed.

The smell of burnt cakes met them at the door. Alain could see little but smoke through the entryway. Marmohec walked past the opening, fanning the air with her shawl and swearing like a soldier. She disappeared into the thick haze. Alain ducked as blackened oatcakes sailed out of the doorway trailing arcs of smoke.

"Head might as well be filled with crap for all I use it," he heard her say. She appeared once more at the door and fanned and swore until the air inside her cottage was diluted to a thin greyness. Only then did she bid them enter.

Her home was small as cottages went, but seemed spacious to Alain. The places he had stayed, if a bit larger, were crowded in with up to a dozen people; a family or two with sons and wives, plus hounds and some livestock, too, for good measure. Everyone would smash together at night, sleeping where room could be found, the warmth of the ever-smoking hearth and the snoring piles of kindred keeping the elements at bay.

This cottage, however, was obviously the home of Marmohec and Marmohec alone.

A heavy-headed axe leaned near the door. Nested in a corner near the hearth, a bed of pine boughs and fresh ferns lay. The other corner was filled by a heavy-timbered table, a stool, and a collection of bowls, pots, cups, and utensils. In the center of the dirt floor, planks covered a hole to a root cellar, and the side of the cottage away from the hearth was given over to industry and supplies.

A huge loom stood next to a pile of dried rushes and a half-woven basket. Hides and pelts lay stacked on another heavy table, and all around lay tools: awls, blades, chisels, adzes, wedges, knives—so many knives—plus the tools to keep them honed and ready. Alain recalled Bronwyn's familiarity with daggers, and thought it likely that she had learned more from Marmohec than line magic.

Marmohec waved away the last threads of smoke from the burnt cakes and set about making some more.

"Did I hear you playing the lines this morning?"

"Yes," Bronwyn said as she squatted at the hearth and began to clean the hard clay surface. At the other end of the hearth, the iron pot of rabbit stew sat in the coals. Steam puffed from beneath the lid in regular intervals. The aroma drew Alain closer to the fire.

"And he must be the new player I heard."

"Yes."

"Who taught him? I don't recognize the style."

Alain glanced up from his study of the stew pot. The women were looking at him.

"Alain," Bronwyn said, pointing to a barrel against the far wall. "Why don't you get us some ale?"

He did that as the women began to bake the hearthcakes, talking to each other in hushed tones that made Alain self-conscious. While they whispered, Marmohec poured a ladle of the thick dough directly on the hearth. It spread to cover a hand's-breadth of the clay dome. Bronwyn moved to the bowl as Marmohec tended the cake. When it began to steam, Marmohec plucked at one edge with a knife and flopped it over onto the other side of the hearth. Bronwyn then moved in to lay down a second cake.

Their movements, done in tandem, were economical and well-timed. Both women were intent on their tasks. Their cooking took on a rhythm, the quality of a slow dance. As Alain sipped his ale, he saw that this was a well-practiced performance, and one that they enjoyed. Their whispered words ebbed away, and they spoke only through touch: a hand on a shoulder, a nudging elbow.

Marmohec began to hum "Brydee and Alda" in a mellow alto. Bronwyn picked up the harmony. The words played along in Alain's head, how Brydee and Alda had sworn their love in youth, only to be separated by the acts of capricious gods.

His exhaustion strove against his hunger for dominance and nearly won, but the rabbit stew kept bubbling and the oatcakes grew in number. Finally, when the stack of cakes was nearly toppling, Marmohec opened the stew pot and filled two bowls full. She handed them to Bronwyn and Alain, along with a handful of cakes, and there followed a spate of serious eating during which no words were exchanged by anyone. Bronwyn ate as heartily as Alain, sopping gravy with the cakes and cracking the legbones to suck out the marrow. He spied Marmohec, eating little, spending her time watching her two guests. In her gaze, Alain saw as much wariness of Bronwyn as of himself. The notion caused him a little concern, but his hunger bested his curiosity and he could not bring himself to care too much about what the old woman was doing.

One huge bowl of hearty stew, two large cups of ale, and half a dozen hearthcakes later, Alain was finally sated, and exhaustion took the upper hand. It tugged on his eyelids and made his limbs heavy. Within moments, lulled by the fullness of his stomach, the warmth of the hearthfire, and the quiet talk of the two women, he began to nod. Empty bowl cradled in mud-caked fingers, he curled up on the floor next to the fire, head pillowed on his arm.

Bronwyn watched Alain's eyelids droop, saw sleep overtake his waking soul and pull him down into depths of slumber. Slowly, his hand released its grip on the bowl. She touched Marmohec and nodded in his direction.

"Finally," the old woman said. "He *is* a headstrong one."

"Poor thing," Bronwyn said. "He's had no rest for two days, and has traveled the lines twice, and still he fights sleep. He amazes me."

"More than that," Marmohec said.

Bronwyn saw her mother's glance switch from her to the sleeping young man. "What?"

"Don't try to fool me, little girl. I see the way you look at him, and I hear the sweetness in your voice when you speak to him. And that little smile on your face, I see that, too. He's taken your heart, has he not?"

Bronwyn did not answer, but she felt her heart speed at the question.

"Hmm," Marmohec said. "So, who is he?"

Bronwyn shook her head. "You won't believe me."

"No?" the old woman said. "Let's see."

Bronwyn shrugged. "He is the bastard of Guihomarc, Count Vannes, from the womb of a woodland witch."

"No. Truly?"

Bronwyn nodded.

"Does the Circle know of him?"

Bronwyn got up to get more ale and brought back a pitcher. "They knew of him once. Before he was born, if his mother's tale was true." She sipped. "But if they know anything of recent occurrences, they learned it from Guihomarc and not from me."

"Guihomarc knows of him, too?"

"Oh, aye, and has sent men for him. *And* those men are dead, though by my hand and not Alain's. I've kept my role hidden, but I fear what will happen if I am discovered."

"Won't the Circle protect you?"

"Rill might, but only if it suits his purposes. Rill protects his game, not the pieces on the board."

Marmohec wrinkled her brow and shook her head. "I care

not for this game you play, daughter of my heart. You sit on too
many sides of the field, and I fear it will cost you in the end."

"There's more," Bronwyn said. "He can cast both earth and
line magic. Of this not even Guihomarc knows."

The old woman turned and stared with sudden interest at the
man asleep on her floor. "He is the Fair One, you think?"

"I don't know," she said. "I hope not."

"Well, does he bear a mark?"

"Again, I don't know."

Marmohec glanced at her in surprise. "No? It should be plain
upon him, if he be the Fair One. Some mark, some blemish. You
didn't notice anything when...." She looked at the sleeper and
back to Bronwyn, a lascivious grin on her face.

"Marmie," Bronwyn warned in a low tone.

"By Epona's hooves; you've not had him yet, have you?"
Bronwyn shook her head no. "He *has* taken your heart," the old
woman teased.

"I fear it may be so."

Marmohec rose and stepped over to Alain. She squatted
down, inspecting him. "Is it wise?" she whispered, turning her
head to better view the young man's neck. "The Fair One—if this
be he—the Fair One will gather danger like flies at slaughter. To
love such a one...tsk...bad enough. But to love unknowing." She
touched his tunic. "This needs mending."

"Marmie, no."

"Not to mention a good scrubbing."

"Marmie, leave him be. I don't want to know."

"But you must know, my darling. You can't leave this
question without answer. Not when it lays so close at hand. You
deal with dangerous people enough not to gain what knowledge
you can, as soon as you can. Perhaps he is not the Fair One as we
fear. Good, then, and we'll know. Good, too, should he bear a
mark and truly be the Fair One, for then we will know that, and
can also act accordingly." She began to tug on his belt.

Bronwyn stood and moved to stop her. Alain groaned
sleepily, his eyes fluttering.

"It's all right, dear," Marmohec told him, dodging Bronwyn
and moving to his other side. "We're just going to launder this
and stitch some of the holes."

"Mm, what?" he mumbled as his belt came off.

"Marmie, stop it." She stepped back and turned away. "I don't want to know, I tell you."

"Hey," she heard Alain say.

"It's all right, young one. I'm just going to—" Bronwyn heard her gasp. "By all the gods," Marmohec breathed.

Gripping Alain's shirt in white-knuckled hands, Marmohec retreated from him as he stood. Bronwyn turned and stifled a moan of anguish.

He was covered. No inch of skin, from wrists to neck, had been left untouched. Scars writhed across his torso like eels in a market basket. They covered his chest, his belly, his shoulders. Whorls and curved lines of raised flesh commanded her attention, would not let her look away.

On his chest was a carved raven, beak open, wings outstretched, feathered tips open to his shoulders. Its tail and clawed feet reached out and down across the flat of his stomach. Around the raven's form twisted vines in full leaf, tendrils curling around his ribs and down his arms. The scars were hard-edged and vile. They spoke of pain and a cruelty beyond anything Bronwyn had ever imagined this side of the Veil. She stared at them, and when she could break her gaze away and finally saw his face, she knew her horror was plain to see.

He faced them, looked from one stricken expression to the other. His jaw tight, he pulled at the ties of his leggings and let the clothing drop. The vines continued down thighs and legs, knotted lines of welted agony. Tears fell to Bronwyn's cheeks as he stood before her, turning to show her all sides of himself. He stared at her with full disdain, his body naked but for the misery that wove its pattern from ankle to wrist to neck. He turned full circle and stopped, his eyes daring her to speak. She did not. She could not. She could only stare at the angry whips snarling about his body, her mind screaming at the crime that mutilated him until, overflowing, she fled into the numbing thunder of the forest and its hidden waterfall.

Alain listened as Bronwyn's footsteps disappeared into the greenery, and as they faded, something within him died, as well. His hauteur cracked, and the confidence that he had only just begun to relish now withdrew, and there remained only shame, embarrassment, and grief.

He reached down and stepped into his leggings, his whole body aflame with humiliation. How could he have even begun to think of Bronwyn in that way? How could he have forgotten the truth of his birth and his upbringing? He glanced up and saw that Marmohec still stood nearby, his tunic hanging from her hand down to the hard earthen floor. He picked up the small bundle of his belongings and held out his hand for the tunic. Marmohec shook her head.

"Do not leave," she said softly, her voice thick with emotion. She gestured, inviting him to sit by the fire, and her expression blended kindness and concern. On another occasion, Alain might have partaken of her pity, but not today.

"I do not wish to stay," he said.

"You must. There is much you need to know. About yourself."

He held out his hand again for the tunic but she begged him sit once more. "What can you know about me that I do not?"

"Your future," she said.

He bowed his head and shut his eyes. "I am so tired," he said. "Of my life. Of my past." He gazed out the empty doorway. "Things start to get better, and life slaps me down again. I don't think I care much about my future, anymore. It can't hold anything more than I've already lived through."

"I think it does," the old woman said. "If you are who I think you are."

"And who is that?"

She beckoned a third time and moved the stool to the hearthside. With a resigned nod, he set down his bundle and took the offered seat. He asked again for his tunic. She pulled a cloak off a peg on the wall and handed it to him, then poured him a large cup of ale. He shrugged the cloak around his shoulders and hid the scars that marked his body. Marmohec went to the far side of the one large room and bent over the items near the loom, searching through the pile and muttering to herself. With a grunt of discovery, she straightened and came back to the fire with a bone needle and a skein of homespun thread. Alain watched with waning patience as she threaded the needle and chose the largest of the tunic's tears to mend.

"You are planning to take some time in telling me this," he said.

She smiled. "Patience. This will not take long."

"Good. Because when you are done, I will be on my way. Alone."

"You think so?" Her voice was conversational, as if nothing in the world was wrong.

"Epona's teats. Say what you have to say!"

"Calmly, calmly," she said. "I will tell, but in my own way. Have some respect. I am old."

Alain clamped shut his jaw and sipped sour ale through tight lips. Satisfied, Marmohec returned to her stitching.

"When the gods forfeited their struggle with men, they left this world for the Summerland. The Fair Folk went with them, too, and when they were gone, the gods drew a Veil across their path to exclude us from their world, except in death."

Alain nodded. "I know all this. Any child knows the old tales."

"And do you know that the Veil is the source of all line magic? That the lines themselves are the threads of the Veil?"

"Of course," he said as if it were the most obvious thing in the world. He did not mention that he had only just guessed it that morning, with Bronwyn. Even now, her confirmation came as quite a revelation.

"But earth magic," she went on, "comes not from the lines. It comes from another source."

"Spirits," Alain volunteered.

"Aye. And the spirits come from...?"

The question hung in the air. It was an idea he had never considered, the source of spirits. "Spirits come from... everywhere. They reside in all things."

"True enough," Marmohec said, biting off a knot and moving on to another of the tunic's rips. "They *reside* in all things. But that is like an echo without a voice. What is their source?"

Alain's stare was vacant. He shrugged.

"From older gods," she said. "Gods older than Epona and Lugh and all the Heroes. Gods with names long forgotten, but who are here still."

"Here? In this world?"

"Aye. Here. In the water, in the air. In the earth beneath our feet and the flames of my hearthfire. They slumber among us. But they are old and weak and can only sleep."

"And the spirits?"

"The spirits are the dreams of these sleeping gods."

Alain sat, thinking. He looked around him as Marmohec's words settled in his mind. The fire was low in the hearth. Outside, sunlight fell through the high-branched trees in slanted pillars. Dreams. He considered the notion.

"Very well," he said with a nod. "What you say seems right, but what has it to do with me? You said you knew my future."

Marmohec pulled her stitch taut and looked at him. She leaned forward, elbows on knees, sewing forgotten. Her gaze was only for him.

"Earth magic comes from the elder gods, and line magic comes from the Veil. They are separate and different; so different that of those who can work magic, they can work only one or the other. Very few can master one. No one can wield both. No one." She paused and let her words sink in.

"No one?" he asked.

"No one."

"Not ever?"

She shook her head. "Never. It is thought that not even the gods can do so."

Alain's mind was awhirl with what she was saying. A season past, he had not been able to work even the smallest charm, but now he was able to pull from lines and spirits alike. He looked at the old woman and tried to judge her intent. If she was lying, he could not tell, nor could fathom why.

"Then how can I?" he asked.

"There has long been a belief among the Fair Folk—a prophecy, some say—that one day there will come a mage who can master both." She closed her eyes and spoke as if reciting something learned long ago. "'And the Fair One will set forth, and bend line and spirit to his will. Man and not Man, he will bear marks, like unto both line and earth.'" She opened her eyes and pointed the needle at him. "That's you, I'd say."

Alain coughed up a derisive laugh. "Me? Hah! Go howl at the moon."

"Aye, you," she said evenly. "Any mage would recognize you, by your talent, and your marks. You, Alain, are the Fair One."

He laughed again. "All right," he said. "And what is this Fair One supposed to do?"

"To the Fey, the Fair One is a savior who will bring about their Return to the lands of Men. To Men, the Fair one is the Undoer, who will destroy the world."

Alain fell silent. "That's not funny, Marmohec."

"Oh, I agree."

He shook his head, looking at her from beneath sandy locks. "And you really believe all this?"

"Yes. And I am not alone. Tell me, why do you think Bronwyn ran from here?"

Alain looked away from the old woman. "Horror," he said sternly. "Or disgust. Take your pick."

"No. 'Twas love."

Alain's jaw opened. He started to say something, tried again, but could find nothing to say. He settled for a befuddled shake of his head.

"'Tis true," Marmohec said. "Though you don't believe it and she won't admit it, 'tis love that drove her out."

"Stop it."

"No, I won't. For she had nearly told me as much. I know her well, young friend. She cares much for you. And now that she has learned that you are the Fair One, she is understandably upset."

Alain did not respond and they looked at each other a long time. Smoke from the hearth curled upward in the space between them.

"Either you are mad, lying, or truthful. In all honesty, I don't think you are mad." He chewed on his lip. "And I do not think you would lie, not about Bronwyn. You love her too much."

"And if I am right?"

"I don't want to think about that. Maybe you're just mistaken." He looked at her hopefully. Marmohec smiled and shook her head, as if in apology. She returned to the mending of his tunic. Alain stood and began to pace.

He walked the length of the cottage. The old woman's words battered him, flailed him. *The Fair One. Bend line and spirit to his will. Undoer. Destroy the world.* He paced, pulling the cloak close, feeling its rough weave on the pattern of his scars. He paced back to the fire. Marmohec glanced up and looked quickly down again. He turned and walked the room once more. At the far end, he stopped.

Could I be this one, he wondered? Am I this Fair One?

There, standing in the dark corner, the smell of wool and thatch strong and thick, he heard Marmohec's words again.

The Fair One will set forth, and bend line and spirit to his will.

Alain reached out with his talent. The dreams of sleeping gods surrounded him. He sought them, found them. They dwelled in the wool that covered his shoulders, slumbered in the timbers of the hut. Their numbers swelled as he looked for them. They were in the trees, in stones, in the earth itself. They were in the animals in burrows and nests. And they were watching him, waiting. He felt the pressure of their regard, the pulse of their presence, as fast as a sparrow's heart, as slow as the pounding of a waterfall on slick, black boulders. His mind followed the sound of the waterfall, a liquid heartbeat that filled the valley. The water of the cataract rushed outward, jubilant at the momentary freedom of flight, happy to come home to bed. And where did it stop, where did it end? It came from the air and swept to the sea. Where Alain drank of it, he, too was one with it. And with the land as well. The spirits came close, crowding in as he pictured the grander scale of the world around him. All one, he thought. All one. He looked within himself, into his darkness and pain, and saw a spark, a ruddy flicker. He felt its smile, saw its joy, heard its agony. It was him, himself, but not him, a part of some other. Part of many. Part of others. Lines, red and harsh, reached out from his center, twined and twirled in the inner darkness. Like ropes, like creeper vines, they encircled, wrapped, and held. The spark grew brighter. The spirits were now behind him as he faced this growing light, as he faced his own inner spirit. *Am I he? Am I the Fair One?* The spark burned white. The roots that grew from it burned white. He grabbed onto them, pulled himself toward the core, toward the incendiary light, toward his own heart. One, he thought. All one. The sound of water pounded in his ears. He pulled, he grew close. The light engulfed him, burning, devouring. The sound of the lines massed around him, the singing strings of unknown viols. He felt future and past, all one. The lines roared. The spirits swept in. He comprehended the mass of the world, took in the light of all the stars, all at once. All one.

All one.

He was cold. The sound of falling water filled his ears. He felt water upon his face.

He opened his eyes and found himself kneeling at the edge of a pool, the air about him heavy with mist. He looked up.

Water filled the air, pouring off an upper ledge and floating airy and free, falling and scattering, until it struck the night-black rocks at the pool's far edge. Gouts of mist shot up through the thundering air to catch fire in the evening light. A double arc of color waved, majestic and ethereal in the sunlight.

The thick moss on which he knelt was wet with watery gems. Beside him, behind him, was the green forest. He did not know how he had come here, but that this was the waterfall he had heard all day, he did not doubt.

A sound pushed through the waterfall's roar. It came again, an animal's call or a shout. He stood.

"Alain," he heard, though faintly. It was a woman's voice, pitched high with fear. "Alain!"

"Here," he shouted.

Bronwyn burst through the foliage at the pool's far edge. Her hair was loose, her eyes wide, and the hem of her dress was wet and muddy.

"Here," he said again, and she turned. Seeing him, she ran around the pool to the rock on which he stood, and stopped before him. He could feel the heat from off her skin, and saw the pulse that pounded along her neck.

"You are...well?" Her voice was quiet, her manner hesitant.

"I think so," he said. "I don't know how I got here. How did you know where I was?"

"Marmie sent to me. She...." Her eyes looked down and her hands played with the cloth of her dress. "She said something was happening. She heard the waterfall like it was in the room and she saw you...fade."

"I came here by magic?"

She nodded. "Line-walking," she said. "Very difficult. Only the most adept..." Her voice trailed off and she would not look up at him.

"Bronwyn, what is it?" he asked, but she only shook her head and turned away. He realized that he had dropped Marmohec's cloak in the hut and now stood half-naked in the chill air. Bronwyn's averted face put the lie to Marmohec's assertion. He took a breath and held it a moment before letting it seep slowly out into the chilling air.

"I'll head out in the morning, then. You needn't travel with me further. My mother's...gifts...can be unsettling."

"What?" She turned and stepped toward him. Her outstretched hand trembled like a too taut cord. Her eyes searched his face. "Leave?" She took another step but her hand came no closer, unable to touch his marred skin. "Leave? Why?"

Solemnly, he lifted his hand to his chest and traced with long fingers the length of the raven's wing from breast to shoulder. He watched her gaze follow as his hand continued, coursing the familiar line that curved down the muscle of his arm and ran beneath the soft hair of his forearm. Her face was a riddle of emotions.

"Look at you," he said. "You can barely stand the sight of me. Your revulsion is plain."

"Revulsion? No!"

"What then?"

She reached out for him but again her hand was stayed before it touched. She withdrew it. "I...fear you."

"Fear me? Why?"

"By all the gods, Alain, you are the Fair One. There can be no doubt."

"Then why fear me? Isn't that really why you came looking for me? Didn't you want it this way?"

Her eyes filled with tears. Parted lips revealed clenched teeth. Again, the hand quested forth. "Don't you understand?" she asked in a broken voice. The hand touched his shoulder, a fluttering contact that ran the welted scar down his arm. Her other hand rose, made contact. A shiver ran through Alain. Her caress was hesitant, but grew surer as she explored the breadth of the raven's wings, the length of the scarry vines. When she stepped close, she looked up into his face. He saw the tears that wetted her cheeks, smelled the scent of her mist-dewed hair, felt the warmth of her arms against his rippled skin.

"I came looking for the Fair One, but I found you." She reached up, her dark eyes steady, her lips flushed. "You," she said, and kissed him firmly, mouth hungry.

Alain's passion ran unchecked. His hands found the sweep of her waist. She pressed herself against him, and they kissed with a fury. A knot was loosened and her shoulders were bared. The beauty of her skin, painted pale green by the dimming forest light, fired his lust and he stood ready beneath his breeches. She twisted in a sensuous curve and her dress fell away. She touched his hardness and he pulled the tie that kept him clothed. She knelt. He followed. She pushed him back onto the mossy rock. The heat of their bodies drove away the chill damp as she, hands braced upon the raven's wings, took him within her. He moaned at the smoothness of her body, the moistness of her love, and guided the swelling blossom of her hips as they loved, merged. Their moans rose and blended, challenging the thunder of the pounding water, until they cried out, and fell to rest.

She lay atop him, a gentle, feather-light warmth, and then rolled off to the side. In the premature dusk of the forest, she became a series of contrasting shapes: the pale shield of her cheek, the dark peak of hair above her brow, the clean pale curve of her buttocks, the dark nebulous warmth of her pubis.

She smiled sweetly at his regard, dark lips revealing white teeth, sadness all but gone.

"Come," she said, and stood. She faced the pool and, toes gripping moss, dove out over the water. He saw her whiteness ripple beneath the surface. With a great whoop that echoed from the rocky ledges, she came up for air in the middle of the pool. She beckoned with a smile that flashed through the growing gloom. Alain stood, remembering summer days in the sum-warmed river near Belvanetes, and dove. The shock of cold spun the breath tumbling from him and he broke the frigid surface spluttering and gasping. Bronwyn came to him, her playful laugh dancing on the water. He reached for her and shivered as they embraced in the dark water. She led him to the shore and there, on a bed of slick grass, they loved again.

After, they bathed in the chill water, pulled on their clothes and made their way back to Marmohec's hut.

Alain could not see her face in the dark forest, but he sensed a change in Bronwyn as they walked. She became silent, and the hand that had touched and guided him along the path did so no longer. When the light from Marmohec's doorway became visible through the trees, he held her back with a touch.

"You are sad again," he said, seeing her face in the glow of lamplight. Her half-smile only accentuated her conflict.

"I am thinking of the future," she told him. She touched his cheek and the stubbly growth of his untrimmed beard.

"You see sadness in the future?"

She nodded. "And pain. For us both." She kissed him gently on the lips. "You need time. Time to learn. Guihomarc will press you, pull you. That is why he sent those men, to bring you to him while you are still raw and untried. Do you understand?"

She was in earnest. He decided then to trust her as he had only trusted one other before. "All right," he said. "Slowly."

She kissed him again. "I do not know what will come, but I know that it will tear at you. Remember, though," she said, most solemn, "that whatever comes, I will be at your side for as long as you want me."

She turned then and walked the rest of the way to the hut. Alain watched her go. He stood there as around him the forest changed persona, moving from day to night, safety to menace. Finally, the cold seeped into his bones, and Alain followed Bronwyn in toward the warmth of a friendly fire.

fourteen

"Get out of my sight, you worthless turd!" Guihomarc shoved the fat cleric aside and strode out the door of his sleeping chamber.

"But my lord," the large man protested. "There is no other way." He lifted the hems of his robes and trotted out after the count. "You must acquiesce." The fat man spoke between wheezing breaths and trotted to keep pace.

"Believe me, my lord—it is necessary—to ensure the departure—of the demonic spirits—that have inhabited your body—these two days past."

Guihomarc stopped and turned on the red-faced monk. He raised a finger and the monk recoiled from it as if from a drawn sword.

"If you said that I had been bested in a tug-of-war with Epona's son, you would speak more truth than anything I've heard from your lips so far this day. Now take your censers and your crosses out of here. Remove him!"

The monk fell back before the count's rage. Guards took hold of the brother's arms and propelled him down the corridor. The count smiled with satisfaction and continued on toward the great hall.

The noise from within the hall carried well beyond its doors. Guihomarc entered to find the great room in chaos. Braziers smoldered on tripods and smoke hung in a heavy haze from ceiling down to men's shoulders. Rowdy shouts surrounded the rattling of dice. Men clustered together in groups, attended by kitchen boys running in with pitchers, and women whose purpose was less culinary in nature. The count's two huge hounds ran back and forth across the crowded room, chasing bones tossed by men intent upon disturbing another group's contest or on interrupting a comrade's liaison in a darkened corner. Tables lay strewn with overturned goblets, heels of old bread, and the pooled wax of burnt-out candles. Guihomarc surveyed the filth and waited for his presence to be noticed.

It did not take long.

Within heartbeats, talk died, dice disappeared, boys and women fled, and all of the count's officers knelt on bended knee, eyes downcast. Only the dogs continued their rampage, fighting over a gristly joint.

"Go on. Out," one man ordered them, but they ignored him, even when he followed his words with a backhanded swipe.

"Wulf, Wegnar," Guihomarc said in a steady voice. *"Tacite."* The beasts froze at his command. With both hands, he beckoned them. The shaggy hounds slunk forward, long heads low, tails tucked. He rubbed their ears and slapped their sides until they rang like ripe melons. *"Via,"* he told them. *"Ite in aulam."* They ran for the open door, Wegnar stopping long enough to snatch up the bone on his way.

The men had not moved.

Guihomarc walked in front of them. He came to one of his troop leaders. Despite his kneeling position, braced by knee, foot and one hand, he still teetered from side to side, sloppy with drink. Beside him knelt another, more junior man. The younger man was less drunk, and held himself firmly. Each time his companion swayed, a smile played at the corner of the young man's mouth.

Guihomarc circled the tottering officer, inspecting him. The man's beard was soiled with grease, his clothes with wine. He stank of sweat and puke. The count completed his circuit and saw him glance upward and immediately down again in fear. Guihomarc lifted his knee and lashed out with a full-soled kick that swept by the troop leader and caught the junior officer in half-smirk. The young man toppled with a howl. Aside from another drunken sway, the senior officer did not move from his submissive stance. The young man lay writhing in the straw that covered the floor, hands covering his broken nose. Guihomarc leaned over to the elder officer and spoke in his ear.

"I would require a greater measure of respect from subordinates," he advised. The officer nodded once.

"Yes, my lord count."

Guihomarc turned to the room at large. "Out. All of you." Men rose and made for the door. The junior man still kicked and moaned on the floor, hands and face slick with blood. "Take that miserable carcass with you." Men grabbed the youth by his jacket and dragged him away.

"Antoine," the count said in a low voice. An old, grey-bearded soldier had been trying to slip by unnoticed. He stopped, drew himself up, and presented himself to his lord. "Explain, Antoine."

Antoine cleared his throat and scratched his jaw. "We thought—We were told—The fat monk said that your lordship would be abed the better part of a sevenday."

"And naturally you and the men took the opportunity to drink and debauch your way into next week?"

"In faith, my lord, the men were somewhat afeared." With a raised eyebrow Guihomarc bid his man continue. "Well, sir, first there was that witch woman, come and gone like a ghost in the night. And then your lordship laid low so mysteriously from within a locked and guarded room. The brother, he spoke of demons and spirits and all such. The men, they were a mite nervous, my lord. I thought I might give them their head, sir, if you know what I'm meaning." He looked around at the wreckage and mess. "It, ah, may have gotten out o'hand. But none were hurt. At least...." He glanced at Guihomarc, regretting his last words. "At least none of consequence," he finished.

"You think me too hard, Antoine?"

The broad-shouldered man shook his head. "Nay. That boy's a problem. A drubbing might have done some good."

"Don't waste your time on him," Guihomarc instructed. "Put him out. He can find his own way back to Morbihan." Antoine bowed, stone-faced. "Oh, and have someone prepare the tower room. First, though, I must visit the kitchens. I'm starving." Antoine bowed again, turned and left.

After consuming a loaf of dark, sweet bread, a finger-thick slab of pale cheese, a quarter-hen, and two large cups of wine, Guihomarc felt nearly whole. He bore no scars from his ordeal along the lines, and felt only a slight tenderness on the side of his head that hit the floor. But he felt faded and grey, and a weakness infused him like a drop of milk in a bucket of water, imperceptible but affecting every part of him.

But the food and wine helped to dispel his enervation. He nodded to the kitchen workers who stood silently along the wall while he ate. Keeping his cup in hand, he plucked a full pitcher from the hands of a surprised serving girl and was out the door and across the yard.

His tower room was cold despite the long days of late summer and the fire that burned in the hearth. He frowned around a mouthful of wine as he recalled the last time he sat alone before a warm fire.

"You may hear me talking," he instructed the new guard. "Pay it no heed unless I call for you." The guard nodded and closed the door. Guihomarc did not know the man, but trusted Antoine's choice. Not like the young officer he had been forced to discipline. He blamed himself for that, having taken the youth into service as a favor to one of the Guild Masters of Vannes. In Guihomarc's opinion, such boys were generally more trouble than they were worth. They neglected all manner of education, drank to excess, tended toward gluttony, and behaved above their station.

Antoine, Frankish-born and Briezh-raised, could take the measure of a man in a blink. He had proven himself in battle as well as in policy. Guihomarc knew he should give more weight to his lieutenant's opinions. He made a note to confer with Antoine more frequently on such matters. He chuckled to himself as he sat cross-legged before the fire; there was one person of whom Antoine made his opinion abundantly clear.

That witch woman, the lieutenant would rumble. *She poisons your mind and sense, she does.* Antoine disliked and distrusted Bronwyn with brash familiarity. Guihomarc had warned the old soldier to take care in voicing such opinions in Bronwyn's presence, but the old curmudgeon paid him no mind on the subject. Antoine continued to speak his mind, and freely, whether Bronwyn was there or not. The count admitted that it made Bronwyn's visits more exciting, not knowing whether the angry twitching of her upper lip would finally erupt into a rage that would murder his old friend.

Tsk, he chided himself. *You're procrastinating.*

He looked into the fire. The wood was green and the half-rounds hissed in protest of the fire's attention. He looked toward the door and considered throwing the bolt, but the memory of his last trip down the lines convinced him to leave them be. Any threat to his safety would not come from outside the room, and he wanted the guard beyond door to have access should the need arise.

He poured another cup of wine and downed it, trying to swallow his anxiousness with the sour vintage. Calling Rill was always a dangerous thing, for a Fey lord was never to be trusted.

The fire made the room's only sound: a steady hiss, the flutter of flame, the crackle and occasional pop of burning wood. The keep was quiet, settling down for the night, and Guihomarc let the tranquility soak into him. The trance came easily, covering him like a warm blanket, coaxing him down to bed like an old and favored lover.

The dark vista opened up and he looked about, his mind adjusting to the non-world as his eyes would to darkness. Lines twirled about him and he could feel the power in them. They towered nearby, rising toward unknown worlds. He felt their call in his blood, but knew better than to follow. What he wanted was not along the lines. It was beyond them in a place to which they could not take him. He called to his desire, bade it come, and withdrew to await a response.

The room was dark, lit only by fire's light. Guihomarc saw it only dimly, a breath of vision over his view of the lines. He felt the response before he heard it. It advanced like a pressure in the ears, as if he had dived too deep, and then with a gentle pop, was upon him.

The figure sat on the floor before him, but Guihomarc could still make out the flames and embers through the translucent body. The visitor was not whole, was not really there, but sitting—perhaps before a similar fire—in a place the distance to which could not be measured in leagues.

The visitor wore a simple gown of pleated gauze, so white as to nearly glow. His skin was fair, rivaling his gown in purity. By contrast, his long, straight hair and large, wide-set eyes were so dark that they seemed to be made of the space between the lines. He nodded to Guihomarc and smiled a smile that showed no teeth. Guihomarc was glad of that, for the grin of a Fey meant no good.

"Count Vannes," the Fey said. His voice was genteel, cultured, with a touch of menace.

"Lord Rill, I am honored. How fare things in Summerland?"

"Don't beleaguer me with banalities. What is it you wish to say?"

Guihomarc bristled but kept his composure. "The boy," he said. "My son. He has come into his own."

"Ah, so it is the boy that we have been hearing. We have been aware of a marked increase in activity. The lines have been ringing as far as the Summerland." Smugness dripped from Rill's voice. "It is a little late in life, isn't it, for him to come into his power? Even for a man-child?"

Guihomarc bit the inside of his cheek to maintain his composure.

"True," he said. "I had given up on him myself. Even so, I thought his awakening talents would be of interest to you."

"Oh? And why is that? Because of our part in his conception?"

It was Guihomarc's turn to be smug. "No, my lord. It is because of the boy's talents. They are quite remarkable. Surely you've noticed."

Rill's eyes narrowed to dark slits. "The view is vague from this side of the Veil. We are not aware of any details."

"Ah. I see. So you do not know." He paused to emphasize his point.

"I tire of this game, Guihomarc of Vannes. The Circle has done you favors in the past—"

"And I have returned them—"

"Do not presume upon our past relationship. Say what you mean to say. Say it all. Be concise."

Guihomarc bowed his head. He had made his point—that he was still a valuable ally—and he did not wish to antagonize the Fey lord any further.

"Two nights past, traveling the lines, I encountered the boy. The lines themselves reacted to his presence. They moved toward him and, more significantly, he created new lines of his own."

Rill's long eyes widened and his narrow chin dropped, revealing long, even teeth. Guihomarc repressed a shudder.

"You are sure? He wove new lines?"

"Absolutely. And if he has inherited any of his mother's talents with earth magic—"

"The Fair One."

"Indeed. And the Return."

"My, my, my," the Fey lord said. His grin diminished and was replaced by a smaller and less chilling expression. "Tell me where the boy is."

"In Briezh lands; Finistére, I believe. I have escorts en route to him even now."

"That is well. I thank you for this news, Guihomarc of Vannes. It has been most...enlightening. Will you be kind enough to keep us informed of future developments?"

"Without question, my lord."

"Most gracious. I shall leave you, then." Guihomarc felt the presence begin to fade. "Oh," the Fey lord added as he left. "My personal congratulations on the birth of your son." He disappeared, his image boiling away like water on a hot stone.

Guihomarc allowed himself a single but deep and satisfied breath. Rill had been well-pleased. Good, the count thought to himself, and dove back down into the lines.

The first snakestone remained silent to his call. Concerns that were only whispers two days past now leapt up, shouting. He moved on to the second snakestone and it came alive at once. In moments, Guihomarc saw the faded outlines of a tavern room.

Richard.

"Your lordship?" the man inquired of the air. He turned to those at his table. "Hush, you! It's the count." His companions fell silent.

Guihomarc sent impressions, the intonations of a question. The soldier understood at once.

"We've stopped for the night in a village. We followed a track out of Manech up into the Montagnes Noires. It was no problem. The lowland boy moves through the forest like a she-bear. We lost him, though, along the deer trails, but we know the direction he's headed. We should pick him up tomorrow."

Affirmation. Approval.

"There's something else, my lord."

Question.

"Pouldou's dead. Bartelme, too. In Manech. The locals said

the boy was taken by a sorcerer. And Pouldou's stone was gone."

Guihomarc felt his heart begin to pound. *Taken! Who was it? Who else would have known? And if he has Pouldou's stone, I should be able to find him. He's blocking me, somehow.*

The man in the tavern squinted and wiped his brow. "I don't understand, my lord."

In a flash of clarity, Guihomarc understood. He called forth the a face and sent the image to Richard, pounding it into his head along with his command. Richard relaxed, the message clear.

"Aye, my lord count. The witch woman. We shall deal with her."

Good. A sound from far-off broke through his trance, demanding attention. Guihomarc broke contact with his man and began to retreat down the lines. His tower room formed about him with the sound of a shout and an opening door. Disoriented, still half-submerged in the sea of lines, he tried to stand.

The room slewed around him and he saw the young officer, the guildsman's son he had disciplined in the hall. The man stepped over the body of the guard and entered the room. His hand, like his face, was bloody, but the blood that shone from his fingers and the blade of his sword was bright and fresh.

"You have dishonored me and now intend to put me out? I'll kill you first!"

Guihomarc shook his head to clear it. The man came at him at a run. Bitterness spilled into Guihomarc's breast and the lines, so close at hand, shouted in terrible fury.

The youth convulsed and fell to his knees before the count. His sword fell, gouging splinters from the wooden floor. Sparks, sun-bright, flew from the tips of his fingers and surrounded his head in a nimbus.

"Traitor," Guihomarc named him, and picked up the fallen sword. Others entered the room only to stand transfixed as the screaming youth was lifted into the air.

Guihomarc stared up at the hovering youth, his features composed, his gaze intent. "I will not suffer traitors in my midst," he said.

Men shouted as he struck with the sword. Entrails spilled onto the floor and the stench of bowels filled the screaming air. Someone stepped forward and he shoved him back with a strong, unseen hand, then let the soldier fall to the floor. He stepped in to grab the man's collar, dragged his victim to the window. The shutters opened with a thought, and he picked up a coil of intestine, looping it, once, twice, three times, around the neck of the moaning youth. A shove sent the body through the window and Guihomarc grunted as the noisome rope slid slowly through his hands until it parted with a wet slap and the would-be assassin fell to the rocks below.

Guihomarc turned to find three men in the room. At his approach, two fled. The third remained.

"My apologies, Lord Count," Antoine said.

"Do not worry on it," Guihomarc said. "None of us thought he would strike down one of our own."

"At least he met a traitor's end."

"May all traitors meet a similar fate."

"All, my lord?"

"Yes," Guihomarc said thoughtfully. "All. I will see her dead, Antoine. Much as it pains me to say it, I will see her dead."

Antoine regarded his blood-soaked liege, the gore and stool on the floor, the dark trail, the smears at the window. He smiled.

"Sanest words you've spoken in a month of moons, my lord."

Dim light, heavily-hued in green and blue, crept in beneath the door accompanied by the alarums of jay and raven. The rumble of the waterfall was echoed by Marmohec's snores.

Alain lay awake, cushioned by pelts, covered by blankets, warmed by the naked Bronwyn beside him. Marmohec had feigned sleep when they came in, had ignored their shared bed, their midnight union. The old woman's approval was tacit but obvious, and it both pleased and disturbed Alain.

The pleasure of it came as he looked about the room. The light, though feeble, showed a home. With the high-roof, the hearth and loom nearby, the goats huddled near the door, and the sounds of sleep filling the space around him, this was truly a place of safety, and not a hut of nightmares or a cottage permeated by a father's bitterness. A feeling of family permeated this place, and Alain bathed in its warm, enfolding spirit of love and acceptance.

What disturbed him as he lay there, conscious of the smooth body of the woman beside him, was the thought of Josselyn.

He knew he should not be troubled. Josselyn had followed through with her intent to marry, had protected her lands by wedding the son of the powerful machtiern. He did not doubt that this was so, but there in the gloom, with the scent of a woman other than his lifelong love thick upon him, his heart felt guilty of betraying an old friend.

He slipped out from beneath the blankets and grabbed his clothes. The goats stirred but did not bleat and he snuck out without waking the women.

He relieved himself in the brush downslope. In the creek, he bathed, and beside it he scraped himself dry and began to dress. He had only just tied the waist of his breeches when he heard the sound of hoofbeats. He grabbed his clothes and ran.

A stone's throw from the hut he halted. Marmohec stood before the half-open door, the goats peeking out like frightened children. Three men on horseback looked down upon her. Their clothing was of good cloth but was soiled with the grime of hard travel. Alain was caught between the desire to act and his lessons of discretion. He could just as easily make things worse by intruding.

"You are Marmohec?" one of the men demanded. "Who fostered the witch woman Bronwyn?"

"Aye, though she's no witch."

The man sneered. "It matters not what you call her. Bring her out, and the boy who came here with her."

Alain tensed. Come after me, he thought, but not Bronwyn.

"She is not here," Marmohec lied. "She and the boy left in the night."

"Don't play with me, old woman. Produce them."

"In whose name do you make demands of me, pup?"

"In the name of Guihomarc, Count Vannes."

"Vannes?" She made a rude sound. "Ha! Guihomarc's arm is not so long as a god's. Lugh might reach across the whole of Morbihan, but the Count Vannes cannot." She shooed at him with waggling fingers. "I hold no allegiance to the county Vannes and neither does my Lord Count Kemper. Go away." She turned and waved the goats back into the hut. The young soldier dismounted and strode up to her, hand on sword.

Alain gasped as Marmohec whirled at the man. In her hands was the axe that rested near the door. The axe's honed edge flashed in the early light and dove deep into the youth's chest. Alain jumped up from his hiding place.

The soldier stood, sword half-drawn, eyes wide with surprise, staring into the old woman's stern visage. No one moved for two full breaths. Then the man crumpled like an ox at slaughter and everyone was in motion.

The other two soldiers shouted and leapt from their horses, swords in hand. Alain ran toward them. The lines chimed and rang. One man fell and lay moaning, but the other was surrounded by a flare of snakestone blue. He raised his sword, and Alain shouted as the man cut. Marmohec raised her axe to ward off the blow, but the heavy arm struck her down.

A scream tore from within the hut. Bronwyn appeared, hurtling herself at the remaining soldier. She hit him mid-section and they both tumbled to the ground. The lines rang again and the clearing was once more lit by azure light. Bronwyn stood in her thin underdress, unarmed, her talents useless, as the man came toward her with a bloody blade.

"Do not move," Alain warned the man. The soldier turned to see who spoke. Alain, bare-chested, was as unarmed as Bronwyn, stood defiantly. He saw the snakestone at the soldier's throat, felt the man's confidence emanate from him like light. Alain closed his eyes.

Spirits answered and came onward. They whirled around the soldier and through him, moths to his flame. The ground trembled. The soldier looked around, confidence gone.

"What is happening?" he cried. What are you doing?"

The soil at his feet erupted in a burst of dust. Roots reached up to entwine him. Alain felt the ropy scars on his own legs burn and the ivy that grew along his arms reddened, brightened. He stepped forward and the soldier raised his sword. Alain lifted his hand and beckoned the memory of the smith's forge. The man dropped his weapon, clutching his seared hand. When he was only a step away, Alain reached for the man's dirk and took it without opposition. The soldier stared at him, skin pallid with fear. He touched his protective stone, but it lay cold and dark in the hollow of his neck.

Alain turned and saw Bronwyn holding the bloodied Marmohec in her arms. Bronwyn's face was red with rage, shiny with tears.

They will come, won't they? he sent to her. *They will come and they will come until I am borne under by the sheer weight of them.*

Her reply was simple. *You are the Fair One.*

"So be it."

He turned to the man, reached out, and clutched the stone at the man's neck. The lines responded to his call, darkness engulfed his mind, and Alain flew through the flashing non-world until he reached the point that the stone called home.

Who? The query was befuddled, sluggish.

Count. It is I. Did I wake you?

Alain? He felt Guihomarc's confusion.

Send no more men, Count. I will be there in good time. He struck with the dagger, driving it up under the man's ribs. Something within the soldier's breast popped and his scream echoed at the ley line's end. The vision went dark, then lightened, and Alain stood in the clearing, his hand bright with blood. The soldier lay on the ground before him, and the horses stamped the sod, whinnying at the scent of violence.

There was a scuff of dirt and Alain looked up. The soldier that had been felled by Bronwyn's magic had regained his wits and stood staring at Alain and the dripping blade.

"Run," Alain told him, and he did.

Alain opened his other hand and found within it the shards of the snakestone. They pattered to the ground as a more earthly darkness overcame him. The spirits swirled about him once and left as he fell to the ground and gripped his head before it split apart with pain.

Marmohec would survive her wounds, though Bronwyn did not know if the old woman would ever use her left hand again. She tended to her while Alain went out in search of herbs and plants for poultices. For several days Marmohec was insensible, and it was nearly a fortnight before she could do well enough on her own for Bronwyn to consider leaving her.

They sat outside in the dancing light of a blustery evening. The wind had risen during the day, threatening a storm. Treetops swayed in the last light of the sun, and Alain's eyes were filled with their patterned brightness.

From inside the hut a long and complex string of curses emerged as Marmohec struggled one-handed with her loom. Alain glanced at Bronwyn. She smiled weakly and he looked back into the darkening wood.

"Summer is nearly gone," she said. "The Feast of Lughnasa is nearly here."

Alain said nothing.

"What bothers you?" she asked. "You've been quiet for days."

Alain sighed and frowned. He stood and paced a short way, considering. Then he held out his hands in the moving sunlight. "They don't look any different, but they are. I've killed a man, Bronwyn. Killed him with these very hands."

"Hunh," she said. "It's not like you stole his goats or horses."

"I know, but...."

"You killed him. That's all. He deserved it. He nearly killed Marmie. And he was going to take you captive."

"But that is what bothers me. He was going to take me captive. He wasn't going to kill me. Yet, I killed him. Worst of all, I killed him when he was helpless, and I did it just to make a point with Guihomarc."

"And you made it, too. Made it well. He was just a man, Alain. He was no one important."

Alain stood. "But he was a *man*. Don't you see? He was a man, with a wife, perhaps. Or even a son."

"And Marmie? What is her worth when judged by your scales? Is she less important because she lives alone? Should the attack on her go unpunished because she raised no son?" Bronwyn rose slowly and advanced on Alain with measured tread. "That man nearly killed her, would have if she'd not been able to defend herself. I am glad you killed him. It was just. Even if it wasn't necessary, it was just." She calmed herself and reached out to touch him. Her fingers caressed his face, attempted to relax the knot in his brow. "You have learned a great deal in these past weeks, but what do you intend to do when you meet Guihomarc? Cook him dinner? If you are to survive that meeting, you must learn something I cannot teach you. You will have to become harder, Fair One."

He turned away from her. "I don't want to grow toughened and heartless. I didn't ask for this." He looked out into the hidden secrets of the forest. "A woman once asked me if I was man or demon. I told her I did not know. Now you tell me which it is I must become in order to survive."

"Tell me," she said from behind him. "Had that Northman

raped Josselyn in the stable, would you have tried to kill him?"

"Of course," he said immediately. "But that was..." He turned, regretting the words.

Bronwyn stood there, arms folded, eyes sharp.

"...Different," she said, finishing his thought. "I see." She turned and walked away.

The journey to Brest was both brief and interminable. The hooves of the soldier's horses made quick work of the uneven terrain. From deep forest to sunny meadow to hills to mountain slope and back to forest they traveled. Each incline was followed by a slightly longer descent as they worked their way down from the slopes toward the seashore.

To Alain, however, the days were unending. Whenever he tried to get close to Bronwyn, he was burned by a crackling frost that added ages to their traveling. She rode ahead of him, unspeaking, pointing only to mark the place they would eat or rest for the night. Their camp, like Bronwyn herself, was cold and without comfort.

But eventually, in the space between the morning fog and the afternoon clouds, the view before them opened and revealed a bay that lay restless between two long, skeletal fingers of green and rocky land. Its water shimmered deep blue with flashes of white, and strewn across it were the bobbing sails of hand-tilled boats.

At the bay's right-hand shore was a dark and somber town with a long pier. Smoke spilled from cottages and homes. Alain looked quickly around but saw no fires, no dragon boats. So many cookfires, he wondered. How many people must there be?

As Alain admired the vista, his horse took the opportunity to stop. His companion had not.

"Bronwyn," he said. She neither turned nor stopped. "Bronwyn," louder this time. She continued on. He rode up beside her. She turned her face away. When he touched her, she slapped his hand away. Her eyes flashed with anger, but also with tears. People traveling with them on the road smiled or frowned as they passed, building their own fantasies about the young man and woman quarreling at the roadside.

"What is it that ails you?" he asked.

She looked at him. He saw a struggle rage within her until some wall collapsed, allowing her to speak.

"I hate her," she said. "I hate that woman."

Alain stared at her, completely uncomprehending. "Hate her? Who? Marmohec?" His confusion did not help.

"Ach! You can be such a fool." The reins creaked in her grip. "Not Marmie. Josselyn. Your precious Josselyn. That's who I hate."

He blinked and shook his head to clear it. "Josselyn?"

"Yes. Josselyn. The woman you love though she has taken another man. The woman you would kill for without a thought, though doing the same for me and mine leaves you whining and crying like a starveling puppy."

"But..." He felt it unwise to challenge her on that point, so he merely asked, "But why do you hate her?"

"Because I cannot fight her. Anyone else, I can fight. With castings, with a blade, with my own teeth and nails and the wits in my head if I have to. But I cannot fight her. She is too well protected. She's safe, locked up in your imagination like a dream lover, clothed in white, a goddess. I cannot fight her, for to fight her I would have to fight you." She looked off toward the steely sky. The land had gone into shadow as the clouds drew their veil over the town, with the bay and the sea beyond soon to follow. "She does not see the man I see. Her only care was for the land she would lose. Poor girl. She might have had to live like you did, and earn her keep every day." Bronwyn looked at him. "And yet you think she loves you?"

Alain sat back on his horse. "I believe that she did, but I don't know about now. But why do you care so much?"

She laughed a soft laugh full of sadness. "Because I love you, too."

She had been so cold, so remote since that day they argued, he had been sure that all affection for him had been driven from her. "I thought," he began, "I thought you had only stayed with me because..." His puzzled expression brought another chuckle from Bronwyn. She shook her head and turned her mount toward the road.

"Come along, Fair One," she called over her shoulder. "The soldiers' coin has served us well thus far, but we'll need more to take us across the sea. The sooner we get down to Brest, the better."

Reins flicked and her horse stepped back onto the muddy

road.

Alain followed, thinking furiously.

They rode down into a town on the edge of the world. Brest was a grey smudge, sooty with smoke and ripe with the smell of mudflats at neap tide. Bronwyn led them between sad, low hovels until they reached the docks, where she steered them toward a rickety structure that seemed more mud than wattle.

"Lady Betina!"

A small round man bustled out the door, his wooden shoes squelching in the mud as he rushed to greet them. The building behind him looked close to collapse. Straw protruded from cracks between the boarding, and the sad memory of a coat of lime was all that relieved the overall impression of greyness and dung. Over her horse's shivering withers, Bronwyn winked at Alain and dismounted. Then she turned to greet the innkeeper.

"Nestor," she crooned and leaned over to kiss both the fat man's cheeks.

"You are back so soon," Nestor said. "An unexpected pleasure. I've hardly had time to empty the pots since you left." Yellow teeth smiled through a thick beard. He wiped his hands on his stained apron and noticed Alain for the first time.

"Don't just stand there, boy! See to your mistress's horse. There's a stablehouse at the end of the row. I'll see her settled into her rooms."

"Nestor," Bronwyn broke in. "May I present you my traveling companion, Lord Alain, heir to the County of Vannes."

Alain felt the blood recede from his face like an outgoing wave. Nestor gaped, blinked, and smiled.

"My deepest apologies, young sir. It is an honor." He bowed from the waist, a ridiculous sight amid the mud, stained clothing, and Alain's vacant stare.

"Come in, come in," the round man urged. "So. What news? Do you travel in secret, my lady?"

"Only while we were within the borders of Morbihan." They ducked under the lintel to enter the inn. "Lord Alain's claim to his father's seat is as yet unrecognized. Now, however, among my friends of Finistére, we may put off such pretenses. You have my things?"

"Aye, my lady, of course." He showed them through a throng

of men and serving girls to two heavy chairs near the fire.

"Faithful Nestor," she said with a touch to his bearded cheek. "Some wine, if you will. And tell the tailor I will need his services this evening."

Nestor beamed and bowed to them both in turn. With a shouted order to the maids, he bustled off into the kitchen.

Alain looked around worriedly. "Lady Betina?" he asked her in a harsh whisper. "Who is Lady Betina? And what are you doing? Trying to get me killed?"

"What?" she asked innocently. "You are upset that I told him who you are? Believe me, Alain, people here do not care *that* much about the politics of Morbihan succession."

"I was thinking more about Guihomarc and his soldiers."

"You told the good count to send no more men, did you not? If any are still in town, I am sure they will keep their distance." She smiled as Nestor appeared with wine and a tray of bread and cheese. "Nestor, please bring my things up to my room. Oh, and would you send someone down to the shore? Lord Alain and I are seeking passage to Sidmouth."

"Of course. It shall be done, Lady Betina."

Bronwyn nodded her thanks and he departed.

Alain leaned forward. "And why does he call you 'Lady Betina?'" he demanded. "Who does he think you are?"

Still smiling she inclined herself toward him ever so slightly. "I would ask that you revise your tone, my Lord Alain. I am not accustomed to being spoken to like some hag-mouthed fishwife." She leaned back. "I am known by different names in different places. In Brest, I am Lady Betina, wife of Lord Monzerole, the spavined old man who controls most of the trade of Tuscan wine to this region. And before you ask, yes, he is quite real. He is also quite rich, and quite, quite far away. He despises the dreary maritime air of our beloved land, and prefers the heated climes of the South. More than that you need not know."

Alain looked at her as if it were for the first time. "Who *are* you?" he asked, wondering how he ever could have trusted her.

She laughed; a quiet, cultured sound like a bright-feathered warbler that flitted from branch to branch. "A short while ago, I was Bronwyn, Marmohec's foster daughter. Today, though—and for as long as I am here—I am Lady Betina of Nantes. And you," she added with a wink, "as Nestor is probably informing the rest of the shopkeeps in the row, are my consort."

Alain felt his face flush red clear up to his scalp. She laughed again and he blushed even more fiercely. She poured wine and he picked it up, looking anywhere but at her. She was so young and yet she carried herself with such aplomb. He envied her the smallest portion of that confidence.

The inn was a fine place, though it had not seemed so from the outside. Large logs burned in the cut-stone hearth. A chimney carried the smoke up and out so it did not foul the air inside. Tables and benches stood in neat rows as they did in most taverns, but they did not bear the usual scars and burns and stains. The surfaces were clean and smooth, their legs were carved and finely finished.

The men who sat at the tables and who stood with one another in the aisles all wore clothes of a similar thread. Tunics of fine wool, thick and dark, covered soft cotton shirts. Leggings tailored close were tucked into short boots of good leather. Wide belts buckled with bronze girdled bellies made broad by good food. Hems waved with satin blue and embroidered green, and on every hand was a signet of gold, a flashing gem, or the wink of silver. The men spoke to one another in the low tones of earnest converse. Merchants, or guildsmen, Alain recognized. He realized he was surrounded by the well-to-do, and that every sidelong glance cast his way was asking a question. Alain became overly conscious of the grime on his hands, the touch of rough wool on his shoulders.

Nestor appeared. "Your room has been prepared, my lady."

"Ah, fine," she said.

She rose. Alain did likewise. Conversation in the room waned. "Do not trouble yourself, my lord," she said to Alain. "Nestor will see to my needs." Alain was stricken by a sharp panic as he realized she intended to leave him alone. *Do not fear,* she sent. *They will not bite you. And if they growl, growl back.* And then she was gone with a bowing Nestor.

A few breaths passed Alain's lips before he realized he was still standing, staring at the doorway. He sat, glanced at the wondering eyes around him, and picked up his untasted wine.

The chair across the hearth from him remained empty. None of the merchants came close enough to spit. The chair's emptiness mocked him. You are either too high or too low, its vacancy said to him, but most definitely, you are not one of us. Worry began to twist at Alain's guts.

A subtle shift in the level of talk warned Alain. At his elbow, he saw an empty goblet held in a ring-heavy hand. Gold thread glittered at the cuff. The hand was part of an arm, was part of a man. A very tall man. He looked at Alain down the length of a long straight nose. His eyes were bluebird blue, his beard the color of wheat. The hat upon his head was black velvet and hung above him like a halo of night. A silence surrounded two of them, spreading outward like a bitter fog until, when the tall merchant finally spoke, his deep voice filled the room.

"Some wine, boy."

Alain glanced at the pitcher on the nearby table. His arm twitched in reaction to the command, but he held back, and felt his heart pound. All the men knew who he was, and what he purported to be. How he reacted was critical, and he could make allies or enemies with a single word. He pointed at the pitcher.

"Help yourself," he said calmly.

"Pour me some wine. Boy." Menace had crept into the man's tone, as had insult. Alain looked the merchant up and down. Tall, yes, broad-shouldered, yes, but with a belly like a hogshead and hands thin and pale as an old woman's. The pommel of the dagger in his belt was carved and wound with braided silver.

A bully, Alain marked him. I have seen your like many times before.

He leaned forward for the pitcher and the man gave an "I told you so" smile to the interested onlookers. Alain poured a splash of wine into his own cup, replaced the pitcher, sat back, and watched the man's smile fade. Alain sipped.

"Please," he said. "Feel free. It is really quite good."

A backhanded slap sent Alain's cup to the floor. The fire breathed through clenched teeth as wine splashed its hot coals. The tall merchant leaned over, a warning digit in Alain's face.

"It makes no difference upon whose arm you arrived, boy. You will still respect your betters. Now *pour me some wine*."

The ley lines were close. Alain heard them whisper to his coursing pulse. But the faces that now looked on—all pretence at disinterest dropped—counseled him to heed Bronwyn's advice: if they growl, growl back. And there was only one language a bully understood.

With one hand, he grabbed the inside of the merchant's knee, and with the other, took hold of the silvered dagger. Alain stood, hoisting the man's leg. The merchant toppled backward. The dagger freed the scabbard and the man hit the floor, flat on his back. Alain leaned over him. The merchant stared wide-eyed at the blade of his own dagger, poised in Alain's hand.

"Forgive me, good sir," Alain said. "I forgot myself." He snatched the pitcher and upended it onto the merchant's face. The man spluttered, then roared. Alain pushed him back down with a foot on his chest.

"I am Alain," he said, and let his anger curl the edges of his words. "My father is Guihomarc, the Count Vannes, and I always respect my betters. However, I have yet to meet one in the town of Brest."

"You scoundrel." The man beneath his foot struggled. "I'll have you flogged!" Alain looked at the mob of silent men. As a body, their faces turned away and the murmur of conversation once more filled the room. Alain dropped the dagger beside the merchant.

"You'll do nothing," he told him. Alain sat down as the merchant gathered the shards of his dignity and rose. He picked up his dagger and glanced at Alain. Alain shook his head slightly, a small gesture. The merchant shot the dagger home into its sheath and disappeared into the crowd.

Well done, came the sending amid the faintness of bells.

You were watching? A test? he queried.

There is more to magic than using it. Knowing when not to cast is also an important skill.

And the merchant?

Rodolfo is a competitor, she answered him. *He has hated House Monzerole for years. His feud with you is an extension of his feud with me. It was inescapable. Do not worry.*

Her thoughts smiled and faded. Alain found Nestor at his elbow, a fresh goblet and pitcher in hand.

"Some of Monzerole's own vintage, my lord." Alain took the cup and tasted. Sharp, woody, it was like no wine he had ever sampled. He despised it. But with a nod, he thanked the innkeeper who bustled off back to the kitchen.

A short while later, a great buzz swept among the merchants. Alain saw them staring. He turned and caught his breath.

Bronwyn's hair was woven with white ribbons. A white surplice shone from beneath the heavy folds of burgundy linen belted by a braided rope of gold and silver threads. Seed pearls and black velvet draped her neckline, and red gemstones winked from her fingers and her ears. Her cheeks were pink, her eyes were bright, and her smile, as it swept the assemblage, was reflected in the mirrors of their faces.

"Lady Betina," several said, and heads were bowed in greeting as she passed. Alain found himself standing, unable to keep his seat at her approach. He bowed, too, as she neared, and felt the force of her personality as he had at no other time.

"Lady Betina," he said.

"Ah. You recognize me at last," she teased. She held out her hand. "Come. The tailor has arrived."

fifteen

"What is it, boy?" Antoine asked.

Guihomarc looked up from the steward's figures. A page whispered in Antoine's ear. Boduos leaned in, too lacking in guile to eavesdrop surreptitiously.

"Very good. I'll tell him. Off wi'ye. His lordship is busy." The page stepped back. Antoine turned. Boduos straightened.

Guihomarc sighed.

"'His lordship is busy.' Feh! What tripe." He shoved Boduos' papers away and sat back from the table. "His lordship is *not* busy. His lordship has been sitting on his lordship's ass in his lordship's keep for nigh on a fortnight. Tell me there is news."

"Aye, my lord," Antoine answered. "There is." Boduos nodded sagely at Antoine's side.

"Lormarc has returned," the steward said, bald head bobbing. Guihomarc ignored him.

"Lormarc?" he asked Antoine.

"One of the men from Richard's team."

"Ah, good. It's been two weeks since Richard was slain. There was no point in driving the boy further when he is already on his way, but I would like to know where he is. What does he know?"

Antoine shrugged. "I cannot tell. He's only just arrived."

"Bring him in. You." He pointed at Boduos. "Out. And don't let me find you listening at the door or I'll have your head in a vise." Boduos managed to look wounded but left. Antoine followed, and in a moment Antoine returned with a young man, tall, lean, with long dark hair and a haunted visage.

"Lormarc, my lord." Antoine stepped aside and the young man came forward.

"My lord count," he said and bowed. His youthful beard was scraggly. His clothes were filthy and worn through at elbows and knees. He reeked of fish and sweat. Guihomarc wondered what the man's last two weeks had seen.

"We know of Richard's death, lad. You're not to be blamed." Lormarc straightened with a sigh. He bowed once more in thanks. "Tell me of the time since then. Have you seen them?"

"Aye, my lord. In Brest. I was working for my passage across the water when they strolled into town like Frankish royalty. She calls herself Lady Betina Monzerole and he—your pardon, my lord—claims to be your son and heir."

"Indeed?" Guihomarc and Antoine exchanged wary glances. "Anything else?"

"Aye. He's bound for here, my lord. They've been waiting for passage on a proper trading vessel, instead of a fisher like the one I took. Before I left, they were walking about town, dining with guildsmen, dressed fine, spending money. Then I left for here. They should sail soon, though. There's cargo due in, probably there now."

Guihomarc nodded. "That's fine, lad. You've done well. Go get scrubbed and fed and have Boduos get you some new clothes."

Lormarc bowed a third time and left. Antoine stepped nearer.

"There's not a speck of good in this, my lord. A public claim? It will have to be answered. Publicly. This is not good."

"I *know*," Guihomarc rasped. "Better than you, I know." He stood and began to pace by the tall windows. Sunlight painted bright squares on the floor, and he strode through them as he paced.

He knew that if Rill learned of Alain's public claim, he would surmise that they were joining forces. That was the last thing Guihomarc wanted the Fey lord to believe. Only Bronwyn's presence gave him hope of gaining the upper hand.

"I've been concentrating on the wrong person," he muttered to himself. "I have spent my energies on him, thinking him to be the more important, the more dangerous." He stopped in a patch of brightness and squinted into the face of the sun. "These aren't his moves. He hasn't the expertise. It's her. She's the one. She's moving the pieces on the board. Whatever her purpose, and for whatever reason, she works against me. I'll have to go after her."

Antoine cleared his throat and Guihomarc turned, suddenly remembering that he was not alone.

"You've always said that she was hidden from you when she was away."

Guihomarc nodded. "Hidden and silent. I could never know where she was." He grinned. "But now I know where she is. She is beside him. And *he* is as easy to spy as a Beltaine bonfire."

There was a knock at the door. At the count's command, it opened and Boduos entered. Guihomarc guessed that the steward had been outside the whole time.

"My lord," Boduos said, still hugging his lists and scrolls. "A man has come. He wishes an audience."

"A petitioner? Some squabble over land? You know better than that. Tell him to come back with the others after the harvest."

"Your pardon, my lord. He says it concerns your heir."

The three men stood there, Antoine and Boduos exchanging glances, Guihomarc staring into thin air, his brows knotted, his jaw tense.

"Show him in."

Boduos stepped out and Antoine came forward scowling. "That witch has sent someone ahead of her. You should not see him. She is forcing your hand."

"Hush!" He regarded Antoine, saw the concern in his lieutenant's face. "I have told myself recently that I must listen more to your council," he told Antoine. "But this time you are wrong. She has outmaneuvered me. If I send this man away, he will say I deny the boy. If I see him, it will lend a small credence to the claim. Either way I feed the flames of their fire."

"Then stall. Say you are ill. It is common knowledge that you have been in poor health this season."

"And how long may I keep him on my doorstep before word spreads of my feigned illness. In case it has failed your notice, Antoine, I am not much loved; not here, nor in Vannes."

"Your lordship is well-respected in his lands. I have seen to that."

"Well-feared, you mean. No. I can ill afford a rise in tribal tempers here. I cannot show weakness. The cunning bitch has outplayed me and that is all there is to it. For now, I must walk the path that causes the least damage."

Boduos's light step was followed by a heavy, darker tread. The steward appeared at the door, nodded to the guardsman, and ushered in a stocky man with a thick mustache and thin, grey hair.

Guihomarc looked closely at the new arrival. The tension he had felt in his chest suddenly unwound like a weaver's spindle. An easy breath brought a low chuckle, a hint of humor that built, growing to fill his lungs. He laughed, threw his head back, and laughed. Through teary eyes, he saw the gaping faces of Boduos and Antoine.

"What can I do for you, Ploughman?" he asked, and the fury that boiled in the face of Alain's foster father made him laugh all the more.

Alain grumbled. He sat across from her. A bowl of stew and a cup of wine lay before him, and a loaf of bread bridged the space between their meals.

"Must we?" He tore off another piece of bread and dipped it in the thick brown gravy. He felt exposed and out of his element. "This fortnight past has been filled with guildsmen and merchants. I've never known a group of men who cared so much about money. Who has it? Where can they get it? How can one get another's? How can one keep his own? Ach." He pointed at her with the sodden bread. "Papa said it to me many a time. There are more important things in this world than money."

Bronwyn smirked. "Spoken with all the enthusiasm of a man who has never had any to worry about. The rich have enough, and the poor don't have any. Only merchants worry about money."

Alain scowled.

She pointed at him with her own piece of bread. "I don't see you complaining about your food. Nor about the wine."

He put down his cup.

"And what of your fine new clothes?" she said. "I didn't hear any refusal of them."

"It was tedious. The tailor was tedious. I said that."

"Oh, aye," she laughed. "So you did. And loudly." She took a bite and inspected him.

He had shaved upon their arrival. It seemed a morbidly

painful process to her, but Alain had insisted. In the end, she was pleased with his choice. He looked all the fine Briezh man. With his clean chin and thick mustache, his blond hair hanging straight to his shoulders, his sharp brown eyes, and his fine new clothes of burgundy and Cornish blue, he was a striking man.

"You are right, though," she said.

Alain looked up. "Hmm? About what?"

"There is something more important than money."

He raised an eyebrow. "And that would be...?"

"Power." She leaned across the table. "Power, Alain. The power to rule. And that is why we must see them tonight."

Alain sputtered. "That gaggle of geese? How are they going to help us?"

"Not us. You. They are going to help you."

Alain waved a dismissive hand and returned to his meal.

"I am serious," she said. "Think on it. Here you are, buckets of noble blood in your veins, and what has it got you? Nothing. Now consider the fact that you can wield more magic that I've ever seen." He looked up at her, interested by her words. "Do you think that will give you power? True power?"

"It will help me take vengeance on Guihomarc."

She gave him an appraising look. "I notice you have stopped referring to him as your father."

"He is not my father."

"But you must use that connection, Alain. To these men, your bloodline is more important than all your character."

He shrugged. "If it gets me close enough to strike him down, I will use it."

She looked back to her stew. "It will, but you must think beyond Guihomarc, think beyond revenge. Once Guihomarc is gone, what will you do? Go on your way? Do you think they will let you? Or will you stand in his place? Do you think you can stand alone against all, should everyone else wish to tear you down?"

"Haven't you heard?" he said around a mouthful of stew. "I'm the Fair One. I'm going to destroy the world."

She frowned. "Don't joke about it."

"All right," he said. "But I still don't see why I need the help of these town rats."

"Guihomarc has been able to retain his power," she said. She watched him as he thought. "And how do you think he has done this?"

The answer shone through the cloudbank of his brow. "With the help of—"

"Merchants," they said in unison. She smiled.

"We will spend time with the guildsmen tonight, and at dawn we sail."

"At dawn," he said, cup raised. She touched hers to his and they drank.

Guihomarc sat before the fire in his tower room, with none other than his trusted Antoine beyond the door. The line-world rumbled and hissed with unspent power, and Guihomarc traced his path along the threads with stealth. Brest lay just a short distance across the channel from Sidmouth, but the lines did not follow a straight path. They took him in a circuitous route eastward, through the blinding nexus of power beneath Stonehenge, and thence beneath the mountain of St. Michel.

Carefully, quietly, he wafted his way through the currents of power until he reached Briezh lands and neared the port town at the edge of Finistére. Finding Alain was simple, for the lines glowed more strongly near him. Alain's presence shone like the evening star, pearly and bright, and the lines reacted to him. They pulsed in his presence, and seemed to even stretch toward him.

By all the gods, Guihomarc thought. He truly is the Fair One.

And then he saw what he had come to find. There, caught in the nimbus of Alain's presence, was a dark spot of shadow, an umbra where the light of Alain's power did not shine, and through which the background glow of the lines did not penetrate.

"Of course I cannot promise it," the man told Alain as he rested his hand and cup on his rotund belly. "But I might be able to sway Count Lorient to your cause. Gregoire has been most displeased with his neighbor's handling of the Viking question. What is your opinion? Would you support an armed resistance to Viking incursions?"

Bronwyn gave his arm the tiniest of squeezes. Alain took a sip from his own cup and looked from face to expectant face.

"Guihomarc, my father, has seen fit to abandon Vannes and the ancient trade roads it controls for five summers now. During that time, I have seen families ruined, women raped, and many men killed. My own landlord, a great friend, was slain, and my home was burnt to the blackened soil. 'Armed resistance' is too weak a phrase to describe what I would employ."

Faces smiled. All but one. Rodolfo stepped forward.

"And how will you succeed where noblemen have failed? And how much will it cost me?"

Bronwyn took a breath to speak but Alain raised his hand.

"A landlord cannot till all his land. He asks the tenants to help, and they enjoy a share of the crops. Likewise, I could not do this alone, but would require the assistance of other counties and the guilds."

"He sees himself as landlord over other Counts," Rodolfo announced to the gathering.

"If that is what is required to keep Briezh lands in Briezh hands, then, yes." A low muttering sluiced about the room. Some merchants pursed their lips and scowled. Rodolfo smiled.

"But tell me, Master Rodolfo," said a well-rounded man Alain knew to be supportive of him. "How much would you pay for unfettered travel from Nantes to Brest? How much do you lose to the Viking's summer raids?"

"I'll tell you what House Monzerole loses," Bronwyn offered. "Over a third of all shipments that travel north of the Loire. And any among you who says you lose less is a liar."

A small man spoke up. "The news today is that the Northmen have settled in East Anglia. And that Frankish King Louis dickers with them for control of Cotentin. Soon it will not be just the summer sun that sees their longboats in our rivers."

Grumbled agreement surrounded Alain. He had heard the rumors as well, though he was still unsure as to exactly where Cotentin was and why it was so important. The men before him did, however, and the room was filled by the sense of common purpose.

Rodolfo, however, was not to be satisfied.

"But this 'landlord' of Counts still does not tell us how he will pay for this bounty. The road from Nantes to Brest may be unfettered under his rule, but it won't be free, I'll wager. What sort of tariffs will this kinglet require?"

Bronwyn's hand squeezed his arm once more, firmly this time. He gave a barely perceptible nod. She had warned him of this subject.

But her grip did not subside. It tightened. He heard her take a hissing breath. His inner ear brought him the haunting tones of seraphim singing through folded wings. Bronwyn buckled and Alain pulled himself back to the real world to tend to her falling body.

"You see?" Rodolfo crowed. "Even House Monzerole faints at the thought of such taxes."

"Close your mouth," snarled one of the merchants.

"What is it?" asked another.

Alain ignored them. Bronwyn was down, legs folded beneath her like a faltering colt. He held her in his arms. Her brow was beaded with sweat and her hands and face were pale and icy.

"I die, my love," she said.

Alain wasted no time. He dropped into the non-world.

Guihomarc!

He sent the name pealing down the lines. Bronwyn's presence was near him, but indistinct. Another was there as well, but hidden, cloaked.

The nearest line came clear. It lay bright with painful light against the darkness. He saw a tiny shadow nearby, a small sphere of darkness that rang with far-off bells.

He has found me, it told him.

Alain could see nothing else. The line in the distance was cold and bright. The dark seed of Bronwyn's soul grew hazy. He could see no attacker. But she could. He dove into the small vagueness beside him.

Pain swallowed him. Lightning crashed across his sight. Pale arms, squid-like, covered him, each one sucking at his vitality. He heard the bells of Bronwyn's failing struggle, the triumvirate chorus that was Guihomarc's attack. The arms swarmed around him. He sought power but could find no purchase, no porthole to the lines. The arms stretched, parried his thrusts. He was trapped with Bronwyn, and began to feel the drain from the grasping tentacles.

He could no longer sense Bronwyn as a separate presence. She existed merely as a part of him, a breath of memory. All else had faded. Guihomarc drained from them both, and Alain fed the little left him to that memory of her. He was rewarded by the chime of a sad bell, faint but alive.

He turned his mind to the life-consuming arms. They would not stop. They would not break. His every move to thwart them brought him into their grasp, pulled him closer to the abyss. He felt for Bronwyn and found her within him. In trying to save her, he had only intertwined his fate with hers. Guihomarc would get twice the price for his efforts.

A thought was born in his mind. He gathered his paltry strength and gave it voice.

Guihomarc, he sent. *You will kill us both.*

His thought was answered by a question, soft and distant. The angry arms ceased to move. Before they could retreat, Alain reached out for them.

All that they had taken, every iota of power they drained, Alain pulled back with force. It slammed into him with a searing light. The power passed into him, through him, and trilled as it coursed into the empty space of the lightless world, singing with freedom. Lines answered from afar, and their song rose like an onrushing wave. Alain held onto the energy. He felt a crest of power above him, below him, like two immense hands. He surrounded Bronwyn's presence with his own and tried to leave. The inn formed in shadow about him: the rush-strewn floor, the yellow light, the pallid shield of Bronwyn's face. The hands met, the waves crashed, and light filled the room.

The flare of power faded and Alain looked around him.

Bronwyn lay in his arms, unconscious still, though color had returned to her cheeks and she breathed evenly. There was the scent of something burnt in the air and Alain saw the rushes were blackened and charred in a circle around him. He looked up with eyes that ached.

The men of the room had all retreated. All stared. Some prayed. Rodolfo made the mystic sign of the Christian god.

"Spirits," said one.

"A demon," Rodolfo said.

"Neither," said Alain. "It is my father. Guihomarc attacks us from afar with magic."

"Guihomarc?"

"The Count Vannes, a sorcerer?"

"I don't believe it," Rodolfo said. "How is it that you know it was he?"

He could not explain away what had happened except by

telling the truth. Resolved, he glared at the merchant. "I am my father's son, Rodolfo, and have inherited some small talent."

Rodolfo's sneer faltered and fled. Alain hoped he had not admitted too much. He looked around the room. None of the assembly had moved.

"You gentlemen are free to worry about your money and your trade. Stay here and weigh the benefits of a familiar evil against the aspects of an unknown. But I tell you, here and now, with or without you I shall protect my own, my home, and my name. I will avenge my mother's torture, my village's suffering, and the attacks on those I love. Oppose me at your peril."

Bronwyn moaned and twisted. Alain pulled her close and lifted her in his arms.

"And when I have completed my tasks, we shall meet once more. At that time, however, you will no longer have the choice of whom to support."

He turned his back and the room was cloaked in merchants' whispers. He left them and climbed the stairs to Bronwyn's room.

"Wait," Bronwyn said from her bed. The weakness made even the single word an effort. It was almost all she could manage.

"I cannot," he said and paced another circuit between door and unshuttered window. He leaned on the sill and peered outside. She saw the setting moon beyond him and heard the complaints of hungry gulls. The smell of salt and the turning tide filled the room. Her stomach ached for food. But most of all, she feared for him.

"A day. Two at most. I'll be fit to travel."

"No." He did not turn as he said it. His coldness had grown overnight. She remembered his attentiveness as they had discussed plans for the evening. Then came the attack. When she awoke, he had been there at her bedside, haggard and wrung out like old, overused linen. He had not smiled as she awakened, nor since. She knew the reason for it, and felt also a fear *of* him, and of the vengeful ire that lay banked within him.

"You cannot go alone," she said and struggled up on one elbow. "He will kill you."

He turned. His eyes were cold, dark, a raven's gaze. He looked at her and he did not blink. "He will surely try."

"But with me—"

No!

The suddenness of the sending startled her. He had not moved, had not even closed his eyes to send his thought through that other world. His raven eyes saw both worlds at once, light and dark. Tears filled her vision.

"You are right." She lay back on the cushions. "You no longer need me."

"It is not a matter of need," he said and she heard a touch of tenderness in his voice. "You are a target." His gaze broke from hers and he looked at the floor. "And a distraction."

"I will take some small comfort from that," she told him. "If it means you still care for me."

Raven eyes.

"Perhaps too much."

Nestor ran the length of the pier. Alain saw the innkeeper's red cheeks puffing as he wove a crooked path between crates and torch-carrying men, around barrels and sacks, through herds of pigs and sheep. The round man ran up to the skipper, a man named Chabot, and Chabot pointed to the bow where Alain stood. Alain met Nestor at the gunwale.

"Is something wrong?"

Nestor swallowed and gulped air. He shook his head. "No, lord. She is well and resting." He held out a cloth bundle. "She sent this for you."

Alain took the bundle. The maroon fabric was thick, but light and supple. He had never felt its like. Unfolding it, he found within a length of tooled leather and a large silver buckle. The metal gleamed in the first blue breath of the coming dawn.

"A baldric, sir." Nestor drew a line from right shoulder to opposite hip. "For your sword. She said you should wear it. As is befitting a man of your station, she said to me."

Alain swallowed a hard bead of emotion.

"You keep her well, Nestor."

"Oh, aye, my lord. A blissful task, that. You'll find her fit when you return. My word on it. Blessings of Llyr upon your journey."

"Thank you, Nestor."

The innkeeper stepped back and bowed. Alain watched him

as he wended a more leisurely path back up the pier toward town.

sixteen

It was dark, but Alain had expected that. He had expected, too, the quiet shush of line-song, the hard light of ley lines against the deep bank of midnight. What he had not expected was the utter solitude.

The world of the dragon lines did not enfold him. It gave neither warmth nor cold against his skin. His hair was not moved by an unseen breeze. He moved his "hand" before his "face" but nothing obstructed his unchanging view of the lines.

Before, none of this had affected him. He had not noticed it, having been entranced by the newness of the experience and distracted by the closeness of his companion.

This dawn, however, with his body shivering on the rocking deck of Master Chabot's ship and the view of Brest growing smaller in his unseeing eyes, Alain traveled the line-world alone, watching as with each rock of the sea-bound boat, the line turned away toward the east. He had entered the other world seeking an answer to the aching in his chest, but he found the pain was only magnified by the sudden and complete isolation of finding himself alone in such vastness.

He sighed deeply and felt the echo of it in his body, now so far away. There came, too, the echo of an unaccustomed weight upon his shoulder.

Her gift, he thought to himself. The buckle of metal was the color of the line beneath him, the sword's sharp edge a bright line in sunlight. He knew his destination, then, and moved his mind back toward Brest and beyond, past the borders of Finistére to his home in Morbihan.

The river was a green mirror and swallows dipped down to kiss their reflections. The rising sun had yet to touch the sheltered vale of Belvanetes, but men toiled in the river-side fields despite the early hour. The season of Gathering had begun and Marrec and Alain's leave-taking meant more work for those who stayed with Josselyn's household.

Alain flew across the grain-heavy fields on borrowed wings. His swallow's heart beat quick and free within him as he pulled air and scythed over the white garden wall.

His jubilance bubbled over in a twisting song. He flew to Josselyn's window, but the room was dark and shuttered from without. She slept now in the master's room, he realized, and flew there. The shutter was open slightly and from within shone a soft warm light. Alain landed on the sill with sharp-toed feet and peered inside.

He saw the end of a mattress, the bunched edge of a heavy blanket, a foot. Hopping in, he found Josselyn lying alone and awake. Around her neck she still wore the snakestone beads. She saw him, or the bird that he was, and smiled.

Josée, he sent, concentrating on the stones. *Josée*.

Her smile was snuffed like a candle's flame. She pulled a blanket over her shoulders.

Josée, he sent again. *Can you hear me?* The swallow flexed its wings, wanting freedom, and Alain let his control of the bird drop away. It flew off and he remained with only Josselyn's gaze to fill his world.

Can you hear me?

"Alain?" Her voice was a breath, a whispered question. Eyes searched. "Is that you?"

Aye, Josée. Aye.

"Are you a ghost? Are you dead?"

No. I live.

"Where are you?"

Far away. And growing farther.

"You truly are a mage, then."

He said nothing to that, but after a moment, sent *You look well.*

She gasped and looked around her, up, down, into corners. "You can see me?"

Aye.

She giggled and Alain saw a spark of the young girl that still dwelled in the mistress's house. "Can you see this?" She pulled aside the bedclothes to reveal the gentle swelling of her belly. It was barely enough to notice, but Alain knew what she was showing him. Her beaming smile injured him.

Charles must be proud, he sent to her, struggling to remain, suddenly wishing he had not come here.

"Yes," she whispered to the empty room. "He thinks that it is his."

Terrors, bonfires, cracks, and ripples laced his mind and *What?* he sent in a heart-pounding rush.

Her smile widened and disappeared behind her covering hand. Laughter followed, joyful and mischievous.

Mine? he asked, more reluctantly.

She nodded and took a deep breath. "Oh, yes," she said. "We did create something wonderful that night."

Her image wavered as the line grew more distant beneath Alain's boat. His mind raced. Thoughts and questions flew through his head. His concentration faltered and he heard Josselyn say his name.

Farewell, he sent her while he could. He did not know if she had heard. The ship formed about him and he found himself far out to sea, the ley line far away toward the rising sun.

A child, he thought. My child. He felt the silly grin on his face stretch even wider and faced the bow to hide it from sullen sailing men.

The sun was up and its light skipped across the peaks of slate-colored waves. The wind was strong from their rear quarter, and clouds were piled high in the southwest. The air that bellied the sails no longer smelled of tidal mud and *garum* vats. Instead, it scudded across the water, clean and cold, and brought only the smell of the salty sea.

"An ill wind, that," complained a voice behind him. Alain turned to find Chabot, the wiry skipper of the ship, staring into the wind that came at them from beneath the heavy cloudbank.

"Really? I was just thinking how wonderful it was. I would think you'd welcome a stiff wind off your stern."

Chabot raked long pale hair from across his brow. "Not this 'un," he said. "Blew all the birds in to port yestereve. This one's brewin' up a storm."

Alain looked from the skipper toward the horizon with its

blanket of suddenly ominous clouds.

"Should we turn back?"

"Och, and spend a waterlogged week in Brest when it hits? I'd say not. No, sir. Oh, we'll outrun it." He scratched the stubble of beard on his chin. "Your landfall is bound to be a wet one, though."

During the progress of the day, Alain watched the horizon. The clouds did not really blow toward them. Fingers of white extended northward and expanded into hands that pulled the storm across the sky, bringing it ever closer. At midday, a dark hand reached out to cover the sun and Alain felt the first drops of rain. The wind freshened and Chabot grinned as he yelled at his men. The boat heeled over and the sails hummed. The ship came alive beneath Alain's feet and leapt into the rolling waves as it outpaced the storm and the sun returned to the deck.

But Chabot could not win. The storm outstrove them and by early evening Alain was ankle-deep in water among the wax-sealed amphorae, bailing collected rain from the open hold.

The weather strengthened as the sun set. Rain stung Alain's cheeks. Deep moaning gusts batted at the ship. Alain was shivering, cold beyond memory of warmth, when Chabot called to him.

"We're off course. I've just spied the signal fires at the Bill of Portland. The storm has blown us too far east. We've missed Sidmouth, and by a good margin."

Alain looked out into the night. He saw only the boat and the dark water. He shrugged. "You'll have to head back."

"Into the teeth of this? Och, no, I'll not risk my cargo on such a fool's errand." The wind whipped them with pelting rain. "We'll go on to The Needles and then to Portsmouth."

"How much time will that cost me?"

"A week, maybe two. It's rough country between there and the Sid, but I've got no choice." Chabot turned and shouted his orders. The ship slewed to starboard, the wind at their backs.

Two weeks, Alain thought, as he gripped the rigging. Two weeks walking through unknown territory. Too long. He tapped Chabot.

"How far from here? To the Sid?"

"From here? Half a day, maybe a bit more."

"Then let me off here."

Chabot looked around as if someone else had spoken. "What? Are ye mad? I'll not!"

Two weeks—if he could even make it back to the Sid—would give Guihomarc too much time. He had to convince Chabot. He sought for a line, but could not find one with the wind and the rain distracting his mind, so he closed his eyes and called instead the storm that rolled above them. He sought the wind and rain and was answered by the voice of an immense spirit. It flew down toward him, and he extended his hand to receive it. When he opened his eyes, his hand was aflame with green fire, and the mast, spars, and rigging danced with light. The fire swirled around his arm, spitting and hissing. Alain looked at Chabot. The captain's eyes were rimmed with white and his skin was as pale as the sailcloth above their heads.

"Please, Captain. Do not refuse me."

Chabot looked at Alain as if he had appeared out of thin air. "Reef the sails! Pull up the dory! Head her into the wind! Our man's wantin' off!" Men leapt to do Chabot's bidding. Chabot's eyes did not leave Alain for a moment.

Alain heard wind and the smack of heavy raindrops. He heard the splash of the sea against the hull and the creak of wet rope against hard wood. Then he heard a boom like the shutting of a stone door in a cavern. As the dory was pulled up alongside, he could discern a crash and hiss of breakers along a hidden shore.

Two men clambered into the slender rowboat. Alain was helped aboard, his satchel of provisions came next.

"Head west along the coast," Chabot said. "When you hit the river, head upstream to Sidmouth."

One man grunted at the oars while the other held the tiller and a lantern. The ship began to fade into the gloom.

"God be wi' ye," were Chabot's last words to him.

The booming was louder now. The steersman set the lantern down. He shouted at the rower and the grunts came faster.

"Can you swim, my lord?" the steersman asked.

"Yes, I can."

"Good."

Rough hands grabbed him and lifted him over the side. The water burned his nose and eyes and he spat the bitter brine between gasping breaths.

"We canna take ye past the breakers. We'll never get back out if we do. Ye'll have to swim the last." He was turned around and given a strong shove. "Swim hard, and don't stop," the steersman told him.

Lantern light disappeared and he was alone in the cold sea, his lungs raw with salty water. The sword and baldric dragged at him, and he lost his bag of provisions at once. The rollers urged him on and he swam. The heavy cloth of his new clothes made his arms leaden. The icy grip of the water made him weak. He saw nothing, heard only the waves, water, his gasping breath, and the boom of the surf. He strove toward the latter until, at last, he felt the water surge beneath him. It picked him up with a gentle hand. It carried him forward. He swam with all his might until the water turned evil and slammed him down with a cruel and pummeling power. He tumbled in the water, up and down lost forever to the battering play of waves. His foot kicked something, then his hand touched bottom. He struggled to right himself, to orient his body to the fleeting touch of shore.

Then the water fled, retreating down the pebbled wash, pulling at him in streams. He found his hands and knees as his back arched in a paroxysm that brought out air and water alike.

Another wave came rushing up and knocked him down. He rose, fighting its selkye pull, and crawled up onto the dark, rain-slick shore.

He ate the air in hungry gasps. Shivers wracked him, rattling his bones and teeth until he could do nothing but shake and breathe.

Will-o-wisps appeared in the deep surrounding night. Alain blinked and the hazy glows came onward. Two. Three. They came near and he shouted as they became ghostly, haze-rimmed faces. Half-men formed from out of the gloom, came at him and held him down.

His mind had been so full he had not had time to think of the lines, less find one. Now, with two men holding him down with feet and hands, with a third man coming near with a knife, Alain had to try.

He dipped down to the non-world and called out. A line echoed as he felt alien hands fumble at the buckle of his baldric. He found the line, a strong one, to the north. He opened his eyes as he drew power from it, but before he could cast, the men released him.

They stood back from where he lay on the hard shore and stared. The torches in their hands smoked, illuminating each passing raindrop like a falling jewel. Alain saw their pale hair was shorn close at the temples. Along the crest of their heads, it was long and combed back like a horse's mane. Their eyes were wide with astonishment. The one with the knife pointed at him. Alain looked down and saw his shirtlaces had come loose. His mother's art shone in the light of triple flames: the raven's head.

"Who are you?" the man with the knife asked. He spoke in the Old Tongue Alain had learned from the Delphine. The man bore tattoos on his hands. Star and moon.

Alain understood, then. The hair like a white horse's mane. The moon and stars on their hands. These men were followers of Epona and the old gods, and were well acquainted with the tales of the marked man. If Alain was to reach Guihomarc, he would need their aid.

"What sort of man are you," the man with the knife demanded.

"By Epona and Lugh," Alain said. "I am the Fair One."

The men stepped back. One stumbled. They all exchanged anxious glances.

"You are not!"

Alain sat up. He pulled back the collar of his shirt showing more of his design. He pulled up his cuffs to show the ivy on his arms. He readied the power he had drawn from the line, and let it crackle and hiss in the rain as it limned his open hands with blue flame. He rolled the cold fire into a ball and sent it soaring up into the clouds with a flare like moonlight.

The man with the knife suddenly laughed at the sky until the light faded. When his gaze came back to earth, his grin was full of childlike glee. He reversed his antler-handled blade and held it out to Alain.

"By all the gods, I have dreamed of this day. I pledge my blade and my undying soul to your service. I am Wrdisten, First Son of Clan Garw, and I am your man, if ye'll have me."

The man's ebullience was infectious. Alain found himself smiling. He reached out for the offered blade and took it. Then, sure it would be an insult to return it, he tucked it in his belt.

Wrdisten was well-pleased by this. He beamed at his fellows, who still regarded Alain with mouths agape. He slapped one of them on the shoulder.

"Well?" he said with a smile. "Why are ye waiting? Go prepare the way." He turned back to Alain. "The Fair One has come among us. The world will be the same no more."

They climbed a switchback path up the shoreline cliffs to a rough hunting camp where the clansman had been sheltering for the night. One man called Pascweten, a young man near Alain's years, ran on ahead. Wrdisten picked up his belongings—a cloak, a satchel, and a short, carp-tongue sword that looked as if it had been brought to the island by the Romans themselves—to escort Alain to his tribe. The third man remained behind to dress the deer they had taken during the hunt.

Alain studied his new-found companion as they walked.

The clansman was older than Alain by perhaps a handful of years, and shorter by half a head. His frame was wide-shouldered and sinewy, and he wore a tunic of heavy homespun belted by wide leather. His breeches were of supple hide and fit his legs loosely down to below the knee, where they were tied closed. His shins and feet were bare, and he walked the forest path with all the ease of a man long accustomed to traveling the woods unshod.

His hair, Alain noticed, had been whitened with a pale powder. The powder had caked in the rain, and Alain could see that, though the man's hair was fair, it was not as white as he had originally thought.

"'Tis nae far," Wrdisten told him. "And it will be a sight more cozy than a camp on the cliffs."

The forest was thick with drooping branches and the calls of night birds. Trees, tall and with massive trunks, were cloaked in moss and lichens like old men out in cold weather. The two men followed a well-traveled path. Wrdisten replaced his torch at caches in the hollows of dead trees along the way.

The clansman guided him, not speaking but to warn of a root or branch in the path. Alain was grateful for the silence. He followed wordlessly and felt exhaustion dogging his heels. He had not slept for two days and nights.

When the third torch had burned and guttered, it was light enough to continue without a fourth. While the forest around him did not sleep, it seemed to sulk as it waited for the dawn. The rain continued to fall in dull drumbeats on the matted forest floor.

For a time, Alain existed in a world of sleepwalking on padded ground, a blankness broken only by cold splashes of rain on his face or down his neck.

Then the forest was gone. They stood on a gently sloping hillside overlooking a dale green with grass and hip-high stalks of pale pink flowers. The sun pierced the clouds and shone down on the two men. For the first time in what seemed forever, Alain remembered warmth.

The forest stood tall behind him, ending as abruptly as if a line had been drawn. Ahead, in the dale, thatched roofs huddled in a wide circle around a common well. Smoke from a dozen hearths rose to meet the grey clouds.

The shaft of sunlight moved on and Alain shivered once again. Wrdisten came to his side and took him by the arm.

"Don't falter now, Fair One. We are nearly there. In the time it takes to boil asparagus, you will be asleep beneath warm furs. I promise."

Alain smiled. Wrdisten nodded. They walked on.

They were announced by the barking of dogs. Men and women came out of their homes. They gathered at the edge of the village, held back by an invisible wall. Children peeked out from doorways and around corners. As Alain approached, he saw gazes drinking in his every move. Mouths were drawn tight, and no one spoke.

The dogs—shaggy mops with bright eyes—came up and sniffed the new arrivals. Wet noses nudged Alain's hand, and then the dogs were off, back toward the village. The people waited at the edge of the muddied ground and all, even now the dogs, were silent.

The sun broke through again as he met them. The clansfolk took silent steps backward to let Wrdisten and his charge pass. Heads nodded greeting to Wrdisten, but there were no smiles. Alain greeted them likewise, but drew no response.

They walked into the village, Wrdisten's people following behind. Wrdisten led the way to the largest of the buildings, a long and narrow structure that Alain took to be a meeting hall. An older man stood at the doorway, along with a woman, a small boy, and the youth Wrdisten had sent on ahead of them. Wrdisten stopped a few paces before the hall.

"This is Retwaltr," he told Alain. "My father."

"I am called Alain." He bowed to the leader of clan Garw.

The old man looked at him with eyes of sleepy grey. "Pascweten tells us that you claim you are the Fair One?"

"I have been called that," he said and tried to stifle a yawn.

"He is tired, Father. He should sleep."

Retwaltr nodded and with an open hand, invited them inside. The hall was dark, with only a fire in the central hearth for light and warmth. Retwaltr, Wrdisten, and Pascweten entered as well. The woman and boy remained outside with the clansfolk.

"Here." Wrdisten placed a soft deerskin down by the fireside. "Take a rest while I get us something to eat."

Alain lay on the supple hide. The deer's short fur was smooth to the touch, and it smelled of hearth and woodsmoke. He pillowed his head on his arm. The fire crackled discreetly and threatened to warm him through and through. He took a deep breath and fell into a deep and sudden sleep.

"But such a claim," the gruff voice whispered. Alain did not open his eyes. He listened to the old man speak in hushed tones across the crackling fire. "I cannot believe it."

"It is true, Father." Alain recognized Wrdisten's voice. "He bears marks on his skin. Pascweten has seen them, too."

"A bird. And vines," whispered another voice. Pascweten.

"And he took the moon in his hands, and threw it up into the sky."

"I saw that as well," the younger man said. "We watched it until it rose up above the clouds."

"He listens," Retwaltr said.

Alain opened his eyes. From across the fire, the three men looked at him with the same face. A father and two sons, he realized. He sat up, rubbed his face, and yawned. His exhaustion was gone, but he still did not feel rested. His clothes, while still damp along his back, were warm and dry across his chest and thighs.

"How long?" he asked.

"A small while," Wrdisten told him. "'Tis not even mid-morn."

The brothers sat on either side of their father. They had applied fresh powder and their hair lay straight and bone-white down their backs.

Retwaltr's hair was white by nature rather than by design. His skin was creased by age, his ancient tattoos were faded, indistinct, and lost among the veins, tendons, and bones of his thin, folded hands. Around his neck, he wore a string of leather from which hung an upturned crescent of gold set with a carbuncle like a drop of blood on an autumn moon. His eyes narrowed.

"Who are you?"

Alain heard the question, and felt it touch his soul.

"Father..." Wrdisten grumbled.

"Who are you?"

Wrdisten began to object once more, but Alain held up a hand to silence him.

Retwaltr, his eyes slits of stormy grey, the red stone winking in the firelight, asked his question again.

"Who are you?"

The thought whispered in Alain's mind like the sighing of a dove's wings. It was not a sending along the lines. It was something else, more like the Delphine's visions, sent down upon Belvanetes. Vague, insubstantial, and somehow unsettling.

Primal.

Old.

He searched the world of spirits, following the nether whisper, the sound of phantom wings. The crops in the gardens surrounding the village, the timbers in the rafters above, the spirits of the stones beneath him were all silent, as if waiting. He let himself fall deeper under the spell of the words.

Who are you? they asked him. The question came from in front of him. From the fire before him. Not from the wood that burned, nor from the stones of the hearth. It came from the spirit of the fire itself. The old man, however weakly, called through the spirit of the fire that lived between them. Alain called it, too, and it came to him.

Power. Ancient. Eternal yet continually reborn. He stood before it on the precipice of Time. It filled the vast chasm. Alain was awed by its size, felt insignificant in its presence, and yet the man across from him used it to ask a simple question.

Who are you?

Alain considered the question. Did he want to know the answer? How much simpler would his life be if he was just Alain?

Who am I? Who am I, really?

Using the same messenger, he answered in the only way he could, giving the sum of his life, his hopes, his fears, his loves, hates, deeds, and his crimes over to the fire and the old man beyond it. He felt the message taken away, consumed by the fire's spirit.

The question ceased. Alain opened his eyes. Retwaltr peered at him still, though his brow bore new seams and his mouth was a thin line.

"I can feel the power in you, the power of this world and of the next. My father's father used to tell me of the days when he was young. Ur-pa said that in those days, a man could feel the gods around him. In the wind. In the curve of a new bride's belly. In the deeps of the wood, and in the breathlessness of a Luguasad dance. He told me that there were moments when the gods would jump inside your skin and make you to do a thing or see a thing or even to feel a thing. And you would feel what a god feels and, for a few breaths of time, you would know what it was like to be a god." He took in a long breath and let it out slowly before continuing.

"I did not know what my ur-pa was telling me. The gods had gone away long before I was born, and I never knew what it was to be a god. Until now."

He turned to Wrdisten. Alain saw the old man's eyes were full with tears.

"You have named him rightly, First Son. He is the Fair One, called 'Soul Eater' in my ur-pa's day. And you have given yourself to him." He swallowed and looked back into the low-burning fire. "Today, I must call you dead. Your wife is widowed. Your son is fatherless. You will travel with the Fair One, and we shall never see you until the Wheel spins us full circle."

Wrdisten sat and looked into the fire, his face a granite mask. Retwaltr and Pascweten stood and turned to go. Alain felt his hands shake and his heart pound. From his belt, he took the knife he had accepted from the clansman and rose.

"Here," he said as he stood. At the doorway, he met them and held the knife out to Retwaltr. "I'd not have taken it if I'd known what he would be sacrificing."

Retwaltr did not turn from the doorway as he spoke. "Fair One, forgive me, but my son was a grown man when he gave his life to you. Even if I could, I would not dishonor his choice by trying to undo it. Now, please let us go; we must tell the others."

They left Alain standing there, the offered knife cold in his hand. He watched Retwaltr and Pascweten walk somberly out to the gathered clansfolk. As the old man spoke to them, jaws dropped and women moaned. After a few more words, one woman, the one Alain had seen when he had met Retwaltr, cried out. Pascweten caught her as she ran forward, and she fell crying to her knees. When she looked up through tangled hair, she saw Alain. Her grief turned bitter on her face. She lunged upward. The brother held her back.

"Monster!" she shouted at Alain. "Beast!" Sobs stole the rest of her curses. People from the crowd stared with fear and anger in their eyes.

Alain turned, overwhelmed by responsibility. He strode back to the fire and threw the knife to the hard-packed earth.

"I did not ask for this." His voice broke and a hand gripped his heart. Wrdisten sat and stared blindly into the fire. Alain grabbed his cloak and sword, and went to the door with large, angry strides. "I did not ask for any of this," he said again and walked out into the diffuse grey of the Cornish noon.

The clansfolk had left the area of the hall and were gathered around one of the cottages nearby. Alain slipped out the door and around the far side of the hall.

A vague brightness in the sky showed him south. He put it to his left hand and started across the fields. Halfway to the forest's edge he heard a shout. He did not look back. He ran.

He ran to the trees and plunged into their midst. Among them, their mossy cloaks told him of north and south and he ran on, continuing west, following no path, hoping to lose his pursuer amid the silent boles. The chill air wrapped around him turning still-damp clothes into icy hands. He ran around trees, through brush, his feet pounding dully into the padded ground. He ran until he ached and his breath came like hot metal, burning in, burning out.

He fell to his knees. His hands touched the ground and angry fingers dug deeply into the mulch. The black soil beneath smelled of ancient secrets. The spirits of the wood were close at hand, pressing inward, impatient.

"Leave me," he shouted and scattered dirt at their unseen presence. "I want no more of this."

The forest swallowed his words. Tears laced hot lines down his flushed cheeks. He bowed his head.

"I do not want this," he whispered to the ground.

"Fair One?" The voice was tremulous, hesitant.

"Leave me be."

"Your pardon, Fair One, I would rather not."

He heard the clansman take a step and lay something on the ground. Alain looked. It was the horn-handled knife.

Alain stared at it, at the blade that lay bright against the dark earth, at the rugged handle worn smooth by a thousand grips. An earthworm, displaced by Alain's digging, crept across the soil. It pulled its way across the cold metal toward the opened ground. Alain watched as it passed over the knife's edge and wriggled down toward its clammy home, its soft length unscathed.

"Am I the worm?" Alain wondered aloud. "Am I the knife?" He looked at his hand, filthy and covered with dirt as it was. "Or am I the hand that wields it?"

"Fair One?"

Alain reached and picked up the knife. He brought the blade close to the worm's disappearing length. He touched it and the worm recoiled from the sharpness. He moved to cut, but stopped, a vague unease staying his hand. With a clod of earth, he covered the last of the worm, burying it, sending it home. He looked up.

"You have given up much, Wrdisten," he said to the waiting clansman.

"Yes, Fair One," came the answer.

"Family. Friends. Home."

Wrdisten nodded.

"Wife and child."

"Yes. All that."

"You have given up everything I have ever dreamed of having."

Wrdisten bit his lip and looked at the ground.

"I did not ask this of you," Alain said.

"No, Fair One."

"It was your choice."

Another nod.

Alain regarded the deep wood around him. "I have been told by some that I will destroy the world. Others tell me that I walk to my death." He rose and stood before the clansman. "If you wish to travel with me, you may. But if you do, you do so of your own free will, knowing your own death may lay in our path." He held the knife out to Wrdisten. "Take this. I wish a companion, not a servant."

Wrdisten pursed his lips and closed one eye. He squinted at the offered knife, then at Alain. He reached for it, hesitated, withdrew.

"Very well," Wrdisten said with a nod. He took the knife and returned it to his own belt. "But a companion may also serve." He held out his open hand. Alain clasped it.

"Good," Alain said. "Now. I seek a man called Guihomarc. Do you know of him?"

"Yes, Fair One."

"Can you take me to him?"

"Yes, Fair One."

"I think I have to rest, first, though."

"Yes, Fair One."

"And, Wrdisten?"

"Fair One?"

"Call me Alain."

Wrdisten sought provender from the forest while Alain gathered wood for a fire. After a few armloads, he stacked some of the smaller pieces in a crude hearth made of smoothed dirt and flat stones from a creekbed. He did not call on the fire directly, but called the spirits of the twigs. They awoke, and did his bidding. The wet wood steamed, then smoked, and with a small puff, caught fire. Alain looked up and saw Wrdisten, his cloak bundled in his arms, his face grinning down upon Alain.

"I would not have believed it had I not seen," he said.

"You know, your father has a small gift for earth magic. Perhaps he has passed it on to you."

The clansman chuckled. "I don't think so. I've been deaf as a stone to his 'echoes.' I am a great disappointment to my father." He laid down his cloak and unfolded it, revealing the bounty of his forage.

Large, pale ears of shelf fungus lay on the dark cloth, their gills pink and unblemished. Young ferns curled beside them, their long spiral fronds a brilliant green. He had also found berries, several misshapen tubers, and, incredibly, two fish, gutted and ready to cook.

Alain stared. He felt his mouth begin to water. His stomach growled, long and deep of voice. Wrdisten laughed and broke off a piece of mushroom.

"Chew on this while I prepare the rest."

Alain did as instructed. The flesh was mild with a flavor reminiscent of pine nuts. He sat back against a tree trunk and watched as Wrdisten buried the tubers beneath the building layer of coals. The ferns he divided in two small bunches, tucked one into either fish, and tied the body closed with a stripped stem. Then he placed them on stones near the fire and soon the thicket was filled with the scent of grilling fish.

"Was that your wife and boy I saw when I met Retwaltr?" Alain asked, recalling the woman who had cursed him.

Wrdisten's eyebrows drew together and he nodded once. "Irouken and Wrmenoc. Wrmenoc is eight years. We lost two others since, a boy and a girl. Wrmenoc is a fine boy, though. Strong and quick. Pascweten will raise him well."

"And your wife?"

"My widow?" His gaze was fixed on the cooking fish. Smoke wafted into his face and he wiped at the corners of his eyes. "She will live on with my father, and that is good, for Father's wives have long since died and he needs a woman to take care of him in his last years." He blinked and wiped his eyes again. "But she will not be taken by another."

His pain was blatant and Alain let the subject drop.

"What of you?" Wrdisten asked. "Does the Fair One have wives and children? You are certainly old enough."

Alain thought for a moment. He could not tell all without dishonoring Josselyn's name.

"I have no wife," he said finally. "A woman from my old homestead carries a child that is mine, but another man will raise it as his own."

"Hm. Our situations seem very similar."

Alain nodded. "Can you never go back? To your wife and son?"

"Our ways say no, for I am dead to them. A man cannot leave his clan but through death. Nor can he return from death except through the turning of the Wheel."

"But what if—"

"No. Retwaltr has decreed it. I travel with the Fair One and am dead. It is done."

"What if I am lying?" Alain asked.

Wrdisten looked up from his cooking. Sadness and loss gave way to confusion. "About what?"

"About who I am."

"But you are not."

"All right, then. What if I am mistaken? What if I am *not* the Fair One?"

"But you are." Wrdisten leaned forward, searching Alain's face. "You do not *believe*. You do not believe that you are the Fair One."

Alain broke off another piece of mushroom and chewed it.

"I do not know what I am."

Wrdisten shrugged his shoulders. "You are the Fair One. That is what you are."

"But I do not know what that means. Am I supposed to do something? Or prevent something from happening? People have named me Fair One, but it is only a name to me."

"You really don't know."

"No. I really do not know."

Wrdisten squatted back on his heels and rested his forearms on his knees. He pointed at Alain with his cooking stick.

"You are the Fair One, and walk between worlds. Other men travel beyond the Veil and back only at the hand of Death. You walk among the gods and return to tell of it."

"I've never done that."

"Nor have you torn the Veil and mended it. Nor traveled to the edge of Time. Nor eaten a man's soul, nor destroyed the world, I'd say." His gaze was frank and adoring, and Alain found himself uncomfortable beneath it.

"No, I've done none of those things," he said.

"And is your life complete that we should end the song of your deeds? Shall we today compare you to the legends of your future, before that future is lived?"

"Do you believe I will do all those things?"

"In truth, I do not know." He handed Alain one of the cooked fish. "But if even only one of them comes to pass, it will be the adventure of a lifetime."

seventeen

The trees held up the sun. Leaves burned with bright greenness, a canopy of color over Alain's head. Occasionally, he glimpsed blue sky between the branches and felt the brief warmth of early autumn. He had slept the rest of the day, all of the night, and most of the next morning. Now, rested and well-fed, he and Wrdisten took back to the trails that the clansman promised would take them to Guihomarc's keep on the River Sid.

The sky and sun wrestled with the overhanging boughs as the men walked. Then, ahead through the pillars of trees, Alain saw light. They continued toward it and the light grew, spreading out to form a pond, a lake, a sea of brightness. When Alain finally walked out from beneath the shadowed trees, the sun washed over him in a blinding wave. He stopped and stood for a few quiet moments, face upturned. The warmth flowed over him, down his face and shoulders to his limbs. He breathed the air and smelled it, warm as summer and full of the moisture of sun-soaked grass.

He and Wrdisten stood atop a long slope that drifted down from the line of trees. It curved first along the right hand and then along the left like a hawk's shallow glide down to the stone-colored river. Upstream, the ground jutted upward in a cliff-edged bluff that commanded the whole of the valley. Atop the bluff stood a palisaded keep, its towers and walls rising above the exposed rock, its whitewashed walls gleaming in the sunlight. Below, at the foot of the rise, near the frothed ripples of the river's ford, a village nestled.

It seemed a view of peacefulness and serenity. A breeze combed the grass along the hillside, and birdsong drifted in the gentle air. Alain shook his head.

"I did not think it would be a place of beauty. I expected dark danger and unfriendly ground. But it is so quiet. It seems like there could be nothing wrong in such a place."

Wrdisten pointed to a place along the river, downstream from the village. Alain felt his blood chill and his bowels tighten.

There, rocking gently in the lapping waters of a quiet eddy along the river's edge, sat four long dragon boats of the Viking raiders.

"Willem."

Guihomarc crossed the busy, sun-filled yard to clasp hands with the huge northerner.

The big man jingled with metal as they met. Chains draped his neck; buckles glinted at his waist and chest. Pins of copper and bronze held his red cloak closed, and white silver and yellow gold girded his wrists. He clasped Guihomarc's hand and turned to beckon forward the men that had climbed with him up to the keep.

"The season was good," he said in his native tongue. The other men brought forth two chests made of heavy wood. Willem opened one of them, sliding off the thick lid. Sunlight flashed from silver bars, plates, and jewelry. "This is your due."

"Cover that," Guihomarc said in Willem's language. "Come inside."

In the main hall, the chests safely stored away, Guihomarc called for food and wine. The two factions, Briezh and Norse, stood ill-at-ease in each other's presence. Antoine stood at Guihomarc's right hand, his expression that of a man who smelled something foul. The man behind Willem kept a close eye on Guihomarc's men, and their cloaks were all worn across their left shoulders, leaving their sword arms free.

Guihomarc poured two goblets full and handed one to Willem. The Norseman took the cup but did not drink. Count Vannes raised his own cup to the Nordic leader.

"To the end of a successful season," he offered and drank.

The Norseman smiled for the first time since his arrival. "And to many more," he said and drank his cup dry as well.

"Come," Guihomarc said, beckoning all the northerners forward to the food and drink. "Come. Slake your thirst and feed your growling bellies. Tonight we feast to your arrival, to your success, and to your safe voyage back to your Northern homeland."

The warriors came forward and wine poured into goblets in thick streams. Willem came up to Guihomarc as the men began to talk and eat. He put his arm around Guihomarc's shoulder and led him away from the soldiers. "I haven't told them yet, but I do not plan to return home this winter."

Guihomarc smiled. "You were thinking that—what?—you would come down and settle, where, in the Vilaine? The Cotentin?"

The big man smiled. "You know me well, Count. My bones begin to ache even now at the thought of the northern ice. I will be calling our families south with the thaw. By the time they arrive—" His eyes bulged and the cords on his neck sprang taut.

Guihomarc stepped into the stricken man's field of view. The ley lines hummed at his touch. Hands of power throttled the Viking's throat and gripped his testicles.

"Perhaps you misunderstood when last we spoke on this subject." Guihomarc spoke calmly, sipping wine. "Let me repeat my views for you and please, this time, pay closer attention. The situation is not yet ripe. I cannot give you the Cotentin. It is difficult enough for me with Harald wintering at the mouth of the Loire. We are not ready." He walked around Willem in a leisurely circle. "Now," he continued, "I *have* heard that there are lands along the eastern shores of this island. My advice is this: call your families south to Anglia. There is fine land to be had, I am told. How does that sound?" Willem managed a stiff nod. Guihomarc released his hold and the Viking leader buckled. Guihomarc caught him and helped him to a bench. He snagged a pitcher and refilled their cups.

"Fine. Let me be the first to welcome you to Anglia, Willem Longsword. You can have the whole besotted island for all that I care. Personally, I hate the place."

Sheep were slaughtered, skinned, and hung to drain. Women were set kneading extra loaves, while men grunted as they rolled casks up from the cellars. Boys roamed the hills collecting grouse and rabbit from their father's snares, and village girls gathered savory, thyme, and greens for the banquet tables.

The hilltop keep was a hive of activity. Four boatloads of Norsemen sat, diced, drank, and snored all about the yard and along the walls. The count's guards joined in the revelry where they could, and by the time Guihomarc descended from his chambers to join the feast, so many personal items had been lost or given to the other side that it was impossible to tell which men where the Count's and which were Willem's.

The large double doors opened as Guihomarc approached, and his two huge hounds yelped and strained at their leads. He entered the hall and a shout went up from the gathered men that sat shoulder-to-shoulder at long tables. The dogs howled in response, and Guihomarc let them slip to run about the hall. He took his seat at the head table, Willem at his right hand, Antoine at his left.

"They look fine," Willem said pointing to the narrow-headed hounds as they fought for scraps.

"I must say, when you gave them to me, I had no idea they would grow up into such magnificent beasts. In the hunt they are absolutely ruthless."

"A harsh land breeds harsh beasts," Willem said.

Guihomarc smiled. "Indeed it does," he answered.

Suddenly there was the shout of ethereal strings in Guihomarc's head. The nape of his neck crawled and he felt the surging sound of line magic.

He stood.

"Antoine!" he shouted. The old soldier was up and ready. "The door! He is here."

Antoine moved in a blur, leaping the table and shouting orders. Four guards leapt into action and followed their lieutenant.

Willem rose, sword unsheathed. "What treachery is this?"

Before Guihomarc could answer there was a booming at the outer door that shook the floor and swung the lamps on their chains. It came again, and once more; three earth-trembling strokes that rung the whole of the keep like a gong.

Swords came out all over the room and the men were suddenly two factions once more. The doors burst open and men cried out. From the dimness of the antechamber, there appeared a tall youth, thin, with a horse-maned tribesman at his side.

Antoine's men moved to grab the intruders. The youth waved

a lazy hand. Green light flashed and men fell back. Guihomarc heard the lines vibrate and felt the air alive upon his skin.

The young man strode forth with a casual air into the dust and silence of the center of the hall.

"Hello, Father," he said.

Five-score swords ringed them, held by snarling Vikings and Briezh guardsmen. Candlelight reflected from edged metal, pounded bronze, hard iron. Wrdisten stepped up to Alain's side.

"My plan was better," he said.

Alain ignored him, concentrating on the man at the head of the hall, the face from his dreams.

Guihomarc stood staring at him. The giant at his side began to demand something but the count silenced him with an imperious hand. The same hand then swiveled and beckoned.

"Stay here," Alain told Wrdisten.

"Oh, nae. I'll not."

Alain glared at the clansman. The clansman glared back.

"I'm here of me own free will, recall? I'll nae be giving that up now."

Alain grumbled wordlessly. The count beckoned again. Alain walked forward to the center of the hall, Wrdisten at his side. The ley line was strong beneath the stones of the keep and he kept his contact with it close and ready. He heard men move behind him, barring their exit.

"My son," Guihomarc said when Alain came close. "You have finally arrived."

The jaw of the Northman dropped open. The big man pointed at Alain and asked a question. Guihomarc nodded. The Northman barked a hearty laugh. He spoke aloud in his language and the northerners around the room nodded and relaxed their ready stances. Half the swords in the room returned to their sheaths.

Alain gave this only the slightest attention. What consumed his mind were the first small words Guihomarc had uttered in front of all present.

My son.

Those two words entered his heart and filled him with disgust. Coming face to face with the author of so much pain, and finding him so oblivious to the result of his crimes, drove from Alain's mind any doubts and galvanized his resolve. This man did not deserve to rule the people of Vannes, and for the attacks on his town, on his family, and on Bronwyn, he would pay.

Guihomarc walked around the long table and came toward Alain. With a few paces still intervening, he stopped, looked Alain up and down, and smiled.

"My son!" he said to all, and a shout filled the room.

Alain looked around the hall. Briezh guards stood cheerfully beside the Norsemen who raided their homes. How can they do this? Alain wondered to himself, and then spied one face that held his sight. Red hair gone roan with gray, eyes blue like sunlit seas. Josselyn's attacker recognized Alain in turn and the man's gaze became as an iron in the smithy's fire.

"I come all this way to meet you, Father, and I find you eating with dogs." He turned to the count. "My mistake was in thinking better of you. I won't make that mistake again."

Guihomarc shook his head. "You are a forward boy."

"It is a requirement for a bastard, if he wants to make a name for himself."

Guihomarc smiled. "Come," he offered. "Sit. Eat."

"I'll not."

"And stand there all evening?" He took a step back toward his seat. "In the middle of the hall? Don't be silly, boy. Come. You needn't sup with me and my guests, if that is what assails you. Just sit. It will make our discussion so much more...civilized." He glanced at Wrdisten. "Your man, too. Come along."

The count walked and stood by his chair. He indicated the seat to his right. Servants cleared the place and laid down a new trencher and goblet.

Alain ground his teeth. What would Bronwyn do, he wondered? But he knew: she would sit and smile and discuss items amicably until all was as she wanted it and then she would thrust in the knife. Alain shook his head, both at the notion in his mind and to the offered place.

"I did not come to dine with you, Father."

Guihomarc sipped wine. All looked on in silence. "Then why did you come?"

"I came to take your place." The words were out of his mouth before he could bite them off. Those near enough to hear his treasonous words cried out in anger, and again the *shing* of freed swords filled the hall. Guihomarc raised a hand and stillness prevailed.

"If that is your intent, your methods are unwise."

"I was not sure that it was my intent until just now. Before I met you, I merely wanted to kill you."

"Ah," said the count. "An ill-timed revelation. But tell me, what brought about this sudden insight, in this, of all places?"

"It was seeing you here, host to the men who raided my village, burnt my home, and killed my friends and family. Seeing them here reminded me of your many sins against my people." He extended his mind to the line deep beneath them and stroked it gently. Guihomarc started as if pricked with a needle.

"I may have inherited your talents, Count, but I shall never be your son. In my heart I shall always be the Bastard Boy of Dead Ox Wood, the ploughman's son of Belvanetes."

The count began to chuckle, then to laugh. He motioned to an older soldier and two guards were sent from the room. He continued to laugh with a mirth that shook his body and brought tears to his eyes. He wiped them away, looked at Alain, and laughed some more.

Alain scanned the gathering. Confusion circled the room; Briezh guards unsure of what to do or feel; Northmen not wholly understanding. The guards returned and all looked toward the door.

Between them was a man, bound and bowed, his head covered by a flour sack. They dragged his yielding form to the center of the hall and dumped him at Alain's feet. The man fell in a grunting heap.

"This man came to me a fortnight ago. I believe you know him?"

Alain reached down and pulled off the sack. Beneath the swollen eye, the bruised face, lay the steadfast features Alain had known from youth.

"Papa," he whispered. He knelt. He held Marrec's shoulders and got the old ploughman off his hands and knees.

"Alain, I'm sorry, son. For everything."

"There's no need, Papa." He sat back on his heels and glared at the count. "Why have you done this?"

Guihomarc's expression shifted. His mouth turned disdainful, his nostrils flared. All humor and condescending grace fell away, cracking like a thin crust, revealing an intensity that shocked Alain and made his heart fearful.

"This man," Guihomarc said. "This creature to whom you profess such an affinity, after learning of your true lineage, ran to me as quickly as his little peasant legs could carry him. And do you know *why* he came? This moral model you hold above me, do you know what he wanted? Can you guess?" He cupped a hand to his ear. "What was that? Honor, is your guess? And I must say no, he did not come to redeem his lost honor. What then? Revenge, you say? And I tell you neither was it that." He spat over the table at Marrec. "No. This pile of refuse that your heart calls 'Papa,' came to me for money. Payment for the years he spent raising you. Do you deny it, Marrec?"

Marrec, kneeling on the dusty floor, stared into space. Slowly, he shook his head.

"Ach, Papa," Alain whispered.

"I was angry, son. An old man's anger." He pursed his lips to hold back his emotions. "It was all I had left."

"And this is the man you value," Guihomarc said.

"More so than I do you," Alain said as he stood. "Even now, more so than you."

Guihomarc's mouth turned feral. He rounded the table at a run. "You little weasel. Look at him!" He pointed at Marrec. "He's nothing. He's given you nothing. I am the one who has given you all that makes you extraordinary. I gave you life. I gave you your talent. Have you never thought to ask yourself why?"

The count's face was flushed, his fists were clenched, and his lips showed white teeth beneath sneering lips. His temper was on the edge, and though Alain knew the reason why—knew the true reason—still he bade the count continue.

"Tell me. Why?"

The sneer became a smile, but one that chilled Alain by its facility. "Why so that I might give you even more. Give you power. Give you station. Give you a kingdom that together we could rule." The hands opened, pleaded, invited Alain into a fatherly embrace.

Alain stepped back and prepared to receive an attack. "I want no more from you," he said, letting his revulsion show. "If Marrec taught me anything—"

The count's roar echoed in both world and non-world. He

reached out with a hand that sang with power but instead of attacking Alain, Marrec went rigid as a post.

"What did Marrec teach you that can compare with this?"

Alain lunged to build a shield. A heavy crunch filled the room and the ploughman screamed. He was lifted to his feet as he screamed again and again. Alain thrust with power but found no grip on the count's attack. His thrusts glanced away in flares of azure. Another scream, followed by a sound like a breaking timber, and the screaming stopped. Marrec fell and Alain caught him, easing him to the floor.

"My son," he whispered, and went limp, mouth agape, dead eyes blank.

Alain stared. He tried to think, but every thought was drowned out by a sound that built in his ears, vague and sibilant. It grew, rising with each beat of his heart as he stared down into Marrec's slackened face. Finally, the sound imposed itself upon his consciousness. It was line-song, the seashell whispering of the lines in the void.

He looked at his hands and saw a pulsing light at his wrists. Blue light glowed along his hidden scars. He had opened a tap on the lines and their power coursed through him, infusing him wholly. He pulled at his sleeves, at the laces of his tunic, and revealed blue fire. His old shame burned. He thought of Marrec and his final shame. He thought of the Delphine and her lifelong shame. He looked at Guihomarc, his father, through the blue light of power and saw the source of it all. He sent his fury forth.

The count spasmed as the power made contact. Alain heard the triple song of his rising response. The shot came, but Alain was ready. Arcs of fiery light lanced away from him, striking sparks around the room.

The frozen onlookers, Briezh and Viking alike, broke from their stunned quietude. Sparks zipping around them, they overturned benches and tripped over themselves in their haste to flee the hall. Some of the older veterans held their ground, but most ran in the face of magic.

The shimmering song of his blood quickened. Alain tried to halt his anger and control the rush of power from the lines, but it only surged into him with renewed force.

Guihomarc took a step back, sensing the danger. Alain lunged and grabbed the count's wrist. The two men fumbled for weapons. Alain's came free first and Jessup's sword was suddenly at the count's throat.

Swords rang behind Alain, but neither man looked toward the noise. Guihomarc tried to pull away.

"Count, didn't you offer me your warm embrace. Is this not to your liking?"

The lines cried out and Alain felt himself pulled like a puppet by its strings. He flew backward into something solid but yielding. A man grunted and Alain looked up to see Wrdisten and an old soldier locked in close press. Alain scrambled to his feet, afraid for the clansman's life, but it was the soldier who coughed and slipped to the floor, his beard stippled with bright blood.

A phantom hand gripped Alain in a chorus of power. Alain lashed himself to the ley line and thrust back. The hum of their battle transcended the worlds. The air in the hall buzzed and spat.

"Wrdisten!" Alain shouted above the rising din. "Flee! Run for your life!" And then he could spare no moment for words or caring.

The vibration deepened. The air grew hot. Alain could feel power crackling along his skin, along the traceries of his body. He smelled the smoldering of his clothes and hair. He saw nothing except two eyes; black depths within deeper black, burning with power and anger. Alain pushed toward them, toward the mind beyond them. He heard a crack and felt the ground tremble. Still, he pushed. The line below him writhed and changed course. The sound of falling stone, the smell of fire, came close. He pushed. The line reached upward, alive. He felt it draw near him. It touched. He pushed. The eyes blinked. The world fell.

The roof rose like a leaf in the wind. With a banshee howl, it shattered and the ground shook Alain to his knees. He covered his head as stones fell and splinters rained from the sky. Dust filled the air. Wraiths of smoke ghosted past. Alain looked around through a pounding pain that thrashed behind his eyes.

The rear of the hall, where it connected to the other buildings of the inner keep, was a pile of burning timbers and smoking rubble. The walls and doors of the front had all been pushed out into the yard by the opposing tides of power. The center, however, where he stood, was clear.

A circle of ground, burnt and free of debris, marked the earth. In it were the pulverized bones of two corpses—Marrec and the soldier that Wrdisten had slain. There was nothing else. Guihomarc was not there. His body was not there.

Immediately and heedless of the pain, Alain sought the lines.

Guihomarc! The word went out, bounced back. Alain sought the reflection. It was close by. At the river bend. The ghosts of ships and running men.

Guihomarc!

One man turned, wincing, and looked up at the pillar of smoke that marked his former home.

"You disappoint me, son," he said. "Our alliance would have united all of Bretagne. The counties would have danced at our whim and even that stammering King Louis would have had to recognize us. And that, my son, is something desired by those even more powerful than I. Such a shame."

I shall be coming for you, Guihomarc. Alain tried to thrust his will beyond the vision and into the thoughts of the Count Vannes. Guihomarc grimaced as he deflected the attack. He shook his head in pain and regret.

"Such a shame." He turned and ran for the boats. In moments, he stood on deck as Northmen pulled at the oars and made for the not too distant sea. Alain could only watch him go.

"Fair One!"

Alain came back to the world around him. He turned, too fast, and went down on one knee, dizzy, pained head in his hands. Wrdisten was there.

"Are you injured? Can you walk?" Wrdisten urged him to his feet once more. "We must flee, for the folk of this place are frightened and angry." He led Alain out past the tumbled walls and burning doors into the yard. The clansman's sword was at the ready.

The yard was empty. Wrdisten pointed beyond the gate of the keep. Then Alain heard the rumble of voices, many voices, beyond the dust and smoke.

The walked onward.

They passed through the gate and smoke and into the fading light of the early autumn evening. Men and women stood along the downhill path. They were peasant folk from the keep and village, as well as a number of the count's guardsmen. Closed and angry faces went wide as Alain appeared in the gateway. A hush fell upon them. Some started toward the pair.

"We must go," Wrdisten said.

"No."

"Really, Fair One. We should go."

"You there," Alain said, pointing to one of the guardsmen. "Were you within the banquet hall this night?"

The man nodded.

"And did you hear how the Count addressed me?"

The man nodded again.

"How did he call me?"

The man mumbled a few words.

"Speak up. How did he call me?"

Another man stepped forward. Tall, thin, bald, he was not a soldier. "I was there, my lord," he said. "And I heard the Count call you son."

The crowd reacted as if burned.

"It is true," the thin man said to them. "Ask any of us who were there. This man is the count's only son and heir. Will any of you men deny it?"

"I did not hear him call the boy his heir," one of the guards said.

Alain stepped forward. "My father," he said, "Guihomarc, Count Vannes, has fled. He has committed crimes against the people of Vannes, and is not fit to rule. By his abandonment, and by his crimes, I call his title forfeit and claim it for myself."

"But you have no right—"

"I have *every* right," Alain shouted. "I am his son. His bastard, to be sure, but his son nonetheless. Tonight, he killed before witnesses and without cause the man who raised me. His evil drove my mother to madness. The northerners with whom he supped are the same raiders who burned my home and ruined my village. I have every right to call him down."

The thin man beside him turned and spoke. "There is more. Your pardon my lord," he said with a bow. "I am Boduos, late of lord Guihomarc's household, and steward of this keep. Not only did those Northmen raid along the Gulf of Morbihan this summer, but they did so at the Count's direction. Two chests of silver lay in the tower, presented to Guihomarc today as his portion of the season's booty."

The crowd found its voice, led by the Briezh guardsmen. This time, however, they called for the count's fall. Alain smiled at the thin steward.

"Boduos?"

"At your service, my lord Alain."

"You know my name?"

"Indeed. In fact, your arrival was most highly anticipated. I was surprised, however, when you arrived with only this man as your escort."

Alain's smile died. "You expected some of the count's men, perhaps?"

"Actually, no. I expected a friend of mine. She was looking for you as well."

Alain's smile returned. "There was a woman who accompanied me as far as Brest."

"Mistress Bronwyn?" Boduos grinned.

"The same."

The steward grew serious. "She is well?"

Alain put his arm around the steward's shoulder. "I hope that she is. She was not, when I left her, and it was her illness that kept her from joining me for the trip across the sea." He began to walk, back toward the gate and the ruined yard. "Guihomarc has fled with the Vikings, back to Vannes if I guess rightly. I need a ship to carry me back to Brest. Do you know where one might be had?"

Boduos nodded. "But it will not come cheaply, my lord. Most of the ships that pass by Sidmouth are en route to local ports to the east. Diverting them will be costly. Wait!" The steward slapped his forehead. "The silver! Guihomarc left behind those two chests. You could raise an army with what is in them."

Alain clapped the man on the shoulder. "Good," he said, relieved that it had all come across as the steward's idea. "We may have to do just that."

Guihomarc sat on the deck abaft, gently rubbing his eyes. He had not attempted a line-walk for many years. His head ached as it never had before and he feared any jar would crack it like an egg. It was, therefore, most unwelcome when he felt the brush of a deep sending.

He moaned and covered his ears as if it could keep the sending at bay. The whisper persisted. Guihomarc opened his mind.

Who? he asked curtly.

Dark eyes filled his mind and the count shuddered at the memory of his recent struggle with his son. A face formed around the eyes; pale skin, dark hair, high-boned cheeks. The ghost imposed itself upon his vision and Lord Rill stood in the gloom of the congealing night.

"What has happened?" There was an urgency in the Fey lord's tone.

"It is the boy." Guihomarc did not try to keep the weariness out of his voice. "He will not be controlled."

"He has damaged the Veil!"

Guihomarc could only nod.

"You knew of this power?" the lord asked.

"I had suspicions."

"And did not voice them? Inexcusable. You should have informed the Circle—"

"To what end?" Guihomarc exploded. "What would you have done that I have not done? I have tried kindness, entreaties, coercion, bribery, threats, malice, power. Name it."

"But you did not succeed," Rill said, voice calm.

"Obviously, I did not." Guihomarc pounded his knee. "He has grown too powerful too fast. Even so, I might have won him over but for that bitch Bronwyn. If she hadn't—"

"Bronwyn?"

The count stopped. He rose and faced the Fey lord. "Yes," he said. "Bronwyn. Do you know her?"

Rill shrugged. "Only by reputation."

"You are lying."

"How dare you!"

"Stop toying with me!" Guihomarc moved closer to the image of Rill. "Do you know her?"

Rill showed teeth and Guihomarc found he did not care about the Fey lord's threats.

"My relationship with the woman Bronwyn is of no concern to you," Rill said.

Guihomarc nodded. "That is answer enough. And it explains everything."

Rill looked down, removed a piece of lint from his gossamer sleeve. "Whither do you travel?" he asked.

"Home," Guihomarc answered him. "To consolidate what

power and strength is still left me. I must prepare for my son's homecoming. It seems, my Lord Rill, that in order to live, I must destroy my only son."

"If you do that, you do so against my wishes and against the desires of the Circle of Merddyn."

Guihomarc stared at the ghostly lord. "To be honest," he said evenly, "I wouldn't give a Frankish fart for the desires of the Circle."

Rill showed more teeth. Guihomarc took perverse pleasure in having caused the Fey lord such discomfiture. He bowed low, a mockery of respect. "If my Lord Rill devises any alternative plans, feel free to contact me." He closed his mind with as much force as he could. The image flickered and went dark. Guihomarc sat down on the cold wood of the deck.

"Get me some wine," he said to the worried Norseman next to him. "Be quick."

Bronwyn was in the common room, sipping spiced wine before the fire, when her cloak of privacy was breached. She swore under her breath and looked around at the other patrons. They were all engaged in their own conversations, but Nestor noticed her glance. He started over, but she waved him back, feigning fatigue.

There was only one person who could contact her in this way. Her mental cloak only hid her from talents on this side of the Veil. It could not hide her from the other side, especially from someone of such power.

"What are you doing?" Rill said, his question forming even before his image appeared before her. "You have endangered the Fair One by pitting him against Guihomarc."

The Fey lord's displeasure was obvious both by his tone and by the distracted expression on his face. Usually so calm, his brow was furrowed and his words came out in a rush.

That is Guihomarc's doing, not mine, she sent in return, not wanting to speak aloud in a roomful of merchants. *Count Vannes is trying to control the Fair One so he can ensure his position of value after the Return.*

Rill's preoccupied gaze found her and focused in. "The Fey will not Return to the world of Men if the Fair One is slaughtered in a duel!"

She had never seen Rill so upset, but she affected nonchalance. *Take that up with the Count. He's the one who is forcing the confrontation. I've worked merely to prepare the Fair One for the tasks that lie ahead.*

"And if Guihomarc is destroyed as a result?"

Bronwyn shrugged. *I will shed no tears over that. You know I wish to repay him for the deaths of my family.*

Rill calmed himself. "And what of my part in the affair?"

Bronwyn shrugged again. *You taught me yourself that there are some battles that cannot be won, and should never be joined. Costing you Guihomarc will be enough for me.*

Rill's laugh was dry and voiceless. "Your honesty is refreshing." He paused for a moment, and Bronwyn felt the intensity of his scrutiny. "Do not tamper with my plans, my dear. I will not risk the long-range outcome. Your past services to the Circle will not carry enough weight to spare you, should the Return be threatened."

Bronwyn sent him a warning note as Nestor appeared at her shoulder.

"Lady Betina, you seem weary," he said as he refilled her cup of wine. "Perhaps you should retire for the night. It would not do if Lord Al—"

"Soon," she said. Though Rill's impatient image was only visible to those attuned to the lines, he still might hear Nestor's words. "Thank you for your concern." When Nestor retreated, she returned her attention to Rill.

Lord Rill, we both know that it is not Guihomarc who is crucial to the Return of the Fey.

"True," Rill said. "But a tool that has proved useful in the past may prove useful again. I will try to save him, you know."

I know, she sent.

Rill had regained his composure, his features serene once more. "Very well. We will not speak again for some time." And he was gone, even more quickly than he had appeared.

Bronwyn sighed with relief. "Fine by me," she muttered, but was concerned.

Had Rill sensed her feelings for Alain? There was a moment when she thought he might have guessed at her true motives. Guihomarc's death would indeed be a great pleasure, but her love for Alain had complicated her plans. Achieving the deaths of both Guihomarc and the Fair One would have been a simple matter, though it was a revenge that would have cost her her life when Rill discovered it.   Keeping Alain alive was going to be much more difficult, and as for the Return, how he would survive it was anybody's guess.   She couldn't plan for that yet, however, and perhaps she never could.   The Fair Folk set schemes that would play out years, decades, even *centuries* into the future.   She did not have the long sight of the Fey.   For her, it was today, tomorrow, and maybe a few years ahead.   It would have to be good enough.

For now.

eighteen

The sun laid its warm hand on the nape of Alain's neck as the smoky town came into view.

"Praise God," said Boduos from his kneeling place. He had spent the whole journey at the gunwale and had brought up more from his stomach than a man two times his size might have held. Wrdisten stood nearby, one arm lashed about the mast. He, too, had not moved the whole of the night and day it had taken them to make the passage from Sidmouth to Brest.

"'Tis unnatural," he said. "A man should ne'er be out of sight of land."

Alain smiled and patted the clansman's shoulder. "You've done quite well. I must say, though, that this passage was much more enjoyable than my last one."

The rest of the ship's deck was filled with a score of Briezh guardsmen. The news of Nordic raiders in their homelands brought concern to many with family left behind. Boduos' assertion that the raids were the result of a secret pact between Norsemen and the Count was enough to turn them all to Alain's side.

"My men," he said to Wrdisten with amazement. "*My* men. I never thought of such a thing."

"You will need many more," said Boduos from the rail. "Guihomarc has a full garrison at Vannes and will raise more from the neighboring lands. He has strong alliances with Counts Lorient and Nantes." He burped and grimaced. "It will take more than my word to turn either of those two, and surely more men than this to defeat them."

Alain sighed. "I hope it will not come to that."

"I would suggest that you raise the might first and worry about the need later."

"Aye," said Wrdisten. "That is wise counsel."

Alain said nothing more. The sun caressed him. The waves sang a salty trio with the hull and the rigging. Slowly, the shore approached.

"Do you see her?" Boduos asked.

"Hm?"

"Our mutual friend. Can you see her yet?"

"Ah, I wasn't looking. She doesn't know of our impending return."

Boduos managed a weak laugh. "You've not known her long, then, if you think that. Where there is news to be had, Mistress Bronwyn will have it."

Alain looked to shore, scanning the docks and along the quay. Men moved in the bright daylight. Masts danced, happily out of step with one another. At the end of the main pier stood a person who was not on any errand of commerce. A robed figure. Alain studied and saw that it was Bronwyn. She did not wave. She just stood at the end of the planking, the wind occasionally lifting a lock of hair or tugging at the hem of her cloak. Patient as the tide.

Hello, he sent and saw her far-off smile. *How did you know?*

After such a racket, it was not hard to guess.

Alain smiled and felt a certain tension within him unknot. Boduos spied her, too, and for a brief moment, mustered the strength to stand and wave.

"Haloo," Boduos shouted. Bronwyn waved back and Boduos collapsed once more.

"That is she?" Wrdisten asked. "That is your companion?"

Alain turned, troubled by the clansman's tone. "Yes. Why? Don't tell me you know her, too."

Wrdisten shook his head. "I cannot say I know her. But I have seen her."

"Seen her? Where?"

"At Guihomarc's keep on the Sid. And at the sacred stone circles, too. She's one to be watched."

"Let me tell you this plainly. Bronwyn has been a good companion during my past months. She has helped me where no others would. I have trusted her with my life."

Wrdisten studied Alain's face. "Aye," he said and looked away. "Well enough. But take care. That woman is dangerous."

Alain smirked. "On that point I will give no argument."

The ship set anchor and began ferrying passengers and cargo to the docks. Boduos was left behind to oversee the transfer of their belongings while Alain and Wrdisten went over with the first boatload.

Bronwyn's smile was a beacon. When Alain climbed the ladder and finally stood on the pier, her smile broadened. Fresh tears joined it. She walked to him, put her arms about his shoulders, and buried her face in the crook of his neck. He held her tightly.

"I was so worried," she whispered. "I have never heard such a battle. The whole world rang with it."

"Guihomarc still lives," he said. "He has fled to Vannes with help of allies from the north."

"Yes," she said. She kissed him swiftly and took his arm. "I know. We'll discuss what comes next back at Nestor's. There is much yet to—Oh, my."

Alain laughed. The clansman stood before her, scowling, his hair bright and his tattoos dark in the sunlight. "Bronwyn, this fierce man is called Wrdisten, late of Clan Garw in the Sid Valley. Wrdisten, meet Lady Betina, whom I call Bronwyn."

Wrdisten bowed from the neck, his mane of hair white and stiff. Bronwyn sniffed.

"I have brought others with me," he told her. "Boduos, who says that he knows you. Guardsmen too, have come along. A score and three, formerly of the count's service."

"Are they pledged to you?"

"No. They are men Guihomarc left behind and who fear for their families. They are against Guihomarc, if that is what you mean."

"Good enough," she said. "For now. But come. I've set things in motion. There is much to do." She touched his cheek. "I am glad you are well."

They walked on to Nestor's, Wrdisten picking up the rear.

"She is wrong," Wrdisten said. He sat on the floor, eschewing the use of a chair. He eyed the walls of the small room suspiciously, as if they were about to leap at him.

"Ridiculous," Bronwyn said. "It is faster if we take the road. Besides, the news will follow the road. Everyone along it will be expecting us."

"To my concern, exactly."

"He will gain support as he travels. I have seen to that."

"And anyone wishing to oppose him will know just where to find him. I say we take the hill routes."

Alain watched the argument proceed, point by point. He wanted to be a leader to this group, but he wanted also their counsel. Neither Bronwyn nor Wrdisten would deign to admit defeat or any validity to the other's reasoning. Boduos, as keeper of the monies and *de facto* steward, sat patiently.

"What do you think, Steward?"

Boduos considered his words before he spoke. "I think that men will fight more cheaply for their own land than for another's. And men who have felt the wrath of a lord's disdain and neglect will fight for even less." He touched a finger to the charcoal markings Bronwyn had made on the tabletop. "What lies between us and Guihomarc?"

Alain thought of his travels. "Kemper," he said. "Then Kemperle, and Lorient. You mentioned Lorient, Boduos. An ally to Guihomarc?"

Boduos nodded. Bronwyn frowned. Wrdisten crossed his arms upon his chest and leaned back looking pleased.

"We take the road," Alain said.

"What?" they all said at once.

Alain reviewed them: clansman, sorceress, steward. "If I am to replace my father, I will need the will of the people behind me. I cannot win that by creeping in the back door like a thief. But neither do I want ranks made up of mercenary men."

Bronwyn leaned forward. "But we shall arrive in Lorient with little more than a color guard."

Alain nodded. "Agreed. But I will not war with Lorient. My disagreement is with Guihomarc and not with any of his neighbors."

"They are his *allies*. Boduos says so."

"Once beyond Lorient and in the vicinity of Vannes, we can send out a call for volunteers. We will regroup at Belvanetes and march on Guihomarc."

"To raise such numbers in such a short time." Boduos shook his head. "I cannot see it done."

"Your pardon, Steward, but you have been far from Vannes for a long time and do not know the timbre of the people in my region. I do not think we will have any trouble." He was sure of his sense of the locals. He stood, and the two men stood with him. "Good. Now, I wish to speak to the men." The others inclined their heads and Alain felt suddenly every bit a leader. He bowed in return and went downstairs.

His entrance to the common room of Nestor's inn was like walking into a hill barrow. The guardsmen sat glumly in a group near the door. Filled cups were sipped slowly and without relish.

They stood as Alain approached. The one named Simon offered up his place. Alain took it and sat, motioning the others to do likewise. They did. Those not at the table came close as well, leaning in to hear. Alain regarded twenty somber faces, all waiting for him to speak.

For a moment the words did not come. He was ready, willing, and anxious to speak to them, but the only words that came to him were the ones he had said as he left Josselyn.

"I left my home in Belvanetes early this summer. I had never been anywhere before that time. I did not leave by choice. I was thrown out. As I left, I said that when I returned I would be a great man." Some of the guards smiled. Simon poured him some wine.

"What I meant was that when I returned, I would be powerful enough to punish them all. I would make their lives miserable because of their treatment of me." He sipped.

"Since then, I have been treated more poorly than at nearly any other time in my life. I have also been treated more grandly than ever before. I have seen what being a great man can bring, and what it can cost.

"Recently, a man offered me his blade. I took it before I knew it would cost him his home, his wife, his son. Just for following me, he gave up these things." He looked at each of them, one by one. "And so I say to all of you: know that I am the bastard son of Guihomarc of Vannes and the Delphine of Dead Ox Wood. Know that by opposing him I forfeit all, and that those who follow me may well do likewise." He stood.

"Those who wish it may collect five silver coins from Boduos and be on their way. Most of you have family. Some even have station, I would wager. I have neither and can lose none. But to those of you who may follow me against Guihomarc, I say this. Briezh lands are for the Briezh people, not for the pillage of Norsemen, nor for the rule of Franks. Marrec, my foster father pushed Charles the Bald back to Angers. I can push Guihomarc at least as far. We make for Vannes as soon as horses can be procured."

He stood and turned to take his leave. Simon faced him. The man was solemn, blue eyes steady. The worry that creased his knitted brow formed the only lines on his youthful face.

"You are an honorable man, my lord."

Alain shrugged.

"No, my lord. Truly. I've seen your father, seen him kill with his own hands. He is cruel. There is no honor in him." Simon held out his hand.

Alain looked at the youth, at the offered handshake. He looked at his own hands and remembered them red and slick with another's blood.

"These hands have killed, too, Simon. I am not free of that particular stain." He looked again at the man, only a few years younger than himself. The hand remained outstretched, and Alain clasped it. "Good night," he said.

He left them.

"Make sure they have what food and drink they wish," he told Nestor. Then he climbed the stairs to the room he would share with Wrdisten for the night.

In the morning, he and Wrdisten descended the creaking stairs. The common room, where the men had passed the night, was empty except for Boduos, seated by the fire.

"They are all gone during the night." The leather purse in his hands chuckled with the sound of silver. "They took nothing, for what comfort that provides. But I had thought better of them. I truly had."

"Do not blame them," Alain said. "They fear for loved ones left behind. Perhaps they fear me as well." He sat across from the steward. "And what of you? On which shore is your family?"

The thin man's smile was bittersweet. "My heart does not fall to women in the way of most men. Thus, I have no wife or child.

But neither does my mind lend favor to sectarian ways, and my years with the good brothers ended with my schooling. The best I thought I could hope for I had already achieved: steward of a minor keep of a powerful lord." He looked up. His voice was thick with emotion. "And then you came."

Alain thought on the ruin he had brought the steward. A life's toil, destroyed. Words of defense came to him but sounded hollow to his mind and he did not speak them. "I am sorry," was all he said.

"No. Do not apologize." The steward leaned forward in earnestness. "You showed me that there was more to which I might aspire. For, more than just the servant of a powerful lord, I might be the friend to a great man."

Alain sat back in his chair. The steward's face was open, honest. Alain could hear no guile in the words.

"I will do what I can to be worthy of such a claim."

There was a sound behind them. Bronwyn entered. Her fancy gown put away, she was once more dressed as she had been when Alain had met her: a simple dress and cloak. She scanned the room.

"You are determined to do this? Without troops? I can raise a double hundred men between here and Lorient."

Alain looked about him as well, as if searching for something unseen. "Why, my dear Lady Betina. I see here all that I need. A fierce warrior, a loyal steward, and a sorceress of politics. What else could I desire?" He stood and smiled.

"Shall we make plans for our travels?"

The journey that had taken Alain a sweat-soaked summer of toil to make took him only four overcast days to retrace. True to her words, each town showed that Bronwyn's news of their coming had preceded them.

On the first day, they passed through Kemper. Shops emptied and homes were left vacant as people lined the road through town. As the four riders dismounted at the well to pull water for their horses, they were met by a retinue of men. Eight armed guardsmen stood behind an abbot and three townsmen of ample girth. A fifth man, dark of both dress and mood, sat astride a horse. Alain dismounted and bowed. The abbot stepped forward from the group.

"You are Alain of Belvanetes, son of Guihomarc of Vannes?"

"Aye, Abbot. I am." The men with the abbot, their clothing less indicative of their office, exchanged glances but said nothing.

"And do you follow the teachings of the Christ?"

"Your pardon, Abbot, but as do many from my home in Belvanetes, I follow the old faith. It was taught to me by my mother. Yet the mistress of the house where I grew up is a follower of the Christ. I bear no ill will toward your faith, and in that I am a good sight better than my father."

"You call Count Vannes a blasphemer?" The abbot's face was red and splotchy.

"Again, your pardon. A blasphemer? No. It is only that my father lacks what I believe is proper respect for your religion. With me, here, is the steward of Count Vannes, who assures me that Guihomarc is no man of Christ. In fact, the last cleric to visit Guihomarc was thrown out on his ear. The Count called the good man...what was the phrase again, Boduos?"

Boduos looked miserable. "A worthless turd, Lord Alain."

"Ach, yes." Alain turned and stared boldly at the abbot. "Quite disrespectful, you would agree I'm sure, Lord Abbot." The abbot took a breath.

"If I may," interrupted the mounted nobleman. "Dear Abbot, excuse me please." The dark man slipped down off his horse. He handed the reins to one of the abbot's colleagues. "Walk with me," he said, leaving behind the fuming abbot.

Alain fell into step beside the nobleman. The man was dressed in fine clothes of black and grey cloth. His pale hair was straight and hung long down his back. His mustache was thick and ruddy brown while his beard had been shaved clean in the Briezh style.

"Do you know who I am?" he asked.

"You are Lord Glímarec, the Count Kemper."

"We have met?"

"No, my lord, but you are known to some of those in my retinue." Count Kemper looked over his shoulder at Alain's comrades.

"I will speak plainly, Alain. I do not favor Guihomarc of Vannes. The merchant guildsmen of this region are blaming him for losses in trade and import. He abandons his lands regularly, leaving them open to pillage and disruption. And he is a pompous sprite who would sell his mother for a Frankish nod." He looked again at the gathering by the well. "On the other hand, I must contend with the abbot and the bishop. They do not trust the ambitions of a bastard, much less one who openly supports the old faith. Nor will they allow me to support such a man, regardless his foe. They want stability in our county, as do I. The church is strong here in Kemper, and I must consider their wishes if I am to rule justly."

Alain stopped. "Perhaps I may ease your mind. My quarrels are with a man in Morbihan and with no one in Finistére. Likewise, the crimes that man committed were done in Morbihan, against people who live in Morbihan. It would not do to take the men of Finistére to a fight in which they have no interest."

"Ah. Just so." His words were solemn but the count could not keep the relief from his face. "It is war, then?"

"I believe so, my Lord Count. And if you will permit us to water our horses and procure a bit of food, we will be on our way to it."

Count Kemper held out his hand. Alain clasped it and sealed their agreement.

"I wish you well, Alain Belvanetes."

They topped the rise between a stand of alder, four lone riders in the sparse line of merchants who drove their wagons and carts down to the crossroads of Lorient. Bronwyn's gaze followed the ancient road of Rome as it cut a swath across rolling hilltops. A quarter mile distant, she spied where a second road left the first and headed downhill to the right. Through trees and beyond fields of harvested grain, she could see the waterfront town of Lorient. Ships plowed the waters of the river mouth and the sea beyond in search of fish and trade. Bronwyn and her companions passed the trees and came to a halt.

"What is it," Boduos asked. "Why have we stopped?" Three arms lifted, pointing to the hilltop to the left of the crossroads. "Oh," Boduos said. "I see. Oh, dear."

Bronwyn peered up at the height. "How many are there?" she asked.

"Half a hundred. Plus a dozen or so on horse." Wrdisten swore. "We should have left this road leagues ago."

"Hush," she told the clansman. "Think toward what we

should do, not what should have been done."

"Very well," he said. "You were the one who wanted to travel this road. What should we do?"

"I don't know. I expected we would have twice their number by this time."

"Stop it," Alain commanded. Bronwyn stopped mid-word. "This place is not our aim," he said. "I will not be stopped here."

"Alain, we need men. Even the savage and I will agree on that." Wrdisten bristled but said nothing to challenge her. "We are in Morbihan now. When do you propose to begin recruiting troops?"

Alain rubbed his brow and frowned. He closed his eyes and took a deep breath. As he let it out, he looked up toward the ridge for a long, lingering moment.

"Now," he said. "I shall begin now." He started his horse forward. "Stay here. All of you."

Bronwyn stepped her horse up to his. "What do you plan to do? Are you going to ride up to them and just ask for some soldiers?"

"Yes, my dear Bronwyn," he said without looking back. "That is my plan exactly."

She watched him ride ahead alone. The men atop the rise stood in the sunlight, watching the road. She and the others were still too far away for their identity to have been guessed.

"Go on," she said to Wrdisten. "Go with him."

Wrdisten sat his horse and folded his arms. He grinned broadly and watched. "I'll do no such a thing."

"You idiot. He can't go up there alone."

"Och, but he can. The Fair One can do many things beyond the scope of mere men."

Bronwyn stared at the clansman. "What did you call him?"

"Fair One." His gaze had not left the lone figure riding on ahead of them. "Though he does not care to be called so."

Bronwyn's eyes narrowed. "Perhaps there is more to you than I thought."

"Ha. I expect I exceed your opinion before I finish my morning piss."

Bronwyn's jaw dropped. She looked at Boduos, but he was busy trying to hide a smile behind an insufficient hand. She heard a shout from up ahead and further argument was postponed.

A man on horse rode down from the hilltop to intersect Alain's path. Bronwyn reached beyond the world to pull a jangling of power from the lines. Alain looked back over his shoulder. He made no overt motion.

Leave it be, came the sending.

"The fool," she said, but while she released the line, she did not release the power she had drawn. She held it, refined it, preparing a hundred sharp shards for flight. She knew they would not stop an enemy, but they would buy her some time. Alain rode up to the rider from the hill. Boduos leaned forward in his saddle.

"I think I know that boy," he said.

"Who?"

"The boy there with Alain. He's a merchant's son from Vannes. One of several who bought a post in service to Guihomarc."

Alain and the rider spoke a few words. Bronwyn saw Alain nod and the two men began riding up the hillside to the gathered force.

"That's enough," Bronwyn breathed. "I'm going to him."

A hand clamped onto her arm. Wrdisten shook his head.

"Please, do not." He released her arm.

Alain and the rider reached the top of the rise. A grey-haired rider moved forward.

"That's old Lorient," said Boduos. "I would swear to it."

Bronwyn stared intently. Boduos was right. Lorient and Alain exchanged greetings. Then Alain said something and the grey-haired man threw back his head in laughter.

"Ach. Epona's mane. He really did ask the old man for troops."

Then the old count, still laughing, turned his mount. Alain's companions watched slack-jawed as the count and three of his riders moved off down the hill, leaving Alain on the hilltop with a score of horsemen and fifty fighting men. Alain waved.

"He says to come ahead," Bronwyn told the others.

Wrdisten grin burst into laughter. He kicked his horse into motion and was galloping through the grass. Boduos smiled.

"Well," the steward said. "That's fine, then." His horse, too, started on its way, though much more slowly than the clansman.

Bronwyn did not move for several breaths. Finally, her mount began to walk of its own accord, undesirous of being left behind.

"Go on," she said to the beast. "Do what you want. There's no point in you listening to me either, I suppose." Her mount shook its head and trotted along to join its fellows.

"See, Mistress Bronwyn?" Boduos was gleeful as she rode up to the crowd on the hilltop. "There's Locmariquer. And there's Simon. Merchant boys all, from the group that we brought with us from Sidmouth. They've come back. And they've brought friends. Isn't it wonderful?"

Bronwyn grumbled softly but otherwise kept her council. She rode up as Alain was speaking to one of the men on horseback.

"We went to our homes," Simon was saying. "All of us. We vowed to gather as many as we could. Simon and me, well, our fathers were more than sympathetic. More are to meet us at Carnac. I've sent a rider ahead to prepare them."

Alain reached and clasped the young guard's arm, just as he had done the night back in the inn. "Well done, Simon," he said, and his smile was reflected in the face of the young rider. "Thank you. Ah, Bronwyn. You've heard the news?"

"You are a very lucky man, Alain of Dead Ox Wood."

"Am I?" he asked. He closed his eyes and sighed. She noticed for the first time the sunken patches of blue beneath his eyes, the tight lines at the corner of his mouth. He looked up into the cloud-strewn sky. "Sometimes I wonder."

At Carnac, three score men stood waiting in the fog, eerie twins to the standing stones that guarded the cliffs above the sea. At Ploéven, they met fifty more. Alain sent riders to the hills to spread the call, and riders ahead to prepare the way.

The harvest was done, and food was plentiful. The count's silver went back into the hands of the people who had lost it. The home-grown soldiers kept their order well under Wrdisten's watchful eye, and every village they passed swelled their numbers by pairs and handfuls.

By the time they reached the road to Belvanetes, Alain rode with Bronwyn and Wrdisten at the head of over three hundred men and riders. His horse carried him up the river road, past the bend in the river where Norsemen had anchored and where swallows still dipped and flew. The fields here lay unworked, though some crops still stood ready for the sickle. He pointed to the low white wall on the far edge of the fields.

"That was my second home."

"It is a fine place," Wrdisten said. "Is that where your child lives?"

Bronwyn gasped and Alain winced. He did not turn, but glared sidelong at Wrdisten. The clansman caught the look, snuck a peek at the lady at Alain's side, and subsided.

"A child?" Bronwyn asked, and Alain gritted his teeth.

"A child yet unborn."

"Hunh," she said, and would say no more.

At the center of the village, they were met by the whole of Belvanetes. Alain, dressed in fine clothes, a sword at his hip, sat atop his horse and looked down on the faces from his youth. He tried to keep the haughtiness he felt from showing. The people of his home were stone-faced and gave him no clue as to his success or failure.

His horse whickered and stamped in the uneasy atmosphere.

With the slightest of nods, he greeted old acquaintances. Erol, Faustin, Amelie, the priest Anton; faces from another time, another life. In the fore of the crowd was Calin. Beside him stood Charles, and beyond him, was Josselyn.

Josselyn's grey eyes smiled upon him, though her lips did not. Her hair was pulled up in the manner of married women, and a dress of fine linen embroidered with threads of indigo and gold, covered her swelling belly. Around her neck, he spied a leather strand with beads of blue and white hiding beneath her collar.

Alain dismounted and walked up to Charles. He was light complected, as were most people of the region, but his hair was dark, curled, almost black, and his face was clean-shaven. He wore garments of fine cloth, a woolen cap, and carried a sword at his hip.

"Master Charles," he said with a nod. "I heard that you have married my longtime friend."

The man nodded in return, but did not bow. Alain heard the creak of leather as some of those behind him took offense, but he stilled them with a backward glance. "Yes," Charles said. "I have. You must be Alain. We have heard much news of your coming."

"Then you have heard that we march on your father's lord."

"Yes. I had hoped to meet you on the field. Your purpose will win you no friends here."

Alain smiled. "I expected none. We will leave you." He

turned to Wrdisten. "Pass the word. Not a speck of food or a drop of wine is to be asked of the people of Belvanetes. We will not bother these good people with our coin or our presence. Make for that ridge up there, and set camp on the far side." Wrdisten nodded and turned to spread the order among the men.

Alain pulled himself back into his saddle. Charles' displeasure was obvious, pinching his brow and souring his face. Alain cared little now how much his own distaste might show. What he noted most was the looks of displeasure that the villagers aimed not at Alain, but at Charles. The loss of the army's silver would not sit well with them.

"We will bother you no more, Master Charles. My best regards to your wife."

A whisper.

Alain set the autumn berries on the stones piled on the grave at the foot of the great tree. The shiny surface of the pond was broken by the snapping of a fish. Spears of sunlight pierced the canopy and water faeries danced along the underside of branches.

Another whisper.

Alain closed his mind, blocking, blanking, dreaming of sky, sea, air, water.

Son.

He felt the quester sift through his thoughts.

You are so easy. I call. You come.

Alain stopped fighting the intrusion. "I come because I wish it—not because you call."

Do you?

"Why couldn't you have been a proper father?"

A pause. *You came to your talent too late.* Then, *Why are you not a proper son?*

"You made me what I am!"

Willful? Disobedient?

Alain relented. He sat, leaning against the tree that cradled his mother's grave. "I cannot do what you wish me to do."

You cannot rule?

"I cannot forget."

A damselfly flew into the sunlight, suddenly ablaze, a stick of hovering fire.

Alain. If you continue, you will make yourself enemies far greater than me.

"I do not care, Father. I have always had enemies."

Not like these.

Silence.

Very well, Guihomarc sent. *But if you must do battle with me, let us do it alone.*

Alain squinted and frowned. "What do you mean?"

If we must meet, let us spare our loyals who will surely die. Let it just be us two alone. We can settle this ourselves.

Alain thought of all the men, the young faces, many younger than his own, who had followed him, joined with his forces. Many would die getting him close enough to Guihomarc to do battle. The garrison of Vannes would not let them walk in unchallenged.

"If you are willing to meet me, I must agree."

Good. Let us meet in the Wood. At dawn. Until then.

Alain sighed, the frown still tight upon his features. He tossed a pebble into the water. The damselfly fled.

Toward evening Alain rested against a saddle and watched Wrdisten cook roots over the fire. Bronwyn and Boduos sat nearby, each gazing into the flames, their thoughts very far away.

Alain's mind touched the ley line under Dead Ox Wood. *Bronwyn,* he sent. *Lend me your thoughts.*

She closed her eyes and he heard her answer. *You wouldn't want them. They are not kind.*

Tell me anyway, he sent.

She looked at him. He heard her falter at the lines, unused to sending while viewing the real world. After a few moments, her thoughts came through. *She is with child.* There was no question in the sending. *The child is yours.* Again, fact, not query.

She says it is mine.

Do you believe her?

He balked. *I...I had not thought to question.*

Bronwyn shook her head. *Always the trusting fool. How long have you known?*

Alain thought back. *I learned just after leaving you in Brest.*

An eyebrow rose. *Just after word of your claim to the county seat would have reached Vannes, you mean?*

He frowned. *Aye.* He caught sight of smiling teeth and

looked to find Wrdisten, arms on his knees, grinning at them.

"The two of ye are talking, nae true? I can fairly see the words flying out yer heads, back and forth. Aye?"

Alain could not help but smile. Bronwyn, too, was amused by the clansman's enthusiasm. "You caught us."

"I *knew* it," Wrdisten said with a shake of his head. "Amazing. It's like sitting amongst the gods."

"Your pardon, my lord." Two men approached. One stood back while the other came into the light of the fire. It was Simon.

"This man," he said. "He says he knows you."

Alain looked closer. "Calin?"

"Aye." Josselyn's steward stepped closer. He was dressed in warm tunic and cloak. In his right hand, he held a thick-bladed sword, its leather scabbard scarred and dark with age. In his left hand, he carried a cloth sack big enough for a few items of clothing and perhaps a blanket; all that he owned.

"Calin," he said, understanding.

"I heard the tale at Erol's. About how the bastard count did the ploughman foul." His toughness crumbled and his face split in a grimace of grief. "Let me fight, boy. Let me fight."

Alain walked to the old steward, feeling his own grief renewed by Calin's blatant feelings of loss. He put a hand to the old man's neck and drew him close, forehead to forehead. He gazed into the steward's tear-filled eyes and whispered.

"If there is to be a fight on the morrow, I promise you a fair portion."

Calin breathed a shaky breath. "Bless you, Alain."

"Wrdisten," Alain said, turning. "Here's a man for you. He fought with my father against Charles the Bald. He may have grown older, but he knows more than a little of the art of war. You and Simon, take him down and put him to good use."

Bronwyn came up beside Alain as the soldiers walked off down the hill. "If there's a battle, he'll die, you know."

Alain nodded.

"Don't you think that's what he wants?"

The ridgeline overlooked the dark vale that lay between his men and the walls of Vannes. Fires marked the corners of the city perimeter, and torches plied the dark void, carried to and fro by unseen guardsmen.

Silently, Alain tended the campfire, his cloak wrapped tightly about his spare frame. Bronwyn slept a few strides away, her face ruddy in the dim firelight. Boduos, unused to such conditions, lay huddled like a hedgehog under a cloak and two horse blankets. Alain gave him a nod of respect, though, for he had not heard a word of complaint from the count's former steward.

Wrdisten had insisted on sleeping—if indeed he slept this night—down with Calin and the men so that he might more closely oversee the patrols and pickets. The young and old who had joined Alain's ranks had taken easily to Wrdisten's command. The clansman, by his fierce mien and oddly accented speech, won their attention. By his example and loyalty to Alain, as well as by a competence at leadership, he had earned their respect. Alain had left the settling of the camp to him and had not been disappointed.

Sleep visited in brief stays filled with visions of violent trees, circles of sky, and precipitous drops from which he awoke breathless and afraid.

When he saw the morning star wink above the sleeping darkness of Dead Ox Wood, he placed the last twigs on the somnolent coals, picked up his sword, and crept off into the dreaming dawn.

The path to the edge of the wood was easily found, guided as he was by the twin lights of moon and star. Within the wood, beneath the skirts of its spreading branches, it soon became too dark and Alain was forced to halt.

He waited patiently for his eyes to adjust to the gloom. Slowly, a blue world rose about him, at first fleeing from his every glance, finally trusting him enough to let itself be viewed.

The gnarled torsos of giants twisted upward toward their branches. He walked among their trunks and listened as the morning began to stir and the nighttime creatures grumbled off to bed.

The wide-eyed songbirds gave first voice to the bluing sky. Squirrels cleaned their faces of dew. An owl wafted her noiseless way back to her roost. He felt them all, the mouse curling in his den, the fish eyeing the dawning light from above, the trees in their silent procession toward autumn.

He walked slowly through the fallen leaves, hearing the creatures of the wood, but sensing something else, as well.

Something new. A vibration that did not belong.

He came to the Delphine's hut and paused. The hut was dark, but it seemed more than dark. He took a step closer in the growing light. The broken door lay on the ground and thatch had spilled from where Reynald had smashed his way inside. Leaves had begun to gather on the moldering roof and within the doorway. It was more than dark. It was dead, the empty shell of a life Alain could hardly believe had been his.

The feeling of wrongness increased as he stood outside the hut. He opened his mind. The lines were active. Their natural song filled the non-world, but the song had been changed, modified. It carried another tone that lay deep and full of power. He traced the sound, turning as he sought its source. Up ahead, toward the pool where the Delphine lay buried. He started that way.

His unease grew as he walked. He listened to the sleeping spirits of the wood, but heard nothing out of order. It was the lines and the lines alone, and he did not know what might be disturbing them.

Blaring sound hit his mind, buffeting him. He fell backward, lost his bearings. He grasped for the line but could not find it. Power hit him again. Guihomarc was there, had been there, waiting to strike.

The massive blow sent him tumbling. He blinked and saw two skies, side by side. He turned his head and saw the pool reflecting light, sky above, sky below. He shook his head and grabbed for power. There was none. The lines were there, he could hear them ringing from his father's blows. They lay below him, deep below the Wood, the heart of the mountain, but something interposed itself, cutting off his access.

He thrust with all his mind and might, trying to go around, to skirt the obstacle. It blocked him, blinding his mind with black cloth. He was helpless, once more the Bastard Boy unable to reach the goal. He rose to his feet.

Guihomarc stood before him, leaning against a tree. The pale light glinted from his eyes and he smiled his perfect smile.

"Hello, Son," he said. The blast hit Alain along every inch of his body, slamming him backward and filling his vision with shouting stars.

Alain reached again for power, the slightest power to ward off the blows, but still met only blankness, numbness where before there had been talent.

"What have you done to me?" he shouted.

"Put you in your place, boy." The next blow came from the toe of a boot and Alain doubled up in agony, tasting blood. He fought for breath.

The lines rang with power each time Guihomarc used them. Bronwyn would hear it, he knew. Guihomarc knew that, too. She'll come, he thought. Why doesn't he finish me? He can't fight us both.

As the thought crossed his mind the lines rang out again, but this time it was Bronwyn: bells pealing with ragged, unprepared magic. Alain looked up. Guihomarc laughed.

"I hope you weren't counting on her, Son. She's quite occupied with the attack."

"Fall back!"

Men ran down the slope as a double rank of Norsemen came howling over the ridgeline. In the vale behind the retreating troops, lines of archers formed, waiting for the enemy to be pushed downhill into range.

"Do something," Wrdisten shouted. "He called you sorceress. Do something." Bronwyn pulled from the lines and sent power crashing into the oncoming men. Two fell, but dozens continued on.

"There are too many," she told Wrdisten. "I can only slow them down."

The clansman turned and shouted to Calin. "Get up behind them. We will hold here!"

Riders bolted to their horses. Calin's voice cut through the sounds of fierceness and terror. "Branch your forces," he shouted to Wrdisten and his troops of boys gone white with fright. "Funnel them in! Fight, you bastards!"

Bronwyn pulled more power. She sent a flock of painful needles into the attackers. Some stumbled but none fell. She pulled more power, more than she had ever wielded before.

Guihomarc stood over Alain and laughed again. Alain felt the old rage rise within his breast.

He planted his feet and lunged. He bowled Guihomarc

backward toward the trunk of an oak. The count hit with a whoosh of air and a shout of pain. Alain drew Jessup's sword and reached one last time for the lines while Guihomarc stood staggered. Nothing. He raised his sword to strike.

An unseen hand grabbed his arm and spun him around. The sword flew from his grasp and stabbed point down in the forest mulch. Alain gaped as he saw a man in a circle of light. Tall, thin-boned, he wore a gown of woven sunshine. His eyes and hair were dark as night. His long-fingered hands reached out.

Bells sounded again and again as Bronwyn fought on the ridge, and the man of the Fair Folk smiled as he came forward slowly, his aura of light extending with his every step, the summer grass growing up through the leaf-strewn floor of Dead Ox Wood.

"My colleague came up with another solution," Guihomarc said as he caught his breath. "You are the key to both our ventures, Son, but he thought you might be more easily controlled from his side of the Veil."

The vibration of the lines, Alain's inability to draw power, it did not come from Guihomarc. It came from the Fey. Alain tried to step back but found that now even his body refused to respond. Panic touched him as the strange man drew closer. Alain recoiled, but only his mind responded, pulling away from the danger of the lines, the Fey, the world. He reached for the only thing left: the spirits of the dreaming gods.

His sight flowed with light and motion. The spirits of Dead Ox Wood surrounded him. He reached for the spirit of the wind. It rushed into his mind and he cried out as it filled him, stretched him, surrounded him. He took it in, fusing with it in point and purpose, and then he aimed it.

The wind's spirit pounced as the solid world returned to Alain's sight. The Fey lord faltered in his approach, buffeted by the sudden gusts. Branches fell from gale-wracked trees, striking Guihomarc and his accomplice.

The Fey's concentration faltered, and Alain could move again. He did so, but Guihomarc came up from behind and struck him to the ground. The man of light stepped forward against the force of the wind. Alain tried to scramble away but found himself bound once more by the Fey's magic. He saw cuts on the Fey's fair cheeks and on his arm where he held it up to ward off debris.

The Fey reached for him. The light moved to surround Alain and he felt the grass grow beneath him. The sound of wind and blowing leaves was muted as the Fey came close and grabbed Alain by the wrist.

Guihomarc hung on to the trunk of a tree, trying to remain upright in the furious blow. The air tore at his cloak and at the length of his sword. Alain glanced over at his own sword, stuck point down in the earth, and called to it as well.

He pushed at the spirit that swirled around them, tempting its ire. The wind spun and blew a course around them through the rattling trees. Then with a focus of desire, he coaxed it into a hand, a fist. It tore through the forest in a flurry of leaves, punching through the underbrush. It hit Jessup's sword at the hilt, and the sword's spirit awoke. Memories of battles raged within it. Jengland-Breslé. Redon. Mayenne. The fierceness of war, the taste of blood. Alain urged it, called it to action. It knew its purpose. It flew to the attack.

The sword shot forward, torn spinning from its earthen sheath. Sunlight from beyond the Veil glinted on hilt and blade as they drove ahead and pierced the Fey high in the breast, just under the collarbone. The Fey released Alain and fell back. Dark blood stained the robes of light. The grass retreated, the light was blown out, and the Fey disappeared into the dawning light of day.

The wind died and Alain pulled for the lines, hoping they were there and found them. He shot a gout of power at his father. Voices sang and the blow curled away from the count's shielding, hitting branches and twisting roots. Guihomarc fell back a step. Alain pressed in, struck again, but it, too, glanced away.

Guihomarc stumbled back toward the great oak and tripped on one of the stones that marked the Delphine's grave. He sent a lance of power at Alain. Alain defended quickly but the count's attack was a feint, and his real blow shot past a shield too quickly lowered. Alain's body convulsed. He fell to his knees and could not protect himself from blows that came too rapidly, one upon the other. Blood flowed from ten wounds. Ragged breath made his ribs creak.

Guihomarc stepped closer. The Delphine's gravesite lay at his feet. Alain spurred the spirits of the wood, called on them, waking them from their slumber. Roots moved, lashing the count's legs. He stumbled. A boar's tooth, buried for a summer at the foot of the oak, flew up from the ground. It hit Guihomarc in the knee with a sound like the snapping of a rotted branch. The count tumbled backward against the oak. A second tooth burst from the ground. The finger-long tooth pierced the count's hand, pinning him to the trunk with its crooked length.

Alain stood. He started forward, but Guihomarc pulled power and drove him back.

Bronwyn threw power as horsemen descended upon the Nordic raiders.

At Calin's command, the riders dashed in by ones and twos, haphazard, following no form. The light-footed Briezh steeds danced away from the ponderous swords of the attackers, danced in again as their riders leaned out to slash and cut. The horsemen ran the length of the line, pushing the raiders downhill toward the stand of Briezh swords. Some crashed through failing ranks, creating greater havoc.

"Pull up your men!" Calin shouted at Wrdisten. "Give me an iron to strike against."

Bronwyn sought a target but could find none in the melee. The horses pranced along the ridgeline, a swarm of spindle-legged demons against the morning sky. They pushed down upon the Viking warriors, who pushed down in turn. The troop of men below fell back with each pass, coming closer and closer to the archers below.

"Wrdisten!" Bronwyn shouted. "Stand. Stand!"

From the vale below came the bark of command, and garrison bowmen put arrow to string. Double-curves arched as bows creaked taut. Bronwyn sent a howling ball of heat into their midst. Some arrows flew wild but most sprang true. They scored the air in graceful arcs, falling among the hundreds that struggled on the hillside. Many found a mark. Men fell. Swordsmen leapt forward through the ranks of archers and six hundred men clashed sword to sword.

Wrdisten! she sent.

The clansman looked up in surprise. She made a sweeping motion upslope. Wrdisten shouted to his men and the command was passed. Bronwyn let fly streamers of power into the Vikings and the attacking garrison. Little damage was done, but the enemy faltered. A shout went up from the ranks beside Wrdisten and the mass of men halted, turned, and pressed uphill.

Calin saw the turn and called his horses into line. The Vikings did not know which way to run as they were charged from two sides.

Bronwyn felt the power burning her hands, and the pain in her head was mountainous. Her vision began to blur. In a short time, she would be of no use to anyone.

Lines sang. The power flowed from Guihomarc like a river. He drew again and again, casting spears of magic meant to kill, blows meant to crush. Alain dodged one, then another. A third hit and he cried out.

Guihomarc, one hand pinned to the oak, stood over the Delphine's grave and threw power with his uninjured hand. Alain fended the attacks and remembered the apples that lay buried with his mother's body. He drew from every memory of every day he had spent in Dead Ox Wood and fed the apple seeds a lifetime of remembered sunshine, rain, and loamy soil. Guihomarc, intent on his offense, did not see the seedlings sprout from the earth beneath his feet. They grew as fast as an old man could rise, pressing upward, until Guihomarc was trapped by them. He kicked at them, pushing them, uprooting them with his free hand, until one snapped but continued to grow, and pierced his side. The count shrieked as the tree continued to grow upward into his chest. The sapling grew taller, its broken tip skewering the count. His screaming grew weak as branches sprouted, thrusting out through his back and belly in sudden leaf. His feet left the ground, and he hung suspended like some grisly fruit.

Alain quieted the young tree's spirit, sending it back to sleep. The count, one bloody hand still pinned to the oak, his body hanging from the branches of a young apple tree, looked at his son with dying eyes. Alain saw the count's lips move, but there was no sound, no last word. He walked up to the count and looked into his face. He reached within, mind meeting mind, and heard the shouting fear as Guihomarc recognized the presence of his own nearing death. Alain folded Guihomarc's mind within his own, engulfing him, and fell with him toward the lines. They pierced the Veil and there, in the final field that separated one world from the next, Alain released Guihomarc and let him sail on into the sun of another land.

Alain stepped back. The dead eyes stared at him, questioning him. He could provide no answer.

The lines rang with the sound of cracking bells. He turned and ran limping toward the battle.

The hillside was strewn with bodies and the shouts and curses of fighting men. Fire burnt in the fields of the vale. Horses ran riderless. The Norsemen were being cut down on the ridgeline but swords and arrows were still attacking Alain's ranks from below. The men who had followed him to Vannes were caught in a vice of edged iron, facing destruction.

He clambered up onto a rock above the battlefield. He stretched his joints, ignoring the blades of pain that cut him, and pulled power from the lines. He released it in a stream of fire that lit the sky overhead.

Men hit the dirt as sound exploded over them. The roar of pure power boomed out across the vale and echoed back from the city's palisades. The cries of men were no longer of rage but of fright. Alain let the lines invade him.

He glowed with the light of a second sun. All eyes turned to view him.

"Lay down your weapons," he said in a voice that filled the vale. "There is no longer any reason to fight."

The body of Guihomarc of Vannes was retrieved from the depths of Dead Ox Wood, though they had to destroy the killing trees to do so. Three clerics, eight guardsmen, and Charles, the son of the count's machtiern, took the broken body down from its arbor of branches. Despite questions, he kept his account of the duel private, but the manner of the count's death was the source of immediate rumor.

While they were there, Alain searched but found no trace of his Fey attacker. He searched, too, for Jessup's sword. It was gone as well.

He walked with the bearers down as far as the rock from which he had called the battle to a halt. The bearers continued on toward the city where the Bishop of Vannes and his priests would spend the night praying over the body.

Wrdisten and Calin walked up to the rock where Alain sat. The clansman's mane was white once more. His arms were wrapped in red-splotched linen. Calin's tunic showed blood at a dozen places. He winced as he walked. Alain waved a hand toward the encampment that still dotted the hillside.

"How did we fare?"

Wrdisten breathed a deep sigh as he looked out over the scattered troops. "We crushed the men of the North, and hurt the garrison severely, but we lost a number of good men doing it. Simon fell. So did Blanchard, Ouen, and ten others. Two score and ten are seriously wounded. Most will survive, though." He cocked his head in the direction of the camp. "Bronwyn sleeps. Her wounds are not of the body. And Boduos negotiates even now with the machtiern. We will enter the city tomorrow, next day at the latest."

Alain nodded. "Good."

"How is your arm?"

Alain flexed his right hand. "Well enough. My ribs ache, but I will live. I will live."

The three men sat on the exposed rock. They were all silent for a time.

The vale echoed with the crackle of freshly lit campfires and the laughter of men heady from surviving battle. Soldiers walked among the bodies of the wounded, the rows of dead. The men bearing the body of Guihomarc reached the fields of the valley and headed toward the city walls.

"Why do you not go with them to bury your father?"

Alain watched the tiny procession pick its solemn path among the trampled fields.

"That man was never my father," he said.

nineteen

Morning came swathed in grey wool. Clouds hung heavy in a leaden sky. A low mist blanketed the plain. The towers of Vannes seemed to float like unearthly rafts on a gauzy sea. Men stirred, moaning at joints abused by battle and stomachs aching for food.

As Alain squinted through the mist toward the city that was his goal, he felt for the first time the true size of the task before him.

"Nervous?" Bronwyn asked as she tied back her hair. Alain nodded.

"There is so much to do," he said. "I do not know where to begin."

"You begin," she said, pointing to the city, "by walking that way."

They walked through a cloud until there appeared before them the wooden towers and timbered walls of the city. The gate lay open to the morning. Alain motioned to Wrdisten who set two pair of men to guard the gate and close it after them.

The city streets were lined with people. Men and women stood with faces drawn tight by fear and the unknown. They filled the street in a solemn crowd.

Ten ranks of soldiers led the column but were slowed by the narrowness of the streets and the press of onlookers. The riders were forced to proceed two abreast. Wrdisten looked around nervously.

"I don't care for this," he said.

Alain sat patiently as his troops wove their way toward the keep. "They only wish to see who it is has turned their lives upside down."

At the expanse of the market square, Alain called a halt. The streets were packed tight with peasantry. In the windows of fine houses that ringed the marketplace the families of merchants gathered. At the far side of the square was the church and abbey. A group of dark-clothed men stood at the abbey gates like a murder of crows.

"People of Vannes," Alain said to them all. "The deeds of my father, Guihomarc of Vannes, are ended. The years of neglect, of treachery, and of pain, are done." They stood and listened to his words. Some looked upon him with anger, some with hope. None, as far as he could tell, looked upon him with hatred.

"As I take his place, I carry no malice toward the people of this city. We have all suffered too long from my father's disregard. To continue to quarrel among ourselves defeats the purpose of my coming. As a token of my earnestness, I absolve all soldiers and men-at-arms who fought in my father's service against me. Their duty was well done, and they will be welcome to stay on in my service, should they so choose." He held up a hand to quiet the voices that rose in support.

"I further pledge to you that our lands shall never again go unguarded. Any invaders—from north or east—will be met and repulsed with all speed." Cheers erupted from the windows and balconies above the marketplace. Alain bowed to the approval. He turned his mount toward the keep.

"On," he commanded, and the column moved ahead. Behind them, glad shouts and laughter filled the square.

The great hall was filled with servants and officers of Guihomarc's keep. Three men stood in the forefront, waiting as Alain, with Boduos and Wrdisten, descended the stairs.

"I know you, Robert Machtiern." The man bowed.

"May I present my son and his wife?"

Alain looked beyond the man and saw Charles and Josselyn. "I have met your son. And Josselyn and I are old friends." He turned to the other two men. "I do not know these men. Who are they, Boduos?"

"This man is Lambert. He commands the garrison." The

thick-featured man inclined his head. "And this man is Main, chamberlain of the keep at Vannes." Main bowed, more deeply than did Lambert.

"Where is the bishop?"

The chamberlain coughed. "His grace was unable to meet you, my lord."

"Unable, or unwilling?"

Main laughed weakly and ended up with only a shrug.

"I see. Is there any resistance in the city?" The machtiern shook his head no. "From the garrison?" Lambert shook his head as well. "Good."

Alain turned and walked to the dais and chair that ruled the far end of the great hall. The colors of Guihomarc of Vannes hung in drapes over it. The finely carved wood of the chair was dark and shiny from years of use. Alain reached a hand toward the chair and listened to the spirits within it. He smiled as they answered him.

"I claim this seat as son and heir to my Guihomarc, Count Vannes. I claim this through blood as well as through conquest." He sat in the chair. Wrdisten took up station at the foot of the dais. Alain looked at the gathered servants.

"Chamberlain." Main came forward, bowing like a broken puppet. "You will stay on, but not in your present capacity." The former chamberlain looked up, startled. "You will now work under the direction of Boduos, whom I place in charge of the entire estate." Boduos and Main gaped at Alain, then at each another. "Step back." Main did so falteringly.

"Machtiern." Robert stepped forward. "Your loyalty to a man such as my father cannot be condoned. You are dismissed and I dissolve the office of machtiern. Your lands are forfeit. For the sake of old friendships, however, I will spare the lands of your son. Go and live with him in Belvanetes." The man's fury boiled behind his eyes. Charles took a step forward but was met by the fierce glare of Wrdisten, hand on sword. Josselyn looked on in shock.

"To the rest of you, there will be no change for now. Please, go on about your tasks."

Josselyn ran forward as the assemblage began to disperse.

"Alain, don't do this! You have ruined me!"

"Ruined you? I've *saved* you." He stood and stepped close,

not wishing his words to travel beyond her ears. "There are those who called for the execution of Robert as well as several others. You and Charles might have fared less well. I have saved you what could be saved. You have kept Jessup's lands. I know how important those are to you."

"Kept Jessup's lands? But you have taken our houses in Vannes and Robert's lands in the valley! I can't pay off my father's debts without them."

"Josée." He closed his eyes as the scent of lavender crept upon him. "Considering the alternatives, I thought you would be pleased."

"Pleased?" She stared him. "You have taken everything. I wish you had slain us all." She turned and fled, pushing past her husband to reach the door.

Alain watched her go. The scent of lavender still hung in the air. He closed his eyes and turned away. "One of us has changed, Wrdisten. But I don't know which one it is." He took his seat once more, knowing that at last he sat in the dark chair of power as Count Vannes.

He gained little comfort from the knowledge.

Alain sat on the precipice near his mother's hut, sheltered by evergreen boughs. Rain thundered over the fields of Belvanetes and tinged the world with a wash of grey. The river bent in its lazy course. Smoke drifted upward against the downpour. The houses of his village seemed to huddle together for warmth. Across the valley, the low white wall sent memories and dreams on fleet wings of desire.

"Why won't you stay?"

Bronwyn pulled her cloak a little closer. "And do what? What would your new subjects think of my presence?" She sighed. "Even Guihomarc never allowed me to visit at Vannes."

"I don't care." He searched for the words he wished to say. "You are very important to me. I need you."

Bronwyn laughed, a small, gentle thing. "You don't need me anymore. Though I liked it better when you were less capable."

"Then stay. Just stay."

"For what? To be second in line for your affections? Or is it third, now that there is to be a child? No." Her voice turned hard as she stared out into the steely rain. "I will not be just an ornament, some frippery to be taken down and admired when the rest of the world proves too ugly."

"I did not mean—"

"You cannot give me what I need, Alain. Or, if you can, then you will not. Your heart is too torn. Perhaps when it is mended." She stood. He looked up at her.

"Where will you be? How will I find you?"

"You know," she said with a laugh. "Sometimes you sound just like your father." She turned and walked off through the silent trees. Thunder rolled across the valley and rain reached the heights. He heard the whicker of her horse as she headed down the mountainside. He dipped down into the lines and followed the bright seed of her mind until, with swift finality, it winked out and was lost to him. She would not be found until she wished it.

He remained on the cliff edge until the rain passed over and the sky brightened with the memory of sunlight. Down on the surface of the river he spied the arrowing trails of three grey geese paddling their way toward the bend. They meandered the breadth of the water's muddy mirror, turning tails skyward in search of underwater greens. Alain heard a footstep behind him.

"My lord Count?" Alain turned to find Gaspar, one of the men who had followed him from Sidmouth.

"Yes?"

"Wrdisten sent me for you, my lord. Night is coming."

Alain nodded. "I'll be along in a while."

"Wrdisten told me to wait, my lord."

Alain chuckled and felt tears hiding behind his eyes. "He knows me well. All right. Let's go."

He walked with Gaspar to the horses. They mounted and headed down the twisting trail. When they came out from under the curtain of the Dead Ox Wood, Alain drew rein and halted.

"My lord?"

Alain gazed down into the valley to the north. The geese carved stripes in the water as they stroked the air for flight. As they rose from the surface of the river, their wingbeats slowed. Shrubs and trees dropped below their wingtips as they climbed toward the sky. Alain watched them as they circled once, twice, a three-point chevron marking the compass.

"Where do they go, do you think?"

One of the birds called out, a lonely cry that was answered by the others, and the geese chose their path. They flew up and over the ridgeline, over the heads of the puzzled soldier and the grinning lord.

He turned to watch them fly on and laughed out loud as the geese flew in an unwavering line toward the city of Vannes.

ABOUT THE AUTHOR:

Kurt R.A. Giambastiani lives in the Puget Sound area with his wife and two cats. Among his other interests are antique pocket watch repair and cooking ethnic cuisine. He works as a lead analyst for an insurance firm in Seattle.

You can learn more about the author and his books at the TimePaths website (*http://www.sff.net/people/giambastiani*) or get the latest publication news at his Yahoo! newsgroup (*http://groups.yahoo.com/group/Giambastiani*).

Coming soon

From Kurt R.A. Giambastiani
and Mouse Road Press

Ploughman King

The story of Alain concludes in
Book II of the Ploughman Chronicles

Unraveling Time

Take a trip in this romantic time-travel adventure
that spans history and the globe.

Beneath a Crystal Sky

The heroes of the Fallen Cloud Saga return in this,
the long-awaited final volume!

www.ingramcontent.com/pod-product-compliance
Lightning Source LLC
Chambersburg PA
CBHW050501260626
47157CB00004B/1137